Love Eternal

CASSANDRA ELIZZABETH

Kissing Camels Publishing, LLC

1653 Lititz Pike #2233

Lancaster, PA 17601

First published in the United States February 2024

ISBN 979-8-9895228-1-1 (paperback)

ISBN 979-8-9895228-0-4 (eBook)

Cover & Interior by Quirky Circe Book Design

Editing by Indie Proofreading

http://www.cassandraelizzabeth.com

To those brave enough to pass through the morally gray shadows into shades of RED.

Content Warning

Spoilers Ahead!

The Immortal Redemption series is a dark paranormal romance saga intended for adults. As such, it delves into dark and intense relationships, moral ambiguity, and features a variety of sensitive subjects, including, but not limited to: *explicit and kinky sex, horror, violence, gore, death, murder, religion, small towns, crappy fathers, off page death of a parent, alcohol, mental health, skeletons & oddities, masks, profanity, body image, and more.*

Playlist

Prologue | **Bullet With Butterfly Wings** *Tommee Profitt*

01 Lieshe | **Under The Milky Way Tonight** *Anakelly*

02 Him | **You Are So Beautiful** *(feat. Brooke) Tommee Profitt*

03 Lieshe | **Saint** *Echos*
Somebody's Watching Me *Hidden Citizens*

04 Lieshe | **Heart Shaped Box** *Annaca*

05 Lieshe | **Waking Up** *MJ Cole & Freya Ridings*
Dragula *Lissie*

06 Him | **One Way Or Another** *Until the Ribbon Breaks*

07 Lieshe | **The Pines** *070 Shake*
Sway *So Below*

08 Lieshe | **Can't Get You Out Of My Head** *Glimmer of Blooms*

09 Lieshe | **Lovesong** *Adele*
Haunted *Adona*

10 Luke | **Can't Help Falling in Love** *Tommee Profitt*

11 Lieshe | **Seven Devils** *Florence + The Machine*

12 Him | **Thirsty** *The Hound + The Fox*

13 Lieshe | **Never Tear Us Apart** *Bishop Briggs*

14 Lieshe | **Possibly Maybe** *Bjork*

15 Lieshe | **No Rest For The Wicked** *Klergy*

16 Luke | **Play With Fire** *Cobra Verde*

17 Lieshe | **Gloria Regali** *Tommee Profitt*

18 Him | **Astronaut In The Ocean** *Masked Wolf*
Home *Edith Whiskers*

19 Lieshe | **The Last Dance** *Peter Gundry*
Unholy *Kim Petras & Sam Smith*

Prologue

"Your move G," the red one smirks.

"You know I hate when you call me that," the white one says with an eye roll like the humans. With a wave of his hand, the queen moves on the red and white chessboard. The simple gesture belies the cosmic implications of the move. "Check."

"You only win if your King comes to her aide," the red one replies with a growl and, with a furious shove, flips the board. The pieces fly into the air where they burst into flames, the ashes drifting down like inky black snow.

While the red one throws his tantrum, the white one glances surreptitiously to the side, lowering his eyes ever so slightly. The lone watcher in the shadows merely dips his chin in response—message received.

Chapter 1

I glance up at the sign hanging above the old green door. The morning sun highlights the contrast of the white conjoined twin skeleton, one body with two skulls and wings instead of arms, against the black background of the distressed wood. In gilt Old English style lettering is the name of my pride and joy, Grimm, named after the German storyteller brothers.

Smiling, I unlock the door with a large skeleton key and turn the wrought iron vintage doorknob. I push open the wooden door and inhale my happy place. Dust, time, and the faintest whiff of formaldehyde hang in the air. It smells like home.

"Come on, Lucifer," I call to the enormous black cat that came with the building. Strutting past me with a twitch of his tattered ear, he jumps to his customary spot in the window, ignoring my existence as usual.

"Good morning!" I call out in a singsong voice to my taxidermy collection and various mummified animals, skeletons, skulls, bugs, and miscellaneous peculiarities. While others may find not only my taxidermied friends but the other contents of my shop bizarre, I have always been at home in the macabre. I find their glass-eyed gazes comforting as they watch me cross the store. They are also far friendlier than my shop cat.

Grimm offers an eclectic collection of curiosities, ranging

from wet mounts to framed prints of crime scenes and death tableaus, as well as uncommon antiques, store merch, and vintage horror movie-themed items. Despite the age of the building and most of my inventory, the shop is tidy and well-organized. I treasure my shining display cases with their thoughtfully curated offerings.

Medical antiques are one of my special areas of interest and take up an entire wall—a nod to my brief former career in nursing. The display includes vintage anatomy prints and sketches, old instruments, pathologic cross sections, and even a wax-injected anatomical specimen prepared by the famous Honoré Fragonard.

I think back on how I came to have such an unusual profession. What had started as a child's love of Grimm's fairy tales matured into a passion for Dracula, Frankenstein, Dorian Grey, and other creatures of the night. I recall my parents being markedly concerned that even as a young girl, I loved the so-called 'bad guys'. My little heart broke when the authors fated them to lost loves and persecution by hordes of angry villagers with pitchforks.

In response to my predilections, my father doubled down on his worldview of good and evil. But to me, life isn't so black and white. Because what is a hero? And who actually are the 'bad guys'? In the end, it's all really just a matter of perspective. The world is so very gray.

One of my formative memories was falling in love with Dracula. Despite my father's best efforts to keep me from "earthly evils," I discovered the ultimate antihero during a stolen moment with my cousin's miraculous cable television. When the catchlight landed on Dracula's face, despite the black and white film, I just knew his eyes would match mine.

While other girls dreamed of white knights and princes, I

longed to be rescued by a creature of the night. I dreamed he would swoop into my bedroom and save me from the tedium of my life. Whisk me off to his faraway castle where we could be alone. My young mind didn't get much further than that, but I knew there was something that followed. Something mysterious and wonderful.

I have had a predilection for anything vampire ever since. I enjoyed countless vampire novels and movies over the years, but my favorite always came back to the original Dracula, and Bela Lugosi is my longest-running crush.

As I grew older and fairytales gave way to gothic fiction and old horror movies, I also developed a fondness for dark, dusty things. Those items others disregarded in favor of what is new and shiny.

Unlike the current societal method of throwing out cheap plastic goods for the latest and greatest, I prefer to upcycle and invest in vintage or quality items that will withstand the test of time. Like classic cult movies instead of the new bloody slasher films.

Even holidays were different for me as I cried over the island of misfit toys at Christmas. Over time, I collected those 'misfits', whether oddities or people, and offered a refuge for all those misunderstood, cast aside, or thrown away.

As my found family grew, both stuffed and alive, my parents and provincial past, neither of which were accepting of me, became more distant. And as I evolved, I became less accepting of who they are, too. As my world expanded, so did my mind, escaping my small town and its imposed constraints.

My father didn't understand my "dark obsessions" and concluded I was "trying too hard to be different." A trait he resolutely believed contributed to both my seemingly permanent single status and my "overactive imagination."

In his rigid puritanical mindset, my sole purpose in life was reduced to marrying and procreating. So, when neither my personality nor looks were conducive to his cause, they just became more disappointments added to his extensive list.

My mother never contradicted him out loud, although in my mind I begged her to. Instead, she was a source of quiet comfort. Although a woman of few words, the ones she bestowed on me were usually loving and supportive. But it would have been nice for her to stand up for me, to show that my worth isn't determined by my father's expectations. To support my ambitions as my own.

After losing my mom, I gave up on trying to navigate a relationship with my father, who doled out judgments over kindness. The strained truce we kept as we cared for her during her illness could not survive her passing. If anything, things were worse than ever without mom as our buffer.

Her passing was also the crossroads of my career. I had quit my nursing job to care for her full time, and after she was gone, I was just done. Done with one of the few careers my father had approved of for an unmarried woman, done with being stuck in that damn town, and done denying who I wanted to be. Seeking comfort, I turned to what I loved, my collection of misfits and knack for finding them.

With encouragement from my chosen family, I took the little bit of money my mom had somehow squirreled away for me and made a down payment on a rundown old building on the outskirts of a questionable small suburb. It was a gamble, but it was thrilling. I finally felt alive again after those terrible years.

Feeling the familiar burn behind my eyes of impending

tears, I lock those thoughts away into the past where they belong and focus on the here and now. Me, successful, loved by my little found family, standing in my beloved Grimm.

Luckily, my macabre tendencies, which once were a source of ostracism, are now popular, or at least popular enough, and my little curiosity shop is thriving. And although my father is far from beaming with pride over my success, my chosen family gives me abounding encouragement.

I couldn't wait to open my email, waiting to hear back from a contact about some information about my upcoming buying trip to Europe, and also needing to check in with my taxidermy restoration friend Wren.

Lady Luck had been so kind as to send her my way, a kindred spirit in all things stuffed and an obvious addition to my found family. Wren was like the quirky Aunt, always out on an adventure, mysterious, and somewhat elusive. But when you were with her—simply fascinating and so very warm.

So many tiny details to keep my shop organized, welcoming, and thriving. My love for all of it makes it easy to sacrifice so much of my life for my shop's success. My computer, something I don't particularly love but is necessary as a business tool, attempts to boot up, leaving me to hope it decides to both work and connect to the spotty Wi-Fi today.

I love the beautiful old building that houses Grimm and my home, but it doesn't seem to embrace modern technology like the internet or even my laptop. It is part of the building's charm, and if I ask nicely for something important, the building seems to indulge me with working electronics.

Like pretty please download this book so I can read it

tonight, or Docs are on sale, come on PayPal! Despite feeling like the store might be magical, I've yet to uncover its secrets.

Thankfully, Grimm's sales always ring through, even if my email won't always load. A running joke is that my business is at the mercy of this building. But I love this brick-end unit, painted in a pale green with a darker green door, black windows and roof.

Standing across the street and looking at Grimm, it would seem as if the builders had gotten to the end of my row and put everything they had left over into this last unit. The roof stands a little taller, the front a little wider, and it has extra finishing details like deep window sills, stained glass, and fancy gingerbread trim.

My favorite feature is the front door's white and gray marble threshold, worn smooth by the passage of feet over the years. I wonder who they belonged to, where they were going.

History fascinates me, so no wonder I also contemplate the stories behind my oddities, wishing they could whisper their secrets to me. Tell me the tales of their past lives.

I wonder who I was in my previous lives. Hopefully someone amazing, like Cleopatra, Tamar the Great, or Florence Nightingale. Maybe a Salem witch burned at the stake for taking in strays labeled as familiars, like my inherited prickly shop cat. I shiver, so many delicious possibilities to lose myself daydreaming in.

My love of history also made it easy to fall in love with this old section of town. Now it is quite up and coming, but back when I had first bought the building, the surrounding area hadn't been as shiny. Gradually the neighborhood has grown more affluent, bringing in businesses, cafes, new homeowners, and, most importantly for my shop, more foot traffic.

The end result is fabulous. I have almost everything I need close to the shop—a thriving small business following my passion—and my investment in my glorious old girl has been a sound one. I am proud to have played a part in the revitalization of this historical section that had been in danger of being lost to the ravages of neglect.

Since the computer is taking its sweet time, with fifteen minutes until I officially open, I decide to dash across the street and grab some coffee from Murray's. Skipping the crosswalk in my hurry, I cast a cautious eye to the overcast sky threatening a downpour.

The door chimes happily announce my arrival as I burst through the door and look around for my favorite barista. I let out a sigh, greeted by the sight of yet another unfamiliar face. Now I will have to train someone new for not just my complicated order, but also to say my name correctly.

Although I love being unique, I wish I had a more conventional name. If I ever have kids, I will give them nice, normal names, like Grace or William. Something easy to spell and say.

My dull senses perk up at the promise of the delicious brew as the aroma of freshly ground beans surrounds me. I only hope the new person can get my order right. It's not that I want a difficult coffee order, just like I don't want a name no one can pronounce. But at thirty years old, I know what I want, and in this case, it is an extremely specific beverage to start my day.

If only the rest of my life was as perfect as my coffee order, I think with a frown, as I wait my turn. I check out the other customers in the shop—a few business folks, a teen with the fastest texting thumbs I've ever seen, a harried mom jiggling a baby on her hip.

Standing in front of me is a couple holding hands and

whispering in each other's ears. Their PDA pokes at my loneliness. I shift my focus to the baby peering at me over her mom's shoulder. Her enormous blue eyes nudge the minute hand of my biological clock, the loud tick reverberating in my mind.

The snap of a newspaper opening pulls my attention to the back corner, where a lone customer is reading. I'd love to see who is enjoying such an archaic delivery form of information, but the open paper obscures their face. Surely, they must be a kindred spirit to relish ephemera rather than be glued to a glowing screen.

Finishing my perusal, I turn back around, eyeing up the baked goods. I rub the back of my neck as a faint prickle skitters across like a goose walked over my grave. After a few more minutes, I approach the counter to order.

"Hi, I'm Lieshe. I own Grimm across the street. Welcome to the neighborhood!" I say brightly with a smile. Normally I'm not so perky pre-caffeine, but I'm trying to charm my way into their good graces and, hopefully, good Joe. The brooding kid stares blankly as I take in their androgynous appearance, vacant stare, and lip ring.

The coffee shop has a high turnover rate since the owner is kind of an asshole. I'd rather not have to greet new people and explain my order, but it's not worth going somewhere else when this is so close. Convenience is a priority, so I ignore the blank face of the newest employee and place my order.

"May I please have a quad espresso with frothed oat milk, sugar-free toasted marshmallow syrup, and six squirts of coconut stevia?"

"What?" the kid asks in a monotone voice without looking at me. They sound like Eeyore. Sighing, I force myself to refrain from giving them a well-deserved eye roll.

"I'm sorry, is Natalie here? She has my order down. I know it's not the easiest one." I offer the apology, attempting to still get the coffee I'm desperate for. Natalie is one of the few baristas tenacious enough to stay put.

She also makes my special drink so impeccably; I haven't been able to replicate hers at home despite having come up with it to begin with. And the best part? She even gets it started when she sees me coming, like I'm important enough that someone knows my usual.

"No," comes the curt reply.

Well shit, no plan B. The silence ticks on for a few beats until I repeat myself, careful to give detailed instructions.

"Ok, that's a quad espresso with frothed oat milk, sugar-free toasted marshmallow syrup, and six squirts of coconut stevia. I know it's not on the menu. You put the stevia in the oat milk before you froth it, add that to the cup, then pour the espresso on top."

I point helpfully to the drawer and attempt a friendly smile, which probably looks more like a grimace at this point, and say, "Natalie keeps my stevia in the drawer under the frother."

My fifteen-minute window to open the shop is closing, but I'm desperate for my morning caffeine fix. This specific concoction I have created over the years is delicious, and I so desperately need it today. I may have stayed up late last night, again, reading a new dark paranormal romance book when I should have been sleeping.

What can I say, I am having a dry streak, and the hot, fantastical antiheroes are really doing it for me lately. Are late-night sinful fantasies and a correct coffee order too much to ask for? Exactly. I deserve both.

The new barista sighs heavily and goes to butcher my order, I am sure. Exasperated, I snag a gluten-free biscotti. I normally avoid simple carbs for breakfast, but my exasperation needs an outlet. Tomorrow, I will start my low-carb kick again. Today is for frustration biscotti.

I nibble it while I wait, but it turns to dust on my tongue without my fabulous latte to dunk it in, so I force myself to hold out for the anticipated cluster of an order. Despite being an asshole, the owner at least stocks gluten-free treats for me, and the coffee beans are fresh-roasted, organic, and always delicious.

At last, the new barista, whose name tag says Charlie, giving me no hint as to their gender, hands me my drink. Charlie could be a purple Martian for all I care, as long as my coffee order is correct.

"Alicia," Charlie calls out flatly.

I audibly sigh. No one ever gets my name right.

"Lieshe," I mumble under my breath. Repeating the same line I've said all my life, I go on to explain, "Like Alicia, but without the A."

Charlie meets my eyes and in the same monotone asks, "Do you know you have two different colored eyes?"

"Yes. Yes, I do," I reply with an even bigger sigh.

I always find it strange that people comment on my heterochromia by asking if I know about it. Of course, I *know* I was born with one solid amber eye and one with a large splash of yellow-green. I guess they didn't know what else to say.

When I was younger, not surprisingly, kids had picked on me about it. When I was in high school, I even wore colored contacts to make my eyes the same color so no one would ask me about it. I never tried hard to be different, as my father accused; I was just born this way. Personality, eyes, and all that came with it.

Eventually, I learned to accept my eyes as one of my many quirks. Although I still struggle with both my confidence and accepting myself, I am making progress. Now, if only I can find some hot guy to accept me, too.

Chapter 2

My light in the darkness shoots across the street like a falling star.

Hypnotic.

Enchanting.

Transcendent.

I can't help following her into the coffee shop. Sitting in a corner, I pretend to read a newspaper so I can hide my ragged breathing at seeing her again. Her every move mesmerizes me, while she remains innocent to my very existence.

I always have an awareness of her. Every time her soul pops back into existence, it's like my world turns back into technicolor. And every time she is gone, black and white silence. Fuzzy static. Agonizing nothingness of years passing by. Sometimes centuries.

My own personal hell.

I've learned over many, many lifetimes to wait in the periphery until she calls to me. The wait is excruciating. I ruminate on every mistake of the last lifetime where I've lost her until I'm invariably torturing myself toward insanity.

Some days, I think I am already there.

Just when I believe my mind will break to match my heart that shattered so very long ago, it is time. And thankfully, my emissaries keep me informed until she calls to me. One of my few tools against the madness that would, beyond a shadow of a doubt, overtake me without her.

I had been called back to America by her presence. This isn't one of my favorite countries. It's too noisy and young. It has purposefully been years since I have last been here.

I have already bought the two buildings next to hers and will convert them to suit my needs while I am here. The other property I still own in America is too far away to be useful.

My mind drifts back to the last time she summoned me here. Memories of her and I caught up in the tantrum of this country, cutting its teeth like an infant. The evil of man never ceases to surprise me, thinking he can hold dominion over his fellow man. Ridiculous.

I have seen civilizations rise and fall, beautiful and ugly, many lost to time and memory. And every single one had fallen due to man's hubris.

I wonder with idle curiosity, but no genuine concern, about the current condition of my southern estate. The Fields, who have served me for what feels like an eternity, manage my properties and affairs around the world. But they could all rot into disrepair for all I care.

Material things are inconsequential to me, acquired only to serve a purpose. I imbue memories into my skin rather than holding on to something physical that will crumble and revert to dust.

My few treasured items that can stand the test of time are always on my body, like my rings. No other worldly possessions hold as much value to me as they do.

My eternal love talks to the barista, and the sound of her voice snaps my attention back to her in the present day. Sometimes the details of her blur from one lifetime to the next, memories superimposed upon themselves. There have been ever so many.

I catch her scent beyond the coffee beans and baked

goods of the shop. The warm note of sunshine mixed with the dark floral of the roses I cultivate to keep her scent with me through the ages. I want to cover her with their petals and nothing else.

Even beyond that, I would recognize her anytime, anywhere. Her face haunts my every day, memories of touching her haunt my every night. Every fleck in her amber eyes, the exact shade of the yellow-green splash in her other eye, even every freckle, seared into my memory. Imprinted into what little remains of my threadbare soul.

I can recall the richness of her laughter and the breathy moans of her release as easily as I can recall the sound of my own voice. I have mapped her body with my hands and lips until her contours were etched into the very fiber of my being.

I'm thankful the newspaper is hiding my face, as I can't imagine the unbridled lust it must show as I picture her spread before me like the finest meal, covered in the midnight red rose petals that bear her scent. My yearning for her knows no bounds.

Memories of the feel of her skin on my fingertips, softer even than the roses, are like a phantom pain in my soul. My mind's eye pictures how her brown curls would tangle in my fingers. I stop myself at the thought of her flavor bursting on my tongue.

Swallowing hard, I peek over the top of the newspaper at her. Some things she does in every lifetime, another nuance that makes it difficult to sort them out in my head. Like biting her lip, as she does now, or showing each thought and emotion on her face.

A half smile crosses my face as I remember a night when I tried to teach her to play poker. She had failed spectacularly, and my victory was sweet. The taste of her, even sweeter.

Her personality changes over the years, and all I can deduce after eons of study is nature controls her physical appearance while nurture nuances her personality. Rediscovering her over and over is like trying different vintages of my favorite wine. I am *starving* for her taste, desperate to sample this lifetime's bouquet.

My little *Rozǎ* makes a face at the barista and then, in response to whatever they say, shoots one eyebrow to her hairline. This particular facial gesture is seared into my brain and is one of my favorites. It's a face she makes a hundred times a day and has made at me a thousand times more than that.

She is irritated with the poor barista, waving her hands around until both eyebrows are stuck near her hairline. I chuckle to myself. My girl appears to be a firecracker this lifetime. Oh, to watch her explode...

I bask in the warmth of just being in her presence. After she leaves, I slink back into the shadows, where I belong. There is no light without her.

Only my darkness.

Chapter 3

Biscotti and latte in hand, I dash back across the street with a minute to spare, bracing for the usual busyness of a Saturday morning. The skies open into a torrential downpour just as I close the door behind me.

"Thanks, angel," I whisper. Part of my "overactive imagination" included sightings of a beautiful man with white-blonde hair and amazing blue eyes. As a child, I was certain that he was my guardian angel, while my parents were certain I was just a lonely and peculiar child with an imaginary friend.

Once they realized I wasn't in danger from a man following me, they shushed me any time I brought him up and reminded me who I should always be thanking for my blessings and looking to for guidance. I quickly learned not to tell other kids or adults about my angel, either. People get real uncomfortable real fast when a child's "invisible friend" is an adult male.

I thought surely my pastor would be able to see my angel and he could convince my parents I wasn't making this up. I was so confused when he told me that wasn't possible, so I pointed out the stained-glass windows in the church and the pictures in my children's bible of the blue-eyed, blonde-haired celestial beings.

In response, he turned a fascinating shade of red above his white robes, and my father just about had an apoplexy. Both men made it crystal clear not only was I not to bring up the subject again, but I was to purge the entire blasphemous idea from my mind.

Seeing the adults so upset, I nodded solemnly in acquiescence while secretly crossing my little fingers in the folds of my Sunday dress. If they hadn't been so pinched in my second-hand black patent church shoes that were a full size too small, I would have crossed my toes as well.

As the years passed, my angel appeared less and less often. As a teenager I had started to think perhaps the pastor and my parents were right; he had never been more than the figment of a lonely child's imagination.

Then one final encounter cemented his significance in my life for all time. I had finally got the nerve to sneak out to a bonfire party in the woods, my last chance to go to one before high school graduation. Time got away from me as I enjoyed feeling like a normal kid, drinking my first warm beer, so I started asking around for a ride home instead of walking back all that way in the dark.

Shocked when one of the popular guys offered me one, I didn't stop to think how everyone had been drinking. Just as I was about to climb into the backseat of his car, a high-pitched laugh had me glancing over my shoulder. Just beyond the group of cackling teenage girls, at the edge of the woods, stood my angel, the bonfire glinting off his white-blonde hair.

We locked eyes and despite the distance, I could see the flames dance hypnotically across endless blue. A slight shake of his head was all it took for me to reconsider my decision and pick a different ride.

To this day, I am thankful for his warning. The car full of kids I was about to get into never made it home. Since that night, nothing. But the childhood habit of thanking him had stuck with me. After all, he saved my life.

Pushing aside the memories, I put down my goodies and check in on my laptop as it chugs along. Since a spinning circle is the only thing my computer has accomplished so far, I turn on my phone's playlist and pop the lid off my beverage. As I stare at the screen, I dunk my morning treat. Eagerly, I blow on the steaming biscotti and take a bite.

"What the–" I exclaim. "Ugh, shitty matcha!"

If I hadn't been trying to multitask, I would have seen my latte was the wrong color before plunging my breakfast in. As I turn to go dump the disgusting beverage, I catch a glimpse of someone out of the corner of my eye. Startled, I slosh green liquid the temperature of liquid hot magma over the side of my hand.

"Fuck!" I scream, racing for the powder room. I dump the shitty six-dollar matcha down the avocado green sink, noting the similarity in colors, and run cold water over my hand.

"What a morning," I mutter under my breath. I hope the rest of the day will be better. Bit by bit, the scald fades to a faint pink under the running water.

I look heavenward, praying for patience, and study the wallpaper covering the little powder room. It had taken me forever to find the perfect one, but the velvet-flocked gothic print was worth the wait.

The paper pattern blurs before my eyes and the present fades away. The burning sensation morphs from just my hand to overwhelming heat as an incredible inferno of fire licks up my limbs. I can just make out an indistinct crowd beyond waves of visible heat erupting around me. My screams echo in my ears.

A desperate voice calls out to me over the noise, "Alice! Alice!"

I turn to the voice, somehow knowing this is my name.

Through the shimmering haze of fire, a set of amber eyes, so like my own, frantically search for me. My heart has already reconciled my fate; he cannot save me. We are out of time.

"I will find you. I will always find you," he cries out, hands outstretched.

His desperate declaration fades away as I push past the sensory overload and reach for the grounding methods I've practiced over the years to carefully pull myself back to the present. I had finally found a great counselor, once I had left my small town behind for college, who had helped me find a few techniques to work through these episodes.

Dr. Samantha was the only one who had been more interested in helping me than pleasing my parents by slapping on a label to force me into a tidy little box. She had been an incredible source of support and helped me along in my transition from an awkward small-town girl to a young woman coming into her own. I still miss her.

"You are safe in Grimm. You are safe in Grimm. You are safe in Grimm," I repeat out loud while firmly planting my Doc Martens into the floor, imagining roots from my feet digging deep down into the earth, anchoring me into the present.

I spin my ring on my index finger with my thumb three times, in sync with each affirmation. I blink hard, and once again, I am staring at my carefully decorated powder room instead of being burned at the stake with a stranger calling me by a different name.

My pounding pulse slowly returns to normal, yet I remain astonished that I've had an episode. I must need more sleep and less stress since I haven't had a waking dream in several years. Not since my disastrous last attempt at visiting my father after my mom's passing. Stress, lack of sleep, and strong emotions can all be triggers. Guess I can add burns to that list now, too.

The dreams are never pleasant, either. Of course, my brain doesn't conjure images of lovely things like puppies and rainbows. Rather, I dream of a thousand ways to die, of shadowy figures, and distant lands. Of profound heartbreak and loss so crushing, I've undoubtedly cried an ocean.

My distressed parents took me to multiple specialists, mostly psychiatrists, with a few religious leaders sprinkled in. I preferred the former, who eventually labeled me with hypnagogic hallucinations, over the latter, who thought I was waging a spiritual battle for my soul. Scary shit for a kid either way.

Since I didn't fit into any other neat little boxes, both my parents and the specialists were comfortable with this label, right or wrong. Merely a sleep disorder—no mental health problems allowed in this family.

I wouldn't have had an issue with an accurate diagnosis, no matter what it was. Especially if it could have helped me receive the right treatment. My parents' generation didn't understand and still attached a lot of stigmas to mental health. And unfortunately, society still does. My brief career in nursing was confirmation of that.

Truthfully, that mouthful of a label didn't at all fit, but I was content to leave well enough alone when my parents started getting more and more worried. After they brought up inpatient treatment or a religious retreat as a last resort, I let them label me with whatever they wanted knowing I was better left to my own devices.

Labels have no power. Or at least that was what Dr. Sam had reassured me. I told myself I simply have waking dreams. During the day and not while falling asleep. But no one else seemed to care about that last bit.

I learned to quit talking about yet another piece of me, and my parents stopped asking. And if I minded my stress and got enough sleep, I did fine. Really. Fine, fine, everything is fine.

The burning fades to a dull throb. I grab a paper towel off the octopus tentacle holder and gently blot my hand dry, followed by the faint sheen of sweat that had broken out on my face, careful not to smudge my makeup. Too bad my guardian angel hadn't saved me from this scald.

Deep breaths, I remind myself, noting my pale and worried reflection in the mirror. Schooling my expression as pleasantly as I can muster to greet the customer, I fill my now empty cup with water to rinse the green splashes from the sink.

"*Mea culpa.* I didn't mean to startle you," comes a voice like honey poured over ice, dark and low, musical and somehow strangely exotic yet simultaneously so damn familiar. In a world where communication happens at lightning speed, the slower and more formal speech grabs my attention.

The timbre caresses my ears, sends a tingle across my scalp, curls around my neck, and licks down my spine. I shiver deliciously. Today might turn out okay after all. The voice sounds straight from the pages of one of my late-night reads and pulls me back from the vestiges of the waking dream to the reality of the moment.

Although I am pissed about my shitty coffee order and the minor burn on my hand, while also worried about the recurrence of the so-called dreams, this voice intrigues me. I finish rinsing out the sink and throw over my shoulder, "How did you get in without me hearing the bells on the door?"

As a happy shop owner, this, of course, is not my usual

greeting. But I'm more than a little thrown off my game. When no one answers, I come out of the powder room and glance around.

"Hello?" Seeing no one, I call out again, "Hello? Where did you go?"

Still, no one responds. Lucifer is sitting in front of the door, staring unblinkingly and twitching his tail. Strange, he rarely leaves his perch in the window, so still that he blends in with the taxidermy critters around the store. Rattled, I wonder if cats really can sense things humans can't.

The massive black tom with a tattered ear came with the building. He is incredibly independent, more of a fixture than something that needs care. I didn't have the heart to get rid of a creature that surely no one would adopt, a fellow misfit. At least I think he stays because of the building.

Although I don't think I have much of a choice in the matter since he comes and goes as he pleases. He largely ignores both me and the customers, but at least his presence offsets the emptiness in my apartment above the shop. When he chooses to come in, anyway.

I shake my faintly throbbing hand and throw the now-empty cup in the garbage. A faint prickling on the back of my neck causes me to check around the store to make sure no one is hiding out. I hurriedly check the small kitchen and even behind the checkout counter, but find no one.

The emergency exit in the back remains locked. There aren't many places to hide. I had converted most of the first floor into one large showroom. It is a long narrow building like the other row homes crammed cheek by jowl on this road.

Besides falling in love with the old green building, I knew the real estate alone would be worth the investment, even if Grimm were to fail. But I wouldn't let it. I am tenacious.

And five years in, I am doing well. I have solid contacts and a stream of oddities coming in from around the world. I am establishing not only a business but a name for myself in the community as a fair but scrupulous and exacting businesswoman.

Albeit one who is losing her mind. I thought someone had startled me and I'm certain I heard a voice. And Lucifer *never* acts this way. He's the laziest and most antagonistic cat I've ever met.

So where is the owner of the disembodied voice? Who is he? I thought I had pulled myself out of my waking dream, but perhaps the voice had been part of it, too. I frown and lecture myself that I need more sleep, less sugar, and clearly less late-night fiction. Maybe even a nicer pet for some stress relief. Too bad Lucifer would probably eat it.

I easily convince myself I had dreamed the whole incident as I hadn't seen anyone distinctly, and it had been a stressful morning. I have an overactive imagination on a good day, even without waking dreams, or so I'd always been told. *Besides, cats are always weird,* I tell myself reassuringly.

The front doorbells jingle as customers come in, and I'm thankful that I can see these people. Lucifer jumps back to his spot in the window, curls up with his tail over his nose, and is once again oblivious to the world around him.

Must be nice buddy, I think, wishing I could hide so easily from my troubles. I shake off the prickling sensation dancing across the back of my neck and direct my knee-high platform Docs to the front of the store, putting my proprietor game face firmly back into place.

Chapter 4

LIESHE

Several hours later, I gratefully plop down on the rickety stool behind the counter. The morning rush is over and my stomach growls loudly. The dry biscotti had been disappointing without a latte and my body is crashing from the lack of caffeine coupled with the excitement of the day.

I need protein and a nap. One out of the two will have to do. My hand is faintly pink from the earlier burn and starts throbbing now that I am no longer distracted by the steady throng of customers. At least the sales were great today.

The new air plants in their glass globes were a hit. They even attracted shoppers who would have normally left upon seeing the inside of my store or waited outside for their more adventurous friends.

Some just had stones or shells to accompany the plants. Others had a darker theme with small skulls or a whimsical touch, like a fairy or gnome figurine. There is a rather large one with a Tillandsia Xerographica and a two-headed skeleton to match my sign out front in the center of the display that I'm not sure yet if I will sell or not.

I had spent a fun weekend with one of my besties, Mindy, putting them together and artistically hanging them in the ever-changing window showcase. They are easy to care for and inexpensive to create, which makes for a great quick sales item. I would have to make a note to order more supplies.

Mindy and I are polar opposites. I'll never fathom how we were matched as college roommates, but I am eternally grateful. She didn't like me at first. In fact, she could hardly stand me.

Neither of us remembers quite how, but somehow, someway, we quickly grew from barely tolerating each other to being inseparable. She was so normal, and I was so, well, so me. She was the first person to just accept me for who I am, macabre warts and all. And there it was, the start of my little found family.

Mindy still doesn't understand my more morbid interests, but she loves me, and crafting, and we are both thankful to find any excuse to spend time together. Despite our busy schedules, we get together as often as we can, which is never enough. I'm hard pressed to recall exactly the last time I saw her.

I should shoot her a text, ask if she wants to do another crafting weekend. I'm sure we would drink too much wine, and I'd laugh as she cringed about our mixed media, gingerly touching bones and taxidermy while making faces. Hopefully, she can get some time away from her kiddos soon.

My mind drifts to other things I need to do for the store, running inventory lists in my head and thinking through the upcoming seasons. I could use a refuel on some taxidermy and mounted small animal skeletons. Many of which I could get from some of my favorite vendors at the approaching Oddities Expo in Philly. Would be nice to find some new things to carry and spice things up a little.

This year's schedule is hectic with attending the convention, my upcoming European buying trip, the local Edgar Allan Poe steampunk event, and then the holidays. Welcome to the life of an oddities store owner. But I need inventory, and it is best to pick up the taxidermy and skeletons in person.

I must be careful with the more fragile oddities. Keeping them safe both in transit to my door and then once in the shop from dangers, such as too much damaging sunlight, is paramount. I think of myself as their adoption agency, trying to send them on to wonderful homes.

Some items I cannot bear to part with, like the baby two-toed sloth in a jar, unless the price is very right. And there are a few things I could never sell, like my dear friend that hangs behind the counter, Van Helsing.

I look over at my articulated human skeleton companion and say, "Well, Van Helsing, that shaped up to be a pretty good morning, after all."

He just smiles his toothy grin at me in agreement. My gaze slides down from his mostly intact teeth to the rest of his bones, taking in the puzzle that is Van Helsing. He is old and yellowed, and I am fairly certain is several skeletons cobbled together.

The large ribcage seems out of proportion to the smaller arms and the enormous femurs would have suited a much larger male pelvic bone. Historically, it had been widespread practice to mash many bones together and sell unscrupulously as a complete skeleton, which is probably why Van Helsing is such a hodge podge.

The oddities trade is full of charlatans and fakes, but I work hard to conduct my business in good faith. I value the relationships I have established to fill my shop with the absolute best things I can find for the amazing customer base I have built up over the years.

Van Helsing isn't for sale, though, and he has so much character that I had knowingly bought him in the shape he is in, with no plans for resale. After all, he accepts me in the shape I am in. I smile to myself at my inner monologue saying, *round is a shape*. My inner monologue can be salty.

Van Helsing is also currently the closest thing I have to a romantic relationship. Sadly, the man I spend the most time with is literally heartless and brainless. At least he can't think with his dick, unlike my last boyfriend.

We hadn't been in love, or even said the word, but we had been together for a couple of months. Long enough I thought it was going somewhere. Until I caught him in a few stupid little lies, and instead of trusting myself, I continued to trust him.

Of course, in time, I busted him in a bigger lie and a compromising position that he couldn't explain his way out of. He had blamed me for holding out on him, so I promptly kicked him to the curb. I wasn't holding out, but I didn't feel like I could be vulnerable with him in the way intimacy required. Turned out it was the right call after all.

Pushing that thought away, I think over my upcoming trips. Everything is almost set, but I dread taking so much time away from my pride and joy, Grimm. My other best friend, Jo, will run it while I am in Europe, and although I trust her completely, it is hard not to micromanage what I worked so hard to build.

Jo could have been the proverbial third wheel of our group when she transferred into the college Mindy and I attended and was added to our sophomore triple dorm room. But one look at Jo, with her innocent blue eyes and mass of honey-colored curls, and Mindy and I both immediately fell in love.

After which, we were promptly shocked as hell when she opened her mouth and started talking. Her angelic looks are in direct contradiction to her filthy mouth. Jo has no filter, which means you get honesty tempered with a fair amount of hilarious commentary. As a result, Jo isn't everyone's cup of tea, but she's my shot of whiskey.

Inseparable from that day forward, the three of us were a self-proclaimed girl gang, ride or die. College with our merry little band was a blast, and I was finally able to do some much-needed growth out from under my father's thumb. I missed those days, and even though we have all moved on to find our own paths, Mindy and Jo will always be my chosen family.

Despite the distance, we remain connected at our core, and it gives me the confidence to entrust Grimm to my friend while I chase down a taxidermy Raven. It is rumored to be from the tower of London itself. I don't want to purchase an item like that, considering its price tag, without seeing it in person, thus prompting my first ever European buying trip.

Ravens eat 170 grams of raw meat a day, plus bird biscuits soaked in blood. They are glorious birds. I could envision the facts smartly written on a piece of parchment next to its mounting, both displayed on a round table with a vintage lace tablecloth, and a few Poe books artfully stacked to the side.

The new display would serve two purposes. First, it would be a showstopper for Halloween, and second, it would help draw the crowd from the upcoming annual steampunk Poe convention in Baltimore, one of my favorite events. I always attend for fun, but this will be my first year as a vendor, so I need to step up my steampunk game.

Jo and I had been emailing back and forth about a full-page ad for the convention's program, since as a designer, she frequently helps me with the store's marketing. I am not yet sure if I will resell the Raven or not, but it is too perfect to pass up.

Thinking of the convention reminds me I want to put together a new outfit for this year's gathering. I better start a list. Even though summer is just starting, I always need to be planning for the season ahead.

Fall is the busiest with Halloween and the start of the Christmas shopping season. I imagine many of the gifts from my store would be a little too dark under the Christmas tree, but I have some die-hard oddities customers who check off a lot on their lists at my place.

Halloween is always a great sales season for me because everyone embraces their inner darkness at least a little then. Outside of the busy fall, I am lucky to also have some fascinating clients who keep me hustling to meet their year-round gift-giving and home décor needs.

I even have one couple that just finished up a stunning gothic nursery done in high gloss black furniture, wainscoting, and trim. They added bright orange linens and walls for an accent and then topped the whole nursery off with raven decor. I can't wait to hear what they name the baby when it is born. My money's on Annabelle Lee for a girl or Edgar for a boy.

My stomach growls loudly again, pulling me from my daydreams. I think about heading back to the small kitchen to reheat my crab cake sandwich, leftover from the darling little gluten-free vegan café down the street. I cannot figure out how they make a vegan crab cake, but it is consistently incredible. That café ruins my low-carb ambitions on a regular basis.

I look down at my curvy body and poke my belly, denting in the stubborn roundness that never seems to want to leave. At 30, I have mostly accepted myself, or so I say in random affirmations when the mood strikes, but still, I always feel like I need to lose ten, or thirty, pounds.

I'd settle for being a medium, not even a small, just a nice, run-of-the-mill medium, I think to myself, not for the first time.

I have never understood this body. It has delicate arms and shapely legs but the most stubborn belly. And that is on top of my two different colored eyes. In my affirmations, I tell myself I am a Botticelli painting, like the "Birth of Venus" in all her voluptuous glory.

But society always sneaks back into my mind, reminding me I am most definitely not a small or a medium, but a large or even extra-large. What a stupid sizing system, anyway! And a tiny piece of me wonders if that is part of what keeps holding me back from falling in love. Both my size and my complete acceptance of myself.

At least shoes don't make me feel bad about my body, so I've amassed quite the collection. Today, I am rocking knee-high platform Doc Martens paired with bright green and black striped tights and a zombie nurse tank dress—vintage Hot Topic.

My weight may fluctuate, but my shoe collection is a constant comfort. My love of fashion is one of the many reasons I transitioned from my previous life as a nurse. I was tired of having to look a certain way when I wanted to wear wild shoes and zombie dresses and embrace my inner darkness.

I miss helping people as a nurse, though I guess I still help people, just differently. And my nursing education is an advantage in my current role, helping me keep an eye out for fakes and reproductions with my knowledge of anatomy. But I never could have worn these shoes to the hospital and risked ruining them.

Being strange and unusual my whole life, nursing was not a good match for my free-spirited nature. Rather, it demands a high level of conformity. As a child, I had enough of that shoved down my throat to last a lifetime. I didn't leave just for the surface conformity; it ran much deeper.

I was successful in school because I am smart and determined. But college hadn't prepared me for reality after graduation, where I soon realized it was not the lifelong job for me. I had no time for the politics and catty environment I discovered myself in.

The only reason I had even become a nurse was it was one of the two careers my father had recognized as suitable for a woman who failed to secure a position as a wife and mother—teacher or nurse. I had chosen nursing over a room full of screaming children.

In hindsight, I could have skipped being a nurse, left my small town, somehow eked out an existence and made my own choices. It's easy to think women can just up and leave if they find themselves somewhere they don't want to be. But there are so many reasons that often can't happen.

For me, I had nothing and no one else to turn to for support. So, I played the role of the dutiful daughter, knowing as soon as I finished college, I could get the hell out of there.

But much to my father's never-ending disappointment in me, for many, many reasons, I left a supremely acceptable career for a woman in my town and instead pursued my passion, Grimm. Needless to say, owning an oddities shop is so far out of the realm of acceptance I might as well have declared myself the Queen of England.

I'd love a good tiara. Would go fabulously with these boots, I think, as I prop my tall Docs up on the counter to admire them more closely. Playfully wiggling my feet side to side as I contemplate my life's decisions and whether or not I could really pull off a tiara, I promptly fall backward off the stool.

I lay on the floor for a minute, stunned, taking inventory of any damage I may have sustained in my fall. Luckily, I missed Van Helsing and the vintage anatomy charts that hang behind the counter, instead, landing on the anti-fatigue mat I have for standing at the register.

"What a damn day!" I groan.

I look up at Van Helsing from my place on the ground to see him staring back at me with sightless eyes. I wish I had Jo here with me already. Although, chaos magnet that she is, I probably would have pulled out a cord when I fell and somehow caught the building on fire only for her to fall in love with a firefighter.

I roll to my side and cautiously come to a sitting position while scolding myself for my daydreaming that caused the fall. Grabbing the rungs of the stool, I haul myself up, graceful as ever.

Lucifer takes that moment to jump down from his perch and stalk over to me. He sits down and studies me judgmentally, clearly wondering why on earth I disturbed his royal slumber. I can almost see his eyebrow raised in disdain. For as much as he dislikes me, I'm not quite sure why he sticks around.

I feel a little dizzy. The morning's events and low blood sugar coalescing into mild disorientation. No longer able to put off eating, I make my way back to my small kitchen to reheat my leftover crab cake.

I fill Lucifer's dish with exorbitantly expensive stinky wet food, the only cat food he will eat. I assume he eats mice or something when he disappears from time to time, but here at home, only the best for his majesty.

I grab a seltzer while I wait for the toaster oven, the fizz dancing on my tongue and tickling my nose, clearing some of the fog from my fall. Sussing out the mystery of the disembodied voice from this morning occupies my mind until, at last, the ding of the oven informs me lunch is ready. I pick up my lunch and drink, heading back out to the shop.

Drink and paper plate in hand, I go to sit down when the same exotic voice from earlier again startles me. I whirl around to face the speaker, determined to catch him this time.

"Hello again," he says with a trace of an accent and a slow cadence. The voice feels ancient, is the only way to describe it. It stirs thoughts of castles, shadowy forests, and leaves in the wind. An image of wolves racing through ancient trees flashes in my mind.

Visceral.

Dark.

Dangerous.

My eyes lift to his amber ones and the hair on my body rises like being too close to a lightning strike. I can almost smell the petrichor and ozone of an incoming storm.

I feel like prey, caught in his amber gaze, his eyes echoing the thought of wolves. Even at this distance, they are striking —bright gold with a darker ring. I wonder if up close his amber eyes, seemingly identical in color to mine, will have the same flecks of green around the pupil. Unlike mine, his are magnificently matched.

As we lock eyes, his pupils dilate and his nostrils flare, like he is scenting me as prey. I feel my heart speed up and know my pupils dilate in response.

My only thought is I would happily sacrifice myself to

this wolf. I realize my mouth is open and wonder just how long I have stood there slack-jawed, awestruck by this gorgeous man.

I tear my gaze back from his intense amber one to take in his entire face. His hair is as dark and velvety as midnight. Tousled like he had been pulling at it and lightly curled around his ears to his collar, just long enough to pull back if he wanted.

Black stubble graces a jaw so beautifully chiseled I could cut myself on the sharp edge of it. He has a straight Greek nose and lush lips with a full bottom and upper cupid's bow. He is entirely too symmetrical, like a marble bust from antiquity. *So, this is the male archetype,* I think.

He must be lost on his way to a modeling interview. He is ridiculously hot, like all the pieces of every late-night romance novel I have ever read rolled into one body of raw and freaking alluring masculinity. I wished I had a security surveillance system solely to watch the footage of this man on a loop, like my own personal porn channel.

My purview drifts over his porcelain skin, in contrast to his dark hair, and takes in the entire image of him. He is well over six feet and seems tall even with my ten-foot-high old ceilings. His shoulders are broad and taper down to a narrow waist.

Sublimely worn jeans encase his thick thighs, and glory be, he has on oxblood docs. I drift my gaze back up his body, trying not to zero in on the serious heat he is packing in the front of his pants.

He has a tight T-shirt that appears soft and weathered. I am jealous of the way the cotton clings to him, framed by a leather jacket. He has one thumb hooked in the front pocket of his jeans, his other hand rests against a tree trunk of a thigh. Light winks off several rings and I'm fascinated by his large hands. I can't help but think how they would feel on my body.

He looks like James Dean and a wolf had a baby that grew up into the hottest damn specimen of man I have ever laid eyes on. I blink, close my mouth before a fly gets in, and swallow hard.

It is audible in the stillness that has lasted through my embarrassingly long perusal. It has been the ogle of all ogles in the history of ogling. But dear God, when would I have the chance to lay eyes on a man like this again?

I try to speak, clear my throat, and try again. My mouth is like the Mojave Desert, while further south it is most definitely Monsoon season. I finally get out, "I'm sorry, you were saying?"

Seriously? Could I have said something lamer to Mr. Tall, Pale, and Handsome? His mouth quirks up in a panty-melting half-smile, and I know this is it. He has ruined all men for me from now until forever. He is H. O. T. with that grin. I dub the mystery man Hottie McHottenstein.

He quirks an eyebrow, and I sincerely hope I haven't accidentally said that part out loud, as I sometimes do. My slips of the tongue are a constant source of embarrassment for me and entertainment for my friends. And the more stress I am under, the more I do it. And this is such a good stress.

"I said, 'hello again,'" comes the exotic voice. There is something niggling at the back of my mind with the accent, but I'm too preoccupied by his looks to pay attention. It is subtle but somehow familiar.

Tomorrow I will not be shallow, I tell myself. But in this second, I am so, so guilty of judging a book by its cover. And I want to devour this book, again and again and again.

Crap, he is waiting for me to respond, and I am so

distracted. I stammer, "I-I'm sorry, I don't think we've met. I'm pretty sure I would remember."

We stand there, staring at each other, the air becoming more and more charged. The store's sound system plays my curated streaming eclectic playlist. As one of my favorite songs, "Dragula," starts playing, the man's half-smile blooms into a full smile.

If I thought the half-smile was panty melting, the full smile is freaking nuclear. I wait for my clothes to incinerate right off my body under the attack.

He takes a step forward and I take one back, his sheer presence pushing the air against me, forcing me into a hasty retreat. I startle when my back is brought up short by the counter and freeze in the face of his intense scrutiny.

His gaze slips down my body to my docs as I stand trapped and then begins a slow perusal back up, taking in my striped tights, zombie nurse tank dress, and I swear lingers on my breasts for just a second too long. Or maybe that is simple optimism.

I could fall easily for this guy. So damn easy. He ticks every item off my checklist as if he were made for me.

I can feel his eyes staring at the pulse point in my neck, which must be visibly pounding, as I can hear the blood rushing in my ears. He runs the tip of his tongue along the edge of his teeth and meets my eyes again. He does not seem displeased with what he is looking at, and I blush furiously.

My skin heats and sweat blooms on my lip. I wonder if this is what menopause feels like. But I'm fairly sure my ovaries just dropped half a dozen eggs at a machine gun pace, so nope, can't be the change.

I realize I am awkwardly standing there with my lunch in hand, so I turn around and set it down on the counter. I surreptitiously wipe my sweaty palms down my dress and take a sip of seltzer to stall from facing him again.

When I spin around, I find him following my every movement with his eyes, reinforcing my earlier feeling of being prey caught in his predator's gaze. I don't hate it.

His stare is intense, forward, and unapologetic in contrast to his words. "I must apologize for this morning. Is your hand better?"

Again, in that mysterious accent and cadence that pools deep into my belly. He holds his hand out to me, palm up, and I feel that I have no choice but to lift my burnt hand to his, the synapses in my brain misfiring.

He takes my hand and brings it to his lips, grazing a kiss over the burn. His hand is cool in my overheated grasp, while his lips ghost over my skin.

I let out a small gasp, electricity zinging straight to my core in this grandiose moment, like the alignment of the universe itself has shifted. This is achingly, hauntingly familiar. I swear I've felt every whirl of his fingerprints on my skin a million times before, know every crease of his lips, felt his words drip down my spine chased by his mouth.

I feel on the edge of a chasm, and I know if I slip into this gaping hole, I will surely fall through the center of the earth and keep falling through all of time and space. Never to recover.

His gaze snaps from my hand to my eyes, and he quickly drops my hand and steps back. The loss is palpable.

I wonder what could have caused his rapid retreat when my entire world has just turned upside down. Had he felt that shockwave, too, or did my reaction cause his sudden withdrawal?

I clear my throat, look at the floor, and then back up at

him. *Get a grip*, I scold myself. He's just a good-looking dude. You are making this out to be so much more than what it is. I blink through the brain fog induced by his presence and focus on his last words.

"You? You are the one who startled me this morning and made me burn my hand? How are you getting in and out of here without me hearing the door? It is quite disarming. Why wouldn't I have heard the bells?"

I have to stop myself from rambling. Disarming? Who says that? What do I speak in Old English now? I internally scold myself, *get it together, Lieshe.*

He shrugs nonchalantly. "You must have missed them. I love your store, it's very, what's the word? Eclectic. I am looking for something—something very specific."

His eyes narrow at me as he says the last word, but I swallow down my lust and turn on proprietor mode. I just want him to keep speaking so I can hear his voice and watch his mouth form the words as they slip from his lips like music. I blink owlishly at him and then realize he is waiting for a reply.

"Well, uh, as you can see, unusual is my specialty. Although specific requests can be difficult to track down, I have some excellent sources. What can I help you with?" I ask with my best smile.

If he notices the quaver in my voice or my racing pulse, he is kind enough to pretend he doesn't. I bet he induces a mild state of hysteria whenever he so much as glances at a woman. He must be used to it by now.

I am used to not grabbing anyone's attention, certainly not the notice of such a fine specimen of manhood. I am dorky and round, hiding behind my thick-framed glasses and enormous mass of curly hair. It's a safe place to hide. Familiar, if a little lonely.

Sometimes my heterochromia, or more rarely, my quirky sense of style or dark humor, would draw someone's attention. Or maybe when they heard what I did for a living. But just me catch someone's attention? I know better. Very few people actually see me and definitely even fewer men.

"I'll know when I see it," he replies, looking me up and down, responding as if he can hear my thoughts of not being seen aloud. This time, I avoid eye contact, not wanting to get drawn back into his magnetic gaze.

I focus on my darling two-toed sloth in a jar just over his shoulder. I feel his heated stare still on me and it is an act of sheer will to not meet it with my own. "Well," I chuckle, "that is pretty vague."

I turn my back to him, my neck prickling with the awareness that I have left an apex predator behind me. My lizard brain recognizes how dangerous this is. A drop of sweat trickles down my spine, and an image of him chasing it with his tongue flashes into my mind.

I audibly gasp and look over my shoulder at him, and that half-smile quirks across his lips again. I narrow my eyes at him, a strange feeling that he knows exactly what I am thinking. I about face and shake my head.

That is not only the most improbable thing that could ever happen between my body and his sweet, sweet mouth, but reading my mind? *Gah, too much fiction*, I tell myself.

My current paranormal romance reading streak tickles my imagination, causing my mind to classify him as one of those super alpha wolves that permeates the shape-shifter genre. But I quickly dismiss the thought.

Despite the predator's gaze, an alpha wolf just doesn't quite fit him. He seems too big, too *much* to simplify into a fictional character. And although I adore fiction, this is real life. He is just a man, albeit an insanely hot one.

"Well, I have a wide variety of oddities, as you can see. I love vintage taxidermy and I'm going on a buying trip soon. So, I can keep an eye out for something specific, but this industry is very hit or miss."

I wander around as I speak, drifting to the front bay window brimming with plants. I know every square inch of Grimm; the familiarity grounds me. The sun is streaming through the clouds so that I can just see my reflection in the glass, framed by the air plants in their glass globes, the vintage baby doll head planters, and dinosaurs filled with succulents.

Surprisingly, the charming taxidermy 'Easter duckling' in the rain boots with a little red umbrella hasn't been sold this spring. It is time to put him away and get ready for summer. Distracted by my thoughts, I'm startled when I sense an intense presence behind me. I spin around, all but planting my face into his broad chest.

That golden gaze stares down at me, forcing me to tip my head up, up, up to meet his eyes. I feel my mouth drop open, my tongue darting out to moisten my dry lips.

He follows the movement of my tongue and then spins and leaves, throwing over his shoulder, "I'll be back."

Just as the door slams, Lucifer makes his way out of the kitchen and runs to the door, hissing. This time I hear the doorbells jingle. I have to figure out why I hadn't heard him come in not just once, but twice today.

What a bizarre interaction. I can't help but wonder at the cause of his sudden departure and Lucifer's reaction. That cat never bothers with any of the customers and although he doesn't actually like anyone, he has also never cared enough to hiss at anything.

I didn't know he could vocalize; I've never even heard

him meow. And he sure as shit hasn't purred. Prickly little thing.

Perhaps I hit my head harder than I thought when I fell. *At least the mystery man didn't ask me if I knew I have two different colored eyes,* I think as I walk back to the counter, eat my now cold again sandwich, and down my seltzer.

Chapter 6

HIM

I hate to cause her pain, yet it has already happened, inevitable as always. Even something as small as a scald to her hand has my cold heart stuttering in my chest.

I hadn't meant to startle her, and then once she had burnt her hand, I had lost my nerve and escaped to the safety of my property next door. Only when I saw she was alone at last was I ready to approach her again.

Her response to my presence pleases me greatly. She is visibly attracted to me. No surprise there. But what is a surprise, and an unpleasant one, is her view of herself.

I can see her fiery true self hidden behind a facade of giant glasses, big curls, and funky clothes meant to pull the eye outwards and away from seeing her. From really seeing *her*.

I wonder if she can even see herself.

Whenever she needs me, I am called to her. There have been many reasons over the years—war, famine, abuse. Over the centuries, the threats have morphed from illness and physical danger to more sophisticated concerns. Like in this lifetime, where she needs to be rescued from herself.

I know her far better than she ever could. I can save her, show her who she is.

My confidence grows. This will be *the* lifetime. There is no alternative. One way or another, I am going to have her. I will not lose her again. I cannot. This time, I will save her. I will save us. I cannot, will not, fail again.

Chapter 7
LIESHE

I have never been so happy to close up and head home. A busy day in the store, interspersed with the stranger's visits, has me beat.

I am so thankful I renovated the two floors above the shop into my unique living space last year. I had left them unused until I saved up enough to really make them the way I wanted. The bonus is, I now have the perfect commute.

Lucifer rushes past me and off on his own errands. I tried to make him an indoor cat to keep him safe, but it was impossible, as he has his own agenda.

I lock the front door to Grimm with my skeleton key and slip down the alley to the back of my building. I am thankful the sun is just setting; the golden glow lights my way, throwing long shadows into sharp relief.

I have always felt safe in this little suburb of Baltimore, but tonight I have that prickling sensation on the back of my neck, like McHottenstein is standing right behind me again.

I hurry a little faster down the alley and around the back stairs. My anxiety continues to ramp up, so I run up them two at a time, breathless by the time I reach the landing. I can't figure out why I am anxious in such a familiar setting, but it has been an odd day.

It is the anxiety of a child—scared of the dark and what is hiding under the bed. As an adult, I framed prints of scary things and resold them rather than thinking they are beneath my bed. But my heart pounds away, and I wish I could hide beneath the covers.

Rather than the vintage skeleton key that unlocks the front door to the shop, with a shaky hand, I take out a regular one and unlock my deadbolt.

As I turn to close and lock the door behind me, I glance out over the back lot and could swear I glimpse a pair of animal eyes reflecting the light back to me. They are too large and too high up to be my cat, though. I blink and they are gone. Weird.

I am exhausted and rattled, in need of a bath and a shot of my favorite tequila—for medicinal purposes, of course. My mind rambles down its rabbit trails, branching off here and there.

Thinking of medicines reminds me of the box of framed antique prescriptions that I had bought on my last buying trip and still needed to display in the shop, if only I can remember where I stashed them.

As my mind continues to run through the store's displays and my to-do list, I unzip my boots and leave them propped next to the door. I turn on my table lamp, a gothic crow with an Edison bulb hanging from a cord in its mouth, and look around my familiar space.

It is reassuring, if lonely. Everything where I left it, only mine and Lucifer's messes to take care of. But I sure wouldn't complain if the oxblood Docs from this morning's hottie were sitting next to mine. Or better yet, under my bed.

I decide to nickname him McHottie, since Hottie McHottenstein is exceedingly long. I wonder what his real name is and hope it is something as exotic and spectacular as he is.

I walk down the hall and start to fill my slipper tub. The

benefit of redoing my space was putting in custom finishes like this one.

I always dreamed of having a tub where I could simultaneously have my feet and boobs under the water, so I put this fabulous one in, and a separate shower area. I add a generous pour of rose-scented oil and leave it to fill.

I traipse to the kitchen at the end of my open-concept main living area and drink some water. After hydrating, I pull down the beautiful blue and white tequila bottle from its spot on top of the fridge. It is my favorite, but hard to find and not cheap, so I save it for special times or when I really need to treat myself.

I grab an ice ball in the shape of a skull from a baggie in the freezer and add it to a copper rocks glass, since I don't want to risk regular glass in the tub. I pick up a lighter from the junk drawer and walk back to the bathroom.

The room is now filled with lovely rose-scented steam and is exactly what I need. I smirk to myself as I light the penis candles around the room. I had bought a case of them cheaply as a novelty for the shop, but then had been too chicken to put them out.

Of all the strange things in my store, penis candles are where I draw the line. Penis anatomy prints, or even baculum jewelry, are fine, but penis candles? Now that's just silly.

I light six of them, softly giggling at the thought of flaming dicks, and slip off my striped tights. The candles are just realistic enough, but not gross.

I never understood why dildoes have ropey veins on them and writers felt the need to describe male anatomy in such great detail in the spicy fiction I liked to read. Maybe I just haven't seen an impressive enough specimen?

For a second, I think about shaving my legs, but dismiss

it just as quickly. It's not like anyone is feeling them but me, and I couldn't care less. Summer is just starting, and the air is still a little chilly.

I could wear tights with my dresses for a little while yet. Without another thought as to the state of my body hair, I drop my high-cut briefs and strip off my dress.

My bestie Mindy laughs at what she calls my "granny panties", but as a curvy girl, I think they are the most comfortable. I unsnap my front clasp bra and let it, too, fall to the floor, letting out a sigh. Although I go for comfort with underwear, I am young enough, and sufficiently vain, to still wear a bra that makes the girls look good.

When you have double D's, that is a tall order. I feel like my breasts are one of my better assets, along with my hair, so I try to play up what I can. I gingerly step into the tub, my skin reddening as I ease down into the heat, the rose-scented steam swirling up around me.

Thrilled with my hammered copper slipper tub that can submerge all of me up to my neck, I slowly sink down into the hot water. I coveted this tub for years, so now I thoroughly enjoy it, as often as I can. Grabbing a scrunchie off the windowsill, I throw my hair up into a messy bun so I can dip even my shoulders under.

Wispy curls escape in the steam to frame my face. I feel sweat bloom on my upper lip and tickle my scalp. The feeling reminds me of the prickling of my neck in the coffee shop, in my store with my strange customer, and then again when I was coming home.

I try to focus on the business aspect and wonder what McHottie is searching for. He was infuriatingly vague. My thoughts wander to how he slipped in and out without me knowing.

I would have to investigate installing an electric door

chime instead. Hopefully, the old green building will allow it to work. There must be copper wiring wrapped in the horsehair plaster with as much electronic interference as there is. This old building, sometimes she is feisty.

Something niggles at the back of my mind, but I just can't put my finger on it. I take another sip of tequila, willing my brain and body to relax. It had been such a strange day.

Yes, I am clumsy at times, but a shitty matcha scald and falling off my stool in one day, followed by the virtual concussion brought on by seeing the world's hottest tall, pale, and handsome stranger is a lot, even for me. What's even more concerning, though, is the recurrence of these damn waking dreams.

I continue to savor my favorite tequila, letting it swirl around in my mouth, and let out a small moan as I swallow. The hot rose-scented water is doing its job of relaxing my body from the outside while the liquor works its way through on the inside.

I love this tequila. It reminds me of a margarita without the fuss. My breathing becomes slow and steady as my mind drifts again, relaxing at last.

Thoughts of castles and wolves inspired by McHottenstein's voice swirl like leaves in my brain. I let my mind wander, recalling his eyes—their fierce amber color, the feel of his intense stare, and how it had dropped to my mouth as I had licked my lips.

My fantasy blooms, imagining that I caught his eye, little old me, who never turns a head. Then he leans down ever so slightly, and I rise on my tiptoes. Overcome with desire, he threads his fingers into my hair, angling my head, and claims my lips in a searing, soul-scorching kiss.

I imagine his hand tightening in my hair, tugging until I

let out a gasp that he swallows with his kiss, darting his tongue into my open mouth to tangle with mine.

He tastes like foreign spices, ancient history, lost souls, and time immemorial. I can taste him as vividly as I can the tequila in my hand, as if I have tasted him a thousand times before.

In my mind's eye, he trails open-mouthed kisses down my jaw to my neck, nuzzling with his nose, nipping at my pulse point. Finally, he wraps my hair around and around his hand, canting my neck to further expose it to his seeking mouth.

As I gasp in a breath at this new vulnerable angle, his canines elongate and he leans in to bite me, piercing the flesh of my neck.

I sit up with a start, sloshing water over the edge of the tub. I can't figure out if this is another waking dream or if the tequila and warmth of the bath water lulled me to sleep. But in my now wakeful state, I realize why I recognize his accent.

My subconscious has sorted through all the day's events and realized his voice sounds like that of my favorite antihero—Dracula—fueling my mind to typecast him as a vampire in my dreamscape.

I chuckle out loud, that poor handsome man being typecast in my brain as Dracula. Ridiculous. Almost as ridiculous as being surrounded by these penis candles.

I drag my sleepy ass out of the tub, wrapping up in a Turkish towel—luxury linens, another of my indulgences. I gladly sacrifice quantity for quality to afford the things I love.

I use a corner of the towel to wipe the ornate antique gold Bordeaux leaning mirror I keep in the bathroom, casting a critical eye on my nude form in the mirror spotted with age.

I admire my shapely arms and legs but critically assess

my breasts. They used to be perkier, but us big-breasted ladies know, perky doesn't last long as a double D. But they are still full and high enough, and I think at least my nipples are a lovely shade of rose and just the right proportional size.

My waist dips in and my hips flare, but man, below the navel is the problem area. Too round for low-cut jeans and tango thongs.

I do look fabulous in a corset, but rarely wear them unless attending certain events or costuming for something with the store. Women figured out long ago, corsets are not for everyday wear. I suck in my belly as long as I can and let out a sigh when I relax back into my usual posture.

Meh. It is what it is. The candles flare and a few gutter. This old building is always a tad breezy. I have a momentary thought about how hard I am being on myself, but let it go. Old habits and all that.

I hear the wind pick up outside. The clouds that had flitted out after this morning's storm had returned in the afternoon, gray and threatening. They amalgamate together, and the downpour starts, thunderous on the old roof.

The rain pings on the window set high into the bathroom and for a brief second, I think I see a bat illuminated in the stained-glass pattern against a flash of lightning.

I really need to get to bed. Now I have vampires on the brain. No more tequila for me. I love a magnificent storm and can't wait for it to lull me to sleep, which I clearly need.

Too exhausted to even grab a snack before bed, I throw back the melting skull ice cube from the cup into my mouth. The coldness is a relief from the steamy bathroom that was starting to feel too close.

I slip on a long, vintage red and black smoking jacket, the silk sticking to my heated skin. I tie the tasseled sash and slip on my memory foam slippers, bought because they feel like little clouds on my feet.

The hot pink rabbit slippers are a sharp contrast to the red and black smoking robe, but I love these little bunnies. They make me smile and this strange outfit is pretty representative of me with vintage and new mashed together.

Comfort mixed with style, a love for the old, with an appreciation of the absurd, as all adult bunny slippers are truly absurd. I couldn't help but give myself some of the indulgences I had been denied in childhood.

I remembered my past in shades of taupe, bland like oatmeal. My parents never wanted to stand out in our small town. They preferred me to be a shrinking violet, which was already difficult with my heterochromia and macabre tendencies.

Something wild, like bunny slippers or hot pink, would have simply been too much for my parents' simple tastes. My "struggles" were just about as exotic as you could get in my family. Though behind closed doors, I'm sure there was a fair amount going on in my hometown.

My bunnies and I go back to the kitchen to put the now empty cup in the sink. I don't love all of adulting, but picking out wild slippers and drinking in the tub are clear winners. The coolness outside the bathroom feels wonderful against my flushed skin.

I open the back door and call for Lucifer, like I do every night before bed. Sometimes he is there waiting, but other nights, like tonight, he is off on his mysterious cat business, so I head upstairs.

I converted the entire attic of the long and narrow row home into quite a lovely bedroom, keeping as many of the little details, like the exposed brick of the chimneys and wood floors, as I could.

Both gables hold original stained glass diamond windows, each one with just four simple colored panes. I love to watch those colors drift across the floor with the changing of the day's light.

Gathered around a fireplace near the stairs is a small seating area. The focal piece is a wonderfully redone chaise lounge with an organic alpaca throw that I love to curl up in and read.

Despite the dark, moody maximalism that is pervasive in my shop, my bedroom is light. The walls are the palest pink; the hue changing with the light. My seating area furniture is emerald green velvet with a white fur rug pulling the little space together.

In the center of my bedroom, hanging from the peaked ceiling, is one of my favorite pieces. A vintage fern chandelier, dripping with crystals that cast rainbows on my walls.

The room is opulent with its pale pink and emerald green color scheme. And the cherry on top is my *pièce de résistance*, a taxidermy standing mount of two flamingos in love.

I have zero regrets about this massive purchase and had them lovingly restored by Wren. She is a whiz with restoration. That had cost me almost as much as the original piece, even with my friends & family discount.

The flamingoes are huge with their necks entwined and heads together, forming a heart. The one I dubbed the girl kicking her foot up like a Hollywood kiss. If a Hollywood kiss had a backward flamingo knee, that is.

I don't just sell oddities—it is my way of life. I thoroughly appreciate the art of collection and display. Perhaps because I had grown up in such a sterile and minimalist environment, discouraged from displaying any more of my quirks, as my eyes had already declared me different to the world.

I make my way to the far end of my room to the antique bed. I always wanted a four-poster canopy bed with curtains, but the roofline of the converted attic would not allow it.

So instead, I fell in love with this old brass one at the local flea market. Jo and I had laughed as we stowed the headboard in my convertible Volkswagen Bug, putting the top down and precariously balancing it in the back seat.

It had been early spring then, and we froze our asses off driving it back to my place. Between the two of us, we lugged it up the two flights of stairs to my bedroom. It was a bitch, but together, we could do anything.

Once we had successfully gotten it up to the attic, we had collapsed in a heap on the floor, laughing. I couldn't wait to see her. It had been too long.

Smiling at the thought of my friend, I walk to my bed and sit on the edge. I kick off the pink bunny slippers and squinch my toes in the plush vintage Persian runner along the side. Finding just the right colors in an antique rug to match the room hadn't been easy, but I loved a decorating challenge.

I put my phone on the wireless charger and turn on my lamp on my version of an end table, a stack of old suitcases, yet another flea market haul. I am so tired I slide under the covers, still in my smoking jacket, barely getting the alarm set on my phone before falling asleep.

I WAKE TO A TREMENDOUS THUNDERCLAP, the lightning flashing white. My bedside light, a replica of a Tiffany's cobweb table lamp, had been on when I had fallen asleep. It is now off, and when I pick up my phone, it is no longer charging. The storm must have knocked out the power.

I roll over to the other side of the bed where there is a candle on the old smoking stand. I grope around and find a lighter for it. The flame provides a cozy and comforting glow in my room, chasing away the darkness. I can barely hear the crackling wooden wick over the storm. *At least it isn't another penis candle,* I think with a smile.

The smell of tobacco and leather fills the air. No girly florals for me. I like my candles like everything else, dark and spicy. I pause on that side of the bed, thinking about what else that table holds.

After all, it is the middle of the night and I am wide awake, startled by the lightning. I quirk an eyebrow, picturing an easy way to relax myself back to sleep.

Well, why not, I think and reach into the drawer to pull out one of my battery-operated friends. I fluff up my pillows and lean back against the old brass headboard. I open the sash of the smoking jacket I had fallen asleep in and slide my hands down to my breasts.

I cup them, appreciating their weight, then move to toying with my nipples. They quickly harden to firm peaks, and I trail my hands down. My mind drifts to the odd customer from today. How could it not? He was some serious eye candy.

I try to recall the good parts of the dream from the tub and shy away from the actual biting part that had startled me sharply awake, but then let my imagination drift to wonder how indeed a vampire bite would feel.

In the massive amount of vampire fiction I've read, and virtually every vampire movie ever made, the bite often seemed orgasmic. As my hands make their way down my body, I realize the candle smells like McHottie—tobacco and leather with the faintest hint of something light underneath, a balancing freshness.

With my left hand, I spread my folds, and with my right, I run the head of my vibrator up and down, the thoughts of Hottie McHottenstein paving the way. No need for lube tonight.

I turn on my vibrator, the low buzzing sound suddenly loud in the quiet of my bedroom. As the storm picks up, I turn up the speed to match the increasing intensity of the raging squall. I can't help but circle back to the thought of McHottie biting me.

I feel the tiniest flicker of guilt for typecasting him as Dracula because of his accent and coloring, but fuck it, every time I have that thought, my hips buck, and the next thing I know I am coming hard with a sudden clap of thunder and flash of lightning, peaking as the thought of his teeth piercing the skin of my neck firmly takes hold in my mind.

"*Mea culpa,*" I call out, repeating his Latin phrase from earlier. My legs shake as I come down from an intense orgasm, the vibrator now too much.

I am completely wiped, wrung out from the day and the best orgasm I've had since I don't know when. I giggle and think to myself, *really Lieshe, 'mea culpa'? Who yells that during an orgasm?*

But I was thinking of him and the way those words sounded coming out of his mouth, his lips wrapped around the syllables like a lover's caress. I grab a toy wipe and clean the vibe, throw it back in the drawer, and drift back to sleep.

Chapter 8
LIESHE

When I wake, the sun is streaming through the stained-glass windows in the gables of my attic bedroom, and I soon realize the angle seems all wrong for the time of morning I normally get up at. I snag my phone to check the time, but it is dead, having not charged overnight.

Damn it, why didn't I have an alarm clock in my room as a backup? I curse my overdependence on my phone while being secretly happy I had snuck in every last possible minute of sleep for my poor brain. I must not have got it perfectly lined up on the wireless charger. *Stupid technology,* I curse.

I sit up and shove my feet into my pink bunny slippers and stumble down the attic stairs to the first floor of my living space. Racing to the kitchen, I drop a pod in the coffee machine. No time to dump a six-dollar drink this morning. Better just to make my own.

Thinking I can't do any worse than yesterday's green sludge, I throw some oat milk in my heated frother, another indulgence, haphazardly squirt some stevia in, and sprint to the bathroom to get ready for the day.

My frizzy hair reflects last night's events—a hot bath and self-tussle between the sheets—and today's resulting humidity from the storm. There is nothing I can do but pile it on top of my head in a messy bun, gathering the wayward curls the best I can.

My premature gray forelock stands out against my chocolate brown hair. I love that it makes me look like the bride of Frankenstein. I pull it out of my messy bun to wisp around my face.

I wrap a handkerchief around my head and knot it on top to catch the flyaways. I brush my teeth and quickly wash my face, followed by some tinted moisturizer. A quick coat of mascara and lip gloss completes my look.

I throw an egg bite in the microwave and race to the closet to grab an outfit. The store opens in ten minutes, and I am running around like a chicken.

Trying to hurriedly pick one out, I end up settling for a pair of high-waisted jeans and a flannel button-down with the sleeves rolled back, thrown on over a Grimm logo tank top. I dig through the closet until I find my saddle shoes and race back to the kitchen.

I cuff my jeans, pour my coffee into my giant Grimm logo travel mug, shove my phone in my back pocket, and grab my egg bite from the microwave. I detest starting my day harried and out of control.

I burst out the back door, clatter down the back stairs, and dart around to the front of the store. I just about trip over Lucifer lying on the front step but manage to open just in time.

Not that I've ever had a customer waiting to get in, unlike Lucifer, but as a small business owner, I pride myself on running a tight ship. I head to my laptop and plug in my phone, thrilled when it charges. Guess the old green girl is giving us a go at technology today.

Hoping this sets a better tone for the rest of the day, I take a bite of my nuked egg and am intensely disappointed when it's rubbery and cold on the outside and like molten lava on the inside.

I marvel that with all of today's technology, microwaves still can't heat evenly. I sigh and set it down. Perhaps the two temperatures will merge, and this will be edible. Or it's the start of another diet.

I walk through the store, running my eyes over my taxidermy friends, sipping my coffee, and smiling. Not as good as when Natalie across the street makes it, but a heck of a lot cheaper, and at least I get my order right. Perhaps I can try the coffee shop again tomorrow.

As I look around the store at the collection I have amassed, I feel a little restless, which is unusual when I'm at Grimm. Perhaps the return of my waking dreams is messing with me, or maybe it's the anxiety that comes with the buying trips coming up. That reminds me, I need to call Jo and firm up the details of her covering the store.

I head back to the counter to check if my phone has charged enough to call her. It's only at ten percent, so I figure I'll let it go a little longer. While I wait for the phone to charge and any customers to come in, I hop online, cheering when my laptop works and zips me right to the online megastore.

I check out the electronic door chimes, but the modern gadget is counterintuitive to the atmosphere I have so painstakingly created in my shop. If I really think about it, there is no way a customer would have been able to get in and out without me hearing the vintage sleigh bells hanging from the doorknob. It makes no sense.

I abandon my cart and pick up my phone. I rationalize that I hate buying from the online megastore, anyway. I'd rather buy used or, at least, local. I phone Jo, but it goes to her voicemail, so I ask her to call me back and hang up.

Turning around, I find Lucifer has confiscated my

breakfast. I roll my eyes at him when a noise that sounds like a jackhammer cuts through the quiet morning.

Curious, I walk out front and stick my head out the door, looking left and then right, to find a construction crew working on the two buildings next to me in the row. And that noise is indeed a legit jackhammer.

The two neighboring units have been various businesses that have fallen in and out of favor over the years. Antiques, psychics, and more recently, an insurance company have occupied them. I suppress a shudder. In a quirky and fun neighborhood like this, an insurance company isn't very enticing for foot traffic.

I head to the sidewalk to better check out the action. There are a dozen guys in hard hats scurrying around, carrying everything from power tools to drywall and doors. It's a frenzy of activity with some decent eye candy. I try to peer in the small basement windows at the ground level to see what is going down there.

When I see them excavating dirt, I hope they know what they are doing. I don't even want to think about how easy structural damage could occur to the old foundation walls connecting that building from mine.

Sensing a looming presence behind me, I whip around. Bouncing off a hard, large body, I would have fallen, but a steadying hand quickly reaches out and grabs me by the upper arm. I smell tobacco and leather and look up and up and up until I meet that amazing half-smile and amber eyes.

I would have been able to place him based on his scent alone and the electricity racing through my blood at his touch.

Fuck me, but McHottenstein is even hotter outside in the daylight. The early morning sun highlights the blue in his black hair and illuminates his beautiful porcelain skin. I will need new vocabulary words to describe this level of hotness.

What is hotter than the term McHottenstein? McSexy? Super Duper Hottie? Hotalicious? *Fuck me,* I think.

"Excuse me?" he says with a quirk of an eyebrow, in his slow, formal cadence.

"What did I say out loud?" I flinch, mortified. I hope I wasn't brainstorming titles of hotness out loud.

"You said, 'Fuck me.'"

Now I need a word stronger than mortification. Why can't the earth just open up and swallow me now? Those words falling from his lips are insanely sexy. His inflection, cadence, and accent have officially made those two words the sexiest thing I have ever heard.

This guy is going to be a never-ending source of material for the spank bank. I'm going to need more batteries. And he still hasn't let go of my arm.

"I'm so sorry. I did *not* mean to say that out loud!" I exclaim, blushing furiously. "Sometimes I do that." I cringe.

He smiles kindly and tucks my white forelock behind my ear with the faintest cool touch. I realize I am still smacked into his chest, every breath brushing my breasts against him.

"Do not be embarrassed. I like a woman who speaks her mind," he quietly reassures me.

I'm dying. Does he think I just asked him to fuck me? I don't know what to do at this point other than change the subject. He doesn't seem put off. Meanwhile, I'm over here falling apart.

"Wh-what are you doing here?" I stammer.

He slides his hand from my upper arm up to the back of my neck and pivots me to stand in line with him, looking at the scene in front of us. The bustling workers are a hive of activity.

"Renovating."

"Renovating?" I stupidly parrot back, distracted by the weight of his cool, heavy hand on my neck. He turns his head toward me and narrows his eyes slightly, seeming to suppress a chuckle.

"Yes, renovating," he repeats.

At this point, he must think I am incapable of intelligent conversation or a bumbling imbecile. He firmly guides me by his grip on my neck, moving me out of the way of the construction workers swarming like ants.

Why does the cool weight of his hand feel so comforting? A thrill races through me at this small public claim.

"Did you get a permit for that basement work? I'm a little worried about the foundation," I say with a nervous glance toward the windows just above the sidewalk.

He slips his hand from my neck to lightly grip my chin between his fingers and directs my face back to his. He looks deep into my eyes and says, "Of course, and don't worry about the basement. I always make sure to build a sound foundation. The attic will be a good place for my bedroom. I imagine it would light up exquisitely in a storm."

My mind drifts back to the storm last night and what I did to go back to sleep. A flash of lightning had accompanied my toe-curling orgasm.

He winks at me. He winks! And somehow, it seems like he knows about my late-night activities. But that's impossible. How the hell could he know?

"I, uh, I'm sure it would. I gotta go," I say, gesturing with my thumb over my shoulder and stepping back to sever our distracting connection.

"Isn't your store that way?" he says, pointing in the other direction.

I'm not sure how it's possible, but I flush even deeper and

just bail at this point. There is no salvaging this conversation. Or possibly even my sanity.

I quickly escape to the safety of my store, dropping down onto the stool. I stare at my computer, breathing hard.

Oh, Mylanta. I try to process our interaction, mentally dodging the part where I sounded like an idiot, and realize he is renovating the two buildings next door. Why? Is he flipping them? Is McHottie a realtor? Or, even worse, a competing business?

Oh no, please don't let it be a competing business. Or something super lame, like a lawyer's office. I'm going to have to get my shit together and string together a few coherent sentences to figure out what is going on. With the mixed zoning, he could do almost anything with the buildings.

I'm saved from my worried thoughts by the sound of growling zombies that serves as my ring tone when Jo calls me. I answer the phone, "Hey girl."

"Lieshe!" my friend exclaims, one of the few people who can consistently pronounce my name correctly. "I miss you, you dirty whore."

She always pronounces whore as "who-re." She is a riot. I swear a little, or maybe a lot, but anything is fair game to come out of her mouth.

"I can't wait to come out there and store-sit. Do you still have the demon cat from hell?"

"Yes. I should have named him Dorian or Gray, since he appears to be immortal. His sole purpose in life seems to be to hate me for all eternity. Thank you for keeping an eye on him as well as the store, Jo."

"It's not like I have to do anything. I've never actually seen the little bastard. I only know him from your loving comments. Cats *are* evil, you know."

"This one is. Although I shouldn't be so hard on him. He's not a bad old guy, he just gives zero F's. He even leaves for days when I'm here, so no hard feelings if he doesn't cross your path."

Jo snorts, "I see what you did there! Black cat crossing my path. Ha. Ha. This is why you're single, my friend."

We laugh like only soul-sisters can and then firm up the details of her upcoming visit. She promises to text me her flight info so I can pick her up at the airport. All too soon, we wrap our call. I really miss her.

I'm so thankful that tomorrow is Monday, the one day Grimm is closed. I have big plans of doing abso-freakin-lutely nothing.

My mind and body need to reset after yesterday and today. I daydream about lying in bed and reading all day, but as divine as that sounds, it rarely actually happens.

Even when I'm not working, I'm still working. There is just always something to do. Or at least that's the excuse I give myself. Because what would happen if I slowed down?

I do not have the mental energy to answer that right now, so squash it back in the recesses of my brain between third grade and asking my mom to take me bra shopping for the first time.

It's a much-needed unusually quiet day in the shop, so I spend some time updating financial spreadsheets and doing my online banking. It feels so good to be successful and have a little money in the bank. I'll check out some shoes later tonight to celebrate the profitable spring season.

As much as I love shoes, it would be nice to have a human to celebrate with, perhaps share an adult beverage and toast my success in my chosen venture. Sure, my few close friends are great and super supportive, but someone to celebrate with me between the sheets sure would be a bonus.

Dating is always a little tricky for me. The circles I move in attract some unusual folks. I know I may not be the biggest prize, with my mop of curls and glasses, Botticelli body, and penchant for retro aesthetics and shoes, but I'm the lid to someone's pot and I'm going to be a little choosy.

Huge hot dudes, like, well, like McHottie, have always been my type. They just never seem to be attracted to a girl like me.

Sure, I've dated, and I've had a few sexual partners, admittedly mostly lukewarm and definitely not on McHottie's level, but I still haven't found the right person to put his Docs under my bed forever quite yet.

Despite being thirty, I'm in no hurry to settle down. I'd be labeled an old maid back in my hometown, where everyone was expected to marry the first person they dated in high school.

Thankful to be out of there, I'm willing to wait for exactly the perfect partner. But it would be nice to not go home to an empty house every night. And I know it sounds desperately romantic, but I really want to fall in love.

I've been in 'like' before. Had the tingle of a new relationship, the starry-eyed infatuation with the sprinkle of lust that accompanies it. I've read plenty about falling in and out of love, and I've seen friends do it.

But I don't actually have any first-hand experience. Sure, I've had crushes, and I've even thrown around an 'I love you' or two, but true love?

Nope. Nothing. Nada. Zilch.

Maybe I'm broken? Hasn't everyone had at least a few loves by the time they reach my advanced age? My parents had married young, like everyone there did. My best friend Mindy was married right out of college. Hell, I even had friends on their second marriages already.

I don't want just any love or to settle, though. I want the kind of love I've only read about, where your souls yearn for each other. To feel the earth move beneath my feet and the other person seep into my very marrow.

I want to not know where I stop and he begins. I know deep in my heart my soulmate is out there, somewhere, just waiting for me to find him. And I will not settle for anything less.

My father's words worm their way into my mind, wrapping icy fingers around my heart. Maybe he's right. What if I am just too different, too odd, to attract my forever love?

I sigh and decide I will go out tonight, just down a few blocks to the corner bar, Jethro's, where the folks are friendly, the food is good, and the drinks are reasonable. That should chase the doldrums away.

Although the days are warm, the nights are still a little cool, so I'm hoping the patio, with its cute white string lights, will be open. I know enough regulars there, I won't feel awkward sitting at the bar by myself.

I'll even grab some indulgent bar food for dinner because I don't want to sit home alone and poke at whatever sad leftovers are kicking around my fridge. Again.

It doesn't hurt that Jethro's makes great shrimp tacos and has the best corn tortillas. Having Celiac disease keeps me on my toes, but I've made it my business to learn what restaurants are safe for me to eat at.

The gluten-free vegan place around the corner is my go-to, but I'm not vegan. I like most foods, obviously, and I like meat just fine.

Jethro's is another of my local haunts, and flirting with Jason, the bartender, always boosts my spirits. He is funny and kind. A nice clean-cut guy who matches my five-three height. I'm not attracted to him, but sometimes I feel like I should at least give him a chance.

As great as his personality is, though, the zing just isn't there, no matter how much I tell myself to make it be. He is the antithesis of my preferred morally gray antiheroes and the beefcakes I can't help but be attracted to.

Closing time is here at last, so I wrap up the spreadsheets I'm working on and collect the cash from the drawer. I don't keep much in the antique register because most of the transactions go through the little plastic gadget next to it. But as valuable as a lot of the shop's contents are, cash would be the most tempting target for a thief, so I deposit it regularly for safety.

I place the money in the bank bag and toss it in my enormous vintage tote. It is one of my favorites, but the thing is like an abyss, and I could probably lose a small child at the bottom. I remember to put my phone in the smaller pocket, so it doesn't get lost.

With keys in hand, I step out the door. I lock up Grimm and zip down the alley to my rear apartment door. This time, I don't run like I'm being chased by the devil himself. Instead, I walk like a normal person, and once inside, I take my time getting ready to go out.

I leave my hair up in its retro do but I swap the jeans for high-waisted sailor button black shorts. I dress them up with large hole fishnet stockings and a red halter top to match my bandana. The shirt looks polka dotted at first glance, but on closer inspection, it has small bats on it.

The warmer weather is just starting, and I am excited about wearing some of my summer clothes. I pop in a pair of dangly bat earrings to coordinate with my copper pendant I had picked up at an art show.

The bat is crafted from copper reclaimed from a church

downspout. It holds onto the black cord with its little clawed hand, so endearing.

My Death's-head Hawkmoth ring goes onto my index finger. It is one of my favorite finds from the last steampunk convention. I love shopping there and can't wait to be a vendor at this year's event.

I touch up my makeup and add a bold red lip to match my shirt and wing out my cat eyeliner a little more. Despite being tired, I look surprisingly good, if I do say so myself.

I head to my closet and peruse my shoe collection, trying to find the perfect complement to this outfit. It is only a few blocks to the bar, so I contemplate a pair of heels but at last go for ease of walking and choose my cherry red Chelsea boot Docs.

Sensible footwear really does make sense, since I have to walk an extra few blocks out of my way to make the bank deposit. I swap my wallet from the bottomless pit tote to my red leather coffin-shaped backpack, adding the deposit bag to drop off on the way.

I took my time getting ready, so by the time I leave, the sky is a little darker than I expected. I put a little hustle in my step and head out.

Chapter 9

As I walk to the bank in the early summer evening, I realize I was a little too enthusiastic about breaking out my warm weather wardrobe. The slight breeze wraps chilly fingers around my legs to caress my skin. I'm thankful I wore boots. At least my toes are toasty.

The stars' feeble attempt to compete with the light pollution from the city while the fingernail moon plays peekaboo with the clouds leaves little natural light. The streetlamps start to space out as I walk, allowing pools of inky darkness to form between their warm glow.

I speed up, wanting to get this errand out of the way so I can get to my end goal a little quicker. The spooky shadows tease me, making a hot meal and a drink to warm up my insides seem even more welcome now than they did earlier.

In a quick ten minutes, the fluorescent glow of the bank's lights welcomes me. My feet hit the empty parking lot and I again get a prickling sensation at the back of my neck. But this prickle is different and uncomfortable, not at all like the McHottie prickle I've started to become accustomed to, even craving it. I can't believe I still don't know his name.

My gut starts to churn, distracting me from my thoughts of the enigmatic stranger, and this feels like trouble. Not the good kind.

I roll my eyes at my overactive imagination, telling myself to just hurry and get the deposit done. Perhaps I should switch to some sweet romance and quit feeding the dark parts of my brain. I contemplate that for a second but then snort out loud at the thought. I love my morally gray book boyfriends.

I straighten my spine, square my shoulders, and widen my stance, trying to appear larger than my five-foot-three frame. I'm again thankful I chose reasonable footwear, but rather than for warmth this time, in case I need to run.

Despite my assurances to myself that I'm being silly, I still want to be sensible and won't totally ignore my intuition. I lift my chin and breathe deep, channeling confidence.

I listen in to the night sounds around me, filtering out the traffic on nearby streets and the other myriad noises expected in any suburb, like distant honking and, further out, church bells. Hopefully, my guardian angel is close, even though it's been ages since I last thought I saw him.

I don't hear any footsteps or an approaching car, but keep scanning my surroundings, looking for the perceived threat setting my instincts off. Swinging my backpack off, I grab the deposit bag and the bank key, then settle my backpack securely back on my shoulders.

I try to unlock the night deposit box, but my hands are shaky and sweaty from nerves, which makes gripping the key and turning it difficult. I feel like this is taking forever.

At last, I get the lock open, drop the deposit in, and close the drawer with a large exhale. Relieved, I try to keep up the charade of confidence, despite my pounding heart. As I turn to walk away from the bank, I catch movement out of the corner of my eye.

Turning back toward it, I see a large shadowy figure emerge from the bushes by the alley behind the bank. In the dark, I can't make out anything other than size. Large. Or maybe even extra-large. It looks like they are coming this way.

I take a deep breath and prepare to make a run for it. There is no way I can take on an attacker who is so much bigger than me. I will fight like hell if I get caught, but running to a more populated area seems the safer bet. My heart pounds in double time.

My hand drifts to my back pocket to grab my phone from its usual spot when I remember I purposefully stashed it in the little pocket of my other bag so it wouldn't get lost. *Damn it, Lieshe,* I curse myself for forgetting to grab it. A low growl interrupts my self-flagellation.

The dark shadow and I both turn toward the deeper shadows in the back of the alley. A pair of golden eyes that appear to glow from within come into view first, followed by the rest of the creature.

A massive black dog steps into the light, growling all the while, with muscles rippling and bunching as it slowly stalks toward whoever is hidden in the shadows. Every hair on my body stands at attention at the otherworldly nature of the menacing sound.

The night has gone eerily silent, highlighting the low throaty growl even more. The enormous beast is positively vicious with its hackles raised, yet I am strangely unafraid. Somehow, I know I am not in any danger from this hell hound, but I can't say the same for the other person.

As I feel my rapid pulse slow and the edges of my vision start to flicker, I think, *oh, no, no, no!* I cannot have a waking dream right now. I begin to spin my ring, but I can't perform any of my usual mantras to ground myself; I am not in a safe situation while the shadowy figure remains.

A pack of wolves briefly shimmers in and out of focus around the dog in the here and now, and I force myself to take in a breath, hold it for three beats, and then breathe it out.

The forced box breathing burns my lungs as I fight my rising panic over having a waking dream in this moment. I keep pushing myself to slow my breathing and count—one, two, three. One, two, three.

Present day coalesces back to a solid image, and I give myself a slight shake. That was a heart-stopper. Moments like this can trigger me, which is super inconvenient. I must be getting better at controlling them if the image just overlaid the present day and didn't take over. Or the dreams are evolving...

I peer closer at the massive beast and all I can think of is that it must be some type of rare breed. My brain stupidly looks for details like dog breeds to focus on instead of worrying about my safety and the resurgence of my evolving waking dreams.

The enormous black animal lunges forward with a ferocious bark, drawing my full attention back to the situation at hand. The shadow person turns and flees into the darkness, hotly pursued by the animal chasing him.

"Yeah, take that fucker!" I yell, pumping my fist in the air like I had anything to do with scaring them away, as opposed to the obviously feral stray dog. How on earth could an animal that big be wandering around on its own?

Muttering under my breath about slacker guardian angels, I bolt in the direction of the bar for my well-deserved drink and dinner. And maybe a second drink. Nodding to myself, I think, *definitely a second drink.*

Before something else can go wrong, I hurry away. There is really no crime to call the police for even if I had my phone. I kick myself for having been so stupid as to go to a bank alone to make a deposit when it is dark out. That is safe girl 101. Duh.

Is it fair that I am vulnerable simply for having a vagina? Of course not. But the world isn't always a safe place, fair or not.

I must be getting overly confident in my quaint little neighborhood, where it's easy to forget there is a big, wicked world out there. Luckily, a dinosaur-sized dog showed up. I've never seen a pet like that. Could be some type of exotic collector animal.

I've been fortunate in my life to rarely stare down true danger, so I'm understandably rattled by tonight's events. To distract myself as I walk, I contemplate the whereabouts of my long-lost guardian angel, but come up with nothing substantial.

I make good time to the bar, my steps fueled by fading adrenaline and chills, as the panic sweat turns icy under my arms. I should have expected the cooler evening and grabbed a jacket. And a weapon. I really need to pick up some mace, like I have been meaning to.

When I arrive, I head to the open patio bar, happy a seat is available near one of the outdoor heaters. I settle onto the high stool and the radiating warmth is blissful. I begin to thaw from the top down, the tension bleeding from my tight shoulders. Apparently, I'm not the only one pushing for a change of season.

Jason wanders over with a smile saying, "Usual?"

I'm here often enough that he knows I always start with an unsweetened iced tea. With a slight quaver to my voice, I reply, "No, I'll need something a little stronger tonight."

He goes over tonight's specials, and I order a medium burger with gouda and bacon over lettuce with a side of sweet potato fries.

I am so grateful they keep a separate gluten-free fryer. As much as I'm loath to admit it, I'm a pretty frequent customer. I know I should cook more at home and probably eat more greens.

Lots of good intentions, but buying food and cooking it for one is just never great. I end up throwing half of the produce away, and that just makes me sadder about cooking for just myself.

Jethro's makes its sauces fresh in-house and the sweet potato fries with dip trio are just so good. The sad produce drawer in my fridge doesn't stand a chance against condiments from scratch.

"Extra dip?" Jason asks with a wink.

I don't know why he asks, so I reply with mock outrage, "Jason, you know I'm a condiment girl! And I'll take an Ocean with two rocks."

"Oh, you're in for a treat. We just got a new voyage."

I love trying the different ocean voyages this bourbon uses as part of their aging process. Each one is just a little different. For a corner bar, they have a nice liquor selection. He brings me a generous pour and goes to put my order in.

He comes right back and probes, "Spill. Why are you starting with a bourbon? I know you're closed tomorrow, but is everything okay? You seemed a little shaken up when you got here."

As I retell the story of the bank deposit incident, Jason's eyes keep drifting over my left shoulder. I reach the end of my narrative and scoff, "Jason, what are you looking at?"

Jason meets my eyes and apologizes. "I'm sorry, but there is a huge guy back there who keeps looking at you. Bummer you had such a scare tonight. Super weird. I always feel safe around here, but you're right, we all need to be aware of our surroundings. And what was up with the giant dog?"

"Right!" I exclaim, gesticulating with my bourbon. "Now I need to be on the lookout for giant feral dogs and assassins!"

I slam my bourbon down with a little more force than necessary, almost sloshing it over the rim.

Jason smiles and says, "Are you sure he was an assassin?"

And thinking back, yes, my woman's protective gut instinct had kicked in, but nothing had actually happened.

"You're right. Probably not an *assassin*, but you never know. I'll be more aware. Maybe I'll catch a ride home tonight. It's only a few blocks, but I don't really feel up to walking by myself. Especially since I want a refill on this bourbon."

Jason's face warms as he smiles, leaning in. We are back to our playful flirting again.

"I'll walk you home," he teases with a wink.

"Oh, Jason," I laugh, "you don't get off until like 3 a.m. I can't hang like that anymore."

And then I feel him.

This prickle I know—this is an awareness of McHottie. I can smell him before I see him. Leather, tobacco, and as a faint undercurrent, anger simmering like heat off the road in summer. The hair on the back of my exposed neck rises.

A large hand descends onto the bar right next to my bourbon glass and a familiar voice says in a low growl, "I'll walk you home."

His voice so close to my ear causes goosebumps to cascade down my side. I feel his breath ghost my neck and my shoulder involuntarily drifts up. I suppress the best possible shudder. Why does his voice affect me without even seeing his face?

Jason instinctually leans back in response to the presence behind me. To his credit, he swallows but looks at me and says, "Lieshe, you know this guy? You okay with this?"

I take in the large hand resting next to my glass, recognizing the scattered rings I had glimpsed just this morning on the street. Closer now, I can see one is some type of dragon signet and the other an ancient and thick rich gold band with years of patina and a stone winking in the light. It is so dark, it is almost black, like a drop of blood at midnight.

His other hand lands on the bar at my other side as he brings his body closer, caging me in from behind. My heart races. I feel like trapped prey, and I don't hate it. Quite the opposite, actually.

He leans into me, placing his mouth right next to my ear again, so close I can feel his lips move and the air leave his mouth as he says my name for the first time.

"Lieshe. Shall I walk you home this evening?"

My name falls from his lips, and not only has he pronounced it correctly, but his accent and cadence make it sound heavenly. As the letters of my name spill from his mouth, I hold my breath. I feel like I'm cascading over a waterfall, mesmerized by its beauty, until I am careening over the crest, dropped into an endless pool below.

I never want to surface, rather I want to let the cold depths claim me without a fight, bubbles silently rising past me. Anyone else saying my name is now ruined for all time, even if they can pronounce it correctly.

I am insanely aroused by this man despite him not even touching me. His nearness, his voice in my ear, the way he says my name. I clench my thighs together, feeling like I have way too many clothes on, and we are in way too public of a place.

I can picture him sliding his mouth down into the junction of my neck and shoulder. I am drowning in his presence, which eats up my oxygen like being caught in the waterfall's hydraulics.

My breathy reply comes out before my brain can even process what is going on. "Yes, of course. Thank you."

I feel him inhale as if scenting me, and then his looming presence is gone as he takes the seat next to me. Despite our proximity sitting next to each other at the bar, I miss the intensity from just a moment ago. I prefer him towering over me from behind, lips at my ear.

"My pleasure. I cannot let a beautiful woman walk home alone. Now you can leave when it pleases you."

I could listen to him speak forever with his exotic voice and formal way of speaking. He prompts me to tell tonight's events again.

"A stray dog, you say? I love dogs. Tell me more."

I repeat my story as Jason moves off to care for the other patrons. I'm thankful for his friendship and for him looking out for me. My new neighbor's face grows tense as I finish, and a little harshly he says, "Promise me you will not put yourself in danger again."

I roll my eyes and say, "Sure," surprised when he grips my upper arm.

"Promise me," he says urgently, giving my arm a little shake.

I meet his gaze, gone darkly serious, and tug my bottom lip between my teeth. His eyes fall to my mouth, watching me worry my lip with my teeth. He inhales sharply and tears his eyes away.

I feel awkward but compelled to respond with the answer I know he wants to hear. I nod and solemnly say, "I promise."

He releases his grip on my arm and his expression is back to normal, as though this grave moment never happened at all. He opens his mouth to speak, but just then Jason arrives with my food. I offer to share with McHottie, but he waves me away.

"I already ate, but I would love to watch you enjoy yourself."

I watch the way his mouth moves around his words, lips and tongue and air creating sounds. I flush, wondering if he means 'enjoy yourself' as a double entendre or if my lust is just projecting. Clearly, he is just being a friendly new neighbor.

After all, he is so far out of my league, we are in different sports on different intergalactic teams playing on different planets. But oh, would I love to score a touchdown with him. Hell, I'd settle for first base. *Stop with the sports analogies, Lieshe,* I scold myself, knowing I have it all mixed up. Sports never were my thing.

We fall into an easy banter as he asks me to tell him all about the neighborhood. I relax into the normalcy of a mundane conversation as I fill him in on the other businesses and residents I know. I wave around my fries as I talk, taking bites between talking.

He seems genuinely interested in what I am saying, asking questions and for clarification. Before I know it, over an hour has passed.

I go to eat the lone fry on my plate, scooping up the last of my favorite aioli sauce with it. I get a little overzealous with the sauce, though, and just as I go to pop it in my mouth, a drop falls, landing on my exposed chest.

McHottie's eyes zero in on the drop. I look down at it, embarrassed to be making a mess in front of my hot new neighbor. But before I can grab my napkin to wipe it off, he reaches out with a lone finger and lifts my chin, so I am looking back up at him.

My face flames as he trails his finger lightly down my throat, across the top swell of my breast, and deftly swipes the drop off my skin. I wait with bated breath to see what follows. Time feels suspended as I fall into his golden stare.

I'm pulled back to the present when Jason comes by to ask if I want dessert. Since I always say no, I think he is actually checking in to make sure I am okay with the newcomer.

McHottie's eyes flash at the intrusion and for the briefest second, he casts a withering glare at Jason. He immediately schools his face back to neutral and asks, "Do you have *crème brûlée?*"

"Yes, coconut is the seasonal flavor," Jason answers slowly. He must have caught that look; I'm surprised he didn't burn to ash under its intensity.

I almost moan out loud. Coconut crème brûlée is my absolute favorite, but I'm always more worried about my weight than I am willing to indulge.

"She will have one please," he replies, turning back to grace me with that panty-melting half smile.

Eek, this guy's voice. Everything is a little formal and oh so freaking amazing that he says. He makes me feel like a fangirl.

As I quirk a brow at him for ordering for me, he turns on the charm to the full megawatt smile and says, "Please, I love to watch a beautiful woman enjoy herself."

How could I resist?

As Jason turns and walks away, I realize I didn't even know McHottie's name to introduce them. And I certainly couldn't call down the street to him, "Hey, McHottie." I feel a little bad for Jason, who has always been such a sweet flirt, to both witness me sitting here with another guy and then catching the evil eye from him.

"You still haven't told me your name, " I say.

"What is a name but the sounds that fall from your lips only to get someone's attention?" he asks.

"No one ever seems to get the right sounds from their lips with my name, yet they still usually manage to get my attention," I grouse with a laugh.

"You absolutely have mine," he confesses, his amber eyes intense.

His words are an exact match to his ardent focus on me. I feel a flush creep up my neck for the second time tonight to know that I am holding his full attention. Jason slides my crème brûlée in front of me, diffusing the intense moment. Perfect timing, again.

I drag my gaze away and check out the dessert. My eyes light up in anticipation of cracking the hard sugar layer open with my spoon. The first crack is my favorite part of the decadent dessert, and this one doesn't disappoint.

I tap, tap, tap it, and scoop up a perfectly composed bite of creamy decadence topped with the slightly burnt sugar that I know will leave a smoky sweet flavor on my tongue.

I contemplate if my tobacco and leather-scented new neighbor would taste the same. If I crack open his hard exterior, will he be sweet and smoky inside? Or I worry, will he leave behind the acrid burnt taste of a broken heart?

I offer a bite to him since he ordered it for me, but he shakes his head and follows the spoon to my mouth. I can't help but close my eyes as I take the first spoonful and let out a small hum of appreciation.

When I open my eyes again, he is staring at my mouth. His nostrils flare, like he is scenting me. I look into his intense amber gaze, finding the moss-green flecks so very much like mine, and watch his pupils dilate.

In every late-night romance novel I read, that is a

response to desire, and I wonder if that is indeed true. Could he really desire me?

Sometimes, I think I pick up on clues that he does, but then my inner voice of reason and doubt replies that is not only improbable, but downright stupid. I must be overanalyzing this simple interaction and turning it into more than it is.

I drop his gaze, mildly ashamed of my thoughts, and finish my dessert. I feel myself start to withdraw, but he quickly draws me back into the conversation, and before I know it, I am reengaged and having a wonderful time talking with him. He just seems so interested in me and somehow so damn familiar.

It's impossible not to be drawn in by his charm. The conversation is easy, and I just keep reminding myself he is just a nice, albeit extremely handsome, new neighbor. Nothing to get self-conscious about, just making friends.

"I would love to try your drink," he says, surprising me. Jason had brought him water when he brought my second bourbon, but it has sat untouched in front of him.

I hand him my almost empty rocks glass and he spins the cup to place his lips exactly over where mine had been. He holds my gaze as he takes a sip.

I am mesmerized by the way his lips caress the glass. The thick column of his throat moves as he swallows, Adam's apple bobbing, followed by his tongue flicking out to lick his lips. How can anyone make taking a sip of bourbon so sexy?

He makes drinking from where my lips had been seem incredibly erotic. I pick the cup up, spinning it the way he had to drink where his lips had been, mimicking his actions. The bourbon seems spicier with this sip, like he has infused it with his tobacco and leather essence. It's even more delicious this way.

Jason comes and places my bill on the bar in front of me, but before I can protest, my new friend takes out his wallet and drops way too much cash down without ever breaking our heated stare. I'm drowning in his eyes as he stands and takes my hand.

I hastily pick up my bourbon glass and drink the last few sips, loving the final watered-down swig. As he pulls me away, I throw over my shoulder, "Thanks Jason, I loved the new voyage!"

Chapter 10

I watch them leave the bar together. I thought I could get to her first, but he had surprised me in his filthy, flea-bitten, mutt form. Virtues don't suit me, but patience is something I have learned over the eons of my damned existence. So, patient I will be.

Chapter 11

As we head out, I try to protest that he had bought me dinner, but he waves me away, saying again, "It was my pleasure."

The way his voice sounds as he says the word pleasure has me squeezing my thighs together, very aware of the effects he has on my body. And he still hasn't dropped my hand.

It is easy to see he is a big man, but standing this close, holding hands, my head barely reaches his shoulder. He must be at least six-three. I could pretend his solid presence at my side isn't a comfort after my near disastrous walk alone earlier, but it is. I'll admit, my vagina is thankful for a penis by my side, for more reasons than one.

I realize while we walk the two blocks back to my place that he has had nothing to eat or drink at the bar other than that super sexy sip of my bourbon. The night has been a whirlwind, leaving me dizzy with lust, liquor, and the earlier adrenaline burst.

I wonder if I should invite him up for a nightcap and then grapple with the implications of that invitation.

On the one hand, my rational mind says, I really don't know him that well. The hedonistic side argues he can't be a serial killer since he has allowed himself to be seen in public with me, paid for my dinner, was worried about my safety on the way home, and is renovating the properties next to mine.

The rational side argues back—he could still be a serial

killer or some type of deviant, or even bury you in the new basement. And then a third voice speaks up and says, ladies —he is not interested in us. He's just a super nice, super hot guy who is being a boy scout.

And then they all frown and sit down, pouting, taking a vote on whether we want him to be a sexual deviant or not. It's a unanimous yes, please! Hedonism wins.

I let out a small giggle at the bourbon-fueled imaginary board meeting in my head.

"What is making you laugh?"

"Oh, um, it's just been a day, and now here we are, walking home, like old friends."

He gently squeezes my fingers with his and says, "Friends..." like he is rolling it around in his mind. "Yes, I'd like that."

We reach the back of my building and walk over to the stairs that lead up to my second-floor entrance. I stand at the bottom, shuffling my feet, and pull my hand out of his grasp to dig in my coffin backpack for my keys.

I instantly miss his cool hand in mine, his palm dwarfing my smaller one. Honestly, my fingers hurt and were falling asleep from his between them, but I would have let them fall off from lack of blood flow before I pulled my hand away from his. The risk of gangrene would have been worth it just to keep touching him, loving the way electricity seemed to zing between our skin.

As a kid, we visited Lancaster County farm country, and I couldn't help but touch the electric fence between me and the cows. I knew it could shock me, but I was just *so* curious. I had cautiously brushed the wire with a long piece of grass, feeling a resulting tingle race up my hand to stand my arm hair on end.

His touch reminds me of that same tingling curiosity. I

wonder how touching the actual live wire of him will be. Incendiary is my only guess.

I peer up at him and as he steps closer, I'm forced to crank my neck back to meet those amber eyes. The moonlight is bright in the cloudless sky, reflected in his unwavering stare. The boardroom of arguing voices in my mind is blissfully silent, and before I know what is happening, my mouth is saying, "Would you like to come up?"

As soon as I realize what I've said, I backtrack. "I mean, I don't know if you have to work tomorrow or—" I am immediately and effectively shushed with his finger against my lips.

"I'd love to," he replies, his voice dark, wrapping me with sinful promises.

I'm shocked that I so confidently and smoothly just invited him up to my place. I frantically try to think if my place is even presentable, but his finger resting against my lips drives all coherent thoughts from my mind.

My tongue reaches out of its own volition and licks the finger that is shushing me. I lick him! I swear it's totally involuntary, just the smallest taste of this man, but he obviously feels it.

His pupils blow wide, the black almost eclipsing the amber of his beautiful eyes, and I'm trapped, motionless, at the chasm again, knowing this time I will gladly fall.

I'm not sure how it happens, but the next thing I know, his hand fists in the back of my hair and I am staring up at the clear night sky. *Oh, there's the dipper,* I think, and then I feel his breath at the base of my throat as he licks the hollow above my sternum, filling in the little dent there with the tip of his tongue.

I can't move, can't breathe, can't think beyond—McHottie licked me. He freaking licked me back!

I am instantly aroused, my nipples hardening in the cool night air, as my blood flow coalesces into my vag. And then I sag against the railing of my stairs, as Mr. Tall, Pale, and Handsome drops his hand out of my hair like a lead balloon and steps back, looking shocked at his own actions.

"Good evening," he says stiffly with a formal nod, as he turns and disappears around the corner of the building.

I stand there, mouth gaping. Had I done something wrong? What the hell? He can't just lick me and walk away!

I run after him, and I swear I am only a few steps behind, but he is nowhere to be seen in the alley. So, I walk the entire way up to the main street and look right toward his property, but he is simply gone.

I dejectedly turn and come back down the alley, dragging my sorry ass up my stairs and in through the door. This night held all the promise of my wildest fantasies until his sudden departure dashed them with a bucket of ice water.

I lean back against my closed front door, thumping my head in frustration. "What the fuck?" I say to the room at large. "What in the ever-loving fuck was that about?"

My frustration channels itself into anger. Of course, McHottie is a fuckface. He gave me whiplash with his actions. And I still don't even know his name. I groan out loud.

I am so thankful tomorrow is Monday. Tonight, I will have a solo nightcap, pass the hell out like a starfish alone in my queen bed, and then tomorrow, I will sleep in like it's my j-o-b.

Then I'll stay in bed all day surfing social media and indulging in an epic pity party. I'll forget about angels and dogs and shadowy creepers. And I will absolutely forget all about hot mysterious neighbors.

I head to my bathroom and swap out my updo and handkerchief for a quick messy bun, wash my face, and smooth on a rose clay mask, hoping it sucks out both my anger and the junk in my pores.

I let my clothes fall to the floor, and with them, the stress of the day. I drop my bra and take a deep breath, feeling my shoulders relax without its heavy binding weight. I throw the discarded garments in the wicker hamper in the corner and change into my long smoking jacket and hot pink bunny slippers.

The silky material of the robe caresses my skin, and the slippers are heavenly on my tired feet. As I move, the silk slides against me like a lover's touch. My little indulgences drag me closer to a more relaxed state, comforting and familiar.

I figure I'll help further my relaxation along and head back to my kitchen. I'm still stuffed from a full dinner and dessert but pour myself my favorite dark red wine, anyway.

Probably not the wisest choice on top of the bourbon I already had, but the anger, hurt, and confusion are simmering just below my surface. I think the wine will be the last item to chase them away completely.

I down the first glass and start a second, just about emptying the bottle with my generous servings and enormous wine glass. I pull up my playlist and send it through the house speakers.

My mask is tight, so I know it is almost time to wash it off. Skin care is another indulgence of mine, and this mask is my favorite. I meander around my open concept first floor, tidying up a few things, putting some shoes away with angry movements to waste time while my mask finishes drying.

When it feels like a piece of old pottery as fragile as my confidence, I head back to the bathroom to rinse it off. I wet a washcloth, wring it out, and then hold it against my face to soften the mask.

I take several steadying deep breaths, each one calming me more than the last. The rose scented air picks up humidity from the warm wet washcloth, and I feel more and more relaxed with each steamy inhalation.

Laying the cloth aside, I bend down over the sink and splash warm water on my face. Between my skin care and the two glasses of wine downed in quick succession, my anger has dissipated, leaving me mellow—if a little hollow.

I gently blot my face dry with a towel and see in the mirror I missed a pretty big swath down on my jawline. I go to rinse it off when I hear a knock at my door.

What the hell? I spin and stomp toward my door. Who on earth would come over this late on a Sunday night? I feel a familiar prickling at the back of my neck, but no, it can't be him after his hasty retreat earlier.

I step up to the peephole, nervous for a second after tonight's events about who or what is on the other side. I remind myself that I have a solid door with a good lock, and I am safe. All I have to do if it is someone dangerous is simply not open the door.

I peer out and can't believe who it is. I stare with one squinty eye at the warped image of McHottie's profile. Even the fisheye glass can't distort this man's raw and primal good looks. What in the serious hell could he want?

Just like I sometimes speak my inner monologue out loud, sometimes when I drink too much, I can get a little snarky. And the emotional whiplash this man has put me through tonight has blown straight past snarky and brought out my inner bitch.

Forgetting my ridiculous get-up, my smoking jacket and hot pink bunny slippers, and of course, the hunk of face mask still clinging to the side of my face now entirely devoid of make-up, I rip open the door to snarl, "What the hell do you want?"

He stands with his hands pressed into the top of my door frame, head downcast. With his arms up like this, his leather jacket and shirt ride up, exposing his Adonis belt dipping into the black jeans slung low on his hips.

I envision biting the thick ridge of muscle and tracing my tongue over the ink that I can't quite make out in the darkness. With the moon behind him, he appears as a dark, fallen angel.

Looking up at me through lowered lashes, he murmurs, "I tried. Forgive me, I tried."

Before I can even process what he is talking about, he bursts through my door and crushes me to him, wrapping me in his arms. I had imagined what his body would feel like pressed against mine, what his smell would morph to at close range, what he would taste like.

My imagination didn't hold a candle to the reality of it all. He is big—bigger even than I had thought. Solid and cool like marble. The man felt carved out of solid rock.

I wrap my arms around him, slipping my hands under his leather jacket and shirt to run them up his bare skin. He shivers, and I feel his muscles tense and bunch as he pulls me even closer to him.

His skin is rough in spots, not the smooth expanse I had imagined. My hands drift up the muscular columns of his back, the width preventing me from being able to even reach his spine.

He threads his hand into the hair at the base of my skull and tugs my head back, leaning down into my face. We are nose to nose, forehead to forehead, eyes locked. I feel enslaved by his amber gaze. I couldn't tear mine away if my life depended on it.

We stand there, bound together, harshly breathing in each other's very essence. He smells like tobacco and leather, and this close, I can pick up an underlying note of his unique scent, a clear and cool note like a rainstorm.

Suddenly, I am the brave bitch I always wanted to be. I am tired of wanting, of thinking I am not good enough or pretty enough or whatever enough. I am ready to step into my own and take what I want. And what I want is standing right here in front of me. And for once, I know, I deserve this.

I.

Deserve.

This.

Whatever tomorrow brings doesn't matter. I deserve this moment to be seen and loved and desired. I feel sexy, powerful, and strong. Riding the sudden wave of confidence, I rise on my tiptoes and crash my mouth to his, licking the seam of his lips.

For a long second, he is motionless, and my newfound confidence balances on a knife's edge. I gasp as he responds by flipping the tables, taking control of the kiss, deepening it until it seems like he is trying to devour my very soul. He may feel like cold marble beneath my hands, but in my mouth, he is liquid fire as his tongue dances with mine.

I've kissed before, but never, *never* like this. It is scorching, consuming, and achingly—hauntingly—familiar. The kiss fills me, seeps into my marrow, flooding into all the recesses of my being.

A tiny flicker of thought that I was right—he tastes like foreign spices, ancient history, lost souls, and time immemorial—flares somewhere in my mind. The intensity of the kiss increases until I feel like I might spontaneously combust.

We break away, panting and desperate for oxygen. He grabs my hand, pulling me down the hall and through the bathroom door. I guess he must have thought it was the way to my bedroom. He looks around, taking in the penis candles, and then back at me with a quizzical eyebrow raised.

I giggle nervously and shrug. "I'll explain later."

His eyes catch on my floor-length antique leaning mirror, and he pulls me over to it, my back to his front. Our eyes meet in our reflection. Seeing us together, his head well above mine, I am shocked by just how much my amber eyes match his, the splash of green standing out in solitude.

I open my mouth to speak, but he covers it with his hand as he leans in and whispers in my ear, "Watch. See what I see."

He reaches up and pulls out my hair tie, letting my curls cascade down. He takes both hands and gently separates the wild mass, dividing it, and pulling it forward over my shoulders where it hangs past my breasts. My playlist over the house speakers switches songs and as the low piano notes start, his movements slow.

He moves his hands back up to my hairline, and I watch him in the mirror as he leisurely glides his cool fingers out along my eyebrows, down the sides of my face, skims my jaw, and traces down to the pulse points on my neck.

I feel otherworldly, seeing him worship me in the mirror while feeling him touch me, the music wrapping around us. It is like an out-of-body experience. I can feel his touch, but it is also like watching a beautiful movie play out, this romantic moment happening to some other person. This girl in the mirror cannot be me.

No, not a girl. This woman. The beautiful woman in the

mirror being worshiped, touched so reverently, followed with the most intense amber gaze. This woman cannot be me.

But I feel every touch and watch her lips part when mine do to drag in air. His hands drift down from my neck to my chest, fingers curling under the edges of my smoking jacket, featherlight touches lighting my skin on fire.

One hand drops to the tassel belt holding the jacket closed while the other sneaks into the robe and settles, covering my heart, a comforting weight and point of connection to keep me grounded in this maelstrom.

I imagine what my racing heart must feel like to him. I'm sure he can feel it trying to beat its way out of my chest. The coolness of his hand is a heavenly contrast to my flushed skin.

As I watch us in the mirror, my gaze drops to where his hand is on my belt and quickly jerks back up to his as it falls loose and the jacket gapes open. Pupils blown, his normally amber eyes are almost black.

I should have worried if he likes what he sees. I should have felt insecure at the thought of my body being on display for him, the thousand negative thoughts a day I would normally have, criticizing myself.

But I don't.

I feel powerful. All that is reflected in his eyes in the mirror is intense desire. And I know this man can see me. Really see me.

I.

Am.

Beautiful.

His left-hand drifts from over my heart to push the robe past my right breast, displaying my entire side to him. He cups my breast and slides his fingertips down the slope, circling my nipple gently. Rolling it between his thumb and finger, I can't help but moan breathily and drop my head back against his chest.

His left forearm presses into my other breast while his hand continues to tease and pluck my right nipple. I could float away, but his arm around me and his hard body pressed to my back keeps me grounded.

His other hand moves from my smoking jacket belt to my stomach. I wiggle my ass back against him to see if I can feel his hardness, see if he is turned on like I am, and am rewarded with the proof that he most definitely is.

He holds my stare in the mirror while his right hand drifts down, sliding sensually against the full curve of my belly and, in this moment, I love my body. I love the way his hands caress my skin, and I love that my body has brought me to this moment. I also love the effect it is clearly having on him.

His hand trails down, exquisitely slow, until he finds the apex of my thighs and sets me to panting. Nothing has ever had me wound up this way before. Nothing I have experienced in my sex life, or have seen or even read, has been as intense as this. And very little has even happened yet.

My hips buck forward of their own volition, desperate for him to touch me. He rewards me by sliding his hand down further. Our stare is molten, his liquid gold around the edge of a bottomless black hole, mine green and gold around endless matching black.

The sight of myself in the mirror, left side covered by my smoking jacket, right side bared and being worshiped by his hands, is so erotic.

He languidly teases me. Feather light touches back and forth across my folds until I could scream, feeling like a live wire, desperate for more. He slips the tips of his fingers through them, finding me soaked. I gasp out loud and he smiles that full megawatt smile.

I bite my bottom lip, tasting copper, and moan as he thrusts two thick fingers inside me. They slide in easily despite their size, as I am dripping for him. I grab onto his forearms, my left hand pulling his tighter into my chest while I push his right arm further down with all my strength, needing his fingers deeper inside of me.

I'm breathing like a freight train, pressing my breast forward into his hand and trying to get enough traction to meet the building wave of pleasure that threatens to pull me under. I am absolutely frantic for him.

If I hadn't been holding on to his arms and caged against him, I think I would be on the floor. His chest feels like an immovable wall against my back. My legs are shaking and I'm breathing in staccato gasps.

He continues to thrust into me with his fingers, with just the right amount of pressure, while grinding the heel of his hand into my throbbing clit. Pleasure spiking, I widen my stance, trying to get more contact with his hand, with anything.

I can't help but dig my nails into his thick leather jacket, muscles tensing, my right hand sliding down to cover his as I grind into his palm. The sounds echo in the bathroom, of not only my breathing and moans, but my lewd wetness.

I would normally be embarrassed, but it is so remarkably erotic, all I can feel is beautiful and desired. My eyes snap shut as I feel myself clenching around his fingers like a vise.

"Watch," he whispers harshly in my ear. I open my eyes and look in the mirror at the most beautifully erotic sight I have ever seen. Him, fully dressed, black leather-clad arms encircling me, one large hand gripping my breast, and the other between my legs.

His colossal size leaves him as an outline around my body, his head topping mine. A wide swath of my skin flushed with pleasure peeks out from my smoking jacket.

His intense, hungry gaze is taking in the same sight and visibly fills with desire for me. As I feast on our combined image, his fingers curl and find a spot inside me that sings.

I'm shocked at the immediacy of my body's response to him. He knows the exact places to touch me, the ideal pressure and speed. His hand on my breast kneads at the optimal rhythm while his other hand provides just the right amount of thrust. Not only does he know where to find my clit, but his thumb expertly strums across it at the perfect angle.

He seems more comfortable with my body than even I am. What should be an encounter with a stranger, instead feels like a core memory, my heart and my body drawn to him, trusting him with my most vulnerable self. Like a physical Déjà vu, rippling through time and space, making it so easy to just give myself over to the incredible sensations.

My pleasure wells up, snaking from my core out to my limbs, spreading like a nuclear blast and leaving me decimated in its wake. Miraculously, I keep my eyes open and focused on his, the erotic sight pushing my peak even higher.

My loud moans echo in the bathroom, the copper slipper tub adding a deeper acoustic layer to the sounds.

"Now you see," he says, as I wantonly ride out the orgasm's last clenches on his hand, smaller aftershocks continue to rumble through me as I bite down hard on my lower lip. He leans down and whispers in my ear, "עֶצֶם מֵעֲצָמַי וּבָשָׂר מִבְּשָׂרִי (Etzem mi'atzamay u'vasar mib'sari)."

I don't understand what he says, but something seismic shifts and clicks into place. Some missing piece I had never even been aware of is sliding home. My racing heart and the swirling feelings fall still. Everything coalesces into a single focus. The entire world seems to stop spinning on its axis.

I can feel everything and nothing at the same moment. I feel the universe expanding ever outward and simultaneously feel it as a single point in the darkness at its birth.

Although I cannot understand his foreign words, I understand the magnitude of this moment, and I know nothing, *nothing*, will ever be the same in my world again. The last words of the song drift into my brain as my breathing quiets, and just like it says, now that I've had a taste of him, I am thirsty.

I turn my head to look at him, rather than our combined reflection in the world of mirrors. His eyes fall to my mouth, and I lick my lips, tasting a drop of blood from where I had accidentally pierced the skin with my teeth.

That second breaks the spell. He drops his hands, looking shocked, and steps back. I stumble with the sudden loss of support from his arms.

"I must go," he says and runs from the room. His loss leaves me cold. I turn to follow, stretching my hand out to him, but before I can even take a step, I hear the front door close, unsure how he could have reached it already.

This time, I don't chase him. I saw his face fall. Something caused his reaction, but I'm puzzled by what it could have been.

Yesterday, or even earlier today, I would have fallen into despair, thinking I wasn't good enough or skinny enough, or that I had done something wrong. But in this moment, despite the splotch of the face mask left over on my cheek and the pink bunny slippers in sharp contrast to my open smoking jacket, I *know* I am beautiful. I am strong.

And I am very, very much his. Judging by his reaction, it seems he knows it, too. And in my newfound strength, I know I can navigate whatever this is with him, and more importantly, with myself.

Chapter 12

HIM

I burst out her front door, running away from my impulsivity. This is not what I had intended. I hadn't seen the Red One in many years and seeing him threatening to approach her tonight derailed my carefully laid plans.

I had planned to woo her, court her, and make her fall madly in love with me. Build trust before I divulge my secrets. And hers. But after I had chased him away at the bank, in my ferocious Cane Corso form, I had to see her and reassure myself that she was indeed safe.

As soon as I had entered the bar, I could smell the desire on the bartender and couldn't resist the instinct to claim her as mine any more than I could resist the compulsion to see her safely back home.

And then at her house, where she flicked my finger with her tentative tongue, I couldn't help but taste her back. One taste, I promised myself, and then I would strategize a path forward.

The second I tasted her throat and heard her blood sing to me, though, I knew I could not stay in control. I forced myself to run away and calm down. But before I fled, I saw her crestfallen face.

By the time I had made it to my new building next to hers, faster than her eyes could follow, I knew I couldn't leave her doubting all that she is, not only to me but to herself.

She is the rarest treasure, her value more precious than jewels, her worth far above rubies or pearls. Although man had destroyed much of the true words, truer words about her had never been spoken. I hear the little jabs she uses to degrade herself, the insecurities she lets slip under the guise of humor.

I want—no, I need—for her to see herself the way I have always seen her. Beautiful. Powerful. Worthy. Cherished. Loved beyond all boundaries of time. And tonight, I showed her. That I could never regret.

Confessing my love in one of my earliest languages, though, risking another lifetime, that I regretted. Those words could easily call the wrong attention.

I am desperate for one, *just one,* happy lifetime together. Just one without pain and suffering. If I were a praying man, I would fall to my knees and beg. But I know better. *He* quit hearing me a long, long time ago.

I need to step back, level set, and logically think through what will give this lifetime the best chance of success. And there is no way for me to do so with her rose smell in my nose, her taste on my tongue, her blood singing to me, and her release on my fingers.

I have failed time and time again. I have no more tears after all these years, no more heartbreak left. All that remains is her and my undying love for her. She will be mine. There is no other acceptable outcome.

I've been told I am obsessed. As if simple obsession could describe the depth of my love and the lengths I will go to for her. I am not obsessed. She is the light. My own lifeblood.

But tonight, seeing that drop of her blood, shimmering red on her lip swollen in pleasure, had been too reminiscent of my downfall. Of the beginning. I had to escape.

I must pull myself together.

I draw my focus inward, calling on my logic and carefully laid plans. I cannot survive another lost lifetime, *losing her again*. This time, I vow to myself, this time will be the last. And if *He* won't listen, I know who will.

Chapter 13

I putz around Grimm, lost in thought. Time keeps passing by since the *mirror incident*, as I refer to it in my head. I had expected to run into him the following day, or even the next.

I had been getting dolled up and dressing cute. Hell, I even shaved my legs. *And other places,* I thought, as I carefully scratched my bikini line.

I had taken to checking the progress of his construction, hoping to glimpse the mysterious McHottie. But he is gone. Vanished for the past few days now.

I didn't want to ask the builders. That would seem so desperate. Deep down, I know we connected that night. I know it in my very soul.

I cursed the timing of the Oddities Expo that I would head up to Philly for, but it couldn't be helped. Despite missing him, I still have a business to run and an overseas trip to prepare for. I have to go about my life, regardless of what happened.

I am trying to be patient with whatever is going on, but my mind constantly drifts back to that night. No matter how hard I try, I cannot figure out what he said to me in that strange language. I blame the alcohol and lack of blood flow to my brain at that moment, but I wonder if what he said is the key.

Otherwise, I feel pretty good. My attitude toward myself has improved. It is as if that night had nudged me closer to self-acceptance. And at 30 years old, that feels so incredibly healthy. Desperately wanting someone to see me, truly see me, made me realize that what I needed all along was to see myself.

Sure, I'm not perfect, no one is, but I am me. And I am wonderful. It is such a juxtaposition to have a seismic shift in how I see myself, but also to be so disappointed and confused about what happened with McHottie.

I finish dusting the display up front, making some last-minute rearrangements. The front display must be frequently changed to prevent sun damage. Today, I put out the remaining pressed carnivorous flowers. They've been a tremendous hit, and I need to remember to pick up some more before Halloween.

I dust around Lucifer, curled up in his usual spot in the window, as his majesty can't be bothered to move himself. Despite his faults, he at least leaves the contents of the store alone, and he really does add to the atmosphere. A black cat is just such a good fit for an oddities store.

I wish he would at least let me pet him occasionally, though. Pausing my dusting, I hesitantly reach out to stroke his midnight head with one finger, but before I can get within a few inches, he lays his ears down flat and twitches his tail, letting out the faintest hiss.

"Rude," I mutter under my breath and resume my duties.

I shuffle around some of the new skulls with butterflies in glass display cloches, trying out different arrangements and groupings until I find something pleasing that also leaves a spot for the undeserving odd cat.

I head out front to view my new arrangement in the window to ensure the display is just as great from the street. I try not to eye up the neighboring building's construction, which appears to be winding up, but can't help myself.

The updates are modern, yet blend seamlessly. Whoever the designer was really had an eye for this type of work. I admire the new windows and front door. They have combined the two buildings into one much larger building.

The builders also left the brick the original red and repointed the mortar. The trim is black like mine, and the copper downspouts and roof accents would weather elegantly to match the green of my building next door. I wonder if that detail was intentional, to link the two buildings together stylistically in addition to their shared wall. Copper is an expensive detail.

I automatically think about the owner from next door and our link. I can sense him in the clean modern lines of the building, updates that hold true to its original character. It fits him, with his stunning beauty and James Dean trappings, his tattoos a modern touch to a classic foundation.

I don't doubt, just like the buildings before me, he and I have a deep connection. I know in my very marrow it is there. But where is he? And why is he gone? I sigh and head back in to close up the shop.

It was a busy day, and I've still got to drive to Philly tonight so I can spend the weekend at the Oddities Expo. My emergency backup worker, Anna, who also is one of my favorite young ladies from the vegan gluten-free restaurant, is going to cover Saturday and Sunday for me.

I'm thankful for her help. I simply can't financially afford to close the store on the weekends, which are my highest sales days. She always leaves things better than she found them, so I'm always happy to return after she works.

I button up Grimm for the night and can't stop myself from taking one more peek at the building next door. I notice one of the upper floor curtains twitch, and I wonder if it is a trick of my eyes or if McHottie is really up there and just hiding out from me.

With that uplifting thought, I head back to my place to pack a quick bag so I can head to Philly. At this time of day, I should make it in less than two hours. I grab my giant Tardis bag, throw in a change of clothes, a few snacks, and a Grimm logo reusable water bottle. I love merch.

I put on my high-top Converse, since I'll wear them to the expo and don't feel like packing a bunch of shoes for such a short trip. Swinging through the bathroom, I snag my makeup, hair tools, and travel toiletries, tossing those in the bag as well.

I run through my mental checklist and realize I'll need a smaller purse for the actual convention, so I grab my new little belt bag and add my wallet. I think I got everything—time to get going.

Bag on shoulder, phone in hand, I lock the front door behind me and head down to my vintage bug. I toss my things across to the passenger seat and give one last glance up at the back side of my building.

Again, I swear my neighbor's upstairs blinds twitch. I throw a stink face toward the window and fire off a double bird salute, in case he is looking down at me, then pull up directions on my phone.

Just for fun, I change the voice on the app to the zombie survivalist option and bring up my playlist. I'm looking forward to the mostly simple drive for some uninterrupted thinking time, though I dread driving in the actual city. I fire up the car and off I go.

As I head north, I realize that uninterrupted thinking time isn't as wonderful as I thought it would be. My brain just circles around McHottie like a whirlpool til I'm tangled up and dizzy in my own thoughts.

I just can't fathom what scared him off. I'm glad to be away this weekend and am hopeful when I get home, he will come back around so we can figure out whatever is going on.

A mental break will be good for me. I worry I'm becoming obsessed, when in reality, it's only been a few days. His silence makes me doubt the deep feelings I had when we were together and the connection I was certain we had forged. Maybe I should brace myself for another notch of disappointment on life's bedpost.

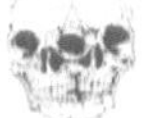

AFTER A RELATIVELY QUICK and easy drive, I pull up to my hotel, thankful for the light traffic. I found this place a few years ago, and it is my go-to place to stay in Philly. The boutique hotel is a tucked away gem near the cobblestone streets surrounding Old City.

There are some great little restaurants nearby, including a fabulous taco place with a fun Mexican wrestler theme. I think I'll grab some tacos and margaritas there tonight. The margaritas will help to beat the summer heat that is in full force today and should also help to clear out some of my swirling thoughts.

I pull the bug up to the valet—another perk of this little hotel in the city—and grab my giant bag from my passenger seat. Passing my keys to the attendant, I head in.

I smile and thank the door man and take a deep breath as I enter the lobby. The hotel's signature scent is incredible. I inhale calming white tea and sandalwood with a faint citrus note.

I breeze through check-in and head up to the fifth floor. It's a smaller hotel, nestled in this old section of town with fun little quirks, like twisting hallways and lofty ceilings. I hop off the elevator after a quick ride up and go down the narrow hallway, making right angle turns to my room.

I walk in and admire the fifteen-foot ceiling. The quiet stillness particular to hotel rooms surrounds me. Faint traffic sounds from the streets below and the hum of the air conditioning form their own white noise. The signature scent of the hotel is more subtle here, but pleasantly present.

I stand there for a minute, quietly absorbing the calm. Taking a relaxing minute, I do some box breathing so I'm in practice in case I need to use it during a time of stress. I love this hotel and the feeling of being in a peaceful bubble it brings me.

Relaxed now, I flop down on the bed with my feet hanging off the edge. The mattress is soft, and the fluffy duvet beckons me to sink into oblivion. My eyes feel heavy, and it would be so easy just to drift off to sleep.

I let myself enjoy a few minutes of blissful solitude. No business to run. No judgmental cats. No mysterious missing McHottie.

But I know I'll wake up hungry in the middle of the night since I skipped dinner to hit the road, so before I can get too sleepy, I drag myself out of the welcoming softness. Tequila calls. And tacos. Oh, how I love you.

I fish out my belt bag so I can head out for my dinner, making sure I have my hotel key and the door is securely locked behind me.

I go back out through the lobby and take a left to the taco place. The foot traffic is light, and I'm happy to find the restaurant not terribly busy for a Friday night, since I'm a little late for dinner and a little too early for the bar scene.

Glorious, cool air conditioning is a welcome greeting after the short walk in the trapped summer heat in the sweltering city. I snag a barstool, so much more comfortable than sitting at a table alone. The vinyl seat sticks to my bare legs, ratcheting up my anticipation of an ice-cold margarita with a salt rim. The perfect summer drink.

I glance over the menu to see if there is anything new and decide to be adventurous with one of the specials—jackfruit tacos—in addition to my usual shrimp. To start, I get guac and a spicy and smoky margarita. I can't wait to try it. This place never disappoints, so I make it a point to stop whenever I am in the city.

After ordering, I absentmindedly play with my phone, texting my friends an update and clearing out some old emails. When my guac arrives, it's expertly seasoned, and the tortilla chips are still warm with big flaky pieces of salt. They are heavenly and I'm so thankful corn is gluten-free.

I'm happily munching when a beautiful margarita with a tamarind straw is delivered. I give my thanks to the bartender and try a sip. It's like a party in my mouth. The spice of the Tajín rim and the tang of the sour mix blended with the smoky tequila induces a delicious, full body shiver.

I may have a new favorite drink. I'll always love bourbon, but margaritas just taste like summer. The first one goes down quickly with the guac while I wait for my entrée. I push my glass back, nodding at the bartender when he gives me the universal signal of the chin jerk with eyebrow raise for 'another round'?

I nod—why yes, I will indulge in another frosty beverage. I dig the expo brochure out of my bag, loosely devising a plan of attack, when out of the blue my neck prickles and I catch a whiff of tobacco and leather.

In true Pavlovian response, the sensation skating across my neck and scent of *him* triggers instant arousal. I whip my head around, ready to lock onto his intense amber eyes, but I don't see him anywhere. My eyes scan the few patrons, and I feel my smile fall at his absence.

I tell myself that it must be wishful thinking, but I can't shake this feeling. And unless I'm having phantosmia, I know I caught the smell of him. I'm not sure if it would surprise me to have McHottie follow me to Philly or not.

What would I do if he did? On one hand, it would be just a little stalkerish. On the other hand, it would be kind of hot to have someone trailing after me. There have been times since he ran out, like the devil himself was chasing him, that I could have sworn he was somewhere close by.

My food comes as a welcome distraction, and I attack my tacos and margarita refill in annoyance. This mystery man has me ferhoodled. I'm seeing twitchy curtains and catching his scent even when he is not around. Ridiculous. When I get home, I vow to resolve this situation one way or another.

I'm going to go knock on his door, and if I can't track him down, then I'll move on. I can't keep mooning after him like a lovesick puppy. Perhaps I really did read too much into this. I blame book boyfriends for setting my unrealistic expectations of love after a single encounter.

I finish up the delicious tacos and suck down the rest of my new favorite margarita and decide to call it a night. More than two tequila drinks and shit will get crazy. Besides, I have early access to the expo tomorrow with my pass and need to maximize my time there.

I'm already a little nervous that the stress of travel and excitement of the expo could trigger yet another waking dream, so I should get to sleep instead of pushing my luck.

Paying my tab, I leave a generous tip, then head back to my hotel. I keep an eye out as I go for Mr. Tall, Pale, and Handsome, although I know in my heart he can't be here. Can he?

Back in my room, I strip down to just my panties. Goosebumps ripple across my flesh as the summer swelter evaporates off my skin. I crawl into the super cozy bed. Sleep comes quickly with a full belly of tacos and margaritas, but it is restless.

I feel like I spend the night in that strange space between awake and dreaming, leaving hazy impressions of a cool body of marble snuggled into me. I try to hold on to the dreamscape where the coolness feels delicious molded against me, but I'm repeatedly dragged back toward awakening.

The next time I drift back to dreamland, the warm breath on my neck is in sharp contrast to the cool body curled around mine, legs tangled. I stretch my neck, wanting more contact, and am awarded with a searing kiss behind my ear.

In response, I arch my back, driving my hips back into a ludicrously hard and obviously aroused male. I grind my ass into my dream man, rewarded with a bruising hand on my hip as he pushes back against me.

I'm pissed when my phone blares Bach's Toccata and Fugue in D minor. Things were just getting good! I haphazardly attempt to smack snooze, and my other arm reaches across the bed to look for my mystery man.

The other side is cold and empty, though. Why would I have expected it to be anything but? I have slept alone for years, so last night must have just been a guacamole and margarita fueled dreamscape.

My wishful brain imagines the faintest whiff of tobacco and leather, and I frown in confusion. I snatch up the other pillow and crush it to my face, taking in a giant lungful. His scent *absolutely* clings to it.

I throw it across the room in frustration and drag myself out of bed. McHottie seems to have broken my brain. Or maybe I have some type of tumor causing phantom smells. I should probably get checked out when I get home.

I head into the bathroom, startled to see dark circles under my eyes. Guess my sleep really did suck. I throw my hair in two braids and tie a red bandana like a headband to contain my frizzy flyaways. Next is some simple makeup, heavy on the under-eye concealer.

I pop my earrings back in from yesterday and pick up my necklace to put back on as well. As I tip my head down and reach around to fasten it, I catch sight of a faint mark on my neck. I turn my head further to the side, struggling to view this odd angle behind my ear.

I head back out to the room, grab my phone, and snap a picture of the area I can't quite get a good angle of in the mirror. Sure enough, there is a discoloration where I dreamed someone had been kissing me.

For a second, I worry something bit me and feel my skin crawl with thoughts of bed bugs. But then I remembered back from my nursing days they leave raised bumps, and this looks more like, well, it's more like a hickey with two tiny scabs.

Did I somehow pinch the skin in my sleep and that prompted part of my hazy dream last night? I shake my head, trying to clear my mind. It's way too early for mysteries and I haven't even had coffee yet. That reminds me to go start up the one cup machine while I get ready.

Shooting for efficiency, I dress to the bubbling of the coffee brewing, pulling on red fishnets, ripped black skinny jeans, a red lace bra, and top it with a black Grimm logo tank. Might as well advertise the store while I walk around. I grab my belt bag, checking it has my wallet, phone, and business cards.

I sit down on the bed to tie my converse sneakers and

notice a jet-black hair on the white duvet. I pick it up and hold it up to the light, like it contains the secrets of the universe. It looks like a McHottie hair, but in all practicality, I'm sure it is just a coincidence. A hair lost by the housekeeper or a less than spotless room.

But after everything that has happened, from the prickling on my neck and catching his scent at the restaurant, to the foggy dreams of last night, and now the more physical evidence of a love bite plus a hair that matches his, I can't help but wonder if McHottie had somehow snuck in and out of my room like he seemed to have done in my store.

My theory makes no sense. How on earth would he be able to get in and out of a hotel room that had the extra safety lock latched from the inside? Shaking off the mystery, I decide I have to get moving and quit playing Scooby Doo, so I quickly stir in the sad powdered coffee creamer and both packets of sugar before heading down to the lobby.

Chapter 14

I'm thankful the morning is still cool since it is just under a mile to the convention center. As I walk, I munch on a protein bar. I know I'm not likely to find a safe gluten-free breakfast here, so this will have to do.

I don't miss gluten, but I miss the convenience of not having to worry about getting sick from food. The coffee is a sad substitute for my usual concoction, but after a night spent tossing and turning, I welcome the caffeine, regardless.

As I walk, I keep rubbing at the mark on my neck, trying to figure out a logical explanation for everything that has happened. I just can't suss it out. There is no way McHottenstein would have been able to slip in and out of my room, even if he had followed me to Philly. Right?

Reaching the convention center entrance, I wave my ticket at the scanner and head into the expo. This is always a good one, and I'm excited to check out the entertainment they have added tonight. The addition of a show is new for this year, and I hope it will be marvelous. I had meant to look it up, but just hadn't had the chance.

I hope there are some burlesque performers in it. I admire their amazing confidence and sex appeal. In my head, I am a sexy burlesque dancer, throwing winks and oozing confidence as I shimmy out of my super cool burlesque outfit down to my pasties, which I can get twirling in opposite directions with just the right shake of my hips.

But that version of Lieshe stays safely stuck in my head

while this version hits the first row of vendors. I make my way around the perimeter, knowing they will cluster the best ones in the center but always having an eye out for a new contact or product. I pass loads of clear acrylic blocks with assorted critters frozen in time, wet and dry mounts of all kinds, and varied other commonly found stock items.

I am just about to start my foray into the inner aisles when I notice a jewelry stand in a darker corner. I wander over, curious, as I haven't seen this vendor before and just love jewelry.

There are some cool pieces—lots of bats, spiders, and various insects. Moving to the far corner of the booth, I find a delightful line of doll heads molded in silver. There are bracelets, earrings, and necklaces in this delightfully creepy style. I know they would sell well at Grimm and hope I can get a fair price on them.

I am so glad I wandered back here to this treasure trove. The owner finishes up with another customer and heads my way. We make some small talk while I find several other pieces I must have, including a line of cicadas I haven't seen before and a really nice spin on spoon rings with skulls, moths, bees, or ants on them.

I decide a larger selection of jewelry will be an excellent addition to my store, especially with the holidays coming up. We chat about pricing and come to a mutually beneficial arrangement. I can't wait for Jo to see these. I even order a few tamer pieces to appeal to everyone.

I am just about to hand my card over to seal the deal when, out of the corner of my eye, I catch the light wink off an unusual ring. It seems out of place, like a priceless antique tucked amongst the mostly silver Gothic offerings.

The red is so dark it is almost black, like a drop of blood at midnight. A heavy gold band sets off the pear-shaped cabochon, which appears genuinely vintage versus a reproduction.

I pick it up and slip it on my left ring finger, where I know it will fit perfectly. The metal feels warm to the touch, and the ring fits the base of my finger like it has been there for years.

I stare down into the stone, the surface appearing so smooth I reach out with my other hand and stroke it to reassure myself that it is truly solid rather than the drop of blood it so realistically resembles.

"What about this?"

"Oh," the salesperson replies, "that's odd. I don't remember ever carrying anything like that before. Can I see it?"

I hold my hand up, admiring it on my finger. The deep red stone catches the light, making it appear to glow warmly from deep within. In my heart, I know it is meant to be mine.

"So strange, I don't recall putting that out. Must be kismet. Are you okay paying the price marked on the tray?"

"Of course. Are you sure?"

She nods. Truth is, I would have paid anything. I feel a little guilty. It must be worth far more than she is charging.

Compared to my customary ornate pieces, this is gold with a simplistic design, but the color of the stone is riveting and vaguely familiar, and I am in love with my new treasure. The gold band has the patina of time, and it just feels so at home on my finger. Kismet, indeed.

I settle my bill and confirm my shipping address, moving away to finish checking out the rest of the expo. I'll ship what I can home, so I don't have to pack up too much. Especially the less fragile items.

As I walk, I glance down at my hand to admire my new

ring and my vision begins to shimmer. *Oh, no, not here,* I think.

Luckily, just ahead is an exit door in the cinderblock wall of this outer aisle. Stumbling the last few steps to reach the door, I lurch through it and slide down the wall to sit on the refreshingly cool concrete floor of the dimly lit stairwell.

I put my head down between my knees, but my head spins until I am forced to close my eyes. I focus on drawing ragged breaths in and out of my constricting lungs, casting about for a grounding technique.

I grasp my new ring with the fingers of my other hand and start spinning it. Instantly, all of my fear and my pounding heart resolve. I feel a different texture against my back than the rough cinderblock wall of the convention center stairwell. Sweet fresh air tickles my noses and fills my lungs, opposite to the stagnant indoor airflow I had just been struggling to pull in.

I blink my eyes open in disbelief at the most intense 'waking dream' yet to find myself seated at the base of an enormous tree. I look up to see a sky of midnight black velvet peppered with the brightest stars I've ever seen behind the enormous foliage of an ancient and twisted yew.

Leaves crunch under my feet on a carpet of spongy moss as I stand. The majestic tree is the centerpiece of a stone courtyard. I cannot see past the shadows of the arched doorways, but I have no fear. This place is so exquisitely beautiful, so magical, I expect the air itself to shimmer.

A noise to my left spins me around to come face to face with McHottie. I brace myself with my hands against his hard, cold chest, reminiscent of that morning outside his house. The bright moonlight highlights his chiseled face and sets his amber eyes aglow.

He takes my left hand in his and kisses my new ring

while staring into my eyes. I am drowning in the twin pools of his endless gaze. He opens his mouth to speak when a loud crash jerks me back to the present, another expo attendee having slammed open the stairwell door.

I stand there with my hand over my thudding heart, wondering how I came to be in a standing position. I've never changed positions or acted out in my waking dreams before, only my mindset usually changes.

This is a new and disturbing development alongside the pleasant one of dreaming about anything that isn't terrifying, horrible, or devastating. What the hell is happening to me?

"Sorry, didn't mean to startle you," the newcomer says, gesturing at me with a vape.

"N-no worries," I stammer out, fleeing the stairwell.

Heading back into the expo feels so mundane after my strange dream, the normalcy a bizarre contrast. I wolf down a bar from my belt bag and head to the vending machines to grab a bottle of water.

I make my purchase and hold the cool bottle against the nape of my neck, gradually starting to feel normal. *Whatever the hell that is,* I think. I chug the cool water and throw the now empty bottle in the recycle bin, feeling good enough to finish out my shopping. I have no choice but to get through this business trip.

I make my way around the outside, working my way toward the middle, where a lot of my usual vendors are. In the very center is a tattoo parlor with a few bold souls starting their day out with a buzzy wake up call. Probably a better way to start the day than bizarre hallucinations.

I'm not sure how I have reached the age of thirty without a tattoo. I love them on other people and even follow a few fine, tattooed male specimens on social media, but I just haven't settled on anything I would want on my body forever just yet.

I spend a few quiet minutes looking over the assorted designs people are getting and wonder if I were to get one, what I would get and where. I would love to see McHottie's ink up close, follow it with eyes and lips and questing fingertips. All kinds of people are getting tattooed, but I don't see anyone as fine as the infamous McHottie.

While I watch on in fascination, I take my swirling thoughts and organize them into neat little compartments. I stash away my worry over my dreams, my frustrations over the MIA McHottie, and focus my attention on the here and now. Today is for business. I do a few rounds of box breathing and then square my shoulders and decide to keep moving.

Leaving the in-progress ink behind, I check my watch and step up my game. I catch up with a few acquaintances from the trade, all of us happy to report we are doing pretty well with sales lately and look forward to the upcoming Halloween and holiday season.

We talk about some vendors, who is new, and who has the best items this year. We speculate about the show this evening that has some type of French name no one knows how to pronounce. It's great to see some of the industry folks, but I need to finish out my shopping list, so I excuse myself from the group and walk on.

I take mental notes on displays I see at various booths to try out in my store window. There are some really creepy dolls out this year, almost too much even for me, and I love dark things. I pick up a few of the tamer ones for my Halloween display and one of the steampunk dolls for the upcoming Poe convention.

I find another vendor I had circled on my map, this one

carrying the coolest rings made of night soil. They will be a colossal hit for both the steam punk crowd and the holidays.

I'm surprised at how beautiful they are, looking more like carved stone than ancient remnants of, how to phrase this delicately, poo. Yeah, there's no delicate way to say that. They make the rings out of outhouse excrement and discarded glass bottles, but the poo is so super old it's not germy anymore. Weird.

I'm so gaga over them I don't actually negotiate that well for a wholesale price, but I know I've forged a new relationship, and that is just as important in this industry. *Today must be ring day,* I think, but push the flash of my waking dream about my new ring down deep to concentrate on the task at hand. Compartmentalization has got me through most of my life.

Further down that same row is a booth full of children's items. The vendor is an incredible artist and has made the cutest prints of baby monsters. Her products feature infant versions of Dracula, Frankenstein's monster and bride of Frankenstein, and the sweetest little Creature from the Black Lagoon.

Her entire series is just darling. I pick up several packs of notecards of the lot and order ten sets of all the prints. I know they are going to be such a great hit. And if someday I ever have a nursery, I now know my theme.

She also carries the cutest bat plushies. I remember hauling around a fuzzy gray bear until I was about eight years old, twirling the tags so much I got a callus. These little soft bats will make a brilliant companion to sit next to my old bear, who now lives on my bedroom chair.

I can't decide between the pink minky plush with contrasting black spider fabric or the gothic skull print one, so I get both for myself and order another dozen for the store. Losing myself in my safe place, falling into the familiar thought patterns of running my business, soothes my frazzled brain.

I pick up one with an Edgar Allan Poe print for my gothic nursery customers back home. It will make a lovely gift for my expecting friends. I also do a custom order for some Baltimore themed ones I know will sell well.

All these thoughts of babies and nurseries make me remember my age. I'm not exactly sure either way whether I want children, but first, I need a partner. I wonder what the offspring of McHottie and I would be like. Would they get his height or my heterochromia? I shake my head, hard to procreate when I haven't seen him since the mirror incident.

I thought we could figure things out, that we had a deep connection, but as time marches on, I'm second guessing my memories of that night. Maybe things weren't as intense for him as they were for me. Or maybe I over read the entire situation, and he just wanted a little handsy time.

But that doesn't quite make sense either. I can't help but believe, hoping not foolishly, that we indeed had some type of bond and there is something larger that is keeping him from me.

I push on, finding my favorite wet and dry mount booth and order a few things that I'll bring home with me tomorrow. The expo has a brilliant hold service for wholesale buyers that allows me to shop efficiently without hauling stuff all over the giant center.

I finish up with my favorite vendor who carries unique pieces, including baculum jewelry. Super unusual and yet always a really fast-moving sales item. I'll put them out for Halloween and bring some to the steampunk convention as well.

The only place left on my list is the one that does the

pressed carnivorous plants. I consult the map and head that way. I find them easily, satisfied I accomplished everything I set out to do today.

I head back to the tattoo section and watch others get inked for a few more minutes. I think through various designs and where they would go on my body if I made the leap. With so many talented artists and styles, I don't know how I could ever choose. And I'd be nervous it would hurt too much.

Chapter 15

Leaving the bustling area behind, I make a final loop through the one aisle I had missed earlier, thrilled when I see a clothing vendor. I've hit the jackpot! There are so many unique offerings—steampunk, gothic, romantic, and even some boho pieces.

I flip through the racks, thinking through what I own already and what I could add to freshen up my outfit for the Poe convention. There are so many other things I would love to buy here, but my closet is already overflowing.

As I slide the hangers across the rack, I discover a beautiful military style jacket. It is blood-red with black silk ropes over the shoulder and flounced with black lace at the sleeves and underneath the full bustled skirt.

I can envision this paired perfectly with my fitted black leather pants with the rivets down the sides. I pull the lovely coat out into the light and admire the heavy brocade of the fabric. It looks rich and sumptuous, with a price tag to match. *I could just try it on,* I think.

I take it over to the mirror, and of course, it fits exquisitely. As I run my hands down the long black velvet shawl collar, I appreciate just how flattering the cut is for my silhouette. I feel sexy and confident. Swapping around accessories could easily allow me to wear the coat for other occasions, too, I justify to myself.

Posing in the mirror, I twist and turn, checking myself

out, unaware I have an audience until the vendor of the booth startles me with a low whistle of appreciation.

I look over my shoulder and my mouth falls open. A fine male specimen is leaning back against a counter. He is tall and lean, muscles barely concealed by his striking steampunk outfit. Although he appears relaxed, he gives off the air of a black panther, ready to spring into action at any second.

My eyes start at his leather Deadman top hat, detailed with gears and goggles, and then drift down to a runway ready face with the faintest smirk. His skin is alabaster as befits his flaming red hair, flowing down from under his hat to almost his waist. Platinum eyebrows frame exotic pale yellow-green eyes. A square jaw keeps his features from being delicate and his nose has an edge like a knife.

His features blend into a rare, severe beauty. The cherry on top is his handlebar mustache which crowns full lush lips, and a pointed thick auburn Van Dyke beard covering his chin directs my gaze downwards. The facial hair brings heart shaped relief to his powerful jawline and an air of rakishness.

His unrelieved black outfit is bespoke, a dapper ensemble. It includes a wing collared shirt, matte silk ascot, and black diamond tie tack, all paired with a vest with a subtle weave. Fitted leather pants are slung low on his hips and a leather belt with a matte raven skull belt buckle highlights his slim waist.

Finally, I take in his matte black leather boots with matching hardware, including spikes and more raven skulls. He even has a pocket watch chain in the same finish, though I can't see the watch itself.

The man knows how to commit to a color. He must have spent a fortune curating this outfit. It could have been cartoonish, but the result on him is anything but. It drips realism and luxury.

He pushes off the counter, stalking towards me like the jungle cat he reminds me of. As he stands before me, I'm greeted by the smell of cinnamon red hearts. My mouth waters and I can almost taste the spicy treat on my tongue.

His smirk grows under my perusal until he looks like the Cheshire cat personified, clearly used to having this effect on people. He reaches out a hand to me and I can't help but slip mine into his, surprised at his scorching touch.

With courtly grace, he bows low over it, trailing his gaze from my Converse encased feet, up my body, and to my face. Looking up at me through his lashes, he playfully winks at me.

Like a true gentleman of years gone by, he brings my hand to his lips, acting as if he will kiss the back of it, but at the last minute he flips it over and presses a searing kiss to my wrist instead, over my pulse, turning an old-fashioned greeting into something sultry and intimate. In my heart, I know this is *no* gentleman.

"*Enchantée, ma Reine Rouge,*" he says in perfect French with a voice like matte black silk as he straightens. His chosen color suits him perfectly.

I blink in response, my hand still in his. I gasp in a much-needed lungful of cinnamon-flavored oxygen, just now realizing he has literally taken my breath away. He is intense, I'll give him that.

Four years of Latin in high school wasn't particularly practical, but every once in a while, it does come in handy. I think he said something about red, maybe because of the color of the coat?

"Luke Devlin, it's a pleasure to meet you," his voice purrs over the word pleasure. Although he has switched back to

English, a slight European accent persists. Maybe his native tongue *is* French? His voice is just so damn smooth.

I try to reply, clear my throat, and squeak out, "Lieshe."

He drops my hand, steps back, and the rest of the world comes into focus. I don't think I've ever met someone so striking and consuming before. It's like being sucked into a vacuum where nothing else exists or matters except his very presence.

I'm not entirely sure I could tell this man no to anything, even if I wanted to. I give my head a small shake, try to force blood flow away from my lady bits and back up to my brain, and attempt some semblance of normalcy.

"This jacket is incredible!" I exclaim and turn back to my reflection in the mirror, taking a break from his intense eye contact. I'm left feeling oddly tired from our interaction, but it has been quite a day.

"What will you wear it with?" he asks.

I tell him my plan, to which he replies, "You must try this."

Mesmerized, I follow him to another rack, where he unerringly picks out a magnificent black brocade corset with matte black buckles down the front and a high lace up back. It complements both his own outfit and, with the deep red pattern of the brocade, also the coat I had found.

"I insist," he says, handing me the amazing garment.

I head into the small changing booth he directs me to, take off my shirt and bra, and loosen the back ties on the corset. My breath quickens as the skin on my back warms where I sense his gaze trailing down my spine despite the opaque fabric of the makeshift changing area.

I slip the corset on, buckle up the front, and adjust my breasts into the high cups. Even without it being pulled tight, it's stunning and damn, I'll admit, I look hot in it.

"I'd love to see you, Lieshe," Luke calls, caressing my name with his silver tongue. It feels deliciously sinful. I come out, feeling a little shy until I see his face light up.

"*Belle fille.* You look incredible. I would love to see the full effect. Come, stand in front of the mirror and I'll pull your laces," he replies. How does every word that falls from his lips sound like a sexual proposition?

I follow his command, watching how his eyes follow the path of his fingertips as they ghost up my arms. Despite the lightness, his touch blazes a trail of fire along my skin. The stark contrast between the inferno that is Luke and the cool air of the expo center raises goosebumps on my exposed flesh.

His eyes lock on mine in the mirror as he traces his fingers across my exposed collarbones and up my neck to take a braid in each hand. He pulls them in front of my shoulders, running his hands sensuously down their length, only to wind them around his wrists.

I'm shocked the mirror doesn't melt under the combined power of our heated stare. Luke bites his bottom lip, and with a wink, releases himself from the bondage of my braids, letting them hang back down the front of my body.

Luke Devlin should be illegal.

He moves his hands behind me and proceeds to pull the laces from the top and then the bottom, making quick and practiced work of lacing me into this Victorian deathtrap. The corset was already flattering, but as he finishes tightening it, I know I'm buying both pieces, no matter the cost.

The corset comes down low in the center and pushes my breasts up high and full. My waist appears narrow compared to my hips, giving me the illusion of Victorian perfection. The buckles down the front add some steam punk flair, but I could certainly wear it for other events.

"*Tu es magnifique.* If you had something to hold on to, I could make this so tight you could scarcely breathe," he whispers like a promise, words tickling my ear with his closeness. His yellow-green gaze meets mine again in the mirror, mesmerizing me. It reminds me of the jungle story and its hypnotic snake.

I lose myself in his strangely colored gaze, noting the striking similarity between the color of his eyes and the splash of color in mine. I've never seen anyone with amber eyes like mine and certainly not with the odd yellow-green color, and now in the span of a week, I've met two men who match my eyes exactly. What a strange coincidence.

My overactive imagination conjures Luke pulling the laces tighter and tighter and my breath coming shorter and shorter, as if I am indeed trapped in the coils of the literary python. He ties off the laces at my waist in an elaborate knot and rests his hands on my flared hips, snapping my focus back to the present where I am free to breathe.

My gaze drops to his too familiar touch, taking in the painted black nails and scattering of rings across his fingers. Another raven's skull, like his belt buckle, but this one carved of black stone, covers almost his entire pointer finger.

I meet his eyes again in our reflection, and his lips curve up wickedly, like the cat who swallowed the canary. And I am quite certain I am the canary.

"It seems a shame to cover beauty such as this," he says as he helps me back into the overcoat.

I can't help but smile at myself in the mirror as he compliments me. The two pieces together are stunning.

"Wow. This is just perfect, Luke. Thank you."

I want to believe that he is just one hell of a salesperson

almost as much as I want to pretend that he has no effect on me. But my traitorous body isn't listening.

Luke induces a strange combination of intense arousal oddly tinged with mild disorientation and fatigue. Like spending the day at a carnival riding the rides and eating all the treats. I'm sure it's just the frantic pace I've set for myself with so much travel.

No wonder I had another dream episode with all this excitement and the rotten night's sleep I had last night. I am surprised by a sudden jaw cracking yawn but thankful it breaks the building sexual tension. Does he feel it, too, or is this just who he is, beauty dripping with confidence and smoldering sexuality?

I laugh behind my hand as I cover my enormous yawn and say, "Excuse me, it's certainly not the company. Just a long night followed by an exciting day. I can't wait to wear this outfit. Thank you for your help."

"I'd love to see you in it again. What are your plans for this stunning beauty?" His eyes twinkle with mischief.

"I wanted a new outfit for the steampunk Poe convention in Baltimore. Will you be there? I'm sure you would make bank at the market."

He smiles his feline smile and responds, "I wouldn't miss it."

"I guess I'll see you again, then." Must be the corset making me sound so breathy.

"*J'ai hâte, mon petit chou*," he says with a small bow. "Until we meet again."

"I should get changed," I murmur, melting in response to his French yet again.

As I take a step back toward the changing booth, I'm brought up short. His hand feels like hot steel circling my wrist and the image of Luke restraining me in handcuffs flashes bright in my mind.

I can't believe the effect this man has on me. Things like tight corsets and bondage aren't usually my style, but for him–I would love to see what happens. My gaze zeroes in on my trapped wrist and then I lift my eyes to Luke and quirk a brow, in true Lieshe fashion.

"You'll need my help," he explains, dropping my arm and motioning to the laces.

"Oh, right," I acknowledge and stand next to the changing booth, clasping the corset to my front while he undoes the laces down the back. My imagination is really running away with me–he was just being helpful.

After he unties the complex knot at my waist, I feel his finger dipping between the laces and my spine up to my neck and then down, down, down my back. Each touch leaves a small, fiery spark and by the time he is done, my skin feels lit up like the fourth of July. I am so thankful he has unlaced me or I worry I would have finally passed out.

He taps my bottom, shooing me forward, in what I could easily interpret as nothing more than a tap between football players. But given his effect on me, I whip my head around in surprise, surprised to see his retreating back.

I frown and step into the booth and get dressed again. The little devil on my shoulder says, he could have spanked us harder. Besides handcuffs, now I'm thinking about him spanking me. The angel on my other shoulder wonders what has gotten into us.

I'm shocked at how much time has passed when I glance down at my watch and realize I really need to get back to the hotel. Before I come back for this evening's entertainment, I need a quiet minute. Or two. Maybe a cold shower.

I walk out and hand Luke the corset to add to my

purchase. He carefully puts it in a nice cloth garment bag emblazoned with his logo. Both pieces are exquisite, but I still swallow hard when he gives me my total. I hand my business and credit cards over to him.

"I really do hope I see you in Baltimore," I tell him, aiming for a friendly, business type voice. I don't want him to know the dramatic effect he has had on me in case he is just being a great salesperson, but it's difficult to hide.

"It would be my pleasure," he says, caressing my fingers as he takes the cards from me, leaving a tingling trail in their wake. He hands me the garment bag with my new purchases tucked inside.

It's been a bit of a whirlwind. Luke Devlin has left me dazzled. Don't get me wrong, I am always willing to take in the sights. But Luke, sweet Heaven above, he has me topsy-turvy as I try to figure out if he is legitimately interested in me or just a flirt.

Before McHottie, I would have blown it off as flirting, but now, with my growing self-confidence, I entertain the thought that Luke really could be interested in me. It's a fun thought. I also realize this is the first time I've thought of McHottie since I laid eyes on Luke.

Chapter 16

LUKE

I watch her walk away, taking the garment bag with her. What wicked fun she is to play with! Lieshe, with her enchanting features—glorious hair, mismatched eyes, and voluptuous body—is a masterpiece of temptation. My love of indulgence extends to my preference for lovers with curves. Today's waifs do nothing for me.

I love seeing my claim on her reflected in her eyes, love knowing every time *he* looks at her, he sees me reflected back at him, my yellow-green stain marring the mirror image of his amber eyes. Oh, the thought of his unimaginable pain is *exquisite.*

Toying with him has been a delightful pastime, meddling with his plans, thwarting his dreams from the shadows. Little nudges here and there to tip the scales in my favor.

Simply knowing I had ruined both of them had been enough in the beginning. But now the stakes are so much higher. A strategic win will require direct intervention. It is time to settle the final score.

I just didn't expect to enjoy the game so much. With her rose scent tickling my nose, her trembling hands and the goosebumps I left in my wake when I touched her, my black heart stirred to life. My inner beast clawed at my skin to burst free. It was all I could do to keep my touch merely warm rather than searing.

But the best part? Her rapid breaths, dilated pupils, and longing looks at me curled my toes in happiness. I can smell the desperation for love on her like a heady perfume. So thick I can taste it, roll it around on my palate. She desires me, wants me. Everyone always does.

There will be nothing more satisfying than making her mine, leaving a wake of broken-hearted souls behind us. The beast within all but purrs at the vision—oceans of destruction and darkness will trail us like a midnight cloak. I will crown her with a wreath of black stars made from their suffering.

As she walks away and is swallowed into the crowd, I can't help but laugh at these mere mortals, going about their daily business like anything they do is of any consequence.

Pawns. All of them. Fucking pawns.

Little pawns happy to be moved around. Happy for any little scraps of happiness or reward. Happy to be sacrificed.

Not me. I will never be a pawn again. I will never beg for scraps. I forged my own dark way.

And now—everything is on the line for the little pawns. They stupidly wander about, smiling, blissfully unaware of the grander game or the stakes contained therein.

I am the King, *the motherfucking King,* and she is *ma Reine Rouge.* I will win and this victory, *this one,* will be the sweetest of them all.

Chapter 17

I trudge back toward my hotel. My ass is dragging. The trapped summer heat of the city is slowly dropping with the sun, but the humidity persists, pulling frizzy flyaways to tickle my neck. The short walk feels longer after so much walking and standing at the large expo center.

I am happy I accomplished my business goals today, but a little uncertain about some of the more personal aspects—like Luke. He is, well, he is *fucking fascinating*. No two ways about it.

I catch a whiff of an unusual smell, like spicy cigarettes, and it makes me smile, reminding me of Luke's cinnamon scent. As I walk, it comes to me.

Cloves, I realize, are the spicy cigarettes. I remember trying them in college and coughing til I cried, but still enjoying the lingering flavor on my lips and being amused at the slight tingling they left in their wake on my tongue.

Luke is spicy and intriguing, like taking a drag from a clove cigarette. Thoughts of wanting to taste him have me marveling at my intense attraction to him. But how can I reconcile my interest in him with my powerful feelings toward McHottie?

I compare the two of them in my mind. Luke is as forward as McHottie is mysterious. They are both tall, but McHottie is beefy and broad, whereas Luke seems strong and sleek. They are both fair, but their hair and eyes are striking opposites. McHottie has been serious and mercurial, whereas Luke seems almost playful in contrast. They really are night and day.

I'd love to see a side by side, preferably naked. The thought lights my face up with a smile so big my cheeks ache. Despite my fatigue, my musings on the two guys who have turned up in my life have passed the quick mile trek back to the hotel in record time.

As I walk through the lobby, I inhale a deep lungful of their signature scent as I cross to the elevator. Instead of enjoying its lightness, though, this time, I wish it were darker and spicy. A mix of leather, tobacco, and cinnamon would be perfect.

"Ms. St. James?" The clerk who checked me in earlier today at the front desk calls out to me, stopping me in my tracks.

"Yes," I reply, walking over, curiosity stamped on my face.

"This came for you," she says, handing me an envelope with my full name beautifully written in bold calligraphy across the thick red stationery.

"Thank you," I say as I take the envelope, frowning at it. I get in the elevator, hitting the button for the fifth floor. I juggle the garment bag over to my other arm. It was heavy to carry the entire way back to the hotel, but I didn't want to leave it with my other items for pickup tomorrow.

I'm dying of curiosity, so hurry back to my room, eager to set down the weight of the bag from my aching arms. I swipe my room key and enter, welcoming the chilly blast of the air conditioning. After I hang my new duds in the closet, I walk over to the window.

I absently rub the back of my neck as it prickles, by now getting accustomed to the strange feeling. I remind myself

McHottie can't be in my hotel room and turn my attention to the enigmatic mail.

I look at the envelope in the sunlight, noting a faint iridescence to the heavy red paper and admire how my name is so magnificent in the bold calligraphy. Wondering what on earth this could be, I turn it over and find a thick gold wax seal over the flap embossed with a stylized raven.

I trace it with my finger and then break the seal to find a ticket inside for tonight's entertainment at the expo. Written in bold letters, I see the name of the show, *Cirque Maléfique*, and the designation of VIP. Flipping it over, I find a handwritten note on the back in the same beautiful calligraphy that says,

I request the pleasure of your company this evening.

That's strange. I thought it was just a general admission. The ticket must be some kind of perk, perhaps for the massive amount of money I dropped today, but how would they know what hotel I am staying at?

I peek back in the envelope for more clues, but it's empty. Curiouser and curiouser. Or maybe when I registered for the expo, there was something about hotel accommodations and I just don't remember filling it out, which is entirely possible. Perhaps everyone got one of these delivered. If so, their marketing is incredible.

I flop down on the bed and toe off my Converse, letting them fall to the floor. Might as well think this through while I relax. I had planned on taking a nap, but the note and ticket have me amped back up now. Why hadn't I brought a cooler outfit for tonight? Or at least better shoes.

What if I see Luke? I'd love to look a little hotter than my jeans and converse. Well, I guess I'll just have to go full war paint then. I spin around and prop my legs up against the headboard and text Jo.

LIESHE

Hey babe, I met a super hot dude at the expo.

JO

Whattttt????? Spill

LIESHE

Think ginger, long-haired model with Van Dyke facial hair.

JO

Ew. You know I hate facial hair. It's like pubes 🤮 but on your face.

LIESHE

Really? That's what you took away from that text?

JO

[sends GIF of Carrot Top]

JO

Does he look like this?

LIESHE

Fuck you, of course not!

JO

😏

LIESHE

When I got back to the hotel after the expo today, there was a red envelope waiting for me with a VIP ticket to the show tonight.

JO

Oooo secret admirer???

LIESHE

Maybe just an expo perk

JO

Maybe, what kinda show?

LIESHE

Some type of burlesque circus thingy, I think?

JO

Send pics. I want to see burlesque titties!

LIESHE

I am not sending you titty pics.

JO

Bish please! You know I gotta live vicariously.

LIESHE

That's what you get for living in the middle of nowhere.

JO

Shit, I forgot. Thanks for the reminder. Go live your life. Be Safe. And please send me pics. I gotta go rake the tumbleweeds

LIESHE

Love you

Laughing at Jo's texts, I head to the bathroom and plug my phone in to charge so I can listen to my playlist while I get ready for the show tonight. A quick glance at the clock shows I still have two hours until it starts, but I want to look smoking hot.

I tell myself it's not in case I run into Luke, but it totally is. To be honest, I'd love to see him again. Something about him is seriously intriguing, and I want to taste his cinnamon candy smell on my tongue. *I could taste a whole lot of him on my tongue,* I think.

I scold myself, muttering out loud, "Lieshe, how many hot guys do you want to be with?"

The little devil on my shoulder replies smartly, all of them. She's not wrong. I do want all of them. Or at least these two. I smile at myself in the bathroom mirror. Perhaps one at a time is a better place to start, though. The little devil on my shoulder chimes in, saying, is it?

Thinking of Luke, I Google what I think he called me back at the expo, but my phonetic spelling must be off, because if this is right it seems, in addition to his "Red Queen," he called me his little cabbage or puff pastry depending on how you interpret it.

Shrugging over French translations, I plug in my straightener and wash my face so I can redo my makeup with a blank slate. I prep my skin with moisturizer and a primer. While that dries, I section my mass of hair for straightening.

I run serum through the sections and start the painstaking process of straightening my curls. I don't do it often, simply because it is so much work, but it is fun to have a completely fresh look.

As I straighten my hair section by section, I continue my earlier thoughts comparing McHottie to Luke. They are so vastly different, but I can't deny I have an attraction to each of them. I'd love to spend more time together, get to know them better.

Maybe Luke is just a flirt, and this entire thought process is a waste of time. Maybe McHottie was a flash in the pan and doesn't actually have the interest in me I thought he did. Maybe I could have both of them and be a Lieshe sandwich?

That thought just about makes me moan out loud. I imagine McHottie's cold marble body pressed to my front and Luke's incendiary touch flush against my back. I've never been in a multiple partner situation before, but I could get into this.

Fantasies of four hands on my body distract me until I smell something burning. I jump and realize my hair is getting singed while I am lost in my daydream.

With tremendous effort, I focus on straightening my hair and thankfully finish it out without further incident. For my full make up look I am planning, I am thankful I always travel with my complete make-up bag, even when traveling light. My playlist is a little slow, so I hit skip until I find something fresh and funky to get ready to.

Setting my glasses to the side, I pop in a pair of contacts I dig out of the bottom of my makeup bag. I prefer my chunky black glasses, but I don't want to hide my face tonight. Contacts will let my bold makeup really show.

I fight to get the slippery little buggers in my eyes and, with a lot of contact solution and blinking, everything finally feels like it's in place. My vision is terrible, so they give me the added advantage of being better able to see to paint my face.

I start with foundation and then layer the various colors needed for contouring. When I'm happy with my base, I build a dark smokey eye. Once the black shadow is flawless, I add a red glitter layer and then finish with thick winged liner.

Next, I add multiple layers of mascara to make my lashes thick and long. I finish it with a white shimmer liner to my inner lower eyelid to make my eyes pop.

I rarely add a dark lip to a flashy eye, but tonight I make an exception. I pull out my favorite lipstick, a deep dark red called Nosferatu. This incredible lipstick lasts a solid 12 hours minimum, even if I drink something or, better yet, kiss someone.

I wish McHottie was here so we could really test out the lipstick's staying power. The image of mussed lipstick not just on me, but on him, is smoking.

I think of Luke's black on black-on-black outfit from earlier today and decide to add black for a vampire ombre lip to represent both of them. I start the painstaking process of lining my lips in black and then filling in the center with a dark matte red, carefully building up the perfect coverage. At last, I cover the center with the glossy Nosferatu.

The make-up gods must be smiling down upon me because the result tonight is fierce. I quirk an eyebrow at myself in the mirror and decide to extend them out just a little. Not too much, just for a little added drama.

I run some hair serum over my ends to keep them silky smooth and finish by spraying on my favorite perfume, a deep rose scent. I've always been drawn to the smell of roses, and this particular scent is dark and spicy rather than floral and girly.

I feel confident and sexy. The woman looking back at me is stunning. I like my burgeoning confidence. It feels so much better than beating myself up. The world is harsh enough and already tries to beat everyone down. Why had I added to my misery by also being so hard on myself all these years?

As I gained weight in high school, I felt more and more pressure to conform to the airbrushed images imposed on my generation, coupled with the poor nutrition narrative that healthy fat was the enemy.

My mother was always dieting, attending group meetings and counting fat. As a result, she pushed chicken breast and diet coke on me, and rather than allowing me gluten-free treats, deprived me of carbs altogether.

Despite her efforts and my father's retorts, my thick frame refused to thin out, and when I got my first job, most of my money went to junk food. By college, I was uncomfortable and unhealthy.

Mindy has changed my life in many ways, and during our first year in college, she taught me about eating for fuel more than for comfort. With her help, I transitioned my diet to real food with healthy fats.

When the third member of our girl gang, Jo, joined us, she introduced me to yoga, and I loved the flexibility and connection to my body that it brought. It also helped with the stress of nursing school.

With the help of my two best friends, I found the middle road between eating garbage and society's obsession with weight. I enjoyed real food, fueled my body, and kept my full figure. And now, I was learning to really embrace 30-year-old Lieshe. Single, curvy, gray streak of hair, and all.

I give myself one more confident smile in the bathroom mirror, then grab my phone and go out to change. I hadn't packed any fun outfits for this trip, but at least I had grabbed a cool shirt to wear home tomorrow. It will be perfect for tonight instead, paired with my red fishnet stockings under my ripped black skinny jeans.

I leave my red lace bra on, knowing it will add a pop of color to the back of my outfit and swap out the Grimm logo shirt. The upgrade is a draped black material in the front that shows a little cleavage, but the back is where the money is with this one. The entire back is a sheer fine mesh, embroidered down the center in white with an anatomically correct spine.

I head back to the bathroom to check out my final look but am disappointed when I see over my shoulder my hair is covering the coolest aspect of my shirt. I think for a second and then I gather my straight hair into a super high pony and add a little rhinestone skeleton hand clip I fish out of my bag to the side of my head.

Now I am ready. I glance at the clock and realize I left myself no time for dinner between the extra glam time and needing to get back to the expo center for the show in time. I'll have to hustle.

Chapter 18

HIM

The problem with transforming to dust is I am aware of my surroundings but powerless to interact with them. But this is the only form that allows me to be virtually undetectable. I watch her face in the mirror as she gets ready to go out.

She randomly grins or quirks one eyebrow at herself, and I wish, as I have thousands of times before, that I had the power to read her mind. I hope her smiles are from thoughts of me. And not of that monster she finally met.

I cannot understand how she could not have seen all along what I see before me. A beautiful woman with a genuine smile and caring heart. I love the way she dances to the music as she gets ready, hips swaying sensuously while her feet stick stubbornly to the ground. She's always loved dancing but has never been good at it. I love to see it, anyway.

The movement highlights the perfect curve of her ass, making me want to sink my teeth into it. I despise her in black, but she swathes herself in it from head to toe tonight. Colors are for the living.

The light winks off her newly reacquired ring, the twin to mine. Seeing it on her finger, where it rightfully belongs, brings me more joy than I have had in so very long.

The ring itself is bittersweet; these are the only two of their kind. And although I love some of the memories of them, the thought alone of how they came to be is almost enough to destroy me.

She rushes out the door, checking her silly little bag and then stopping to make sure the door is closed securely behind her. Like that could stop me. Oh, her innocence. If only a simple door could keep the monsters at bay.

I feel a faint twinge of guilt over hiding here to watch her, but I can't get the compulsion to be near her out of my mind after all this time. Our souls call to each other, across time, across space. I can no more resist coming to her than a compass can refuse true north. I am drawn to her. Always.

Just like last night, she had looked so innocent in her sleep—face relaxed, breathing deeply. I couldn't resist carefully crawling into her bed and wrapping myself around her as she laid on her side. I had been scared to even breathe as I had stealthily moved a single muscle at a time until her back was flush against my front.

Home.

Holding her is home.

Her body had felt so warm after so many years away from her fire. As I twined my legs through hers and fit my rapidly hardening cock into the cleft of her fine ass, I had to bite my lip to stifle my groan.

With the reserve that could only come from eons of time, I had kept myself still instead of grinding and thrusting into her. It would have been easy to sneak her panties down and slip into her tight, wet warmth.

But I needed to look into her eyes when we joined ourselves again. I needed to see her, her to see me. So, I took pleasure in the simple nearness of her and the way our bodies fit together, carved from the same flesh.

I ghosted a fingertip down her hair and then over each vertebra of her spine. Feeling her flesh ripple into goosebumps was the most exquisite torture. I longed to follow my questing fingertips with my tongue.

I desperately craved to taste every inch of her, explore every texture of this lifetime with a kiss. But I forced myself to be satisfied for now with these stolen touches. I mapped the topography of her body with a single fingertip, across the top of her panties to her elbow, up over her arm, and down to her exposed stomach, luxuriating in the softness of her skin.

I really had been attempting to exercise considerable restraint, but when she ground her perfectly round ass back into me and let out a breathy little moan, I hadn't been able to stop myself from a taste of her. Just one taste, I promised myself, as I opened my mouth where it laid behind her ear.

Her essence flooded my mouth, consuming me, thrumming through my veins like liquid light. She tasted like the promise of hope. She tasted like the fruit of the garden. She tasted like mine.

Soon, my love, my light. Soon, my *Roză*.

Chapter 19

Rushing to get out the door, I grab two protein bars, throw one in my belt bag, and put the other in my back pocket to eat on the way. I make sure I have my wallet and hotel key.

Just as I walk out the door, I whip my head around to scan the room behind me. I have the strangest feeling of being watched. Seeing nothing, I shake my head at my imagination and head out. I open my bar in the elevator and am finishing it up by the time I cross the lobby and am out the front door.

There are a fair amount of people out walking around at this hour. The heat of the day has faded, and a slight breeze makes for a pleasant summer evening. I'm thankful the humidity has dissipated, so my freshly straightened hair doesn't get any ideas.

I wish I had brought some more stylish shoes than my Converse, but at least they are comfortable to walk back to the expo center. I head back in that direction, noticing it's one of those nights where couples in love are everywhere—twosomes are strolling hand in hand down the street, sitting together holding hands across a cafe table, or taking a selfie in the city.

It makes me feel maudlin and more than a little jealous. My life is wonderful in so many ways. My confidence and happiness are growing. I am proud of the business I have built. My little found family is amazing.

But.

I'm lonely. My friends have become understandably busy with their own lives over the past few years. My cat barely tolerates me. My father—well, is my father. I'm ready to find my other half and have a partner to share my life with.

Hell, I'd even take someone to fight with. We'd have some silly argument about something stupid, like hair in the sink, and then end up having fabulous make up sex. I'd even be willing to tolerate someone's mess in my little home above the shop.

So, when is my time? Where is my person? My doubts about McHottie resurface, and I decide if he doesn't show back up when I get home, I realistically need to think about moving on. I can't mourn the loss of a nameless man, no matter how hot, forever.

Especially after starting to build a relationship in my mind over what, in reality, has been a single physical encounter. My steps slow, the excitement over my strange VIP ticket dimming, as I continue to focus on my lack of a love life.

This pattern is nothing new. I meet someone, get hopeful, and build a relationship in my head like a castle in the sand. And then the wave of life comes crashing down, reducing my beautiful creation to a sad, unrecognizable blob, and I'm left devastated. Thank goodness I've never actually fallen in love. I don't think I could survive the fallout.

And maybe, just maybe, that's what keeps me in love with impossible, imaginary men like Dracula and lusting after ones, like McHottie and Luke, so far out of my league I don't know why I think they would even consider me.

My steps falter, and then I remember Luke's feline smile and his earlier compliments, and they buoy me back up. Perhaps I'll even see him again tonight instead of the far off

Poe convention. And with that thought, my stride picks back up, carrying me the rest of the way to the expo center.

There is a short line, since I'm still pretty early. I wanted a good seat so had timed it just right, not entirely sure what the VIP ticket even meant. Perhaps my earlier thought was correct and everyone got one, just a marketing ploy after all.

But as I glance around at the others standing in line, I don't see anyone else with a red envelope. I dig my ticket out of my belt bag so it's ready when I get to the front.

My curiosity builds as the queue inches its way forward until, by the time my turn comes to hand my ticket over, I have butterflies in my stomach waiting to see what will happen. I hold it out to the two incredible women taking tickets.

I think they are some type of gothic clowns, in completely black and white costumes, with black-and-white striped corset dresses. Each has one white and one black leg, thick white stage makeup with creepy black eye makeup and lipstick. Even their hair is half black and half white. I can't wait to see the rest of the costuming, and the show, with this as the preview.

The ladies exchange a sideways glance and then each give me a chilling smile. Out of the shadows steps a large figure in a hooded black robe. Peeking out of the hood is the beak of a long plague mask. As the ladies turn toward the figure, I see they each have a raven tattoo on the back of their shoulders, like the one that had been on the seal from the envelope.

I guess I'm supposed to follow the hooded figure who comes to stand in front of me. Given his size, I assume he is a man, but I can't see anything of him except part of the mask and the swirling black cloak.

This isn't scary as shit, I think. I hope this isn't the start of some weird kidnapping movie. He turns and starts walking. After a brief hesitation, I follow. It's either that or get left behind.

The butterflies have multiplied, and I am both super nervous and super excited. As we turn and walk down a dim hallway, my palms start to sweat. The figure turns into a stairwell and starts heading down.

I hesitate because this is getting creepier by the minute. He pauses on the landing and looks up at me, staring in silence while my pulse thunders in my ears.

My vision dims and I slump against the wall, trying and failing to ground myself with the feeling of the cold cinder block against me. Before I can attempt to ward it off, I'm thrust deep into another waking dream.

For the first time, one has found me *in flagrante delicto*. The details are so vivid, I can feel the soft fur clenched in my hands and cushioning my knees from the stone floor below. The ferocious heat of an enormous open fireplace to my side causes sweat to drip down my neck and roll down my breasts, where it drips off my nipples to the furs below.

I gasp, realizing with startling clarity that I can feel each finger in a bruising iron grip on my hips, holding me at the mercy of someone's punishing pace. The rising need in me urges me to arch my back further, desperately trying to get closer but held immobile.

I'm so fabulously full, but something is missing—I need more. I can feel this has been a marathon session, from my ragged breathing and quaking muscles, bathed in firelight and sweat.

One hand leaves my hip to gently caress down my spine, making a series of sharp slaps landing on my ass even more surprising, but just what I need to bring me one step closer to cresting this flaming peak. My mouth drops open in a silent scream, flooded with the salt of my own tears and sweat from this exquisite and unrelenting torture.

I toss my head, dislodging the long curls that cover my face like a curtain. I must see the face of my tormentor who is keeping me on this razor's edge of pleasure. I strain to look over my shoulder at the man who expertly thrusts behind me, shocked to find him wearing a stylized raven mask.

He fists my hair, keeping my gaze on him. The exquisite pull of my hair, coupled with his anonymity, pushes me over the edge. I feel my inner walls ripple around him, triggering him to swell and explode inside me, the sudden filling warmth pushing my own release even higher.

I barely recognize the animalistic sounds falling from my lips, only his iron grasp on my hip and hand tangled in my hair keep me from collapsing bonelessly into the furs beneath me.

He thrusts impossibly deeper, riding out the end of his orgasm and pushing me into aftershocks of my own. He stills, reaching up to rip off his mask.

The shocked gasp from the doorway reveals I am not the only one surprised to see Luke Devlin behind me, eyes fully black and smiling his cheshire grin like a well-pleased demon. It snaps both of our attention to a desolate McHottie, who collapses onto his knees, arms outstretched, reaching for me.

As fast as I succumbed to this dream, I'm back from the castle-like room to the present-day stairwell and feeling fine. I reach up to wipe the dream sweat from my forehead, but of course, there is none. None of it was real, yet I feel my pussy still pulsing with arousal.

Odd, I've never snapped in and out of a dream so quickly. Usually there is some type of transition period. They seem to be evolving. This was more like some sort of vision and less like my usual dreams as I know them.

Or was it a memory, I wonder. But it can't be. I barely know my new neighbor and I just met Luke. I sure as shit have never had amazing masked sex with him.

The robed figure cocks his head, catching my attention. The hood slips back enough with the movement that in the light of the stairwell, I can see the plague mask is actually a stylized raven's mask with exquisite details. The same damn one I just saw on Luke.

"What the fuck?" I mutter under my breath.

This night is getting strange. I have two options: turn around and run or continue to follow him. The thought of trying to outrun this robed and masked figure is the scarier of the two. So, I follow him.

The only noise is my feet clattering down the stairs. The figure I'm following is as silent as the grave. *What a horrible saying,* I realize as I break out in goosebumps.

I can't decide whether I should be thrilled about this adventure in my otherwise relatively safe life or be scared out of my mind in anticipation of some Hostel-like shit happening. We go down one floor and then enter another dimly lit hallway. Fluorescent lights flicker dimly, and exposed pipes line the ceiling.

Maybe following wasn't the safer option. I feel like we are in the bowels of the expo center now, and I couldn't find my way out alone even if I had to. *Super reassuring, Lieshe,* I scold myself. The cloaked man turns into another stairwell, and now I'm wondering if he is just fucking with me.

But I continue to follow him—up two flights of stairs this time—my legs burning a little with all the climbing and walking. I'm thankful for my sneakers now.

When we exit the stairwell, I catch sight of a circus tent

erected within the expo center. It is like something out of a nightmare. Instead of a cheery red and white big top, it is black and white with multiple asymmetrical curling towers. It is darkly fantastical. Our strange detour has somehow landed us closer to a side entrance, well away from the crowd waiting to get in.

From my vantage point, I can still see at the front of the lengthy line of people waiting to get in is a fearsome entrance—an enormous devil's mouth, complete with spiky teeth and a handlebar mustache. The red of the devil's face is a startling contrast to the black and white tent. The eyes are shining brightly in the otherwise dim interior of the expo, lit from within.

I see the cloaked figure ahead of me now circling around the tent, and I scurry to catch up, not realizing the sight had rooted me to the spot, gawking. I follow him to a side entrance guarded by two enormous guys in old-fashioned strongman outfits. They don't spare either of us a glance and I shadow him, hot on his heels, thankful to not have to enter through that creepy ass devil's mouth.

He leads me into what is clearly a special roped-off section. Instead of the tiered stand seating I can see around the perimeter of the tent, this area has tables and chairs set up on terraced levels. Eventually, we reach the bottom level, and he spins, robe flaring, holding out a hand to show me to the first table in front of the round stage.

I take the proffered seat, wondering who will sit in the other chair, if anyone. I look around the inside of the tent as the general admission seats quickly start filling. The lighting makes it hard to see anything beyond the seating area and the central stage, creating a feeling of being at the center of a vast nothingness.

The air is buzzing with excited conversation, and I feel a

little awkward sitting in the forefront of the VIP section alone as my guide vanishes. Apparently, the whole VIP ticket actually was some type of exclusive thing. I just do not know how I got picked.

Maybe it's because I spent so much damn money at the expo on my new clothes, I think to myself, smiling. I wonder who else is in this area, craning my head, trying to see behind me.

I'm startled to find a little person in front of me when I turn back around. She is stunning, with her ebony skin in contrast to her snow-white hair in victory rolls. Like a pinup girl in a black and white outfit, similar to the ladies who had taken my ticket.

She passes me a drink with a dazzling smile and a wink, then sets a plate of snacks on the table at my elbow.

"Oh, I didn't order anything."

"On the house darlin'," she replies in a beautiful Southern accent. "Gluten-free, of course," she throws over her shoulder as she saunters away.

Now this is just getting weird. I take a cautious sniff of my drink and wonder if it is actually a good idea to accept it. What if someone is trying to drug me? My mouth waters. The bourbon looks incredible and is a generous pour over two rocks, just how I like it.

I glance at the snacks she put down and my stomach rumbles. It's like someone has read my mind or at least done a decent job stalking me. The plate is a delightful little charcuterie board with artfully arrayed meats and cheeses, nuts, pomegranate seeds, dried apricots, preserves, honey, and mustards.

I recognize my favorite gluten-free crackers and figure no one is likely to go to this much trouble just to drug me, in public no less. It makes the second protein bar in my bag seem very unappealing. I love charcuterie. Nothing beats making a meal out of snack foods.

Fuck it.

I decide to go with the adventure and go all in. I use the 'Kentucky Chew' to taste the unfamiliar bourbon. First, I pick up the rocks glass and swirl the amber liquid, then I delicately put my nose in the glass and inhale with my lips slightly parted. I smell vanilla and caramel notes, with a spicy black pepper undertone. I don't immediately recognize it as anything I've had before.

I take a tentative sip into the middle of my palate, then chew it. The bourbon starts off with a surprising amount of heat up front and then mellows to the vanilla and caramel notes I smelled.

What I didn't expect from the bouquet, or the world of bourbon, is a surprising fruity finish. It's definitely an unusual tasting one, but absolutely delicious, with a smooth finish despite the heat upfront.

I lightly smack my lips, trying to puzzle out the fruity flavor at the end. Is it apple? Pomegranate? It's hard to place. The lingering note is reminiscent of a cinnamon candy apple.

"Whew, that's bottled in bond," I mutter on a spicy exhale. I nibble my snacks, glancing around as the general admission seats fill and check out the VIP area behind me. A few other tables in this section are now seated with a wide variety of guests.

I see a few suits at one table, a gothic couple at another, and a giant mountain of a man in a three-piece suit of unrelieved black in the very back. I turn back around, surveying the stands closest to me, startled to see a man looking right at me.

Although, at this distance, I can't make out the precise shade of his eyes, in my mind, I can picture them exactly. He looks disturbingly like my long-lost guardian angel everyone had insisted was an imaginary friend.

Without warning, the lights dim and anticipation of the upcoming entertainment swirls in my belly. I forget about the blond man reminiscent of my past in my excitement over the show. I can't wait to see what's in store just from the few interactions and performers I've seen so far.

Chapter 20

The volume of the crowd drops with the lights, leaving everyone quietly buzzing with excitement. I steadily work through my charcuterie plate, savoring the burst of flavors on my tongue from the pomegranate seeds, then relishing the smokey meats and sharp cheeses. I dip a cracker in the honey, surprised when I pop it into my mouth to find it's spicy.

I take another sip of my bourbon, enjoying how well it complements my snacky meal. When I see the same server pass by, I wave her over to ask for water. I'll need to pace myself with as strong as this is.

Haunting music starts as the whole interior fades to black. The audience lets out a collective gasp as red spotlights come on along the edge of the circular stage, directing their swirling beams of light upwards.

We all look up, eyes searching for the start of the show. The spotlights fade away, save a single red one illuminating the figure dropping from the ceiling.

An oversized birdcage holds an impossibly contorted woman. The cage slowly lowers, eerie in the red light. As it makes its way down, the music swells. The cage sits in the center of the rotating stage, showcasing just how contorted the woman is—a mass of red and black and flesh.

I recognize the two men coming down the aisles as the huge guys who had been at the side door. They each spring up onto the stage and grasp opposite sides of the cage.

I feel the whole tent holding its collective breath, waiting to see what will happen. The strongmen lift the cage into the air, muscles straining as if they are trying to rip it apart.

Suddenly, long red silk swaths of fabric fall from the ceiling, hiding the performers. Pyrotechnics shoot up plumes of sparks around the edge of the stage and the strongmen fall to their sides. The cage mysteriously vanishes.

A strong back light comes on and the outline of a woman becomes visible through the red fabric. The crowd erupts into cheers as the red silk parts and out steps the most stunning redheaded woman.

She has on an exquisite costume of a female ringmaster with a miniature top hat cocked to the side. A long red and black silk jacket covered in gold swirling embroidery ripples around her. Her black over the knee stiletto boots have echoes of the same gold swirls from her jacket. I'd kill for this outfit.

I've never seen a redhead pull off this much red before. Even her lips are colored to match her outfit. As she steps forward and bows with a flourish, her coat fans out.

"Welcome to *Cirque Maléfique*," her sultry voice easily carries out over the crowd. The music changes from ethereal to a faster beat and the strongmen sneak up behind her, ripping off her fabulous coat and little ringmaster hat, leaving her in a black satin corset and short skirt with ruffled bustle.

She feigns shock and embarrassment, then dramatically runs forward away from the men and launches herself into the silks, sailing out over the audience as the fabric retracts into the ceiling. The crowd goes wild as she climbs up the long lengths of red silk, escaping the strongmen who circle threateningly below.

Spotlights follow her into the air as she winds in and out

of the silks, moving ever upwards, and I unconsciously hold my breath, scared at just how high up she is. The silks stop retracting, their ends fluttering above the stage.

I'm amazed by her strength as she anchors herself in the silks and then swings out in ever-widening circles. The two strongmen join her at the bottom of each silk, like they are trying to keep her from flying away, and I can't help but stare at their rippling muscles as they move their bodies gracefully across the stage, even becoming airborne at times.

The guys use the silks like ropes, holding themselves out perpendicularly and then returning their feet to the stage and moving to the edges, anchoring the ends of the fabric to swing them in circles. The control they have over their movements adds to the realism of the pantomime and highlights the truth behind their nickname of strongmen.

The beautiful redhead continues to wind herself higher, almost out of sight in a theatrical escape from her dramatic attackers. The music builds, holding the audience's rapt attention. My mouth dries in anticipation of what will come next, prompting me to take a sip of my forgotten bourbon.

The song reaches a crescendo and abruptly stops. The tent is silent, the crowd holding their collective breath, and then the aerial performer falls through the air, tumbling down the silks until she catches herself upside down, the tip of her long red hair just touching the stage. After a second of stunned silence, we all jump to our feet, thundering applause and cheering.

She flips upright, dropping into the arms of the strongmen as the silks retract back into the ceiling. She makes a show of comically smacking them on the head, so they put her down. Walking the circular perimeter of the stage, she blows kisses to the crowd, who are all now completely in love with her.

The fellas jump down and stand next to the stage. Four more guys come running down the aisles between the stands and the six of them form human stairs at the edge.

I give them credit. Despite her walking down them in her stiletto boots, they don't flinch or even grimace. I watch her beauty and confidence, her incredible strength, and I think she might be my spirit animal.

She descends the last 'step' of the strongman pyramid, directly in line with my seat, meets my eyes and walks straight up to me.

She is even more stunning the closer she gets and is somehow vaguely familiar. She continues her sexy strut toward me, and if I wasn't so enamored by her, I would probably remember to be shy that I am now under the spotlight with this breathtaking beauty in front of a crowd.

Up close, her burlesque costuming is even more exquisite. I can see the intricate embroidery in shades of gold on her boots and her corset is a beautiful black satin. Her makeup is fierce, her lips covered in red rhinestones, twinkling under the bright spotlight.

She straddles my legs and sits on my lap, making a show of wrapping her arms around my neck to the wolf whistles and catcalls of the audience. I've never been attracted to a woman before, but I am not at all put off by the close contact of this stunning beauty. Besides, I tell myself, this is all part of the act.

She leans into my ear and whispers in some type of glorious exotic accent, "Now I see what all the fuss is about."

I'm still catching up with her words when she nips my earlobe and leans back with a sultry smile. She brushes the faintest kiss over my lips and then picks up my bourbon, knocking the rest of it back to the hilarity of the crowd.

She winks at me, then gracefully gets up and ascends the

VIP section to sit with the mountain of a man in a black suit at the furthest table. A made man if my late-night fiction bears any weight.

The spotlights, now white, track back to the stage, where the six strongmen put on an incredible display of balance and strength. Their muscles ripple and pull while they toss each other around and pose precariously. I sip on my water, since the fiery redhead drained my bourbon, and eat some more of the charcuterie plate.

I'm so thrilled I got this VIP ticket. The show is just getting started, and it's already been an amazing experience coupled with dinner and drinks. I continue to marvel at the strongmen, surprised when four hoops descend from the ceiling, each containing a gothic clown.

I recognize the two from the ticket line, and there are two more, similar in appearance and costuming. The guys finish their performance to tremendous applause and bound up the aisles as the music changes over and the hoop act begins.

The server comes back with fresh water and another hefty pour of bourbon. I'm thankful since the fiery red goddess downed the rest of my drink, and I want to have some more of its unusual flavor.

As I watch the hoop performers in awe, I hardly know where to look next. Each of them is so incredible, their talent and strength are simply magnificent.

The hoopers finish up their act, but instead of getting down, their hoops retreat into the ceiling while they are still on them, and I wonder how the hell they will get down.

Amazing act after act graces the stage, each one more surprising than the last. The performers are flawless. Some acts are pure sensuality, some are hilarious, all are unique.

I finish my charcuterie plate, thankful I had more to eat than a protein bar since I'm on my second bourbon. Feeling pretty warm, I suspect this really is bottled in bond, which would make it one hundred proof. I remind myself to alternate sips of liquor with sips of water so I can make it back to my hotel tonight.

The last act's applause fades and the music starts back up with a pounding beat. The crowd claps along. It's infectious, and the next thing I know, I am clapping with them.

The spotlights swirl over the stage, faster and faster. They start to strobe, the noise and lights rising to a fevered pitch until I need to squint my eyes against the crazy visual onslaught. Abruptly, everything goes still and silent.

I can almost hear the crowd breathing as one in the darkness, like we've become a combined living entity in our united experience and anticipation of what is coming. On a collective inhale, pyrotechnics fire towers of sparks, lighting up the darkness and breaking the silence.

The bright flash briefly reveals a robed figure standing in the center of the stage. I think my eyes are playing tricks on me until a red spotlight shines straight down onto the stage, proving it really is him, the masked man. I shiver at the eerie sight.

A primal beat with a low singing voice starts in. The suspense builds until the hooded man drops back his hood, revealing the raven mask. The crowd goes absolutely wild, as he spins, raising his arms as if embracing us all. With a flourish, he whips off his robe and flings it to the circling strongmen below.

This guy is magnificent, tall and lithe, heavily muscled but not beefy. He has on tight leather pants and struts across the stage to stand facing me. I look from his masked face, down his upper body, rippling with muscle and crisscrossed with a leather harness that looks like it was custom made to highlight the dips and valleys of his body. Light glints off his nipple piercings.

I can feel his heated stare through the mask. Something niggles at the back of my brain—I should know who this is. Wait, it can't be. Can it?

As if in answer to my unvoiced question, he rips the mask off and tosses it to a waiting strongman below.

"Luke?" I gasp his name out loud, shocked to see him on the stage. There is no way he should be able to hear me over the music, but he meets my eyes, and in the red spotlight, his smile is demonic and sinful. He leans down to grab a whip in each hand from his helpers off stage.

Fuck, this is hot on the heels of that dream, or vision, or whatever that erotic happening in the stairwell was. He winks at me and spins, showcasing his magnificently inked back. An enormous raven covers his rippling muscles, and as he lifts his arms, it appears ready to take flight. It's stunning. He's stunning.

Like a Viking warrior, he had braided and pulled back his long hair. He struts along the perimeter, swirling his whips, wrapping one around his body while he does some cracking work with the other and then with both together.

The sound of them is deafening and each crack ratchets my heart rate up. Once he whips the crowd into a frenzy, literally, he makes his way back to stand on the edge, facing me again.

He hands the whips off to another of the strongmen and they pass him a fresh set. He spins to face the audience and yells, "Do you want to burn?"

The crowd goes absolutely wild.

"Do you want to burn?" he yells again, tendons in his neck straining, spinning in a circle.

I yell along with the crowd, "Yes!"

We all want to burn with him. I feel the mad mob mentality taking over, all of us swept up in the show's drama. Yes, we want fire from this gorgeous man. I swig down the last of my bourbon, the fire on my tongue matching the mood of the crowd.

Yes, I want to burn with Luke.

He faces me again, staring directly into my eyes. I can't breathe, can't blink, as he lowers the tips down to where the waiting strongmen light them up. The flames lick up the length of the whips, and he sprints to the center of the stage and starts cracking them in an impressive display of speed.

They crack in quick succession, breaking the barrier of sound. He dances around, wielding the whips with speed, precision, and so much damn showmanship. It feels primal. Raw.

The poppers sail through the air, cracking repeatedly. He looks like controlled chaos as his body moves, in complete dominance over the fire whips and the audience.

The noise from the crowd surges louder and louder, almost overpowering the sounds of the cracking. The firelight flickers over his body as he spins. His nearly naked torso ripples and flexes, sweat dripping down. I want to chase the drops with my tongue.

I think every person here is ready to tear this man apart. He pivots again and meets my eyes, moving the whips faster and faster until the flames extinguish. We all leap to our feet, yelling and cheering.

Luke spreads his arms wide and drops his head back, yelling, "Do you want more?"

Fuck, yes. I want more.

"More, more, more," immediately breaks out, a massive chant from the audience. He's awakened the beast in all of us and we all want more fire. More Luke. It seems to appeal to the caveman part of the brain in all of us.

Fire.

Heat.

Lust.

He keeps his arms spread wide and swaggers to the edge. He drops the whips down and turns and faces the middle of the stage. The spotlights point back up, swirling through the air, to illuminate the redheaded goddess again. Instead of a cage, this time she is descending on a swing.

As she drifts down, she swings it out over the crowd in a large circle. They gasp as she flips backwards, almost falling, but catching herself with her legs at the last second. She wraps one around one side and drops the other leg, arcing over the audience like an upside-down ballerina.

Her mass of wild red curls hangs down, catching the light, and I realize this is why she looked familiar. She is the female version of Luke, down to the exact shade of their hair.

We are all so distracted by her coming down that people are just now noticing the hoopers from earlier are rising up amongst the stands, their legs strapped into a contraption mounted on long poles. They whip out over the audience, narrowly missing the circling swing. Every time I am amazed by this show and think it has reached its zenith, they kick it up another notch.

The women are now in black leather strappy bralettes with capped sleeves and tight leather leggings that lace up the sides. They are like fierce warrior princesses with their hair in braids like Luke's.

The cheering is non-stop as people reach out, the ladies whipping around on what must be some type of carbon fiber poles, coming so close it seems like you can reach out and touch them.

Everyone reaches their arms up toward the performers. Finally, the fiery redhead circles more narrowly and lands on stage, Luke lending a gallant hand for her dismount. She is in a similar leather strappy bralette and pants, but hers are a brilliant red.

Hands raised, the handsome pair stalks across the stage to stand in front of me. He twirls her in and out like a dancer, and she sinks to her knees, facing me. He stands behind her and gathers her glorious hair and winds it around his hand.

I imagine him winding mine with his fist like that behind me, reminiscent of when he wrapped my braids around his hands. I frown and wonder if they are actually lovers, jealousy rearing its ugly head. He quickly secures her beautiful tresses, and I'm left wondering why.

He raises her back up, and they face each other, touching their foreheads. In profile now, I question if they are twins as they look so alike. They grin at one another and then fiercely spin away, moving into a lyrical dance, spinning and twisting dramatically.

Every eye is riveted on them. The pounding primal beat of music starts and instantly the lights drop. As we all cheer yet again, my voice hoarse from yelling so much, the lights come back up to show every performer is now on the stage. The strongmen are back, also encased in leather, making the ensemble appear like a badass dance troupe. Or a band of lethal assassins. One of the two. Or both.

They leap off the platform and four of them turn and offer a hand to help the ladies down. They walk halfway up the aisles and then spin to face the stage. The two remaining strongmen head straight for me, and my mouth goes dry.

Chapter 21

They stop right in front of me, each extending out a hand. I realize with a sinking feeling what is happening. I haven't been on a stage since my sixth-grade choir concert where I almost barfed.

Both petrified and ridiculously excited to see what is in store for me, I wish I would have had a third bourbon as I take their hands and allow them to lead me. They lift me up like I weigh nothing and deposit me on the edge of the stage.

From up here, I thankfully can't see the crowd past the lights, but I can hear them cheering me on. I let their excitement fill me and it makes me feel brave.

Luke stands in the center and holds out a hand, beckoning me closer. I cross the stage with steady feet, but a pounding heart, and place my hand in his scorching grip once again.

My fingers are trembling and I'm thankful that his hand closes around them tightly. I sense his partner come behind me, where she pushes me to my knees with her hands on my shoulders. Luke drops my hand as I kneel and brings it to my chin instead, tilting my face up to look into his eyes.

They are alive with mischief, glittering green. He isn't even breathing heavily, despite the physicality of his performance. My hair is gently tugged, making me realize she is behind me, securing my hair. I can't help but wonder what is coming next.

Why leather outfits? It feels like she has braided my hair

and wound it around itself, turning my high pony into a topknot.

Luke raises me up by my chin and his eyes smolder at me. As I stand there, staring back at him, I sense his female counterpart dancing over to hand him something.

I catch a flash out of the corner of my eye and turn my head to see each pair of performers in the aisles. The men are all breathing fire in sync, shooting impressive plumes up into the air. The fire is so hot and so big I can feel the air warming around me.

Each couple stationed in the aisles performs with a different prop, from wings to swords to sticks to ropes. I did not know so many things could wield fire. I've heard of fire performers, but I've never seen them live until Luke's display. It's incredible. I turn my head to look back at Luke.

"Do you trust me?"

"I have no idea," I answer, voice breathy.

He smiles his sinful, wicked smile and says, "We're about to find out. I wouldn't move if I were you."

My eyes widen as I see his partner dance by, stopping to light the fire poi that are hanging from his hands from the scythe she is carrying. I hear the flames spinning by as she dances around the stage in a whirling glory of flames. I lock my eyes onto Luke's and don't dare move a muscle.

He spins his fire poi around me, each with three balls of flame, the heat and light flashing by. This is the single most exhilarating experience of my life. The fear and excitement bleed together into a heady mixture of lust.

I am desperate for this fiery man. His face is alternately cast into light and shadow, the flickering image searing into my retinas. His face appears both devastatingly handsome, followed by pure evil in turns as the flashing firelight comes and goes. It's a shocking yet thrilling sight.

I should probably be scared shitless, but the only thing I feel right now is extreme, unadulterated lust. My core throbs and my chest is heaving with my deep breaths as I fight to remain motionless. Intense heat passes by me with every spin of the poi, leaving me sweating and then alternately cold.

All I want to do is take the half step forward that is needed to close the gap between us and crash my lips into his. The crowd pulses with excitement. I can smell the fire, the burning fuel smoky in the back of my throat. And underneath it all, the spice of cinnamon.

I'm desperate to taste him, to see if Luke will burn my tongue like those little red candies he reminds me of. Everything is red. His face, the air, my blood thrumming through my body. Red. The thought resounds in my mind and pulses in my veins.

Red.

Red.

Red.

He gives me an almost imperceptible nod and I inch forward. He tilts his chin down, the fire spinning by flashing wickedly across his sinister face, one corner of his mouth inching up. I feel a shiver work its way down my spine, a sudden urge to flee in the face of his eerie countenance.

Luke narrows his eyes at me and offers me the smallest shake of his head, as if he can sense the panic trying to well up within me. I take a deep breath to steel my nerves and his smile widens.

I can't hold back any longer. My feet inch forward of their own accord. He looks so very satisfied as I am pulled into his orbit. Closer and closer.

Time feels like it slows. The cheering of the crowd fades away. The firelight drifts slowly across his face as the poi appears to spin slower, the whooshing past my ears dissolving into tiny separate sounds instead of one quick swoosh.

Every detail of his face comes into sharp focus. His smooth forehead. Platinum eyebrows. His strange yellow-green eyes, framed by thick lashes. They are white at the roots and flare to auburn at the tips.

My eyes follow down the harsh knife edge of his nose to his curled mustache. Finally, I find his lush lips, tipped up in his signature feline smile.

I see the red tip of his tongue sweep out along his bottom lip and I'm done for. I don't remember closing the remaining gap between us or the first brush of my heaving chest against him. All I know is his searing hot mouth is on mine. His cinnamon flavor bursts to life on my tongue like it is the first flavor I have ever tasted.

There has never been a taste before his fiery cinnamon, and I never want another taste after. I don't know which of us started this kiss, but I am so exceedingly thankful. I was absolutely starving for it. For him.

He bites down on my bottom lip, hard, and I taste the coppery tang of my blood. Red. It startles me into opening my eyes and I find him staring back at me. Then he sweeps his cinnamon tongue into my mouth and its scorch chases away the copper.

I feel consumed by the fire that is Luke. I'm worried all that will be left in his wake is the burnt husk of my body—nothing but an ashy shell. He consumes my oxygen like fuel, and I have to break the kiss as stars dance behind my eyes, breathless.

He never blinks.

I suck in lungfuls of air, and time abruptly returns to its

normal pace. The firelight flickers across his face, his eyes completely black, just like in my dream in the stairwell.

"Turn around," he commands darkly. I obey without hesitation. He steps forward and plasters himself against my back. He puts his lips next to my ear and says, "Dance with me."

The heat radiating off his body feels like a sunburn, even through my clothes. This angle is thrilling and terrifying. Instead of staring into his eyes, I can see the flaming poi spinning in front of my own.

I keep my arms plastered to my sides as he brings his hands together and spins the poi in various configurations. In my periphery, I see the other woman dancing; her scythe cutting through the air. I can't see beyond the stage, but I can still hear the crowd going as wild as my heart.

He pushes further into my body, and I can feel his hard length against my back. I'm a little shocked, but also thankful that I'm not the only one of us so affected by being part of this performance with its scorching fire kiss.

He nudges me forward, and like a dancer, I follow his lead. Before I know it, we are miraculously moving in unison, spinning in a circle while he expertly handles the fire poi. It seems as if we've been doing this for hours, but in reality, it must only be a few minutes.

"On your knees," he rasps in my ear.

Gladly.

I fall to my knees, and he dances around to face me, his leather-covered bulge tauntingly in front of my mouth. Faced with his hard length straining against his pants, my mouth waters.

I'm just about to stretch forward and undo his pants when I remember I'm on stage in the middle of a show. Instead, I reach back into my addled brain and pull out some of my late-night fiction reading. I place my hands on top of my thighs, palms up, and slightly spread my legs, sitting back on my heels.

"Good fucking girl," Luke growls out, looking down at me. I shiver and feel my pussy flood my panties. No one has ever called me that before, and although it sounded hot when I read about it, to hear that phrase roll out of Luke's mouth, I'm just about ready to have my first public orgasm.

He glances down at me and repeats, "Don't move."

He steps forward just a bit, bringing his crotch even closer to my face. Tease. He brings his hands together above his head and spins the poi at lightning speed, putting the fire out. He throws them off the stage and snags the bottle out of the air that comes sailing toward him.

He reaches out and grabs my braided top knot with one hand while he squeezes fluid from the bottle into his mouth with the other. I can only watch him as he holds me by my hair, effectively immobilizing my head. He winks at me and then tilts his head back and shoots an enormous length of flame up and out like a damn dragon.

I marvel at how he breathes fire, but then I'm overwhelmed by the deafening sound of the house coming down around us. The lights dim on the stage, and I can see the audience now, standing and cheering.

The performers circle the stage and Luke helps me to my feet, leaning in and quickly licking my mouth, pulling away before I can even respond. I lick my lips and taste burnt smoky cinnamon. I will forever crave his unique flavor.

Next thing I know, both he and the beautiful redhead take my hands and raise them above our heads, and then the three of us bow. We spin and repeat the process several times, applause raining down on us. It's a heady feeling.

I hardly did anything, yet I feel the adoration of the

crowd, and it's intoxicating. They cheer and roar. The performers all wave as the people shuffle out, the show now over.

I imagine many of them are heading out to get lucky. I can taste the lust filling the very air. The show was so hot and sexy. I'm still trying to come down.

Luke spins me to face him, reaching up with his other hand to hold my face. We lock eyes and I bring my hands up against his chest. I simply must touch him, stabilize myself in this whirling world.

He's lightly covered in sweat, skin blazing. All I can think about is tasting his chest to see if it carries the same cinnamon flavor as his mouth.

He takes my hands and brings them behind my back, gripping my wrists with one hand and leaning me back over them. I feel my balance slipping, but his arm at my back feels solid like steel.

He uses his other hand to tip my head back, my neck stretched to its limit. He leans over my arched body and trails his nose up the center of my chest and over my throat, inhaling as he goes.

"Mmm," he hums. "*Délicieuse.*"

"Luke, introduce me to your new pet."

I stare upside down at the redheaded goddess from earlier. She walks toward me like a runway model, sex on stilettos. Luke meets her eyes above my head and snaps me back up to a standing position, making my head spin.

She sidles up next to him, leaning into his side and draping herself over his body. She tilts her head and studies me, her green-eyed gaze looking me up and down. They both have a feline air to them and have their heads titled at the same angle.

"Are you twins?" I ask, curious, with the smallest twinge

of jealousy.

They quirk their mouths in the same half smile, their mannerisms strikingly similar and movements in tandem.

"Of a sort," Luke answers mysteriously.

The woman gives an uncharacteristic snort. I look back and forth between them, thinking they must have some amount of shared blood. I can't imagine how any two people with this exact coloring could not be related.

She flashes me a dazzling smile and turns and walks away, throwing over her shoulder, "You should bring the pet."

I can't help but admire her red leather clad ass as she saunters away. Her hips don't lie.

"Are you ready to continue your adventure?" Luke asks, snapping my attention off his maybe sister's ass and back to his face.

"Uh, maybe?" I squeak.

I can hear some voices out in the distance, but only the two of us seem to be left on stage, standing alone in a pool of black. He reaches out and grips my chin between his thumb and index finger, turning my face side to side as if searching for the truth.

"Maybe?"

His piercing yellow-green eyes burn with intensity, one platinum brow quirked at me. It's all I can do to think. I can smell the burnt fuel on his hands and his unique cinnamon scent underneath it. I wonder if this is what Hell smells like.

I'm still riding the high of performing, drunk on the adoration of the crowd. I debate my answer. Tonight has been wild. I can't believe I was on stage!

The night feels surreal, and I should probably say no, walk back to my hotel so when I wake up, I can head home in the morning. It must be getting late, and I ought to get to bed. Be responsible. I've had my fun, and this is a business trip, after all.

But.

I look at Luke, his fiery hair slicked back in braids, a streak of soot down the side of his face. He looks like a Viking warrior in all his leather, and fuck me, but I'm going the whole way down this rabbit hole.

I recall the deep satisfaction I felt earlier when he called me a good girl and the response rolls off my tongue before I can even think it through. It feels so incredibly good to be wanted, desired, pursued.

"Yes, Sir."

Luke's eyes turn black, and he drops his chin and stares straight into my soul. "Be careful, *ma petite fille coquine*. You're playing with fire."

I instinctively step back, nervous that I've opened the lid to Pandora's box, and I'm not sure how I'm going to get it back on. I had felt confident with my pithy response based on late night fiction, but suddenly I think I'm way out of my league here. Then Luke smiles, breaking the serious moment, and holds out a hand to me.

Damn, I love to perform. The crowd fuels my cravings, filling me with their energy as I feed on their lust. Their adoration swells my pride, their greed for danger and destruction fills me, as does the envy of the men who want to be me. I avoid their wrath, as they'll still get their rocks off from the lust I funnel back to them.

And my darling little morsel here, staring at me while she debates taking my hand, I will feast on her like a glutton. The stolen taste from her sweet lips already has me wanting more.

Nothing makes me smile like hitting all the big seven in one night. And that is why this *Cirque Maléfique* will never get old. It tickles me in all the right places. And I do love a good tickle.

I take a deep breath and place my hand in his, cementing my decision. He gives me a dazzling smile and walks me to the edge of the stage. I stand there looking down, wondering how the heck I'm going to jump that far without breaking an ankle, when Luke jumps down like a jungle cat, turns, and raises his hands toward me.

I lean down and put mine on his shoulders. He grabs my waist and swings me down in one graceful movement, setting me on my feet like I am the *mon petit chou* he calls me. Luke wraps his hand around the back of my neck and steers me down a back aisle out of the tent.

He stops to grab a long leather coat from a costume rack at a back door and slips it on. He is incredible in his leather pants and matching coat, the harness over his bare chest peeking out.

He places his hand back on my neck and leads us out into a rear hallway, where we pop out a set of metal double doors into the balmy night air. Several giant murdered-out Cadillac Escalades are idling at the curb, followed by a rose gold car. The engine revs and the alluring woman from earlier waves.

"What is that gorgeous car?"

"Audi," Luke mutters, steering me toward the end of the motorcade. Just then, a sleek red sports car pulls in behind her. It has a long nose and is undeniably sexy. One of the strongmen gets out and tosses Luke the keys. He snatches them out of the air and says, "*Grazie.*"

I wonder how many languages he speaks as I'm reasonably sure that was Italian. The strongman heads over to one of the SUVs as Luke walks to the latest arrival and opens the passenger door for me. I slide into the low seat, scared to touch anything in the interior. It smells like money, and the red and black leather feels like butter. It utterly suits him.

Luke leans in and fastens my seatbelt for me, which I find endearing. He closes my door and rounds the car, shooting me a wink through the windshield and then slides into his side. The car appears to be an extension of him, like it was custom made to fit his long form. The engine purrs to life as he starts it.

"What's this one?"

He flashes me an excited grin and says, "Maybach."

"I've never seen a car like this before."

"One of a kind, like you," he replies with a smile. His playful side is charming.

Despite not being a car aficionado, I can't help but be impressed with the engine's throaty purr as he revs it. As the convoy takes off through the night, I watch Luke's face flash in and out of shadow and light as we pass streetlights and businesses. He fiddles with some buttons until music swells around us through the incredible sound system.

"Take your hair down."

I reach up and find the clip securing the top knot and unwind the length, finger combing out the braid, so it is back to its original high pony. I wonder at his accent. It's subtle, but I'm fairly sure it's French.

"I said down," he drawls, deathly quiet.

Oh, shit. This tone of voice packs an even more dramatic impact. I pull out the hair tie straightaway, eager to please him, and finger comb it again, hoping it looks okay. I gently massage the roots in relief at it being down and to add some volume to the crown.

It falls around me like a cape of soft waves from having it braided. Being able to run my hands through it is one perk of straightening it. When my hair is in its usual curly state, it's impossible to do so.

"Good girl," he growls, and I shift in the seat, the seam in the crotch of my jeans suddenly a little too tight for comfort, yet not tight enough.

He reaches over and rests his large hand on my knee, warm even through the denim. I'm quickly developing an addiction to this phrase and the heady feeling it triggers. Sure, I like some spice in my fiction, but I'd never experienced anything in real life. I can see the draw to this praise kink I've read about.

I turn and stare out the window, at the city whizzing by, when I feel his hand trail up my leg. He reaches the top and tucks his pinky into the crease of my leg. I'm worried he will feel the heat radiating out from my core like a nuclear meltdown, but swallow down my nerves.

He idly plays with the strings of my fishnets with his index finger, hand over one of the higher up tears in my jeans. His fingertip feels hot compared to the cool night air.

"I like your eyes on me," Luke says softly, sounding oddly vulnerable, so I turn and face him once again. He gives my leg a squeeze, and it's all I can do to not grind against his hand.

"Better," he says with a smile, after I'm facing him again, without his eyes ever leaving the road.

I take in his profile, the outline sharp against the night. Light and shadow chasing each other over his face. He is beautiful, lounging like a big cat in the driver's seat, one hand carelessly draped over the wheel. Although he is in repose, I again sense he is ready to spring into action like a panther, a restlessness ever present under the relaxed facade.

Soon the caravan turns into a parking garage, driving down level after level until I feel like we are being swallowed up by the earth itself. The cars stop while an enormous gate retracts to allow us into a separate private parking area.

Luke pulls the car into a space and says, "Wait." He gets out, walks around to my door, opens it, and holds out a hand to me. Pulling me up out of the low seat, he says, "I'll get you home later. For now, just enjoy."

The performance crew and a slew of other folks pour out of the caravan and walk toward a bank of elevators. I glance at the SUVs as we pass by. Show business must be really profitable if their vehicles are anything to go by. The value of this small fleet must be astronomical.

The group stands in front of the elevators, and Luke pulls me to his side. Everyone is busy chattering amongst themselves and although I see a few curious glances directed my way, for the most part, my presence is simply accepted.

They all take turns piling into the elevator, but Luke tightens his arm around my shoulders when I go to step forward. I pick up on his hint and wait as car after car goes up.

In time, it's just him and me standing alone in the garage. It's quiet and warm, and I take slow, steady breaths as I feel the faint edge of claustrophobia creeping in. Parking garages have always confused me; they feel like some type of Escher drawing, so going down into an underground one tickles several of my fears.

I'm a little claustrophobic, but this feels tomb-like, kicking my usually mild distress up a notch. Strong emotions can trigger my waking dreams. I try to will them away—now would be a terrible time. I'd become lax as it had been so long since I had one, but the bombardment by them this week and their newly evolving nature prompts me to be more vigilant going forward.

I focus on standing here under his arm, his heat radiating toward me. I wait to see what he will do, willing to follow his lead. I'm happy to be pressed into his side, a perfect fit, breathing him in, and if I just zero in on that, I can forget about being deep underground while we wait.

I stay blissfully in the present as the elevator doors open and we step in, alone. He pulls a card out of his jacket pocket and scans it, hitting the only button on the panel.

The mirrored elevator reflects us into infinity, showing me every angle. I'm happy for a peek at my hair, which surprisingly looks great, softly waving around me.

I'm busy enjoying seeing the reflection of Luke's leather clad body, discreetly trying to check out the back of him in the mirror when he surprises me by walking me back, caging me against the elevator wall with a hand on either side of my head.

I meet his unflinching yellow-green gaze and feel myself blush, filled with heat at his proximity. He steps forward, bringing his hips into mine, nudging a leg between my thighs. He reaches one hand into my hair at the base of my skull and tugs sharply, angling my face up to his.

He grips my entire lower jaw with his other hand, fingers over my mouth. He slowly drags his hand down, eyes following its path. He tugs my lower lip down as his fingers slide over it. I hear it pop back up, shockingly loud in the elevator's silence, interrupted only by my heavy breathing.

He continues to drag his hand heavily down my throat, pausing to squeeze directly over my pulse points ever so slightly. My pulse races in response as he continues his heavy-handed caress straight down the center of my chest.

I'm fervently hoping he takes a detour, my breasts aching for his touch, but he firmly continues his descent. A frustrated whimper escapes my lips, pulling his heated stare back to my face.

He devours me with his eyes as finally his hand trails down to grip the front waistband of my jeans, while the other tightens in my hair, startling a gasp out of me. He twists the fabric in his fist, pulling it even tighter into my apex, the seam of my jeans highlighting the throbbing pulse of my sex.

Hitching his thigh further into my apex, he uses his grip on my jeans to push and pull me along his hard thigh. My jeans slide easily along his leather encased leg, and I greedily wish for more friction. That damn seam of my jeans presses directly against my clit, making me frustrated and needy.

I move to slide my hands up his chest, desperate to touch him, find an anchor. Seeking a way to gain some semblance of control while chasing this orgasm.

Instead, he growls, "Grab the railing."

I'm impatient to feel his skin below my fingertips, but eager to comply, I reach to my sides and grip the railing that runs the perimeter of the elevator walls, the metal cold in my heated grasp.

He gives me his wicked smile and leans into my ear, sinfully murmuring, "Good girls get rewarded. *Bonne fille.*"

He releases his grip on my jeans, sneaking his hand around to grab a handful of my ass, using that instead to grind me into his hard thigh. I feel torn between the savage grip at the base of my skull, tugging delightfully on my hair, and the harsh handful of ass he is using to grind me into his leg, delivering delicious friction into my core.

My loud breathing echoes in the small enclosed space.

The sensations are incredible and I'm loving the erotic novelty of making out in an elevator, but it's just not enough.

I ride his thigh, grasping for a way to get more pressure on my throbbing pussy. All I can think about, though, is being filled by him, the sensations from the stairwell dream teasing me with their absence.

All too soon, he chuckles and says, "Out of time, *mon petit chou. Bientôt, je réaliserai tous tes rêves les plus sombres.*"

He steps back just as the doors open, leaving me sprawled against the elevator wall, panting. I'm thankful for my grip on the railing, or I think I would have fallen forward with his abrupt departure. What I wouldn't give to understand the damn sexy French he keeps caressing me with.

Asshole.

He holds a hand out to me, like he didn't just tease the shit out of me. I ignore it, brushing past him as I step out and try to covertly pull my jeans back out of my crotch.

We've arrived in an enormous penthouse, where a raucous party is in full swing. I'm amazed at the diverse crowd of people. I stand there awkwardly, not quite sure what to do now that we have arrived. Thankfully, Luke takes my hand and leads me over to the small kitchen.

"Hungry?"

I shake my head at him mutely. I couldn't eat with all this excitement and don't want to risk eating the wrong thing and getting sick.

"Drink?"

I nod, my mouth feeling dry from all the heavy breathing I was doing in the elevator. He hovers his hand over various bottles and then reaches up into a cupboard, pulling down a bottle of bourbon.

"How did you like this earlier?"

"Um, spicy, with an interesting finish, if it's the one from the show. What is it?"

He smiles as he picks out two rocks glasses and adds two large ice balls to each glass, the way I prefer mine. I'm not surprised, but I do wonder how he knows so much about me, from my dietary restrictions to my ice preferences. There's no doubt in my mind he set up my drinks and snacks with the VIP ticket.

He pours us both a generous double and hands one to me. Smiling, he says, "It's mine."

"Yours?"

"Mine. Brimstone."

"Brimstone." I let the name roll around my mouth like a taste of bourbon. "Suits it. And you."

I take a drink to cover my sudden uncertainty. I had felt so confident getting ready for tonight in the safety of my hotel bathroom. But standing in this penthouse in a pair of converse sneakers, surrounded by interesting people and performance artists, riding here in what I'm sure is a ridiculously expensive car, and now drinking with a gorgeous man who has his own label?

I'm feeling a little, well, boring. Plain Jane. My newfound confidence withers under the question, why me?

Luke steps closer, distracting me from my spiraling thoughts. "And just how does it suit me? *Vous pensez que vous me connaissez? Détrompez-vous.*"

I look up at him and back up to lean against the counter, overwhelmed by his nearness and dazzled by his words. "Spicy," I whisper, answering the part of his question I can understand. As his eyes heat, I continue, "Bold. Adventurously unconventional."

He smiles his feline smile, tapping his glass to mine. "Beautiful words from a beautiful woman. *Santé.*"

"*Santé,*" I repeat back, the foreign word slippery on my tongue. I take a sip of the bourbon, again marveling at the spicy finish. I wheeze out, "Bottled in bond?"

He takes my glass and sets it down with his. Wrapping his hands around my neck, he tips up my chin with his thumbs. I'm not sure why I continue to be surprised by his incendiary touch, like living fire is just below the surface of his skin.

He leans in, eclipsing the party around us. I drown in his eyes, the intriguing yellow-green color pulling me under. If eyes truly are the window to the soul, some semblance of self-preservation has me scared to look too deep.

Luke knows no such fear, the depth of his gaze probing the very essence of my existence as he slowly slides his hands from my neck to my shoulders and down my arms until his hands encircle my wrists like hot iron shackles.

He tucks them behind my back, forcing my breasts up and out as I arch back over the counter. Dropping his head, he licks a slow, burning line from my exposed decolletage, up my throat, and finishes by lightly nipping my chin.

"Always in bond," he whispers against my lips, so close I can taste his cinnamon flavor.

He gives me a smoldering smile. My cheeks heat in response as I feel stupidly naïve when he hints at things I think I want but have no real-world experience with. Each frantic beat of my heart pulses through my body as his heavy gaze feels like he is weighing the value of my soul and deciding my fate.

He seems to arrive at some sort of decision and releases my wrists. Picking both of our glasses up, he hands mine back to me. The glass feels so cold against my hand, a stark contrast to the fiery man before me.

I blink the rest of the world back into focus, taking a big

sip of the bourbon as I search for equilibrium. I'm starting to feel closed in by the party and his overwhelming presence.

As if he sees this, Luke places his free hand on the small of my back and guides me out of the kitchen and out onto a large balcony that wraps around the penthouse. Music pulses in the background and a group near us breaks out into laughter.

I'm thankful to be away from the bulk of the crowd, the noise and the heat. I take a few large sips of my drink, thankful the ice has watered it down, smoothing out the spicy finish.

We walk to the end of the balcony where Luke confidently leans on the railing, looking out over the city. I sidle up to him, enthralled by the glittering skyline, but when my gaze falls to the streets far, far below, I step back. My palms immediately start sweating. The penthouse is *stupid* high.

Luke laughs, and it's a low, sexy sound. I want him to do it again as much as I want to hear that severe, dominant voice drip from his lips and every sound in between. I want to explore his mind and his body, unwrap this uber sexy package to see what is underneath.

The mystery of him simmers below his surface. He spins to face me, leaning too far back against the railing for my comfort, balanced like the dangerous panther he reminds me of.

"Luke," I gasp, reaching a hand out toward him as he leans precariously. My knees go weak as I force myself to take a hesitant step closer to him.

"Are you scared for me?" he challenges, face blank, eyes locked onto mine.

"Of course! Please come away from there," I plead, holding my hand out to him. A calculating look flashes across his face so quickly I'm not sure I can confidently say it was there.

"Luke, please," I implore him, inching forward, stretching my hand toward him. After a beat, he gives me his sinful smile and pushes off the ledge, stalking toward me. I step back as he invades my space, tilting my head back to accommodate his height at this close range.

"You would worry for me," he murmurs, staring into my eyes, head cocked.

I silently nod.

"You're cold," he says as he slips off his long leather coat and swirls it around my shoulders. It carries a massive amount of heat, his cinnamon smell, and a hint of lingering burnt fuel from the show.

I turn my head into the leather and inhale deeply, closing my eyes, trying to burn this memory deep into my amygdala. I want to bottle the sensations, smells, and emotions of this night to savor throughout my life. I can't imagine another night will ever be like this.

The warmth seeps into my tight shoulders, my racing heart begins to slow as my muscles relax. My mind is anything but. I never know what I am going to get with Luke—sweet, dominant, aloof.

The only constant with him is sinful. The smell of the leather triggers a memory—unlike the rest of his crew, he was able to just spout fire into the air only using fuel, no lighter.

"How did you breathe fire without a lighter?"

"A performer never tells his secrets," comes his playful reply.

He wraps his arm around my shoulders, tucking me into his side. It's becoming my favorite spot with the way we fit perfectly together. I can't fathom how he still radiates heat in nothing but a leather harness and pants, yet he does.

I had been chilly in the humid late-night air that is partial to these early summer nights, but between his long leather coat and his body heat, I'm cozy as we stroll along the balcony wrapping around the penthouse. I am thankful we are walking closer to the building than to the railing. I really hate heights.

We wind further around the penthouse, leaving the small groups gathered outside behind us, until we reach a seating area with a low table. A flickering fire dances down the center over the top of glass stones that shimmer in the light.

Luke pulls me over to it, and we sit together on the couch. I lean forward and warm my hands by the blaze, not cold now that I'm wrapped in his leather coat, just comforted by its heat and light.

Movement in the shadows catches my eye, and I could've sworn I saw a black cat slinking by. I'm just about to ask Luke about it when he distracts me with a proposition.

"We could find the hot tub," he suggests with a wink.

I feel my face flush and take a drink of my bourbon to cover my silence. Do I want to get into a hot tub with Luke? Great question. This calls for a bigger sip of liquid courage.

On the one hand, we just met. On the other, he is smoking hot, and it's been a magical night. I'm not sure what to say. I'm a little rusty on the dating scene. Is getting in a hot tub an automatic prelude to sex, or is it literally just getting in a hot tub?

I remember the time I asked Jo if she wanted to 'Netflix and chill' and she burst into raucous laughter. Apparently, it does not mean hang out and watch TV, which she explained in between fits of giggles so hard she was crying. Is this like that?

"Lieshe," Luke purrs softly.

I look from the fire into his eyes, seeing the dancing flames reflected there. Tonight has been such an adventure. I'm feeling dazzled, between this party in a luxury penthouse, the fire performance, and then being brought almost to orgasm in the elevator.

We just met. I have no idea who he really is, but somehow, there is a familiarity to him. I get the faint sense that somehow Luke has been trouble for me before. But after everything that has happened today and his strange role in my stairwell dream, I guess that only makes sense. Especially the part about McHottie being devastated to see us together.

Although with his recent absence, he clearly has no interest or claim on me. I'm a free woman, free to live the only life I have to the fullest. Fuck it. Let's do this.

Maybe Luke is a player, fucking around with a girl in every city his show performs in. And maybe tonight, I don't care. Maybe I want the adventure, even if it is just for one night. I want to be the one he chooses. I want someone to want me.

I meet his eyes, and damn, I want him to keep looking at me like this. Taking a deep breath, I stammer out, "I, uh, I'd like that."

His lips curve as he jumps up, taking my hand and pulling me along. Apparently, he would like that, too. As we head toward the far end of the balcony, he nods at two of the strongmen standing off to the side, saying, "Boys."

They fall in behind us until he gives them a slight wave of the hand, signaling them to stop, and they about face with crossed arms. I guess we have bodyguards. We continue on. No one else from the party is over here and apparently the 'boys' will ensure we have some privacy.

Faint city noises reach my ears, but this high up, the rest

of the world seems so distant. Tucked into a corner, surrounded by beautiful landscaping and soft white lighting, is a sunken hot tub. Luke pulls his phone from his pocket and messes around with it until dark, moody music floods the area we are standing in, and the hot tub water turns red with underwater lighting.

I turn back to Luke to see the flickering firelight reflected in his eyes and highlighting his face. It reminds me of being on stage with him. Feeling bold, I step toward him, reaching up to trace the light and shadows on his face, whispering, "Tonight has been incredible."

"Oh, *mon petit chou*, tonight has just begun."

He turns his face into my hand and presses a kiss into my palm, then gently presses down on my shoulders until I am again sinking to my knees before him. I'm getting frustrated that I keep coming face to face with his leather crotch without getting any action.

I desperately want to see him and find out if he tastes like cinnamon everywhere. He smirks, as if he can hear my thoughts.

Luke's hands are gentle in my hair as he gathers it up and twists it on top of my head, securing the high messy bun with a hair tie he pulls from his pocket.

Stepping back, he reaches behind him, and the leather harness drops off his chest to the ground. I hold my breath, wondering what he will take off next, fervently hoping he finally drops his pants.

But to my disappointment, he grips my upper arms and pulls up, encouraging me to stand. He removes his coat from where it rests over my shoulders, and I shiver without its heat.

"Turn around."

I drop my belt bag onto the couch and dutifully obey,

hearing movements behind me that sound like he has finally taken off those damn leather pants. I'm disappointed I've yet to see him in all his naked glory.

He steps into me, and I feel his incredible heat at my back. He grabs my hips and slowly slides his hands up my sides, gathering my shirt as he goes. I instinctively put my arms up as he pulls my shirt up and off.

I guess this is happening. He drops my shirt on the ground, and this time when he steps into me, I gasp, feeling his hot skin pressed to mine. Yup, those pants are gone. He feels very naked and very aroused.

I won't have sex, everything but, I tell myself, drawing a line in the sand in my mind. But as his hands ghost up my arms and down my back to undo my bra, I'm not so sure I'll actually be able to stick to my guns.

I feel the sudden freedom of an unhooked bra and stand motionless, fighting the urge to clasp it to my breasts to keep them covered.

Luke moves his hands to my shoulders, sliding the straps down until the whole thing simply falls to the ground in front of me. My nipples instantly peak in the cool night air, a slight breeze playing over my flushed skin inducing shivers.

Luke returns his hands to my hips and then slides them around to the button of my jeans. I wait for him to pop it open, but he surprises me by running his hands up my stomach to my lower ribs.

I suck in a startled breath as he pulls me back against his chest. He nuzzles behind my ear, and I tip my head to the side to give him more access.

He drifts his hands up the underside of my breasts, pushing them up and together like a corset. He growls low in my ear and thrusts his hips into me, grinding an impressive erection into my jean covered ass.

I drop my head back as he kisses his way down the curve of my neck, offered to him like a sacrifice. He kneads my breasts intensely, and although it borders just this side of the pain, it's delicious. All too soon, his hands are moving back down, leaving my breasts bereft and exposed to the chilly air.

He finds the waistband of my jeans, the button popping open sounding loud, and drags down my zipper. I toe off my Converse in anticipation of removing my pants, thankful that I wore decent underwear tonight—red lace to match my bra. Luke skims his hands down my legs, sliding my jeans down.

He squats behind me, tapping my ankle to get me to lift my foot so he can slide the pants off each leg. I'm left in my red fishnet stockings and panties. He leans in, nuzzling my backside with his face. I'm motionless, mind racing.

He lightly nips my ass with his sharp teeth and moves his hands to my hips as he stands. "Leave these on."

I guess I'm getting in the hot tub in fishnets and panties. At least this will make it easier to stick to my weakening resolve about no sex. I feel his heat dissipate and turn around just in time to catch his fabulous ass walking to the hot tub.

It may be the finest ass on a man I've ever seen. It's high and tight and I want to sink my teeth into it. Strange thought, I've never wanted to bite anyone's ass before.

He throws his feline smile at me over his shoulder, as if he heard my very thoughts. I follow him to the hot tub like the pied piper. The raven tattoo covering his back is even more beautiful in the low light, lifelike in its details.

He steps down into the bubbling red water, steam curling around him, like he is descending into the legendary river Styx. Luke turns and watches me advance toward him.

I'm half tempted to reach up and cover my breasts but remind myself to be bold. I walk confidently to the hot tub and step in, following in his earlier footsteps. He offers me a hand to help me sink down into the warm depths.

The swirling bubbles obscure the sight of him. Bummer. I was really hoping to glimpse full frontal nudity and take this up to an R rating. I ease down onto the ledge, submerging my shoulders in the steaming water. I instantly relax and feel the bourbon course through my veins a little quicker.

Luke sits on the ledge across from me and for a while we just sit there, studying each other's faces. The music and bubbling steamy water provide the perfect backdrop and fill the companionable silence between us. I scrutinize his face for clues to his thoughts, but all I see is his faint smile.

My breasts float and I admire their weightlessness. Luke stands, the water sluicing down his chest and abdomen, the water level so close to letting me see what my mouth has been watering over all night.

I'm jealous of the way the drops get to cascade down his body and run down the deep V of his abs when I want to chase them with my tongue. I stand and step toward him. Luke takes my hand and turns me to face out.

This far back from the edge, I am comfortable enough to enjoy the scene in front of me. The skyline is impressive, twinkling lights and a soft glow against the midnight sky. I can feel the night wanting to make the shift to the break of day.

Luke guides me so we are standing at the main jet as we take in the view. He sinks to his knees, pulling me down by my hand with him. He pulls my upper body back against his and puts his hands on my hips. The water laps up to my neck.

"Put your feet up on the bench," he says in my ear. I follow his instructions, sucking in a breath as the hot tub jet now blows precariously close to my lady parts. If I moved just a few inches, it would be better than a handheld shower.

"Wrap your arms around my neck."

I reach back and wrap my arms behind his neck, linking my hands, my head resting on his shoulder. It arches my back and brings my breasts out of the water like they are on display.

Luke releases my hips and cups his steaming hands, repeatedly pouring the hot water over my nipples. The interplay of the cooling night air against the water dripping on them is mind-blowing, like some sexy version of water torture.

If he keeps doing this long enough, I might even be able to orgasm from it. Luke leans in, nibbling my ear lobe. I've never liked someone's mouth on my ear before, but apparently no one else knew how to do it right. Because the way he uses his teeth has my pulse racing. I feel his sharp teeth nip at me and hiss in a breath.

"Look at you, *mon petit chou*. Spread out for me like a feast."

He quits teasing my breasts with the water and changes over to torturing me with his hands. Using his grip on my breasts, he moves my body slightly in the water until the jet is dangerously close to my core.

He continues to massage and knead my breasts, whispering a torrent of incomprehensible but utterly bewitching French into my ear until I can't help but beg, "Luke, please!"

"Luke? No, *ma petite fille coquiner*, what do you think you should call me?"

His voice is soft in my ear, quiet and restrained in juxtaposition to my current predicament. I'm trying to think, but my brain feels so fuzzy. How can he expect me to think when I'm walking the edge of this precipice?

"Sir," I call out, getting desperate for something more than what he is giving me. I think it's a damn fine guess. It must be good enough to get me what I want. He tsks in my ear.

"Closer," he says as he moves my lower half infinitesimally nearer to the jet.

"I don't know," I whine, my body demanding release. The entire night has been waves of foreplay, and I'm at the end of my rope. I try to move my hips closer, but his grip is iron. My arms tense, my hands frantically clasping each other behind his head, tangled in his braids.

"Master?" I guess, impressed that my synapses are firing at all now. I can't keep my eyes open, feeling like I am going to implode in on myself in my desperation.

"Closer," he chuckles as he again minutely moves my body. He reaches down his hand and grips the crotch of my fishnet stockings and pulls, ripping them apart with primal passion. He returns his hand back to my breast and whispers darkly into my ear, "Reach down and spread yourself open for me."

Fuck, his dirty talk is killing me! I follow his instructions, reaching down with one hand to pull my panties to the side, too far gone in my need to even feel embarrassed or question what he is telling me to do. My other arm clings to the back of his neck.

He moves me just right and the jet bursts over my exposed clit. I spread my lips further, moaning at the jets rushing across me.

I get so close, but he firmly moves me just to the side, away from the force of the jet. Panting, I'm both loving and hating being on this razor's edge, not knowing how much more I can take. Luke grips my breasts harder, breathing heavily into my ear.

"When you come for me, you will scream 'my Lord'. You worship at my altar tonight. Understand? Say, 'Yes, my Lord.'"

"Yes, my Lord," I grind out between clenched teeth. Rewarded with returning to the intense rushing water.

"Louder," he demands harshly, his voice losing the restraint he had been so carefully clinging to.

"Yes, my Lord," I call out. I'm so close, I can feel the pressure building deep inside me, ready to burst out to the surface. I would have called him Jesus Christ Superstar if he had asked.

He repositions me just a fraction of an inch away. It takes me a minute to realize the keening sound is coming from my mouth.

"Again," he says louder and more forcefully, just as he pinches my nipples hard and sinks his teeth into my neck.

He shifts me back into the full force of the jet and the combined sensations of pleasure and pain coalesce and gather in my core to explode out. The teasing throughout the night and edging were all worth it for this explosive moment.

"Fuck, my Lord!" I scream into the night air, oblivious to anything around me, existing purely in the moment of this intense, earth-shattering orgasm as it pulses from deep within my belly and licks out along my limbs like the fire of his whips.

Luke slides his hand down over mine and cups my pussy, helping me grind out the aftershocks away from the intense blast of the jet. They keep rolling through me as he gathers me against his chest.

"One more," he growls and slips his hand past mine,

sliding two fingers deep into me and curling them forward to some secret magic spot. His fingers feel like live fire inside me. I'm surprised this new onslaught has me coming hard again, unused to multiple orgasms.

I can feel myself clamping down on his hand, my walls fluttering around him. My body feels like it is melting away, filled with his heat and surrounded by the steaming water. I'm on fire.

He captures my cry with his mouth, plunging his tongue inside, fucking my mouth with it. I can imagine what kind of lover he would be, raw and brutal, so passionate and fearfully wild.

I don't know if I could survive him. And I don't know that I want to.

I can feel his impressive erection digging into my hip, and I have the craziest thought of just straddling him and impaling myself on it in my post orgasmic bliss. I must move to do so when Luke pulls back, nuzzling my nose with his.

"*Non pas encore ma chérie.*"

Bone deep satiety and fatigue drag me down to rest my head in the crook of his neck, feeling a little dizzy from multiple orgasms at one hundred degrees on the heels of hundred-proof bourbon. I sneak my arm behind him and wrap my hand in the braids cascading down his back, curling my other hand under my chin.

I just need to close my eyes for a moment, I think as I try, but fail, to hold back a jaw-splitting yawn.

A SUDDEN AND shocking change in temperature startles me awake as Luke lifts me bridal style out of the hot tub. I sleepily worry he will slip, trying to carry me, but his arms feel like iron bands encircling me, and he carries me like I weigh nothing. He returns to the conversation area and holds me on his lap.

I blink open tired eyes to watch the firelight dance over his face. He drapes me in a thick, plush towel, leaving himself exposed to the air without so much as a goosebump.

He gazes out over the night skyline, looking almost lost without his wicked and sinful smile. No crinkles around laughing eyes. No playful words spill from his lips. As he stares into the night, unblinking, he appears ancient.

Unable to stand this look on his face anymore, I reach up and tentatively lay my hand on his cheek.

He drops his forehead to mine and inhales deeply. When he pulls back, his familiar, devastating smile is back on his face, but now it reminds me of a mask. What is he hiding?

"Stand up," he softly commands.

I get to my feet between his legs. I grip his face gently between my hands and bend down to kiss the crown of his head, disappointed he no longer smells like fuel and fire, back to his usually spicy cinnamon by itself. He rests his hands on my hips, neither of us moving for a minute until he clears his throat.

"Let me dry you." He takes the towel and gently slides it over the front of my body. "Turn," he says, and I do, facing the fire, offering him my back.

I feel him tracing a fingertip in an intricate pattern over my back and peer over my shoulder at him. "What was that?"

It almost felt like he was drawing an image on my skin. But instead of answering, he drags the towel down my back, erasing the feel of his touch. He stands and wraps me in the large towel, then walks away.

I whip my head around but only catch the sight of his fine ass moving away from me and stepping back into his black leather pants.

He turns and stares at me as he closes and fastens his pants. I did not know watching someone get dressed could be so sexy. The leather pants highlight the deep V of his abs, and the flickering firelight showcases the ridges and valleys of his long, lean form. Fire and shadows suit him.

The light illuminates his hair, making the red seem to dance and flicker like the flames themselves. It's as if Luke is a creature from another world, crafted from fire. He stalks back toward me, and I shiver in the night air, the towel no match for the breeze.

He stops in front of me and drags the tip of his finger down my forehead and off the tip of my nose before dropping his hand.

"Come in when you're dressed."

I watch his sexy ass retreat and debate whether it looks better naked or encased in leather. My fishnets are mostly dry, and despite the big rip in the crotch, I leave them on. I can throw them out at home. Or I might keep them as a souvenir of my magical night at the *Cirque Maléfique*.

I shimmy into my jeans and find my discarded bra and shirt so I can finish dressing. I take out the messy bun Luke had put in my hair and shake it out.

It is helplessly frizzy after the hot tub's steam, so I pull it all over my shoulder and plait it into a thick, messy braid, securing the end with Luke's hair tie. I'm happy to keep something from him and am struck by a sudden pang of sadness when I realize I don't know when, or even if, I'll see him again.

Sure, he said he would be at the steampunk event, but that isn't for quite some time yet. Tonight was almost magical. Luke is an enigma of fire and shadow, and I want to dissect his layers and discover what lies at his very core.

I sense there is so much more to him under his mask of calm confidence and charm. I can't help but speculate what fires forged him and what experiences have tempered him.

I give the cityscape one last glance from this safe distance, retrieve my belt bag from where I had dropped it on the couch, and head back toward the penthouse. No one else is on the balcony now, and I wonder what time it must be. I can feel the day hanging in the brief span between dark and dawn. I shudder as I wonder if this is the witching hour.

I make my way back in the door and note the crowd has markedly thinned to just a few small sporadic clusters of people. I don't see Luke anywhere, so I go wandering about, looking for him.

It's an open concept floor plan, but I don't see his red hair beckoning my attention anywhere. I frown as I head back toward a short hallway with a few doors off it. I hear voices raised behind a closed door and I freeze.

Not wanting to eavesdrop, I begin walking away, but stop because it really sounds like Luke and his 'maybe sister' are arguing. I pause for a beat, trying to decide what to do. My answer comes in the form of the door whipping open, and I'm met with the scowling face of the female equivalent of Luke.

"Bathroom?" I say with a shrug, a totally plausible reason for lurking down this hallway.

"Last door on the left," she replies coolly, narrowing her eyes at me. I think she sees right through my lie.

"Thanks," I reply, backing down the hallway. She slams the door closed and I turn around to walk the rest of the way forward. I use the immaculate white powder room and head back out to the main area without pausing at the door, not wanting to get busted a second time.

I wonder what that was all about. As I wander back into the kitchen and grab a fancy bottle of sparkling water, I'm shocked to see the time on the clock is four in the morning.

One of the 'boys' from earlier comes over and says in heavily accented English, "I'm to take you back, Miss."

"Oh," I mutter as my stomach falls to my knees. I thought Luke would be returning me to my hotel or even ask me to stay. I seem to have a new and terrible effect on men.

They give me an incredible orgasm—or two—and in return, they run screaming for the hills. Apparently, I have a King Midas in reverse pussy where it's turning all my love interests to shit.

Schooling my face into a flat mask, I follow the strongman out, back down the elevator, and climb into one of the SUVs from earlier. I tell him the name of my hotel and stare out the window until we pull up a brief time later. I numbly walk through the lobby, into yet another elevator, and trudge to my room.

Physically and emotionally wrung out, I pull up the hotel app on my phone, request a late checkout, and set an alarm for noon. I peel off my clothes, draping my damp jeans over the back of the chair, and leave the destroyed fishnets and wet panties in a heap on the floor.

I flop face down onto the bed and drag the other side of the comforter over my body, too tired to even crawl under the covers.

I clench my teeth so hard I'm surprised they don't crack. Looking at my 'sister' is like looking in a mirror and seeing a female version of myself staring back.

She's the only one who has ever dared to challenge me, and for that, I begrudgingly tolerate her. I can only stand so much kowtowing and usually that is all I am surrounded by. Where's the fun in that?

Idly, I watch her pace back and forth in front of me, clutching the poor black cat to her chest. I almost feel sorry for the creature as it wisely tolerates her grip, merely twitching its tail.

I'll let her wear herself out. It's the most effective path of least resistance. I'm thankful she is winding down, but when she drops the cat, who wisely slinks away, and wrenches open the door to see the girl lurking there, she starts back in all over again.

Thinking I should have escaped with the creature while the getting out was good, I roll my eyes at just how long eternity is. She spins around, catching me in the act.

"Infatuation is not a good look on you," she hisses, glaring at me with fire in her yellow-green stare, a mirror of my own. She is so beautiful when she is angry—those perfect lips drawn into a pout, cheeks flushed, heaving bosom, hands on hips.

I could give a fuck about her beauty. It's her soul that is so exquisitely ugly, so stained and delicious, that calls to me.

Lucky for her, she continues to entertain me, but my tolerance is waning with her criticism.

I scoff in disagreement. I am resolutely not infatuated. However, for the first time in an exceedingly long time, I'm mildly curious about something besides winning.

Maybe.

But I'd never admit it. Especially to her.

"Don't be such a cunt. The only thing of interest to me is winning," I sneer. "And I. Will. Win."

I punctuate each word with a step closer to her until I invade her space, looming over her petite frame. She cowers the slightest bit, so marginally that only I who know her so well could even spot it.

Buoyed by the trace of fear I can smell, I spin and walk away from the more annoying, and honestly more viscous, version of myself. I close the door behind me just as something smashes into it, shattering.

I roll my eyes and leave her to her tantrum. I'll go play with someone else. There are more than enough who are willing to feed my monster.

Chapter 26

HIM

From the corner of her hotel room, deep in the shadows, I watch. I don't trust myself to get in the bed with her again, knowing the smell of that fucking bastard on her skin would drive me insane until I claimed her as mine, covering every square inch of her with my touch to erase his.

I stay suspended in particle form, my restraint a hair's breadth away from snapping, unable to trust myself as a man right now. She rolls over, quietly mumbling in her sleep, and the comforter she hastily threw over herself slips off her shoulders, revealing the creamy expanse of her back to me.

Seeing his mark desecrating the perfection of her skin fills me with boiling hot rage. My world narrows to a tunnel vision of that damn raven, inky evil black, wrenching away the last vestiges of my control.

Before I destroy this city in my anger, I must leave, lest my *Rozǎ* be caught in the crossfire. Her safety is the only thing that anchors me in this moment as my sanity balances on a razor thin edge of rage and revenge.

Dreams of drowning in red attempt to pull me under as so much of his presence is in this room, filling my nose, my mouth, my lungs until I can't breathe. Escape the only option, I slither over her skin, goosebumps rising in my wake, and filter out under the door.

Chapter 27

I bolt upright in bed, disoriented in the dark room, heart racing. Wildly, I look around and realize I'm in my hotel room. Eyeing the clock, I'm thankful to see I have an hour yet until checkout, even though now I'm too wired to go back to sleep.

I turn off the alarm on my phone since I'm already up and stumble into the bathroom, cringing at my reflection in the mirror. My hair is reminiscent of Medusa and my makeup is making its way diagonally off my face.

I decide to take a quick shower to work on this mess and clear my head for the drive home today. This hotel has their signature scent down, but I'd need about ten of their little conditioner bottles to get my hair back under control.

I do the best I can with the provided toiletries since I hadn't planned on showering here on such a short trip. After I wrestle as much conditioner as possible from the tiny bottle and into my hair, I wash off the remnants of yesterday's glamorous makeup.

I crank up the water temperature, pile my hair on top of my head, and stand under the spray, letting the heat hit my tense shoulders and cascade down my body.

The hot water makes me think of last night in the hot tub and I'm left confused all over again by how it ended. Maybe my initial fear was spot-on, and Luke really does hook up with a different girl after every show, then leaves his crew to dispose of them to avoid any uncomfortable farewells.

Until that time, I was having the most amazing night of my life. At least I hadn't done anything to put my health, or my heart, too much at risk. And yes, Luke is fun and intriguing. He's so smoking hot. If not for the odd send-off, I would be falling head over heels for him.

I really do want to fall in love, but this doesn't feel like love. Right now, it barely even feels like, well, *like*. And I am fairly sure that's a stepping stone on the highway to love.

If I'm honest, it feels like lust. Sure, I'd love a healthy dollop of sexual chemistry when I hopefully do fall in love. But love and lust—they aren't the same. I'm not that naïve. Or that desperate. I need more than fireworks. And I will not be disrespected like my mother. My voice will be heard and valued.

I tip my head back, rinse the conditioner, and then gently wring my hair out. I turn off the water and step out into the steamy bathroom. Looking at the fogged mirror reminds me of McHottie and our intense experience in my bathroom.

As I stare at my cloudy reflection, I face the reality that maybe I am wrong about everything. Maybe I am not the beautiful, strong, confident woman I've been playing at. Maybe my soulmate doesn't exist, and I don't get a happily ever after. Maybe I don't even get a happy for right now. The run of rejections sting.

I reach out and draw a sad smiley face in the condensation on the mirror where my face would be. As the water coalesces from the little eyes I made, running down like tears, I give myself a small shake.

This is going nowhere good, fast. I realize I can't wait to get back to my little sanctuary, where I can lose myself in my work, surrounded by my macabre taxidermy and oddities. Hang out with Val Helsing, who won't give me emotional whiplash with sinful smiles and magic hands. I can distract myself by tracking down the next big thing for my store and finalize my plans for Europe.

I'm suddenly desperate to get the hell out of Philadelphia where they can shove their brotherly love crap where the sun don't shine. My shop is safe. I know the rules. My business hopes and dreams are attainable. I know what I'm doing there.

Why do I push myself to reach for more? To be more than I am and believe that I could snag one of these awesome guys and what, ride off into the sunset? There's a reason I've always been a little snarky and sarcastic. This right here, this is the reason. *Stick to your wheelhouse, Lieshe,* I chide myself.

I barely dry my hair and throw it into a quick braid. In my rush, I don't even put on my moisturizer, despite my usual devotion to skin care. I stomp around the room, shoving things into my large bag with huffs of annoyance at myself for leaving stuff strewn all over the room when all I want to do is get home.

I slip on my Converse, give the room one last glance to make sure I have everything, and head down to the valet station. I check out from my phone on the hotel app while riding the elevator down, throwing my key in the return box as I pass through the lobby.

I toss a tight smile and a five-dollar bill to the valet when he delivers my VW beetle back to me. Slipping into my vintage car brings a modicum of relief to the tightness in my chest and swirling in my veins. I begin to build my armor back up with layers of familiarity.

I bring up directions on my phone and head back to the convention center, yet again, to pick up the purchases from the holding service that I am not having shipped from the vendors.

Navigating the mile of traffic quickly, I pull around to the back where the pickup area is. Half of me hopes Luke, or someone from the show, will be there packing up, while the other half hopes in time, I can just keep this as a memory of a fantastic adventure and tease out the feeling of being cast aside. Forgotten.

As I reach the pickup area, there are just a couple of cars loading up, no sign of anyone from the show anywhere. I head over to the warehouse gate and give my name, thankful for the nice young guy who helps me load some boxes into my car.

I'm happy I could ship most of my purchases, since there isn't much room in the bug unless I put the top down. I get back in the driver's seat and buckle my seatbelt when my phone chimes with a text from Mindy.

MINDY

Hope the expo was good. You doing ok?

No. No, I'm not. Trust Mindy for perfect timing. I don't know that I want to get into it right now, though, when I need to spend the next few hours on the road and escape back to the safety of my own little world.

LIESHE

It was fine. What's up with you?

MINDY

Just thinking of you and missing you.

LIESHE

Miss u

MINDY

Get together soon?

I'm hit with a wave of loneliness, making the rush to get

home feel less appealing. I wish, as I do every day, that I could call my mom. Sure, I wouldn't have given her all the spicy details, but I could have confided in her. And she would have known just what to say in her own quiet way.

I miss her terribly. Like so many others in her family, she had inherited a fatal neurological disease and slipped away fast. I had spent as much time with her as I could between nursing shifts, caring for her, and ultimately quit my job to stay with her in her last few months.

I would sit in the recliner next to her bed, and when she couldn't sleep, we would talk quietly about so many things. Those midnight moments let us bridge the gap from my childhood. I'm so thankful we were able to find meaning and love before I lost her forever.

I realized she had done the best she could as a woman who was the product of a small town and a strict upbringing herself, struggling to meet the demands and needs of a husband and a family. She was by no means perfect, even admitted as much, but she had tried, and in the end, that was enough for me. It had to be.

Part of being an adult child was realizing some parents, like my mom, did the best they could with what they had. And some, like my father, just had nothing to offer. And although I can't pick up the phone to call her, I can have a conversation of the heart with my mom. What would she say?

With a sad smile, I think of exactly what mom would say. As much as I love my store, I realize I don't need taxidermied critters or my skeletal best mate, Van Helsing.

I need a real live human with listening ears and a beating heart. I need the safe landing of a familiar shoulder to cry on. When I had tearfully asked my mom what on Earth I would do without her, she patted my hand and said, "Oh, honey.

You are so strong. Lean on your girlfriends. That's what women do when we lose our moms."

She was right. I may not feel strong right now, but I know I can lean on my found family, my rocks, so I can take all these shattered pieces and mold them back together. Mindy and Jo are the glue. Mom knew that. And now I know what I need to do.

LIESHE

Get together now?

MINDY

🙂 what do I always tell you?

LIESHE

Real friends don't need invitations.

MINDY

Drive safe.

I blink my now teary eyes and bite down on my lower lip as it wobbles. Missing Mom, coupled with the blow to my newfound confidence, feels like too much to handle. I can't help but feel rejected by both guys, and it makes me freaking mad-sad.

Two hours, I tell myself. Keep it together for two hours and then you can fall apart. I dig deep for strength, bring up an upbeat playlist, and enter a new destination into the GPS app. I can keep my shit together for two hours.

I head north to Mindy's instead of south to Grimm and focus on driving out of the city. Once I hit the interstate, I wish my vintage bug had cruise control. This part of the drive is easy. Just go straight for miles and miles, so I turn my thoughts inwards.

I had clicked on an upbeat playlist, but the universe is

conspiring against me and sappy song after depressing one about heartbreak and loss comes on. I hit skip so many times I run out of skips. Frustrated, I kill the music and drive in silence. This is the price I pay for being too cheap to buy any of the subscription music services.

I look out the windshield at the verdant green of the passing mountains, like sleeping giants curled on their sides. Above is a brilliant and clear summer sky, endless blue. If I didn't have inventory in the backseat, I would pull over and put the top down. Instead, I crank down my window and let the summer air whiz by my ear.

I breathe deeply and imagine the warm sunshine filling my lungs and diffusing out to every cell in my body like little molecules of oxygen. I visualize breathing out doubt, anger, sadness, and any other negative emotion renting space in my head.

I repeat this process, and after a few minutes, I feel a little lighter. I decide to put off sorting through my thoughts and feelings about Luke and McHottie until I can do it with someone with some amount of objectivity.

The scenery continues to whiz by while I steadily make my way to Mindy's. The next thing I know, my GPS app reminds me my exit is coming up. I follow the directions through winding back roads, keeping an eye out for her hidden driveway when I get close. Even the GPS has a tough time finding this remote location.

There it is!

I buzz my little beetle up her driveway and am met by an explosion of dogs, cats, chickens, and kids. I get out, laughing and bracing for impact from past experiences of small people tackling my legs and animals getting underfoot.

True to form, her twins race over and wrap themselves around my legs. I make them squeal in delight as I walk stiff-legged, a kid sitting on each foot, sadness evaporating away with every step.

I pet whichever dog is butting my hand with a wet nose and make my way to Mindy's back patio where she stands grilling. With this many human and animal mouths, someone is always eating, and she is always cooking. The normalcy is a balm to my sore feelings.

"Snacks on the table," she announces, and all the kids take off running, the dogs chasing after them, leaving just Mindy and I in a few moments of stolen quiet. She grabs me up in a crushing hug, BBQ tongs still in hand. "You're here now. Everything will be okay."

Basking in the nearness of my chosen family, the last vestiges of my earlier funk disappear. "What can I do to help?"

"Open the wine."

I head into the house and raid her stash, pulling down the Christmas glasses we use no matter the season. The familiarity of my longest friend and the little traditions we have are comforting in this time of uncertainty.

They cement me to the core parts of myself that are unchanging—friendship, loyalty, resilience. A dark and wicked sense of humor. I focus on the positive personality traits I love about myself and feel them solidifying internally, leaving me a little less fragile than when I was escaping Philadelphia.

I grab two bottles, one of each of our favorites, and head back out to the patio. Mindy's wine stash, filled from our many trips to the Finger Lakes region together, makes me want to plan another excursion. The wine is good, but the little Airbnb we stay at is even better. Time spent together, though, that's freaking priceless.

I open the bottles and pour each of us a glass. Perhaps

our next trip could be on a beautiful summer day like this instead of November, when it's freezing. We try to hit their big annual Christmas winery tour, which is a lot of fun, but we always freeze our asses off.

I sip my red, remembering the time Mindy, Jo, and I were all up. We had on obnoxious flashing necklaces and ugly Christmas sweaters, having the best time. As we staggered through the parking lot and loaded into our mini-tour bus, the New York ice knocked me on my ass.

Mindy and Jo couldn't figure out where I was since I had been right behind them before I suddenly disappeared. Finally, they leaned out the door to look for me and found me lying on the ground, laughing. The next day, of course, it wasn't quite so funny. I missed my girl gang and our antics.

I head back out and sit down just as Mindy yells for her husband to take over the grill duties so she can sit next to me. We link arms on the loveseat and lean our heads together, sipping wine and staring out at the fading sun trailing over the mountain that is her backyard.

The benefit of having a best friend this long is the ability to sit in silence, talking without breathing a word. Silence until the kids and dogs burst out the back door and run past, intent on some type of game that involves a lot of running and shouting.

Mindy gets up to shut the door, yelling, "Shut the door, wildlings! Get ready for dinner!"

I go back inside to grab the paper plates and handfuls of silverware. I know we will talk when the house is actually quiet—the dogs and kids down for the night. Dinner on the patio is a raucous affair with lots of laughter.

Mindy's house is noisy and full and fun like you'd expect from a house filled with people and love and pets. I enjoy visiting but am always happy to get back to my quiet little life.

We build a fire in the firepit, and I load the kids up with marshmallows as fast as they can burn them and scarf them down. I sneak in a few myself, the sickly sweet, sticky mess making me nostalgic for summer as a kid, when there are endless adventures and bedtime gets later and later as the summer sun lingers.

Soon enough, the children start to settle down, a sure sign they are ready for bed, and the dogs are all asleep around the fire. The cats are off doing whatever it is cats do at night and the chickens are tucked up in their coop.

Mindy herds her brood off to bed, leaving me staring into the flickering flames, looking for the answers to the mysteries of life. Eventually, she comes back out and passes the bedtime baton to her husband. He disappears into the house, probably trying to get the twins settled since they wind each other back up.

Finally, *finally*, it's just us.

"So," she prompts, clinking her wine glass to mine.

I take a sip and attempt to organize my thoughts, but, as if they have a mind of their own, the words spew forth in a torrent of verbal diarrhea. I start at the beginning and retell almost every detail, weaving a convoluted tale that is even hard for me to follow as the storyteller. Mindy waits until I run out of steam, then reaches over and squeezes my hand.

We stay holding hands, sparks flying up toward the heavens where they wither and die. The quiet of the night envelops us, the stars amazingly bright away from the light pollution of more populated areas.

I stare up into the inky blackness, fascinated by the twinkling lights, the faint rustling of leaves in a slight breeze and the crackling of the fire our musical background.

I envision the earth spinning under this starry sky as it loops around the sun, the solar system and galaxy all functioning perfectly in their own little corner of the universe.

The feeling of everything being as it should be is as grounding as my best friend's hand in mine. I appreciate the time she is taking to plan a meaningful reply.

"Ok. So, you're living your life, full steam ahead. Non-stop, too busy to even stop and think. So many of the things that make you amazing, also make you your own worst enemy. Your drive and ambition. Your empathy and good-hearted nature. You love *so big*."

She continues, "It makes you an awesome friend and a lovely human. It also makes you vulnerable and leaves you feeling lost when others don't have the same emotional depth or wear their hearts on their sleeves like you do. You give your entire self away."

"Yeah," I sigh. "You've known me forever. You know me better than I even know myself."

"As a mom, I have learned you *must* save a little piece of yourself just for you. You simply cannot give away one hundred percent. Deep inside, there has to be a sacred space, a safe spot for your soul that is just for you. You keep that little spot whole, and you protect it. What are you doing to take care of you?"

Damn, she is wise. I've always had big feelings and have been super empathetic. The downside, though, is my heart is easy to break, and I am constantly exhausting myself.

Even this year, I'm on a frantic trajectory of the expo, the trip to Europe, and then the steampunk convention during the busy retail season of Halloween through Christmas. Why am I pushing so hard?

"I'm not," I say slowly as I realize what she is saying is

true. I'm not taking care of myself at all. "I'm pushing so hard and I'm exhausting myself. Why?"

"Why indeed? What happens if you just stop?"

I picture what stopping and relaxing for a hot minute would be like. When was the last time I just relaxed? I think it may have been after nursing school. Or maybe even before that. Which means it would have been in high school. Which also wasn't my best years.

Nursing school had been frantic. Then I was a new nurse, which was brutal. Mom got sick, so then I was caring for her and working until I broke out of the hospital and launched my nonstop business.

I had set a grueling schedule for myself, covering all the store hours alone plus doing all the buying trips. The only time I was away from the store was usually for business, barring a few rare weekend getaways with my girlfriends. But, more often than not, Mindy or Jo would come to my place, and we would work on something for the store. They never complained, though.

I tried to think of the last time we had even gone up to wine country and sadly realized it was probably going on a few years. If I really thought about it, I don't think I've done anything not work related for at least three years.

I weigh her words and realize Luke and McHottie aren't the actual issue. I'm the issue. It's me. I need to make time for myself and get back to being me. Because I *am* a beautiful, confident, strong woman.

I don't need a man to tell me that or reassure me. I need to reassure myself. Yes, I still want to see both of them, and I'd love to see what could happen. Yes, I want to fall in love. But more importantly, I need to come into my own. I've worked my ass off to be where I am at.

"You're right. This is not sustainable. And I can't depend on a man for my self-worth. I need to be enough for me."

Mindy clinks her glass to mine and says, "And there you have it."

I look back up at the stars and silently tell my mom I love her. And although I miss her inexplicably, she gave me the best advice. Lean into my friends. It feels good to do so and also to make space in my heart for myself.

Now I need to make space in my life for me. And I've got to get some fun in. I'm 30 years old, for goodness' sake, and I have no life outside the business.

Mindy continues, "So, we've established you don't need a man for self-worth. You are your own champion. But is there one you want more than the other?"

It's a brilliant question. They couldn't be more different. "I mean, maybe whichever one sticks around for more than a minute?"

We laugh, and it feels good. There isn't an answer. I do want to get to know each one better. And I want to get to know myself.

I tell Mindy that when I get home, I'm going to think about having someone pick up one or two days a week at the store so I can have some time to myself and to focus *on* the business instead of being *in* the business every day.

"Do you want me to come down to make up some more pretty dead things," she deadpans.

We break into belly laughs. Mindy is great at crafts, but dreads seeing what materials we will work with for my version of art projects. She also says my taxidermy gives her the willies and swears Van Helsing has a trapped soul.

She must love me a lot to keep coming to Grimm. I vow to visit my friends more. I need to be a good friend in return. Although, now that I think of it, we've never been to Jo's house out in the middle of nowhere. I'll offer to visit her next since she is coming out to watch the store for me.

We sit talking into the night, watching the fire die and drain our bottles of wine. Mindy taps out and collects her sleepy dogs, but I stay for a little while longer, enjoying the quiet sounds of the night and the glittering stars overhead. Soaking in the peace of the moment, I just breathe without thinking, what's next?

I stare out over the mountain. The fading sun reduces the surrounding woods to dark and then darker shadows. I scan their purple depths, delighted to see the first flickers of the year's lightning bugs. I watch their strange blinking pattern, frowning when I see something that doesn't quite fit.

Nope, definitely not fireflies. Further up the mountain, far from the light cast by the fire, I see two golden glowing eyes.

I blink, but the eyes remain, staring. And t*hat's my cue for bed,* I think as I make my way to the safety of the house. Mindy has bears on her mountain, and I'm not ready to be a bedtime snack.

Or at least not for a bear, anyway. Now McHottie or Luke? I'd be happy to be their bedtime snack. If either of them could get their shit together.

Chapter 28

LIESHE

Someone prying my eyelids open pulls me from sleep. I pretend to snore loudly and Mindy's littlest ones, the twins, break out in giggles. Acting as if I am still asleep and dreaming, I sweep them up and tickle them. It's all fun and games until two of the fluffy golden retrievers pile on and then it's bedlam.

I extricate myself from the pile and go in search of coffee and Mindy. I need to get home. This detour has added a few hours to my drive home, but I'm so happy I came. The time is worth the clarity Mindy gives me.

I find her frothing oat milk next to the coffeepot, since I have her hooked on my concoction, too. She hands me a travel mug and says, "Hit the road, Jack. Go live your best life. Let's get together soon. I can't go so long without seeing you again."

"Me neither," I say, blinking back tears as I squeeze her tight. Taking the mug, I say goodbye to the endless stream of pets and kids as I make my way back out to my car. The early sun feels warm on my head, hope from the possibilities a new day brings bubbles up inside of me.

I'm so thankful for Mindy's friendship. Her no-nonsense but supportive approach was exactly what I needed. The new day and new perspective have me feeling more centered and less fragile.

Acknowledging being confident and true to myself independent of a relationship is a pivotal moment for me.

263

Yes, I want to fall in love. But more importantly, I need to be the best version of myself that I can be.

I pull up my favorites playlist since the station labeled upbeat yesterday was such a disaster and hit the winding roads that will lead me back toward the interstate. One of my favorite driving songs comes on and I crank down my window, turn up the volume, and sing at the top of my lungs along with the Violent Femmes.

Great song after great song plays as I sing my way south. I'm looking forward to giving my schedule a hard reboot, starting by asking Anna if she wants to pick up a day a week.

Working only five days a week sounds like heaven. And if I can swing it financially, she could pick up a second day, and I could take one day to devote to working on the business *and* have a day off.

If I am strategic and use that time to grow the business, like finally figuring out all the social media like I've been meaning to, having her there should pay for itself. I feel good about this plan, excited to get home and iron out the details.

The drive flies by, and soon enough, I'm pulling in behind my beloved Grimm. Normally, I would have raced around to the front and immediately checked in on Anna and the store, but I decide to trust in her and take some much needed time for self-care. Nothing would change in the next hour.

Proud of myself, I head up to my place and unpack my small bag. I putter around, getting laundry started and changing clothes, since I had slept in the ones I had on and wore them home.

I tame my hair while I'm at it and then look in my fridge, not surprised when there isn't much to eat. I figure I'll go down and check in with Anna and then go find some grub. Grabbing my small belt bag, I bound down the stairs, zip around the building, and head toward the shop door.

As always, I get a small thrill of pride to see it. I head inside, happy to see Anna helping a customer choose between two different wet mounts. While I wait for her to finish, I head back to the storage area to make room for the new purchases I brought home with me.

I shuffle some inventory, organizing some of the holiday merchandise a little when my stomach reminds me all I've had today was coffee. I head back out to the store to talk with Anna just as the customer is leaving.

"How did it go?" I ask.

"Oh, it was great! The weekend was pretty busy, but I had so much fun. How was your trip?"

I pause, thinking how to answer. "I turned out to be exactly what I needed. Thank you so much for covering. Could you help me bring some stuff in from the car?"

"Of course!" she says.

Anna jumps up, and we head out the back emergency exit, which is closer to the car. She is young and exuberant. Her friendly nature will be an asset to the store, and her energy is contagious. I feel myself smiling just from her presence.

I prop the back door open so we can ferry in the boxes. We get things settled into the back storage room and then both stand back, hands on hips, and survey the packed space. It feels good to have a wide selection of inventory for restocking, but I will also need to stay on top of it since more will arrive soon.

"Did you bring in my garment bag?" I ask Anna as I look around, but don't see it anywhere.

"What garment bag?"

"The big black one with my new jacket and corset."

I frown, retracing my steps. Now that I think about it, I

don't recall taking it out of the hotel closet or putting it in my car.

"Oh no! I forgot it at the hotel!"

I had been so distracted when I was leaving, I had forgotten to grab it out of the closet. Disappointed in myself, I really hope I can get back the expensive pieces I fell in love with.

"Quick, call the hotel!" Anna exclaims.

At the sound of the sleigh bells on the front door, she scurries out to greet the incoming customer, leaving me shaking my head at myself.

I hope Anna is right, and they put it aside for me. Although I am not looking forward to driving to Philly and back just to pick it up, it is a small price to pay, as shipping would be a fortune because of the weight.

Besides, I wouldn't want to ask the hotel to ship it and chance it getting lost in the mail. I groan and quickly pull up the hotel's phone number and dial it. I'm thankful it's a boutique hotel, so I don't end up in some centralized call center.

The front desk picks up and I explain who I am and the situation. They politely ask me to hold. I tap my foot impatiently and start chewing on my thumb cuticle as I worry. After what feels like an eternity, a new person comes back on the phone.

"Hello, Ms. St. James. I am so sorry to tell you this, but I checked with housekeeping, and they recalled seeing a garment bag and putting it on their cart to bring to the lost and found. But before we could call you, someone must have called the business number printed on the bag and it was picked up."

"I'm sorry, I don't understand. Who picked it up?"

"Someone from the business. They assured us they

would get it to you. I am so sorry for the mix-up, and I hope you will stay with us again soon."

"Sure, thanks," I reply flatly and end the call with a groan.

It isn't the hotel's fault I forgot the bag, but I'm frustrated, nonetheless. Thankfully, all is not completely lost. However, I am also anxious about how I can get the items back.

Does this mean I'll be seeing Luke again? I'm not entirely sure where his home base is. I don't want to wait until the Poe convention to get my corset and jacket back, but I'm worried about seeing Luke again after he didn't even say goodbye and had one of his 'boys' drop me off.

My poor thumb cuticle that bore the brunt of my worry is now bleeding and throbbing. I grab a napkin from the little kitchenette and hold pressure on it. A torn hangnail is the least of my worries.

I feel my heartbeat pulse in my finger as I hold pressure on it and feel sympathetic toward the poor confused organ in my chest. I feel a little hollow inside to be reminded of Luke.

I channel my inner Mindy and do some deep breathing, focusing on this moment, and ask myself what I need to do next. Worrying won't solve anything. As Jo would always remind me when I got anxious back in college, "Worry is the illusion of control."

I will give Luke's company a few days to call me about returning the items, and then, if I don't hear from him, I will be very professional and contact him about it. Surely, I can find the info for his business online. I smile in response to how utterly practical and grown-up I am being. *I got this.*

I also stop to think, *what else do I need right now?* The new inventory is under control. Anna has the store until closing, and what I need is food followed by a nap. A nap sounds glorious. I've gotta start taking better care of myself, as the resurgence of my waking dreams indicates, and Mindy has reminded me.

First, I will offer Anna a part-time position. She did an excellent job this weekend and is such a wonderful help, great with the customers, and easy to get along with. *Please accept,* I plead in my mind.

I walk back out to the front of the store as she is ringing out yet another customer. I think I could have her put out some of the new stock during her next shift, too. That will get her familiar with the restocking and the inventory.

Looks like I now need an inventory management system since I won't be the only one working here. I had always just kept it all in my head, but that will no longer be practical with more than one person handling everything.

As soon as the customer is back out the door, I approach her with my offer.

Fueled by my commitment to take better care of myself, I decide to head to the store to pick up some groceries. As I hop back into the bug, I think over my conversation with Anna while I make the short drive.

Not only was she thrilled with my offer, she somehow talked me into two days per week straight away and would research not only inventory management, but was excited to develop our social media accounts.

I had been hoping for some time for myself and time to work on the business, and now I've not only met those goals, but Anna is bringing bonus features. She also promised to do some gluten-free cooking!

Hiring her is brilliant, and as much as I love Grimm, I am thrilled to not only grow the business with someone to help me, but am also enormously relieved to not be carrying the load solely on my shoulders anymore.

In my head, she already seems more like a partner than an hourly employee with all the great ideas she bubbled over with. I feel a renewed sense of excitement over the business I've loved for years now.

Buzzing on a second wind, I walk around the store, actually picking out some healthy foods since I'm energized enough to think about cooking. I even buy some green vegetables.

I still get drawn in by the freezer aisle and pick out a few assorted flavors of my favorite gelato. I can't wait to try the new strawberry champagne flavor. Feeling magnanimous, I even grab a bag of treats for my hateful cat.

I check out and load my bags into my car and head back home. The sun is shining brightly in an azure blue sky and, for once, the perfect summer temperature warms my skin without suffocating me.

I'm on top of the world. This is my time. I feel, well, I feel great. I drive back to Grimm with my hand out the window, letting the air make my hand fly. It reminds me of being a kid, pretending my hand was a bird as I made it go up and down as the wind rushed by.

I gather all the groceries in my arms, committed to making just one trip, no matter the price. Lucifer helpfully picks this time to show up and wind his way between my ankles as I precariously make my way up the stairs. I juggle the bags as I unlock the door and my cat bolts through ahead of me, probably disappointed he wasn't able to knock me down after all.

I walk through the door, surprised by the intense aroma

of roses. I look around and am shocked to find vases upon vases of roses on the counter, the end tables, the coffee table, and the kitchen island. I drop the groceries on the floor and go to the closest vase, reaching out to stroke the petals.

The flowers are a deep dark red, the color so rich and velvety they bleed to black. I have never seen roses like this. They are simply stunning.

Their smell is intoxicating without being overpowering, exactly like my favorite rose perfume. As I caress the petals and stare into the velvety depths, I jerk my hand back, realizing that someone has been in my house.

Someone has brought roses into my home! I search around my open-concept main floor, but nothing else seems out of place. The TV is there, and I doubt a burglar would break in to steal things and leave this many flowers behind. That would be the most bizarre theft in the world's history.

I glance over at the stairs up to my bedroom. There could be a psycho killer hanging out up there. I guess this could be some strange, elaborate murder set up, but that doesn't quite seem plausible.

"Lucifer, stop that," I scold the cat as he happily chomps on an arrangement on an end table. Oddly, I don't feel nearly as scared as I presumably should. Still, probably isn't the smartest idea to walk up the stairs by myself though.

I grab my cell out of my back pocket and call Jo for backup. Not that she can do anything other than ring the police if I am attacked, but it seems like a good plan.

"'Sup bish."

I whisper yell, "Seriously? That's how you answer the phone?"

"Caller ID. I knew it was you. How was Philly? Did you go to pound town with Carrot Top?"

"Jo! Shut. Up. This is serious. I need you to focus."

"Why are you whispering? Wait, does Carrot Top have you locked in a closet? Press the number nine if you need help."

"I should have called someone else. Anyone else," I mutter.

"No, really, I'm here for you. What's going on that you're acting so weird?"

I sigh, "Pot meet kettle. Okay, listen. I came home to find my house filled with the most beautiful roses I've ever seen."

"I'm sorry. You're calling me because someone filled your house with flowers?"

"Yes," I whisper-shout.

"Lieshe, I don't get it. What's the problem?"

"Jo! A burglar snuck into my house and put flowers all over the place."

"Huh. That's weird. Wouldn't a burglar normally take something?"

I take a deep breath. I should have just walked upstairs to see if there was a killer. It would have been less painful than this call. "I need you to stay on the phone with me while I check my house to make sure there isn't a killer hiding."

Once I say it out loud, I realize just how dumb it sounds. I'm not thinking straight, clearly. Maybe the roses are also poisoned, and the toxic fumes are already damaging my brain. Shaking my head, I think, *really, Lieshe? Not just roses, but roses with aerosolized poison?*

"You're doing that thing where you talk out loud again when you're stressed. I doubt they are poisoned, but I'm glad you called me. I mean, yeah, I'm like eight states away, but I'm here for you. I guess if I hear screaming, I'll call the police. But you know you'll be dead by then, right? Do you think you should just call them now?"

She has a point. Should I? "What would I say? 'Hello,

officer, someone broke into my house and left roses everywhere.' And the officer would say, 'Oh no—not roses!'"

"Yeah, that would be a running joke at the department. Okay, go check it out. I'll be on standby. Maybe get a weapon?"

Oh, good idea. I'd probably stab myself by accident if I grabbed a butcher knife. Do I have some pepper spray in the junk drawer? I keep meaning to buy some. I head to the kitchen and root around, but all I can find is silly string.

Covering the label with my hand, I clutch the can and hope it seems frightening enough. Walking down the hall toward the bathroom, I call out, "Hello? Anyone there?"

Jo whispers, "Did you find a weapon? Is anyone answering you?"

"All I could find was a can of silly string," I whisper back. Jo dissolves into a fit of laughter until she is out of breath and all I can hear is her high-pitched gasps between wheezing giggles.

"Oh shit, I just peed my pants. By all means, please proceed with your silly string. Aim for the eyes." She barely gets the words out between laughs.

I scowl at my phone but inch down the hallway until I throw the bathroom door open. No one is there, just the same old bathroom, penis candles, and all.

"The bathroom is clear," I whisper, like this is some type of cop movie.

I head back out to the hallway and burst through my closet door. The only thing there is my usual mess of clothes and shoes. I go back into the hallway and tiptoe toward the stairs to my bedroom.

I'm thankful for the open concept main floor with few places to hide. I'm almost done. I just need to check my bedroom by breaking the most basic rule of horror movies by going up the stairs.

My heart is pounding, but I'm still not as scared as logic would dictate. Maybe because the flowers are so pretty, they seem harmless? As long as they're not poisoned, anyway.

"Hello? Anyone there?" I creep up, holding my silly string out like pepper spray.

"Status report?" Jo asks, recovered from her laughing fit.

"More roses," I tell Jo incredulously as I reach the top. There are more vases up here, one on each side of the bed, one at the base of my flamingos in love, and on the coffee table in my little conversation area is an enormous basket of roses. There must be a dozen dozen roses in it. "Literally, a shit ton."

"And you don't know who could have filled your entire house with flowers?" she asks.

"No. No clue. Oh, wait! The giant basket has a note."

I hurry over, put down the silly string, and pick up a small envelope. Opening it, I find a heavy cream-colored card. I pull out the note and read aloud the elegantly calligraphed words,

Love Eternal.

"Oh," she gasps. "I love a good stalker romance."

"Are you crying?" I ask incredulously.

"No, I'm not crying. You're crying." Jo blows her nose over the phone. "Who could it be?"

"Jo, you have the strangest sense of romance. I have no idea who. Well, no killers here. But I'm getting my locks changed. Today."

"Good idea. Keep your phone close and call me if you

need me. Or if you figure out who the delivery man is. See you soon!"

We hang up and I flop down on my chaise lounge, staring at the enormous basket of flowers. Who on earth could have sent them? And how did they get into my house?

I google a locksmith and arrange to have the locks changed. They can't come until tomorrow, but I'm sure I'll be okay until then. After all, I have my silly string.

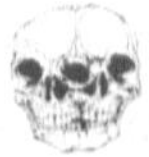

I spend the night tossing and turning, startled at every tiny noise. I wedged a chair under the knob of my front door as I'd seen on TV. It made me feel marginally better, but my sleep was still totally jacked.

Despite being exhausted, I was up with the dawn, the rising sun chasing away the fears that come in the dark of the night. I'm so thankful the store is closed today.

After I get my locks changed, I am definitely going to need a nap. I'm dragging even though I've already had two enormous mugs of coffee. I fire off a quick text to Jo to let her know I've survived the night.

I sit on a bar stool at the kitchen island and pull out my planning notebook to work on my European buying trip. The distraction will help to pass the time until the locksmith shows up. I still like working on paper for many reasons, including a vague mistrust of technology and a penchant for a bygone era.

I've already purchased my flight and written the details on the first page of my notebook. I make up a page for each day to include lodging, transportation, and contacts for that day's destination.

I've worked in a little time for sightseeing for some can't miss items since I'm not sure when, or if, I'll get back to some of these places. I'm really excited about going to Loch Ness, on the top of my top bucket list.

My stomach growls since all I had for breakfast was copious amounts of coffee, so I take a break to whip up a turkey lettuce wrap and slice up some fresh fruit. I've got to use up the produce I bought when I was feeling inspired to eat better. The gelato in the freezer is calling my name, but I promise it to myself as a treat tonight for making it through the day.

I sit back down at the kitchen bar, writing more notes as I make my way through my early lunch. I send some emails from my phone to confirm with the contacts I haven't spoken to in a bit.

Feeling good about the plans for my upcoming trip, I stand and stretch, then take my plate to the sink and grab a seltzer. I crack it open and hear a knock at the door. Taking a quick sip, I set it down and go open the door for the locksmith. I'll sleep so much better tonight with my locks changed.

Chapter 29

I stand at her front door and curl my lip in distaste.

I can smell that fucking dog. The disgusting odor curls up into my nose and sneaks down into the back of my palate. I all but gag. Guess I'll just have to piss on my territory.

With a smirk, I reach out and trace a raven onto her door with my finger, infusing it with my power.

"Take that, you filthy mutt," I mutter under my breath.

I plaster a pleasant smile on my face and knock. I can't wait to chase this taste out of my mouth. And I know just the flavor I want instead.

A delicious cocktail of equal parts innocence and desperation, with a dash of shame, garnished with a slice of lust. My mouth waters in anticipation. This will be better than my own bourbon.

Chapter 30

I open the door and my jaw drops, shocked when I don't see the locksmith on the other side.

Luke in bespoke steampunk is hot.

Luke dressed as a robed raven-masked fire spinner, is enthralling.

Luke standing at my front door with the sun behind him, casually leaning back against the railing of the landing in a t-shirt and jeans, is fucking *exquisite*.

The light glints on his loose red hair as it cascades down his shoulders like a halo of fire. He looks like Hephaestus limned in sunlight. My eyes trace down his fiery locks, taking in the tight t-shirt straining over his lean muscular body, down to the black matte raven belt buckle at the waist of his fitted and artfully ripped jeans. Even his sneakers are awesome, black leather high tops covered in small spikes.

He holds up the missing garment bag with a wink. "You forgot something."

I stand staring at him, shocked he would have driven it here today.

"Aren't you going to invite me in?" he asks.

"I'm sorry, yes, of course. Please come in."

I step back and gesture into my house. As he passes me, I turn to watch him. He moves with such purpose and grace, every step powerful and controlled. It reminds me of the way he moved on stage. As he walks, I can't help but notice the bottoms of his cool black sneakers are red.

I ask incredulously, "Are those Louboutins?"

He doesn't answer, just stalks to my kitchen bar and lays the garment bag over it. He studies my open notebook for a moment and then hops up on a stool facing me and leans back on the counter on his elbows, fancy sneakers propped up on the rungs.

"What's with the flowers, *mon petit chou?*"

He peers around the room until his intense gaze lands on me. I feel drawn to him, like a moth to a flame. Before I know it, I am crossing the room to him, my feet with a mind of their own.

"Long strange story," I reply a little breathlessly. Did Luke do this? I try to keep the hint of suspicion out of my voice as I ask, "How did you know where I live?"

He smiles his Cheshire smile at me and says, "You gave me your card, remember? Since your shop was closed, I came around back and took a chance you'd live here."

Sure, that makes sense. I nod at him, smiling. It is easy to fall under his spell. He is captivating. I vaguely recall being perturbed with him about something, but for the life of me, right now, I can't recall what he could have done to upset me.

He is here and smiling at me and this feels so right. My feet continue to propel me forward until I am standing just in front of him. He slides his knees apart and gives me a smoldering look.

"Come."

The dark dominance in his voice is commanding, and I obey without thought, stepping in between his legs. The intensity of his stare is dizzying, causing me to reach out and steady myself with my hands on his hard thighs.

His skin feels hot even through his jeans. I run my hands further up his legs, wanting to explore him.

"Aren't you going to thank me?"

I nod my head. Yes, that's exactly what I should be doing. He reaches out and collars my throat with his hand, heavy and calming, pulling me to him until our noses are all but touching. His green-eyed gaze is too intense, forcing me to close my eyes, my breath quickening.

"Lieshe," he whispers in front of my lips, so close I can feel the hot air escaping his mouth and tickling over mine.

I suck a breath in through my mouth, wanting to swallow the way he says my name. Devour his cinnamon scented dominance.

"Thank you," I whisper back, hoping when I speak, my lips will brush against his. I slide my hands up his thighs, desperate to feel him. Instead of my hands getting to continue their exploration, he releases my throat and picks them up in his.

"You're welcome," he replies with a pleasant smile. He gently pushes me away from him with our combined hands and stands, dropping them.

My mouth falls open. This is not where I thought this 'thank you' was going. I feel like I have lady blue balls as I watch him cross my living room and head for my front door.

"Wait," I cry. I cringe at the desperation in my tone. I need to play it a little cooler, so I clear my throat and try for a sexy voice instead of the desperate one that had escaped.

"I, uh, also wanted to thank you for the other night," I say bravely to his retreating back, hoping he picks up on my thoughts of just how I can express my gratitude.

Dirty talk has never been something I could do. Really interested in, yes, but never comfortable with. I'd love to sound super sexy and spell out exactly how I want to thank him, but I would probably die of embarrassment first or choke on my words.

"Oh?" he tosses over his shoulder, one hand on the doorknob.

"Um, yeah, I had an amazing night."

He angles his head, looking at me over his shoulder.

"My pleasure."

"You could stay for a while," I blurt. "If you want, I mean, I hate for you to get right back on the road. Can I at least get you a drink?"

Luke turns to face me fully, his beauty punching me in the chest.

"Okay."

"Okay?" I parrot back in surprise.

"Sure, I can stay for a while."

"Great. What can I get you to drink?" I offer awkwardly. Now that he is here, what am I going to do with him?

"Is that tequila I see on top of your fridge?"

"Yeah, my favorite. I'll pour us some." He gives me his feline smile and I don't know how I'm going to manage to pour anything. "On the rocks?"

"No, I like it just the way it is," he responds smoothly.

Everything he says sounds sinful, like there is some deeper meaning I should be able to suss out. I feel my face flush and busy myself returning to the kitchen and pouring him a drink, neat, and one for me with ice.

While I do, Luke makes himself at home on my couch, gracefully draping his arm along the back and crossing an ankle over his knee, an alpha male position if ever there was one. It suits him. No bravado here, just pure, powerful masculinity. I cross the room and hand him his glass and then sit safely on the opposite end.

"Well, now that you have me here, what are you going to do with me?"

Shit. Good question. I have no clue. I hadn't thought

about anything beyond asking him to hang out. Luckily, there is a knock at the door, saving me from having to answer. He quirks a brow at me as I stand up and answer it.

Now the locksmith is here. I had completely forgotten he was coming. Great timing dude. I cross the room and open the door to find a friendly looking older guy in overalls with his name and company logo emblazoned on the chest.

"You missing a big black dog?" He jabs a thumb over his shoulder.

"No," I reply with a frown. "I don't have a dog. I have a black cat."

"Huh," he grunts. "I'm here to change your locks," he says, handing me a business card.

"Wonderful. Please come in."

"No need. This will only take a minute."

He leaves the door open and gets to work, rekeying the locks on the doorknob and deadbolt, while I stand there awkwardly between him and Luke. I can feel Luke's heated gaze on me as I wait. After a few minutes, the locksmith hands me the new key and a copy.

"That's it. Sign here."

"Seriously? That was quick."

I sign the screen on his tablet and off he goes. I toss the keys on the end table next to the door and turn around to see Luke sipping his tequila, his hot yellow-green gaze laser focused on me. Shockingly, Lucifer is curled up on the back of the couch at Luke's shoulder.

"I can't believe that cat is sitting with you. Lucifer hates everyone. Even me."

"Cats always love me. Why did you name this sweet thing Lucifer?"

"After the mean cat in Cinderella."

Lucifer lifts his head, looks at me haughtily as if he

knows we are discussing him, and blinks his yellow eyes. After a brief stare off, he stretches, bumping his head against Luke before jumping down to stalk off. I glare after him. That damn cat I so kindly allowed to stay with the building has never even acknowledged my existence.

I shake my head and return to my seat on the couch and take a sip of my tequila, rolling it around in my mouth, savoring the flavor. I swallow and lick a drop off my lips with the tip of my tongue. Luke's eyes follow the movement, and he groans.

"Fuck it," he mutters and uncrosses his legs, taking the foot that was resting on his knee and using it to kick the coffee table away from him. He scowls at the vase of roses as it teeters precariously. Turning his gaze back to mine, he points at the floor in front of him expectantly.

Oh, shit. I have a feeling I'm about to lose the lid to Pandora's box completely. I take another swallow of tequila for courage and rise from the couch.

"Lieshe," he draws out each letter of my name so that it falls like sin from his lips. "*Je veux croquer la pomme.* On your hands and knees. Crawl to me."

Yup. There goes the lid. The French is *killing* me. I drop to my hands and knees as gracefully as I can and crawl the few scant feet, so I am in front of him.

I hope to hell I look sexy, but what I feel is awkward as fuck. I'm trying to please him by following his commands, but I can't help but wonder if there is a sexy way to crawl or if just the act itself is enough.

"Get in position," he says.

Position? What position? I rack my brain, trying to think of what the hell he is talking about, and move to the only position I can think of. I kneel before him like I did the other night and smile up at him.

His face is stern, but his eyes are heavy-lidded with lust. A thrill races through me at pleasing him. I might not have any experience with this kinky stuff, but I start to feel a little cocky if the expression on his face is anything to go by.

Giving myself a little pep talk, I think, *I can do this! I'm a sexy bad bitch.*

"How do you want to thank me?" Luke's voice drops an octave and rasps over me like hot smoke, his accent more pronounced.

The sexy pride I had felt falls away and my mouth feels like cotton. What does he want me to say?

"Use your words," he prompts.

It's like he can see into my mind and unravel my secret fantasies. I always wanted to try out some of this kinky stuff and dirty talk, but never knew what to do or say.

Here's my chance, but I feel so intimidated. There are so many words to choose from. I always think in terms of medical lingo due to my nursing background, but I don't think 'penis' counts as sexy talk.

"Lieshe," he growls darkly, pulling me from my musings on the merits of various vocab for male anatomy. I lick my lips and swallow, turning options over in my mind. "What do you want to do?"

"I, uh, I want to put you in my mouth," I stammer out, and it sounds more like a question instead of a statement. I chicken out, wanting to say something bold and spicy like 'cock,' but I don't know that I can get the words out.

"What do you want to put in your mouth?" he questions with a quirked brow, his smile deepening. It's clear he is enjoying my discomfort.

"You know," I squirm, looking away. I need a break from the intensity of his yellow-green stare. I am surprised at just how turned on I am while feeling so embarrassed. Is being embarrassed a kink, too? Or does Luke just make everything feel this way?

"No, I don't know," he reprimands. Then he challenges in a low sultry voice, "I want to hear you say it."

Every syllable that falls from his lips feels purposeful, like its reason for existing is only to slip from his beautiful mouth. I look up at him, straight into his unusual eyes. I want his lips to caress me like those words. I want this. I want him.

"Shall I give you a list, *mon petit chou? Bite, nœud, pine, queue, zob. Comment dites-vous en anglais?* Wood, rod, spear, arrow, sword, phallus, sex, beast of desire? Or something more serious, perhaps? Erection, penis, shaft, manhood, cock, dick, or my personal favorite, velvet-wrapped steel?"

I sputter, my face burning, thankful Luke broke the rising tension with his wicked humor. Damn his French, it gets me every time. He gives me his Cheshire cat grin, eyes crinkling at the corners.

His smile shoots to my core. His eyes trace my tongue as I lick my dry lips and his face turns deadly serious. I can't believe he spouted off so many damn words for dick, including the infamous velvet-wrapped steel. I am *not* saying that.

"Lieshe," he purrs, bringing my attention back to the task at hand.

Finally, I am getting a chance to play out some of my deepest-held fantasies and I don't know if I'll ever get another one. I quickly snag my glass off the coffee table behind me, slug down a mouthful of tequila, and turn back to him.

I lift my chin, square my shoulders, look him straight in his mesmerizing eyes, and before I can overthink it, I say boldly, "I want to suck your cock."

I did it!

I am instantly aroused. I said sexy words *out loud*, and I feel amazing. His gaze smolders impossibly hotter as he leans forward off the back of the couch and reaches behind his neck, ripping his shirt off in one smooth move.

Oh. I'll have to try this more often when this is the effect. I drink in the sight of his naked upper body as he takes my tequila from me. He takes a sip without breaking our intense eye contact and then drips a few drops from the glass onto his chest.

I rise up on my knees and chase the drops with my mouth. He tastes exquisite, like fire beneath my tongue. His skin turns my favorite smooth tequila into a smoky mezcal. I want to make him into a cocktail. *Cocktail,* I giggle in my mind. That's where I'm heading.

I kiss my way down the center of his chest, chasing the tequila, down his abs flexing into an eight-pack under my tongue. I boldly change course and nip at his Adonis belt, my favorite part of the male body that I have always wanted to bite but have never been close enough to do so. His skin is flawless and smooth in its porcelain perfection.

With trembling hands, I undo his raven belt buckle, pop the button on his jeans, and slowly drag the zipper down. I'm incredibly nervous, but I really want to impress Luke. I've had his leather-covered crotch in my face multiple times as my mouth watered, but now that I'm faced with the real thing, I can't help but be a little intimidated.

I raise my eyes to Luke's and feel my shyness evaporate. The visible heat in them shows I'm doing just fine and should continue. I reach up and grasp the waistband of his jeans. Just as Luke lifts his hips and I start to drag his pants down, a loud knock comes at the door, startling us both.

"*Bordel de merde.* Who the hell is that now?" Luke snarls.

"Maybe it's the locksmith again?"

I get up and race to the door. I peer out the peephole and let out a shocked gasp when I see who is on the other side. My hand flies to my mouth, and I turn to Luke with enormous eyes.

"I knew I smelled dog," he says cryptically as he stalks to me with his shirt off, fly down, pants precariously clinging to his hips.

Shit! I have no idea what the protocol is in this situation. Do I pretend I'm not home? Do I answer the door and introduce them? Hiding in my closet seems like the best choice at this moment. Maybe a portal to another dimension will emerge to swallow me whole. Or the building could collapse. Anything but this.

Luke glances from me to the door, expectantly. I guess I'm opening the door. I reach out and grab the doorknob, stalling, dreading the confrontation. Luke's eyes are on me, waiting.

And honestly, it's not like I've done anything wrong. In fact, I realize I haven't done shit wrong. And I won't be ashamed of spending time with someone else. Feeling my ire rise, I whip open the door.

My anger fades the second I see the shocked look on McHottie's face. It's identical to the one he had when he discovered us together in my waking dream in the stairwell.

Luke leans into me and wraps his arm around my shoulders, pulling me into his side. He drops a kiss on top of my head, drawing the other man's gaze, and says flatly, "What can I do for you, *chien*?"

McHottie's eyes narrow and his hands clench into fists. The air smells like ozone and sulfur, causing my eyes to scan the clear blue sky for an impending storm. But I see nothing.

He swings his eyes back to me, saying, "I was hoping we could talk."

"I'm sorry, now's not a good time," I say.

His face falls at my words and then hardens as he swings his gaze back to Luke. He goes to step forward but abruptly stops, his eyes darting to my open door. He huffs and shakes his head, fuming.

Shooting a last dejected glance back at my face, he turns and heads down the stairs without another word. I reach out my hand toward him and go to step forward, to call after him and apologize for what, I don't know, when Luke grasps my other wrist.

He tugs me back inside and closes the door, slowly backing me up against it. I had been so excited to explore Luke and see where this could go, but right now, all I feel is immense disappointment.

I'm not even entirely sure why. But that whole interaction had been a major lady boner killer. So now here I stand, with a hottie in retreat and a hottie in front of me, most definitely not the Lieshe sandwich I had fantasized about.

Luke cages me against the door, and instead of feeling turned on, I feel trapped. When I don't react, he steps back and lifts my chin gently toward his face. His eyes look back and forth between mine as if he is trying to read my mind.

Eventually, he says, "Who was that, *mon petit chou?*"

"My new neighbor," I say, but it comes out more like a question. I'm surprised when he leans in and gives me a tiny kiss on my nose and then spins around. He walks back to the couch, pulls his shirt on, and fastens his pants.

"Thanks for the drink."

"Luke," I start. But I don't know what to say. I'm torn

between asking him to stay and letting him go. He decides for me.

"*À plus.*" He gives me a half smile and walks to the door. I follow him, locking the door behind him. I guess I could have tried to stop him, too.

But I'm not sure that I want to right now with this hollow feeling in my chest where all the intense attraction had been just a few minutes ago. I walk back to the couch and flop down, curled on my side. I can still smell Luke on my sofa. Cinnamon layered in with the bouquet of so many roses.

I look at the vase on the coffee table in front of me and frown. The roses are all wilted–petals falling as I watch. That's strange. Glancing around the room, every other arrangement is just as beautiful as when I found them. Had Lucifer had been chewing this bunch, too?

I wonder why McHottie had shown up. I wonder why Luke had left. Until ultimately, I wonder no more and let sleep claim me, a nap the perfect escape from this strange day and my fruitless thoughts.

Chapter 31

LUKE

It was all I could do not to clap my hands in delight. I knew I smelled dog below the stench of all those damn roses. Sure, it had been petty to zap the ones on the coffee table, but I hadn't been able to help myself. They were all I could see behind the head of the little one who looked like she was ready to devour me in her desperation for love.

My face twists at the word, like it is a sour, bitter thing in my mouth. Love is a stupid concept humans use to justify violence and lust. Love, pure love, does not exist. I learned that eons ago.

Lieshe, though, that's a taste I could get used to. Her innocence is intoxicating, her corruption so delicious I can taste it high on my palate, like the tickle of champagne bubbles. So much better than the other times I've sampled her.

I knew *he* would be furious when he saw her door. I only wish I could have seen his face when he saw the same raven I traced on her back. Things couldn't have been scripted more perfectly if I had tried.

This time, I will win. There is no doubt in my black, scorched heart.

I.

Will.

Win.

Chapter 32

I had been filled with hope as I walked next door, anticipating her appreciation for the flowers I had filled her apartment with. After I had smelled Luke on her at the hotel, all I could think of was erasing his stench. What better way to do so than with her roses?

She has always loved flowers, and I thought rather than a single bouquet, I would fill her apartment in an epic display. I imagined how much she would love them. How much this would prove to her I loved her.

Instead, Luke's presence has ruined everything, as it was in the beginning, is now, and as it ever shall be. Destruction and ruin surround him like a miasma. The blast radius of his evil ripples through the very fabric of time and space.

He marked her door like he was pissing on his territory, as if it wasn't bad enough that he had already left his evil, inky black stain on her back. Fucking fucker. I am not sure what his endgame is, or if I will be able to bargain with him as I had planned as a contingency.

I desperately want nothing to do with him. However, I will stop at nothing to save her, save us, in this lifetime. I will give everything for her, for us, even if that means a bargain with that demon.

But thinking of what he has already taken from us leaves me seething with hatred. There are no words to describe the rage that pushes out into every last corner of my being. Each beat of my dead heart resonates with a burning fury until relentless anger threatens to devour me.

I feel the air around me crackle, reflecting the depths of my malevolence. My *Roză* has no idea. None! She is oxygen, and she is playing with fire. He will consume her where I would only complete her. Complete us.

I need to find the courage to tell her the truth and figure out a way to bring her back into my life. I thought by building her confidence in herself I could help her be stronger, more equipped to hear the hard truths I need to share with her.

But my work in showing her the beauty I have always seen in her is so close to being undermined by *him*. I thought she would love the roses and, foolishly, thought perhaps she may even remember them.

I thought I could surround her with their beauty like she surrounds me with hers. There is just never an easy way, a bulletproof way to tell her. All this time, I've yet to find anything that consistently works to convince her of our story.

I don't understand this world, this society. The rules keep changing, and I try to grow with it, try to update myself, but it feels impossible after so long. I have been so many people, lived so many lifetimes, I barely know who I am anymore.

All I know, from the foundation of my being, all that is left that I have unshakable faith in, is that she is mine. From me. For me. And I am hers. This I know as the most basic and unbreakable tenet of my soul.

Maybe I don't completely understand her. Women are different today. She is different. She carries a deep beauty and strength despite her fragility. Yet even if I don't understand her, I *know* her. I have always known her, seen her.

This lifetime is as different as she is. Or at least, that is what I tell myself. Because this time *must* be different. But everything is falling apart now.

I have failed her, failed us, time and time again. I cannot fail again. I cannot survive one more lifetime without her. My God has abandoned me. My *Roză* is abandoning me. I cannot let that asshole have her.

He will destroy her. Destroy us. Destroy any chance we have of happiness.

I storm down the alley, leaving my heart behind with them. There in the shadows, I fall against the wall, sliding down to sit dejectedly. Red pulses in my mind, floods my thoughts, until red is all I can think of.

Hearing her door open and close again has me racing around from the alley to my front door. I cannot see him, allow him to see me in this wrecked state.

Too late.

As I reach to open my door, I can sense *him*. I leave the door closed and spin to face evil, leaning my shoulder against the door, striving to appear nonchalant as he makes his way toward me. Despite the rage coursing through my veins, urging me to swift and severe violence against my oldest enemy, I school my face to cool detachment.

We lock eyes and I clench my jaw, my only visible sign of anger, while his mouth tips up in a smug smirk. He stands at the corner and I'm thankful he doesn't come any closer. I know I cannot defeat him, but I also don't know if that knowledge alone is enough to stop me right now with the state I am in.

The sight of him evokes so many vicious memories. After all, he is the very reason for our predicament. His silver tongue ruins all that is good and precious. His lies are the destroyer of man.

He stands at the corner of the road and the alley, surveying me with his reptilian stare, then hisses at me like the snake he is and disappears with a wink. Those yellow-green eyes forever haunt my every waking moment.

Exhausted, I let myself into my newly renovated house and head toward the basement doors. I scan my finger on the discrete biometric lock and head down the stairs. Walking through the finished basement to the bookshelf, I pull a volume to activate the locking mechanism, stepping back to allow it to swing open.

At the hidden door, I scan my fingerprint again and enter a complex numerical code. The final security door swings noiselessly inward. The false wall of the finished basement hides my secret resting place. I close the door and hear the locks engage. Nothing can reach me now except memories.

Despite the modern security measures, this impenetrable room is sparse. Glass blocks filled with dirt dredged from the places of my past make up the floor. Every spot my *Roză* has fallen, from the first to the last, I have taken a handful. Most I leave at my one permanent residence; some I bring with me to new construction like this.

A minute amount, I add to the extensive scarification on my back. I have lost too much to the ravages of time. Marking memories into my body is the only way to truly ensure their survival.

My mind drifts back through the years of body modifications. Although immune to sickness and death, I am not immune to pain. I welcome the modern trappings of modification, so quick and easy now compared to some of my earlier work.

Faint memories of flickering firelight and intense pain deep in the heart of a forgotten jungle tickle the edges of my mind. I close my eyes and can almost hear the cacophony of night animals and insects behind the people chanting and feel the fire on my skin.

Memories of the coppery scent of the blood as it drips down my back surrounded by a people lost to time, unspoiled by exploration, who welcome me through the centuries. Their leader takes great pride in bestowing their ancient rites of scarification onto their god. I'm no god, I started as a man, but they cannot understand any other explanation of my presence and power.

The memories swirl and build upon each other, edges blurred by massive doses of the hallucinogenic brew they mixed with their offering of blood to me, the only way to withstand the pain of their rituals, even for one like me. I reach back and drift my fingertips over the upper part of my back, the bumps and ridges comforting in their familiarity.

Pulling my mind back to the present, I walk to the only thing in this room, a fridge, and pull a bag from the large supply within. I rip the top open with my teeth and drink down the contents. Still reeling from my encounter, I down two more bags in quick succession, but they do nothing to fill the hollowness in my soul.

Feeling empty, I slide down the wall and sit above the dirt on the floor, elbows on my knees, face clutched in my hands. I let the outside world fall away and retreat into my mind, reaching back through the ages, sifting for clues through memories like a slideshow carousel.

Searching for a path forward. Searching for a way to save us both.

Chapter 33

LIESHE

Sweat trickles down my back, soaking the khaki cotton of my life's uniform. I take my hat off, fanning my face, the pitiful breeze doing nothing to offset the jungle's heat. Curls have escaped my tight braids to stick to my forehead and neck, adding to the tickle of dripping sweat and insect wings.

I wish for the millionth time I could dress like our guides in barely there clothing instead of being swathed head to toe in the most boring color on the planet and heavy boots. *At least it keeps the bulk of the mosquitoes off,* I think as I slap a juicy one that came in for a bite on the back of my neck.

I know I should have gone back to camp with the rest of the group, but I am positive the rare orchid I am hunting is close to this small creek. If I can just go a little further, I know in my gut I will find it. And my gut is always right about plants.

I hack at the foliage, pushing forward, following the creek. The sweat is flowing freely down now, no longer a trickle. I pause just for a moment, draining the last of the water from my canteen, the faint metallic taste wrinkling my nose.

The heat is oppressive. Coupled with the humidity, the air feels like a wet sponge. I mop my face with my wet handkerchief, achieving no more than just rearranging the grime on my face. Soldiering on, I follow the curve of the stream, my machete neatly carving out a path in front of me.

The rhythm of slash, step, slash, step allows my mind to wander. Only one more week to find my precious flower before we go home. My parents are wrapping up their excavation, which means we will all be packing up soon.

I dread our return, having no interest in dresses, debutante balls, or marriage. I want to be left in my trousers to explore the jungle, free to wear my hair in braids and stay up late, stealing sips of my father's bourbon by the fire and a puff of his cigar. I will not be caged, no more how golden the bars.

Oh, how I wish I were a man and could remain here at camp with my own crew. As progressive as my parents are, and as much as they encourage me in my study of botany, a lonesome woman simply cannot be left behind with nothing but a jungle crew.

As I round the bend, I am brought up short by the sight of two Indigenous men. I must have walked further than I thought; there are no local people here that we were told of.

My eyes widen as one aims his spear at me. They gesture at my large machete, and I place it on the ground, keeping my eyes on them. I see the second man lift his blowgun and then the darkness claims me.

My head is swimming like a carousel and my mouth reminds me of our Egyptian dig two summers ago. While I fight to open my eyes, someone holds a cup to my lips. I greedily take a mouthful and immediately struggle to spit out the bitter brew when a hand clamps over my mouth and nose, leaving me no choice but to swallow.

I force my eyes open and see I am in a low building, next

to a fire surrounded by women. I fight down panic as understanding dawns on me–not only am I not back at the camp, but my family has no idea as to my whereabouts.

For the first time in my years traipsing the globe with my parents, I am afraid. Truly and unquestionably frightened. Damn my distracted independence.

I begin to feel the liquid I was forced to drink seep through my system. My last coherent thought is it must be some sort of hallucinogenic, given the way the firelight starts to dance hypnotically and my fear bleeds away.

I allow the women to undress me and fit me with a rough skirt, leaving my breasts exposed. They adorn me with some type of paint, from my face to my toes, swirling patterns of dots and lines.

Some deep thought tries to surface about how strange it is to feel so many hands slipping over my body and breasts, but all I can focus on are the designs pulsing with my heartbeat as if fueled by magic. The cool mud worked into my hair feels heavenly after the heat of the day.

The entire mass is piled on top of my head, and I shiver in the cooling night air, goosebumps breaking out across my flesh. One of the women shows me my reflection in a broken shard of mirror, one section of my body at a time.

I am shocked at my exotic appearance, the paint and patterns on my face highlighting my mismatched eyes, the splash of green vibrant in the amber.

She tilts the mirror, and my warped mind cannot process what appears to be crude fangs and dripping blood painted around my mouth. A line from one of my childhood favorites drifts into my thoughts—curiouser and curiouser.

They offer me a cool sweet drink and I accept, rational thought gone. Could be more drugs, but at this point, I don't care. At least it tastes better. One of the women takes me by the arm and leads to the main fire, where some type of ceremony has started.

I try to capture the details and store them in my mind to tell my parents, as I'm sure no one has yet discovered this group of people. I stupidly think, *my parents would be fascinated.*

The people are all small, shorter even than my five foot three frame, but most startling are their feet, wide and spread. I try to puzzle out why this adaptation would happen, but my thoughts are too busy swirling up into the sky with the sparks from the fire. The details I try to recall from even a minute ago simply slip away, up, up, up to the stars.

Arms outstretched, I spin in a circle and laugh wildly, imagining myself a spark of flame dancing in the wind. I am led away from my impromptu dance next to the fire to a seat and watch in rapt fascination at the ceremonial dance playing out before me.

It appears to be a pantomime of my capture and possibly my sacrifice. Fascinating.

The central fire builds and builds as more dancers join and more fuel is added. The loud beat of the drums and rise and fall of the chanting voices almost drown out the jungle noises of frogs, monkeys, and insects.

Soon the young men are leaping through the enormous blaze in their grass skirts, each trying to outdo the last. The women watch at the circle's edge, whispering behind their hands. The drumming builds to a crescendo and stops. The abrupt silence is deafening.

I try to replicate their beat by drumming on my thighs, I'm not ready for this party to end. The woman next to me stills my hands and shakes her head at me. Party pooper.

As one, everyone falls to their knees as an elder comes

forth, heavily draped in animal skins with an elaborate headpiece. I watch, frozen, as he comes to stand before me.

At close range, I realize the adornments are made of small bones and teeth. We lock eyes, and I realize through the haze of the fading hallucinogenic coursing through my veins that I am in danger. Mortal danger.

Years of fieldwork with my parents sends a chilling realization down my spine. Fear brings startling clarity to my mind, dusting away the hallucinogenic cobwebs. Those aren't just animal parts. In the jumble of macabre bric-a-brac, I can pick out human phalanges and molars.

The withered and decorated leader withdraws a long, wicked pointed blade and reaches for me, cementing my fears that I am indeed going to be sacrificed. As my primal instincts kick in, crowding out the last vestiges of the drug, a scream bubbles up from my throat and out of my mouth.

Once I start, I can't stop. I scream and scream until all hell breaks loose.

An enormous man bursts forth into the clearing and my heart soars. Someone has found me! His pale white skin marks him as a foreigner, his size looming in the shadowy light of the fire.

My excitement is short-lived, as I'm not sure how he can fight his way through the warriors descending on him with their spears and poison blow guns. I know this is my only chance out of this debacle.

He swings his arms like an angry bear, dislodging the men throwing themselves at his towering frame. He fights his way around the fire toward me until we lock eyes. I'm shocked to see in the firelight, their amber color is a mirror of my own, minus the yellow-green splash of my heterochromia.

I reach out my hand toward him and take the first step to

run to the salvation he promises when he is rushed by a fresh onslaught of fighters. He falls like Gulliver covered in Lilliputians.

I cover my mouth, sobbing at the loss of my rescuer and hopelessness of the situation. My mind is finally crystal clear, my trembling limbs no longer leaden. I can't decide if this clarity is a blessing or a curse.

Deciding it's only a curse if I am caught, I search for an escape. While everyone is distracted by the fray, the men running and fighting while the women wail, I spot one. I can slip back through the jungle and into the night. If I can make my way back to the stream, I might be able to retrace my steps back to camp.

This is my only shot. I look up at the night sky, the full moon shining brightly to light my way. I'd rather take my chances with the jungle than bet on the success of my would-be rescuer. I take a step toward the safety of the trees, then hesitate, stopped by my conscience.

With a sigh, I realize I can't abandon the man who came to help me. Shocked by either my bravery, or my stupidity, I'm not sure which, I search around for a weapon. Next to an elaborate chair I suspect is meant for the elder, the firelight glints off my machete.

Someone must have given it to him as the spoils of my capture. Seeing a piece of me, of my life, casually handed over, enrages me. Digging deep into my rage for strength, I stealthily make my way over to it, thrilled when the familiar hilt is in my hand.

Out of habit, I rub my thumb over the pink leather and beads my father had lovingly wrapped around the handle when he had gifted it to me, along with the advice to always keep it with me in the jungle.

Now I see how right he was. I tighten my grip, and my

resolve, and look at the fighting mass of bodies, trying to find a point where I can help. All I can see is a writhing mass of limbs and gore. The screams and battle cries combined with the smell of blood threaten to overwhelm me.

I drop into a crouch, breathing deep through my mouth, narrowing my focus to waiting to spring into action. I see an opening and get ready to charge, knowing my rescue mission may well be a suicide mission, when my rescuer suddenly lets out a ferocious roar and stands.

The night goes deathly still as the warriors begin to back away, wide-eyed and frightened. The firelight shines behind him, but even in the dim lighting, I can see multiple blow darts and weapons lodged in his body.

His shirt hangs in tatters, revealing a blood soaked and battered body. Blood covers his mouth and drips down his chin. There is no way he should be alive. *Could* be alive.

He calmly starts to pull the implements out–knives, spears, and poison-tipped darts casually drop to the ground. As his wounds begin to heal before all of our eyes, the elder comes to stand in front of him. He reverently whispers a word in a language I've never heard and kneels at the man's feet.

The entire village falls to their knees and presses their foreheads to the ground. I look around in awe. I question, *what the hell is going on here?*

My savior pulls a few remaining darts from his body as he stalks toward me, ignoring the events around him. He doesn't spare a glance for anyone but me. I'm drawn to his intense amber gaze, riveted on mine. I must be in shock. Or maybe the drug is still warping my thoughts after all.

There is no way this man could have not only fought his way to me through an entire village, but also have his wounds heal before our eyes. He comes to stand in front of me, his face in shadow with the firelight behind him.

I'm forced to crane my head back to meet his ferocious face. This can't be real. Tentatively, I reach up a hand and swipe a finger through the blood coating his lips, black in the shadows. I bring it closer for inspection, rubbing my fingers together, disbelief propelling my actions.

The fluid is sticky between my fingers, and the smell of copper hits my nose. It is definitely blood. I look up at him, eyes wide and mouth open, blood coated fingers shaking in the moonlight, and promptly pass out.

Chapter 34

I blink my eyes open to the fading sunlight and stretch. Nothing like a nap to escape reality and refresh the soul. I love naps. I have a faint recollection of a bizarre dream that doesn't quite make sense, flickering firelight with chanting and dancing. I chalk it up to so much damn stress lately.

I sit up and my focus catches on the singular dead floral arrangement on the coffee table. How odd. I pick up the vase and carry it to the kitchen, pull the roses out over the sink, and dump the water.

I catch a strange smell and bring them to my nose. Overlaying the slightly cloying scent of the decaying flowers is sulfur. I eye my drain suspiciously. Must be the garbage disposal got funky again. Puring a big glob of soap down it, I turn it on and let the water run while I walk the roses over to the trash can.

I head back to the sink, but it smells fine now, so I turn off the horrible grinding noise. Since I'm in the kitchen, I might as well whip up some dinner. I turn on some streaming music from my phone to dance while I cook.

Poking around the fridge for inspiration, I rustle up some sad spinach in the vegetable bin. I throw that on the counter and keep digging, coming up with some heavy cream that is surprisingly not expired and a hunk of parm.

Looking over the mishmash of ingredients, I think I'll mix them all together into a pasta dish. I scrounge some spicy

Italian sausage from the freezer and throw that into a pan to thaw, while I continue to dig through my pantry. I pull out a box of the cassava pasta I keep on hand and root around in the back for something fun. Jackpot—sundried tomatoes for pizzazz.

While the sausage thaws in the pan, I dice garlic and onions. I haven't cooked like this in a long time, and it feels good. Dancing around the kitchen, I stir the sausage in my streamlined attempt to get it thawed and cooked. I'm not a chef by any means, but I'm optimistic about how this will taste.

Once the sausage looks like it's on its way, I get the pasta started. I excitedly realize I have gluten-free garlic bread in the freezer, so I pop that in the oven, too. My mouth waters in anticipation.

I sauté the onions and garlic, get fancy by deglazing the pan with some chicken stock that should be used up, and finally mix everything to let the flavors simmer and the sauce thicken.

The heavy cream sauce seems so decadent that I can't wait to try it. I think I'll call it Lieshe's pasta. Guessing it's done, I wilt in the spinach and realize I have made an inordinate amount of food.

I transfer it to a serving bowl and pull the garlic bread from the oven. *How will I ever eat all this?* I think. I wish, not for the first time, that I had someone to share my life with. Or at least this much food with.

And then it hits me. I have a very handsome, and I think more than a little sad, next-door neighbor. He said he wanted to talk. I have a ton of food. Maybe this could be a two-birds, one-stone situation.

How should I approach this? If I invite him over, he could say no, but if I bring the food over there and he says no, I could still leave some of it there. Although I was upset that I hadn't heard from him in so long, he could have any number of reasonable excuses why.

If I really think about it, I am not giving him much of a chance. I had felt such a deep connection to him after the mirror incident that I feel that I at least owe him the opportunity to talk to me as he had asked, and this peace offering is the perfect olive branch.

I cover the pasta, then wrap the garlic bread in foil to keep it warm and balance it on top. I pop into the bathroom to freshen up my hair and decide to spend a quick minute on my makeup.

And, what the hell, I head into the closet to change up my outfit. I put on a matching bra and panty set to boost my confidence and throw on a summer dress printed with bats, a pair of knee highs, and patent platform boots. I toss my phone, wallet, and keys into my red coffin backpack so I can have both hands free to carry the food.

Picking up the precarious tower, I head over to my new neighbor's house. The sun highlights the clouds on the horizon, pink and purple in its descent. As I turn from the alley to the main road, the brilliant light of the golden hour gilds the Grimm sign above my store.

I am filled with pride over my successful oddities business and the work I've put in over the years to get to where I am today. My pride bolsters my confidence as I approach McHottie's front door and knock. If I can be a kick ass business woman, I can knock on his door.

I wonder what he will say and then I wonder if he is home at all as the minutes drag by until he comes to the door, and I wonder no more. His mouth falls open for a beat when he sees me standing at his door. Then his face lights up with a glorious smile, crinkling his eyes that are flooded with warmth.

I *feel* his joy infuse into my marrow, sliding home as if it was created for me. It's the same feeling as when I fit the antique skeleton key into the lock on the door of Grimm. Two pieces created to form a perfect union together, whose only purpose of existence is to be joined.

I ponder this revelation as I see him standing there in the golden light of the setting sun. It brings out the blue highlights in his black hair and sets his amber eyes on fire. His white button down is untucked and has a couple of buttons undone to expose some of his chiseled chest. I can just make out some swirls of dark ink through his white shirt. I'm desperate to explore his tattoos and their meaning.

The dark jeans seem to emphasize the length of his legs. My gaze drops to his bare feet, feeling oddly intimate. Like I've caught him truly relaxed.

Blown away by the picture he cuts and the feelings he conjures, I stammer out, "I, uh, I made a lot of dinner and was hoping for someone to share it with?"

I hold the food out toward him like the peace offering it is. He holds my eyes for what feels like an eternity until, at last, he steps back, inviting me in.

I walk past him into his home, surrounded by his leather and tobacco smell. The faintest hint of rain teasing at my senses as I brush past him. I stand in his entryway, admiring the dark masculine colors and framed art. He walks down the hall and I follow him into a beautiful, modern kitchen.

I set the food down on a large island, appreciating the elegant black marble countertops. The room is exquisite, with deep green cabinets and black tiles offset by gold hardware and fixtures. The pendant lights are gold mercury glass with Edison bulbs. It's magazine-worthy and exactly what I would have picked for this building.

I wonder if he is an amazing cook in the face of this fancy kitchen and worry about the dinner I haphazardly threw together. I kick myself for not tasting it before I brought it over. This could be a disaster of epic proportions.

"I just realized I didn't even try this. I hope it's okay," I blurt out, suddenly unsure of myself.

"I'm sure it will be perfect."

He holds my gaze as his words wash over me. It's been so long since it was just him and me, that I wonder anew at his beautiful accent and the slow, measured cadence of his words.

"White or red?" he asks.

"Um, white?"

He turns and goes to a wine fridge set under the counter. He returns with a bottle and two stemless glasses, then gathers plates and utensils. I stand idly by, watching his shirt strain under muscles that flex and ripple with his movements. I selfishly hope he splits a seam.

He makes up two plates and pours two generous glasses of wine. He tucks the bottle under his arm, picks up the plates, and heads down the hallway with them as I follow behind with the wine glasses.

We enter an exquisite open concept living area with exposed brick and light fixtures like the kitchen. Reclaimed hardwood floors gleam in the low light, and he sets the two plates on a natural wood living edge coffee table in front of a low leather sectional couch.

His entire place is opulent and masculine. So stunning I wonder if he has a professional decorator. I sink into the buttery leather couch and hope I'm able to eat dinner and drink wine without spilling anything on myself. Or his beautiful couch or rug.

He picks up his wineglass and meets my eyes. Lifting his glass to me, he says, "*Noroc.*"

"Cheers," I reply, gently tapping my glass to his and taking a sip while I ponder hot guys who speak foreign languages. I never could roll my R's like that.

The white wine blooms bright on my tongue, not too dry or too sweet. It's like the goldilocks of wine. Sunshine and magic explode on my palate. This is not like the boxed stuff in the back of my fridge.

"This is incredible," I gush.

"Like you. It's an 1811 *Château d'Yquem.* There's no one else I would rather share it with." His eyes blaze with sincerity.

I take another sip and savor the delicious wine before I swallow and then pick up my plate, digging into my pasta, surprised at just how good it is.

"I'm so happy we could share dinner together. I was, uh, feeling bad. You know, about earlier."

He takes another sip and sets his wineglass down, turning his body to face me head-on. "You have nothing to apologize for. I am the one who has failed you."

Wow. I thought I was hard on myself. "I mean, I was kinda surprised when I didn't hear from you for a while, but I wouldn't say you failed me."

He gives me a thankful smile and picks up his plate. We eat in companionable silence for a while, and even I must admit, this dinner is fantastic—the company and wine are the perfect complements.

Half way through my plate, I feel the need to break the silence and say, "Your home is beautiful. Did you hire a designer?"

I look around the open room, appreciating the rich, dark colors and unique artwork on the walls, some exposed brick and some matte black. He has multiple pieces from Dante, including "Dante and Virgil in Hell" above the leather sectional where we are sitting.

In the dining room, he has Van Gogh's "Skull with Burning Cigarette." The artwork appears to be super high-quality reproductions. They could almost pass for the real thing. I'm seriously impressed with his taste.

"I'm glad you like it," he replies as he tops off my wine glass.

I mop up the remnants of the sauce with my last bite of garlic bread and set down my plate, stuffed. I lean back into the soft leather sofa and swirl the last of the lemony yellow wine in my glass.

"I thought that was a famous Van Gogh painting, but now I see it's not quite the same." It looks like it could be a companion piece to it, though.

"You are right," is his vague answer.

I take the final sip, savoring it. We've polished off the bottle and I'm happy that he seems to have genuinely enjoyed the dinner. It was delicious. I'll have to make it again.

"Thank you for sharing dinner with me," I say sincerely.

This dinner together has been lovely. It feels so, well, comfortable is the only way to describe it. Like we've done this a thousand times before. I didn't feel awkward eating in front of him, wondering if I was chewing too loudly or eating too much. We just ate and enjoyed each other's company. Like an old married couple.

"My pleasure."

His voice practically purrs over the last word, and I feel it deep into my core. We angle our bodies to better face each other, leaning in at the same time. Our faces inch closer together as we both fall into a heated stare.

"I should probably go," I murmur, breaking the moment. But what I really mean is, I want to stay, and I hope he tries to talk me into it.

He glances at his watch, which looks suspiciously like a Patek Phillipe, and replies, "It's early. How about a movie and some gelato a little later?"

I'm such a sucker for gelato. I challenge, "What flavor?"

He scoffs, "The only one that counts. Pistachio."

Oh, a low blow. Pistachio is my absolute favorite. "You had me a gelato. What movie?"

His answer could be a deal breaker. If he proposes a rom-com, I'm out, gelato or not.

"I was hoping for something scary, so you'd have no choice but to jump into my arms," he replies with his panty-melting smile.

This new playful and flirty side of him is fun to see. I feel so relaxed and comfortable with him, especially now we seem past any hard feelings or lingering tension from the early disastrous confrontation between him and Luke.

"Okay, but none of the new modern nonsense."

He mocks being affronted. "Of course not. I was thinking of a classic horror movie like Frankenstein, Night of the Living Dead, or perhaps Dracula."

He waggles his eyebrows at me as he says Dracula and, with his accent, I dissolve into giggles. He laughs softly and stands up to clear the plates. I move to help, but he motions me back down, so I pull the luxurious throw from the back of the couch across my lap.

I unzip my knee-high platform boots and drop them to the floor so I can curl my legs up under the blanket. After a few minutes, he returns and holds out a hand to me.

"Can I bring this blanket?" I might just steal it, obsessed with the serious fluff.

"Of course, but let's head to my theater room."

Uh-oh. Is this a Netflix and chill situation? I wrap the amazing throw around my shoulders and follow him up a set of stairs to the second floor, where we enter an entertainment room.

There are vintage horror movie posters on the walls above a popcorn maker and bar along one wall. A leather loveseat with an end table on each side faces an enormous big screen TV. I really love his place.

"This is incredible. I'd watch movies here all the time!" I exclaim.

"It's more fun with someone to enjoy it with."

He's not wrong. He sits down on the leather loveseat and hits a button on the side to recline. I sit next to him and do the same, throwing the soft throw I've carried up with me over both of us.

He lifts his arm in invitation, which I gladly accept, burrowing into his side. Reclining the chairs, we can really sprawl out, which is good considering his tall frame takes up most of the space, even with his body angled well into mine.

I sink into the supple leather, in the most comfortable theater seats to exist. If I had this setup, I'd never go out. He pulls up a menu of movies and starts clicking through.

"Oh, Night of the Living Dead! I haven't seen that in forever."

He clicks on it, and we watch in companionable silence. I'm thankful for the posh blanket since snuggling into his cool side steals my body heat. As the movie plays, our bodies naturally gravitate toward the other, and the next thing I know, our legs are entwined like a pretzel.

About halfway through, I let out a few yawns, so he hits

pause and smiles at me before untangling himself to grab the previously promised gelato.

He brings me back a bowl of the best pistachio gelato I've ever had and then makes two Old Fashioneds and sets one down next to me. I am impressed to see a real cherry rather than one of those red dye monstrosities.

I offer him a bite of the gelato when he sits again, but he shakes his head. I enjoy the creamy treat as we sit together, watching the end of the vintage horror movie.

"Last chance," I say, holding the spoon out. He again shakes his head. I scoop the last spoonful into my mouth, saying, "Your loss."

"I'd rather taste it off your lips," he says in a low, gravelly voice.

I whip my head to face him and see the heat in his eyes. Inspired to take decisive action, I take the spoon and scrape up the last few drops, painting my lips with them as he watches.

He holds my eyes as he slowly and deliberately takes the bowl from me and sets it on the end table next to him. Their amber color looks like fire with the desire I see reflected in them.

Before I can process what is happening, he dives across the loveseat, fisting his hand in the back of my hair and licking his warm, wet tongue over the seam of my lips.

I gasp at his sudden tackle, and he takes advantage of my surprise, thrusting his tongue into my mouth and moaning deep in his throat. I come alive under his touch, tangling my tongue with his, nipping at his lips.

Wrapping my arms around his narrow waist, I skim my hands up the corded muscles of his back, again wondering at the rough texture of his skin. The lingering bite of the bourbon on his tongue cuts through the sweetness of the gelato I just ate, turning the kiss into a heady combination.

We make out like teenagers as the credits roll, all roving hands and grinding bodies. Our clothes stay on, but that somehow adds to the thrill of it all. He kisses me as if he is starving for me, touches me as if he is trying to pull me inside his own body. Finally, we break apart, panting.

"That was some good gelato," he quips with a smile that crinkles his eyes.

After Luke's intensity and domineering nature, this is all so normal and real. And good. It feels really good.

I have a brief thought about what making out with two guys on the same day means. The reproach I envision from my father tries to worm its way into my head, trailing shame in its wake like a dirty oil-slicked puddle on the side of the road.

I firmly push it from the corners of my mind, saying to myself, *you have no power over me.* In my heart, I know I'm doing nothing wrong as both interests, for lack of a better title, are in their infancy. It feels good to claim my sexuality and my body as my own, separate from my past and the societal paradigms forced upon me.

But I also know that as happy as I am to reconnect with McHottie, and as much as I've enjoyed appreciating each other's bodies, I'm not ready to take things any further tonight. I need time to process, not for my dad or for society, but for me.

As we break apart and return to a sitting position, it feels amazing to be back under his arm. No pressure, no huffing for 'teasing', just two adults who enjoyed a good old-fashioned make-out session.

I pick up my drink now that I have a free hand. Even with

the melting ice, it's one of the best cocktails I've ever had. The movie long over, I stand and straighten my clothes.

Making out was great, but I don't want to overstay. My eye is drawn to his crotch as he adjusts himself, not quite hiding the bulge in the front of his jeans. Before I can get second thoughts about not hopping on his disco stick, I start my goodbye.

"Thanks for sharing dinner with me. It was nice not to eat alone," I tell him sincerely.

"You should never be alone," he replies in his slow, musical way of speaking. I could drown in his voice. "It's still early. One more movie. I'll fire up the popcorn maker and fix you another drink. Besides, it's not like you have to drive home."

Twist my arm. I pretend to mull it over. "Well, it is a pretty good offer. I mean, you do have popcorn. And bourbon."

His face lights up, and I feel ten feet tall that I made him look that way. He walks over to the popcorn machine, and I follow him, watching curiously as he gets the kernels ready, followed by both ghee and coconut oil.

"Trust me, I've got this recipe down."

He looks at me earnestly, and I get the strange feeling that he's talking about more than the popcorn. Like he *needs* me to trust him, and it is absolutely imperative to him to have it. Before I can overthink it, I step into him and reach up, cupping his face.

"Ok, I'll trust you."

I barely know him. We just met. But I feel something deep in my soul that wants to meet him halfway, wants to satisfy his craving for my trust. The deep feeling flutters and I think, *is this it? If I open my heart, will this be love?*

He leans down, bringing our foreheads together, noses

touching tip to tip. We breathe each other in for a few heartbeats, basking in the breaking dawn of something new. Something beautiful and precious until we are startled apart, laughing, by the popping of the first kernels.

I lean against the bar and watch him make two more cocktails while the popcorn pops away. This time, he makes Manhattans while I check out his impressive bourbon collection. He grabs a bottle of Pappy Van Winkle and starts to put it into the drinks.

"Seriously, you're going to use that as a mixer?" I squeal, interrupting him.

"Why not? It's to enjoy, not sit on a shelf."

"Oh dude, this is some serious sacrilege. I'll take a taste of the Pappy and then we can use an everyday sipper as the mixer."

He smiles and rolls his eyes good-naturedly, fetching a Glencairn and pouring a generous measure of Pappy. I can't believe he was going to use it as a mixer. Sacrilege, truly.

I take the Glencairn and do the Kentucky Chew to appreciate the unicorn bourbon that I'm certain I'll never get to have again. It's smooth and delicious, with notes of vanilla, cherry, oak, and, of all things, candy corn. The finish brings notes of oak and raspberry.

Huh. Now I see what the fuss is about. Still not sure I would pay market price for it, but glad to have had a taste. I feel his intense stare and turn to look at him.

He reaches out and traces from my temple down to my jawline with a tentative finger, saying, "I want to sample you like you sampled that bourbon. I want to breathe your bouquet and savor your taste on my tongue."

My eyebrows shoot up into my hairline, the fine bourbon drying to dust in my mouth. I don't know what else he could have said that could have shocked me more. A small breathy reply slips past my lips, "Oh."

Our eyes lock in a smoldering stare. My imagination runs wildly with abandon, as I can picture all too clearly those amber eyes and black wavy hair peeking up at me while his mouth is blissfully engaged elsewhere.

"Shit, the popcorn!" He turns and begins finishing up the popcorn right as it starts burning.

I giggle at hearing his usual formal speech break into the vernacular. I'm thankful he saved the snack because I need something in my belly to soak up all the booze he's plied me with. It is also a welcome distraction after so much tension.

I pick up our drinks and set them on the end tables on either side of our fancy recliner seats. We sit back down, the bowl of popcorn a safe barrier between us. He starts up my favorite movie of all time, Dracula, and as I snuggle down into the blanket, I must admit, this feels like fate.

He lets me eat the lion's share of the popcorn as we sip our Manhattans. Once the bowl is empty, he sets it aside, and we end up snuggled back together. Despite the massive difference in our size, we fit together perfectly, like two pieces of the same puzzle.

Feeling his eyes on me, I turn my head to him, shocked at the way he studies me—eyes lit with pure adoration. I blush and duck my head, not used to feeling beautiful or worshiped.

Butterflies take wing in my too-tight chest. I inhale a shaky breath of familiar tobacco and leather, and the subtle, clean scent of rain that I can only catch at close proximity.

I climb into his lap and stare deep into his amber eyes, losing myself in their mystery. *Why are our eyes the same?* My focus drifts back and forth between his, as if their amber depths hold the answer to my question.

He threads both hands into my hair and pulls me into him, placing featherlight kisses on my forehead, each closed eye, my nose. Everywhere but my mouth.

Between each kiss he murmurs with heartbreaking sweetness, "Любовь моя. Свет мой. Я прешел вечность, чтобы найти тебя, лишь чтобы потерять тебя снова и снова. Останься, моя любовь, останься. Моя душа не может выжить без тебя. Прошу тебя, не оставляй меня во тьме снова. (Lyubov' moya. Svet moy. Ya preshel vechnost', chtoby nayti tebya, leesh' chtoby poteryat' tebya snova i snova. Ostan'sya, moya lyubov', ostan'sya. Moya dusha ne mozh-et vyzh-eeht' bez tebya. Proshu tebya, ne ostavlyay menya vo t'me snova)."

His foreign words somehow feel familiar, deepening my desire for him, for us, until his touch finally drives all the questions from my mind as together we explore the greatest mystery of all time—how two bodies can fit together so perfectly.

I'm frantic for his lips to meet mine and can't help but grind down into him, seeking friction. His pecs are cool and hard beneath my hands. After what feels like eternity, his lips find mine and he gently kisses me.

Small kisses turn heated, and as impatient as I am to kiss him deeper, I let him lead our mouths in the slowest dance. The sweetness is killing me. He leisurely increases his passion one single degree at a time. The building tension is almost painful, and when he finally licks the seam of my lips which bloom open for him, I'm lost.

The butterflies from my chest take flight and soar. Suddenly our passion knows no bounds, and we are kissing like there was no yesterday, there is no tomorrow, there is only this moment, here and now. And the only reason for our existence is *this* kiss.

I fall into him, our kiss deepening until I don't know where he begins and I end. This! This is what I had always thought love would feel like. Losing myself, becoming one. Before I know what is happening, my hips are grinding against him of their own volition.

My mouth seems to know every inch of his, my hands recognize each dip and ridge of his hard muscles beneath me, like we've mapped each other's bodies a thousand times before and kissed a thousand times more than that.

Bone deep recognition echoes through my body and I know, *I know*, beyond a shadow of a doubt, this is not the first time our souls have met. I know him. Truly know him. Is this what destiny feels like? Is this what it feels like to have two halves finally become whole?

Recognition amplifies my rising need, and I wantonly thrust against him, seeking purchase in this maelstrom. My hands are fisted in his shirt as I try to absorb him into my very being, rational thought giving way to pure animalistic need.

A claiming. I don't want him. I need him like I need air to breathe and light to see.

I.

Need.

Him.

He snakes one arm around my waist, aiding me in my frantic writhing, and anchors the other hand in my hair, tilting my head where he wants it. He moans into the kiss as he impossibly deepens it.

As my pleasure rises, I'm forced to break away from his intoxicating kiss, gasping in desperately needed oxygen. He sharply pulls my head back further, exposing the long line of my neck only to run his nose over my pulse point, inhaling deeply.

I'm so damn close. I feel pleasure building deep inside my core and fervently wish we didn't have on all these damn clothes. Despite my desperate movements and our rising passion, I need something to push me over the precipice through our layers of separation.

As frustrated whimpers fall from my mouth, he must know exactly what I need as he traces my pulse point in a heated, open-mouthed kiss. I shiver in delight as his mouth is searing in contrast to the usual chill of his skin.

So.

Damn.

Close.

I chase my orgasm, grinding my pelvis into him, finding the edge of his hardness trapped below me. I let my head tip back, rewarded when his kiss morphs into a sharp sting followed by absolute, exquisite, soul-drenching pleasure.

This. This is what I needed.

My mind flashes back to my dream when we first met, of his vampire's kiss. With that image in my mind and Bela Lugosi's voice in the movie playing in the background, I finally ride the wave of pleasure to its peak and crest, grinding out my release against him, my empty pussy clenching in perfect harmony to the flexing of his lips against my neck.

Flashes of the two of us, climaxes superimposed on each other, flip through my mind like a high-speed slide show. Thousands of images, each one like a small spark extending my pleasure until I bite my lip, breathing hard, no longer able to hold back my keening cries as I ride out the last fading spasms.

As I rejoin the land of the living, frantically trying to catch my breath and figure out what the hell just happened to my brain, he whispers sweetly against my neck, "*Roză*."

Although earlier I was happy to let his sweet but incomprehensible whispers wash over me, this single word brings my swirling thoughts to a screeching halt. I give up trying to figure out if I just had some type of visual hallucination or seizure, as this single word takes root in my melting brain.

I think he just called me some version of Rose.

Rose. Why is this concerning?

Alarm bells go off as I try to figure out why I'm bothered he would use 'Rose' as a term of endearment for me. That doesn't even sound like my name. Maybe that is something from his language?

My brain stumbles over thoughts of how roses could somehow be connected to me until at last a vivid image of me reaching out and stroking a midnight red petal crystalizes in my mind.

Oh, shit. Was it him? Did he fill my home with flowers? Did he break into my house?

"What did you call me?"

I watch the passion fade from his eyes.

"What?" he asks.

He knows exactly what I am hinting at. I'm convinced he does.

"What did you call me?" I enunciate each word with artic chill.

Time slows, my languid muscles start tensing until my entire body is rigid with fury. My brain starts ringing warning bells while my heart, my poor heart, breaks into a million shattered pieces.

My mother had few pretty things, too worldly, but she had one beautiful Waterford crystal vase. One day I had been playing make believe with my dolls, wishing I had a real Barbie. A brand name Barbie from a pink box with blonde hair and blue eyes rather than the generic, church-sanctioned, far less sexy version approved by my father.

That sparkly vase on the top shelf of the China cabinet full of boring white company dishes was so pretty, and in my child's mind, it would make the most amazing addition to the sad cardboard faux-Barbie house I had made.

I pulled over a chair and carefully climbed up. I stretched and stretched until at last, on my very tippy toes, I hooked my little fingertips into the thick rim of that vase. I carefully inched it toward me, and just when it was in my grasp, my father yelled my name. As I spun around in surprise, my fingers slipped off the rim, and it fell.

I dropped the only beautiful thing my mother had. A wedding gift from her mother. And down, down, down it fell, scattering rainbows on its descent until finally it hit the floor, shattering on impact and sending crystal shards everywhere. I was hysterical with fear of my father, but even worse was the incredible sadness I felt at causing my mother pain.

Her special vase lay in a million jagged pieces at my feet. It was gone and there was nothing I could do. Just like now, all I can do is watch my heart fall to the floor at my feet and shatter into a million jagged pieces, just like that fucking vase.

A pile of beautiful, worthless shards.

"*Rozǎ*," he breathes, not letting me go.

I narrow my eyes, staring back at the uncanny amber so reflective of my own. My voice breaks and I barely get out, "Was it you?"

He looks abashed. "Was it me what?"

"Was it you who filled my home with roses? Was it you who broke into my home, violated my trust, and scared me half to death? Was. It. You?"

My chest is heaving, my voice rising in anger as the longer I talk, he doesn't answer. But I already know the truth.

There's no going back. I couldn't put the vase back together. I couldn't take away my mother's sob as my father told her with relish, throwing out my only faux-Barbie, declaring it the devil's doll. And now, I don't know how I will be able to glue the pieces of my heart back together either.

Damn it.

Fucking damn it to hell. Of course, he's a stalker. Of-fucking-course I would attract the crazy hot guy. Not the regular hot guy or even the average-looking but blessedly normal guy. He's a unicorn. The hotness and crazy are exponentially related.

I can't believe I started falling for the crazy stalker man. With rising dread, I realize, the crazy stalker man who is my neighbor! I can't escape him if I wanted to.

"Please let me go," I whisper.

My chest gets tighter, and those poor butterflies taking flight? They die. I'm filled with death's-head hawk moths. Dead ones at that. Of course, no freaking sunshine and rainbow butterflies for me! Of course, no happy fucking endings.

I kick myself for, once again, reaching for more, thinking I could be more, have more.

Pushing off him, I spring off the loveseat and stomp down the stairs. I sit down on the couch to get the damn knee-high boots back on, once again cursing my fashion sense for interfering with practicality.

The boots are a serious impedance right now to my dramatic exit. I finally get them back on and continue my stomp, which sounds much more satisfying now with the solid soles on, to the front door.

He chases after me. "Please. Lieshe, please stop. Let me explain."

I continue my angry stomp. His voice is like a hammer on the broken crystal shards of my heart. If I let myself, I could hear the pain, the absolute devastation in his voice. But I can't. I'm too busy trying to keep one last little piece safe for me.

One last little piece to keep my heart beating. I need something to push the blood through my shaking limbs, to keep my rational mind pushing me toward safety. I latch on to my anger to get me through.

"At least let me walk you home."

"Nope," I sass, popping the p. "I'm fine to walk by myself," I throw over my shoulder. I know I sound like a petulant toddler right now, but I can't even stop myself. I'm angry. Betrayed. Hurt. And so extremely disappointed.

Deep down, I know I really will be fine. I'm always fine. I've survived worse and fallen back on that stupid word a million times before. Home is right around the corner, and I think the most dangerous thing in the neighborhood is now pursuing me down his hallway.

I don't let the sneaky feelings of how nice it is to have someone worried about me and wanting to protect me worm their way into my head or heart. Nope, stalker man doesn't get to make me feel cherished or wanted. Not after what he did.

He follows a few feet behind me as I stomp the whole way to the corner, down the alley, and up the stairs leading up to my door. All this stomping feels a little foolish, but I can't stop now. I'm committed.

As I start up the stairs, I look over my shoulder to make sure he isn't following me. Because I don't want him to.

No, really, I don't want him to have a reasonable

explanation for any of this or follow me up and salvage what was a beautiful burgeoning beginning. Of course, he is still standing at the bottom of the stairs, staring at my door and scowling.

"What?" I snap crossly, wrapping myself in anger like a sad attempt at fixing that vase with scotch tape.

"Nothing. Good evening," he murmurs as he turns and walks away.

I throw open my door and slam it closed, racing across to the kitchen windows, so I can watch him walk back to his place. Just one more look at this man that I had been falling hard for. But after several minutes, I still don't see him. He could have gone for a walk or something to blow off some steam.

For some reason, not seeing him makes me far sadder than it should. I shake off the strange disappointment, double-check the lock and deadbolt on the door again, and head to the bathroom to get ready for bed. Fuck this day. Fuck my life. And fuck him.

Chapter 35

HIM

Seeing Luke's mark on her door enrages me all over again. She is mine. I miss the days where there was no end to my ability to exhaust my anger and I could paint the world red with it. But the world is a different place now, and I had turned away from that dark time, vowing to never become that monster again.

Yet the darkness of the night calls to me, so I walk around the windowless alley where I know I will not attract the wrong attention and let myself shift into my bat form, fluttering up in graceful swooping arcs that feel like a direct contradiction to the despair pulsing in my veins.

As I soar up into the cold, clear night, I let my mind drift back, long before this time, to the first time I had shifted. I had wanted to escape that time into the cold, dark sky as well.

Back then, crystal clear stars filled the night, so unlike the murky skies of today. That flight had felt like I was soaring amongst the stars themselves, leaving my human form behind with its bleeding heart.

I had flown deep into the desert and into the safety of a cave, far from anything. And there I stayed for years and years, lost in my misery. Until I felt her calling me from my self-imposed exile. I pursued the strange pulling sensation, following it to the source.

I had watched her from the shadows, confused, scared to even breathe, hoping against hope that it was my beloved, returned to me. She had been gathering water from a well, but paused and looked out into the setting sun, shielding her eyes. In the shadow of her hand, I saw them, the same golden eyes I had lived and breathed for, and knew it was her.

The pools of gold were different now, one stained with our curse. With him. But I recognized her soul despite the change in her eyes. *I saw her.* And in my excitement, I ruined everything in that lifetime through a string of clumsy and clueless mistakes. Not just that one, but so many others. Stuck on repeat, my torture knows no end.

I swoop in a few more lazy arcs, bringing my mind back to the present, and come to rest on her roof, right where I know her bed to be. I lay above her, feeling her soul pulse below me.

I transform back to my original form as a sorry excuse of a man and work to calm my breaking heart by imagining her essence pulsing in my veins, coursing through like iridescent honey. I envision it chasing away the darkness and the anger, leaving pure love and light in its wake.

My body responds to every thought of her, but I push the physical feelings away and retreat into my mind, losing myself in lifetimes of memories. And once again, I fight the desperation that I have ruined yet another one. Because I cannot fathom surviving any longer without her. One way or another, this will be the last time.

One day slowly plods into the next. I go through the motions of my life, but my mind is stuck in rumination mode. I turn over each moment I spent with McHottie and analyze it for truths and lies, hidden agendas, and motivations.

By turns I am suspicious, sad, angry, irritated, and everything in between. I'm also thankful that I hadn't fallen completely in love with him, but it had been a damn close call.

All has been quiet on the Luke front as well, though I'm not surprised after the disastrous way our last encounter ended. I'm secretly grateful. I need to focus on myself and my internal growth. Both of these infuriating men are so damn distracting.

I also consider resuming counseling with the childhood memories and insecurities that have been dredged back up. Between that and the waking dreams that have returned, I know if I stay on this path without intervention, I could spiral. Finding the time is the hardest part, but this isn't optional.

I surf around and choose an online app with good reviews and book an appointment. I really miss Dr. Sam, my college counselor, but I know she would be proud of me for reaching out for help when I need it.

I continue to firm up details for my impending trip to Europe, but even that cannot cheer me up. The entire thing now feels like one big to-do list rather than an epic adventure.

As the dog days of summer hit, so do a week of thunderstorms, which suit my mood just fine. They slow down the foot traffic of the seasonal tourists, but I'm not upset with the disruption in business.

I really need the time to think, to force my body to move faster when it feels like I'm in quicksand. The downtime also allows me to do my counseling intake appointment. I'm incredibly proud of myself for prioritizing my mental health.

I double-check all my reservations and have heard from everyone except Wren, which makes me nervous. Meeting up with Wren is one of the main reasons I had planned this trip.

She is my go-to taxidermist and preservation specialist. When she told me she would be in Europe and would meet me to check out the taxidermy raven I was going to purchase, I was ecstatic.

I emailed her a few days ago but haven't heard back, so I decide I'll try to call her instead. Email is not foolproof, yet another reason I fall back on the old-fashioned method of communication—the phone.

I never know where Wren is, so I figure I'll just call and see if she answers, hoping it's not the middle of the night wherever she is. She may be out of touch, tracking down some obscure oddity in a far-flung corner of the world.

If I didn't have a brick and mortar, I'd be tempted to do the same. She has the most incredible stories of her worldwide travels and comes back with amazing treasures. I'm sure it sounds way more romantic than it actually is.

I'm not surprised when I get her voicemail, so I leave a message for her to call me back. However, I am surprised when, just as I hang up, my phone rings.

"Wren!"

"Hey, sorry, I've been in and out of service chasing down some cool things. We're still on for Europe, right?"

"Of course! I can't wait to see you again. It's been a minute."

"Lieshe, it's been way too long! You sound a little off. Is everything okay?"

I sigh, debating how I want to respond. "There's been a lot going on here. But I'm really looking forward to seeing you."

"Well, I've been thinking. This might be too much added stress, and if so, let me know and no hard feelings. But it also may be exactly what you need, since I know it's always been a dream for you. Romania is not too much further from where we'll already be."

"Romania? Why would we go to Romania?" I gasp.

"Dracula's castle! I know Dracula is one of your favorite movies, so we could check the castle out. It's only a couple hours away by plane, and I have a few extra days to spare. How cool would it be to bring back some real Romanian oddities for your store?"

Dracula's castle. I could see the real Dracula's castle. I feel goosebumps skate over my skin. Wren's right. When else would I get the chance to do this? This is exactly the distraction I need. Something just for me.

Between Jo coming to cover the shop and now having hired Anna on, I could have the extra time away. And I could really use something to cheer me up.

"Abso-fucking-lutely brilliant Wren, I'd love to go!" I don't even have to overthink this. I have always wanted to, but never dreamed it would happen. I have no excuses not to go and every reason to go.

This new development has me excited about my trip all over again. Now I will have something to direct my energy into. The perfect distraction from the man whose voice made me think of Dracula. Or will it be the perfect reminder, I wonder?

I will not mope. It's time to move on. I'm not turning down one of my bucket list items because of stalker-boy's voice. I will not deny myself the happiness I deserve. If anything, this is a wake-up call. I can hear Mom in my heart saying, "Onwards and upwards, honey."

We wrap up our conversation, with Wren assuring me she will shoot me the details. I set up a group text with Anna and Jo to send out the new dates for the trip. I'm thrilled when they both text back those dates work for them. The adventure is far enough out that I can still tweak my flights, so I log on and change my return flight.

I'm amazed at how everything is falling into place. I can't believe I am finally going to see Dracula's castle. For the first time in weeks, my face cracks into a true smile. I say out loud to Mom, "Onwards and upwards, Mama."

Lucifer startles at my outburst, casting some serious side eye toward me from the barstool, but still follows me as I head into my closet. I unearth my suitcase, which he promptly claims as his new perch and start pulling out potential outfits to pack.

I get a few foundation pieces picked out when I hear my phone chime with a text message. Looking down, I expect to see another group text about the trip, but an unknown number comes up.

UNKNOWN

Miss me?

LIESHE

Me, who?

UNKNOWN

3 guesses

LIESHE

I literally have no idea.

What the hell? I'm not up for games. My gut churns, wondering if this is Stalky Hottie.

UNKNOWN

How utterly disappointing.

Exasperated, I think about just blocking whatever creeper this is, but my curiosity gets the best of me.

LIESHE

FFS just tell me.

UNKNOWN

Now where is the fun in that, mon petit chou?

I audibly gasp. Of course, he would just pop back up.

LIESHE

Luke?

UNKNOWN

There's my good girl 😈

He sends his contact and I save it to my phone, laughing that now when he texts, it pops up differently.

MY LORD

Now, have you missed me?

Have I missed him? Absolutely. I also am kinda irritated, wondering where he has been in the couple of weeks since I saw him. With everything that has happened, I feel a little snarky and decide to mess with him as retribution.

LIESHE
Kinda

I see the three dots pop up to show he is typing and then they stop. They appear and then disappear again. Crap. I wonder if I overplayed my hand. I cringe and then he replies.

MY LORD
Kinda? I'll remember that.

I type several messages and then delete them before sending. I don't want to appear clingy, and he owes me no explanation as to where he has been. But he also deserves some shit for his disappearing act.

LIESHE
You didn't seem to miss me.

He doesn't even read my reply, and after five minutes of anxiously staring at my phone, I toss it to the side and go back to packing in a huff. I feel like an epic failure as a flirt. I hate technology. From shoddy Wi-Fi to not getting the tone of a text right, we just don't seem to get along.

I crank up some music and make good progress on the first round of my packing. I always over pack, so I've learned to gather everything I want and then do a few rounds of editing.

I want to be efficient, since I'll be traveling so much on this trip. And now I've added another country. I'll have to start a new page in my binder and do some research on the weather of Romania during our visit and what I'll need.

After pulling out some outfits that include layering for all weather possibilities, I shuffle my trip stuff to the side of my closet to edit tomorrow. For now, I'll reward myself for getting started.

I head out to the kitchen and dig in the fridge for something to eat, but really nothing sounds good. With a sigh, I pull a frozen pizza from the freezer and toss it into the oven. To cheer myself up, I pour a small glass of my favorite tequila.

I swirl the golden liquid around the glass to get it chilled from the two skull ice cubes and take a sip while I scroll through our new social media accounts Anna set up. The oven timer goes off, and I pull out my sad little pizza. I cut it into fours and throw half of it on a paper plate. I'm eating high class tonight.

I keep scrolling, getting drawn in by book reviews and funny memes, and absentmindedly take a large bite. I drop the phone and start panting as cheese the temperature of liquid hot magma hits the roof of my mouth. Lucifer stares at me with judgmental unblinking yellow eyes, unamused by my open-mouthed breathing.

I grab my drink and fill my mouth with ice cold tequila. *Social media really is dangerous,* I think. I scowl at the offending pizza and decide to let it cool while I grab a seltzer. I hear my phone chime with an incoming text message and my heart races, wondering if Luke is replying.

I snatch it up only to see another unknown number. Curiosity piqued, I swipe my text messages open.

UNKNOWN

I'm in town. We're going out, little pet.

Pet? Who the hell would call me that? I wonder how everyone is getting my phone number. Is it scrawled on the bathroom wall somewhere I don't know about?

LIESHE

Who is this?

An incoming contact comes in and when I click it, a stunning picture of a redhead wearing devil horns pops up with the name Fire Goddess. How on earth did Luke's 'maybe sister' get my number? And more importantly, why on earth would she invite me out when she obviously doesn't even like me?

LIESHE

Out? You know where I live?

I question my sanity as I entertain the thought of going out with this girl. I really don't know her at all. But I know that if I say no, I might regret not going for the rest of my life. I just know she has to be absolute trouble when she's out. Like arrested on the front page of the news trouble.

I'm also intrigued by the possibility of getting some insider info on Luke. I look at the clock. It's already eight and I'm on my second tequila. I'll need it to face her. Fuck it, let's do this. Apparently, it's a "yes" night and I'm up for anything from international travel to local mayhem.

FIRE GODDESS

30 minutes. Be ready.

LIESHE

I didn't even say yes yet! Where are we
going?

She doesn't reply. Poor communication must run in the family. Guess I'm going out–somewhere. I take a chance and text Anna to see if she can cover the store for me tomorrow since I have a feeling I will get in a little late. Or a lot.

I pick up my now lukewarm pizza and fold the two pieces over on each other into a giant sandwich and head back to my closet while I wolf it down.

I stare at the disarray, trying to figure out what the hell to wear. Anything will seem like a burlap sack next to the "Fire Goddess." I really need to get her name since I am *not* calling her that. I admire her big dick energy, though. She could teach lessons. Maybe hanging out with her will do me good.

I finish my pizza while flipping through hangers, quickly dismissing almost everything I own. It doesn't help that I do not know where we are going. I don't want to be completely off, so settle for a black skater dress and pair it with my red Chelsea boots and red coffin backpack.

I think it's cute and flattering. I would normally have worn my red fishnets with this outfit, but someone ripped the crotch out of mine, and I hadn't gotten around to replacing them yet.

I rummage through my drawer to find the perfect bra and panty set, hoping to channel some big dick energy myself, then sprint to the bathroom to do my hair and makeup. I change into the lingerie and do a quick curl refresh with a spray bottle and conditioner.

Leaving my hair to air dry, I start my makeup. I glance at my watch and see I only have fifteen minutes left until she is supposed to pick me up. Rushing to finish, I pair a smokey cat eye with a bold red lip. I'm just about to get dressed when I hear a brusque knock.

Of course, she's early.

I hurriedly throw my dress on and head to the front door. Since she's early, she is going to have to wait for me to finish up. I answer the door to her staring down, texting. She is wearing a draped fringe dress in her signature bright red. I'm convinced there no lining since I'm pretty sure I can see her nipples peeking out.

She brushes past me, saying, "Nice door," as she bumps my shoulder.

I look at my door and frown, not understanding what she is talking about. It's just a door. McHottie had also cast disparaging glances at it. Weird.

I turn around and follow her into my house. She puts her phone away and looks at me with a raised eyebrow. Before she can get off a snarky comment, I defend myself, saying, "You're early."

"What are you wearing?" She gives me the once over with a blank face.

"A black dress? You never said where we are going," I say as I look down at myself. I think my outfit is okay.

She crosses her arms, pushing up her already impressive cleavage, and rolls her eyes, saying, "It's not only exceedingly boring, but inside out. Take me to your closet."

"Take me to your leader," I reply in my best robot voice. She just stares at me, not so much as a twitch of the mouth. *Awkward.* I thought I was funny.

As I lead the way, I smile to myself as I picture her as the sexy, glamorous Barbie doll I always wanted as a child. If Barbie was a redhead from hell with the attitude of a succubus. Then I think, *maybe she asked me out tonight because she needs a friend.*

My mindset thaws a little as I think of her as having a hard outer shell of rock-solid confidence but a sweet and lonely center. Like a chocolate-covered cherry. By the time I open the closet door, I'm smiling at my analogy and planning to be her best friend.

"What a fucking mess," she huffs at me, again bumping

my shoulder as she walks past me and starts rifling through my clothes.

Okay, friend might be too strong a word. We can start as acquaintances first. She spies the black garment bag toward the back and pounces on it like a cat.

"Aha!" She spins to face me, her feline smile so like Luke's, I can't believe they aren't twins. "I bet there's something positively dripping in here."

She hangs it on the back of the closet door and unzips it, pulling out the corset. "Now this is more like it."

"I'm not sure I want to go out in a corset," I say with hesitation, but she seems so excited about it.

She narrows her eyes at me and the side of her mouth quirks up as she says, "Oh."

Giving a little shrug, she starts to zip up the bag. She singsongs, "I just thought you'd want to surprise Luke by wearing it."

"Luke? We're going to see Luke?" She's got me. If I'm going to see Luke, then I want to knock his socks off after the weird exchange earlier. "Well, I guess I could wear the corset. But what should I wear with it?"

She claps her hands excitedly and gives a little bounce. I can't keep up with her shifting mood. She is a mercurial little thing. Turning toward my rack of skirts and pants, she quickly flips through them, coming up with a leather skirt.

I vaguely recall buying it and shoving it in the back. I haven't even worn it, as I was never brave enough to wear a skirt that laced completely up the sides. So much skin.

"Are you sure?" I squeak out.

"Trust me," she replies, handing me the pieces.

What underwear do I wear? I have a set of lacy boy shorts on, but I don't think that will go with the skirt. And I'm clearly losing the bra since I'm wearing a corset. My usual briefs won't work, so I turn and start digging through my unmentionables drawer.

"What are you doing?"

"I'm trying to find underwear to go with that skirt," I reply, rooting around.

"Why on earth would you do that?" she asks incredulously.

I spin to face her, my mouth open and closing like a fish. Finally, I blurt out, "I can't wear a skirt that short without underwear!"

She twirls, thrusting her perfect peach shaped bottom out at me and shoots over her shoulder, "Do you see panty lines on this ass?"

"Well, no," I say reluctantly.

She smacks her ass with a loud crack and says, "Exactly. Let's go."

I can't help but laugh at her antics. She is funny. Intense like Luke, but funny. Am I really going to wear a corset and short skirt with no underthings?

It feels so scandalous. And dangerous. As I look at the fire goddess in front of me, I think, *well, I wanted to learn some big dick energy.*

"Fuck it. Let's do this!" I reply with far more confidence than I feel. I'll fake it till I make it.

She gives me a huge smile, clapping her hands again. With a little hand gesture, I realize she wants me to take the black dress off. Okay, well then, guess we're heading to friendship first base.

Pulling the dress off, I try not to be embarrassed, but she is already working on getting the corset ready for me. I step into the black leather skirt and fuss with the laces. I look back up at her and she holds out the corset.

I take it from her and step into it, sliding it up my body.

Once my breasts are covered, I slip off my bra and adjust myself into the front of it. She gestures at me to spin around and deftly does up the laces.

I'm thankful she does them tight enough to be flattering, but not so tight that I can't get a deep breath in. I spin back around, and she gives me a slow up and down perusal. My skin heats under her stare and I can't help but blush, wondering what she is thinking.

She drips sex and confidence and I ooze—well, I guess, okayness? Yeah, I could learn a thing or two from her. She steps out of the closet, and I walk to the bathroom to take a peek in my big mirror.

I give myself a once-over and I gotta hand it to her. I'm smoking. I turn to check out the profile and realize she's right. Undies will not work, so I slip them off from under the skirt, and the outfit looks perfect. Scandalous, but perfect.

As I stand there looking into the mirror, I can't help but think back to Stalky Hottie. Maybe wherever he is from, stalking is different, or breaking and entering isn't a crime.

With a small shake of my head, I give up on trying to understand his motivations, determined to have a fun time tonight despite still not knowing what we are doing.

I head out of the bathroom to find her standing in front of my closet door, holding a pair of stilettos out toward me in one hand and Lucifer in the other.

"You, too? Lucifer hates everyone but Luke and now you. I can't believe he let you pick him up."

"Cats love me. Don't they, sweet boy?" she croons as they nuzzle foreheads together.

"That's what Luke said," I mumble under my breath. Louder I say, "I am not wearing those shoes. I don't care where we are going or who we are seeing, I draw the line at stilettos."

She pouts at me and says, "Then why do you own them, party pooper? Fine. Pick out your own then."

She drops the shoes carelessly to the floor but puts Lucifer down gently. He winds himself around her ankles as she passes me the black clutch she must have unearthed from my closet.

I prefer my coffin backpack, but she's right, the clutch is better with this outfit. I put in my ID, some cash, and a credit card. I grab my phone to add it, happy to see a reply from Anna confirming she can work tomorrow. Now I really can let loose tonight.

I add my phone to the clutch and then go dig through my closet until I find my cherry red knee-high Docs with the black ribbon laces.

It may not have been what she picked out, but the outfit still is great, even with these shoes. It has my sense of style and I'll be able to walk in them. I head to the kitchen and down a glass of water so I can stay ahead of hydrating since I'm guessing tonight will involve some level of drinking.

We step out into the night where I see parked next to my little bug is her glamorous rose gold Audi. I tuck my spare house key into the porch light beside my door before walking down to the cars.

She clicks the key fob and we both slide into the luxurious leather seats. Turning and smiling at me, she starts the car and revs the engine like we're waiting at the starting line of a car race.

Shocked, I look over at her as she slams into drive, peeling out like the devil himself is chasing us. I brace myself against the seat with one hand and the door with the other and squeak, "If I am going to die tonight, I should at least know the name of my killer."

She lets out a disturbingly childlike giggle as she weaves

in and out of traffic, steering us toward the highway. She flies up the on-ramp, slipping between two tractor trailers and into the far-left lane. Looking at me, she smiles and says, "You're a funny little pet. I'm Lilith."

She holds my gaze longer than seems safe at warp speed on a busy freeway. I look forward and then back at her. "Eyes on the road, Lilith!"

She shrugs one shoulder at me and faces front, fiddling with some buttons on the steering wheel until some type of French rap with a fun back beat fills the air. She dances in her seat, singing loudly in perfect French.

I'm seriously questioning my sanity for jumping in a car and going out with a virtual stranger. Yet, I can't help but believe tonight is going to be something. I cannot even begin to guess what that something might be, but it's definitely going to be something.

She continues to drive like a bat out of hell, singing along to every song, no matter the language. Her chair dancing is amazing. I worry that's where we are going, which I secretly love, but I'm super self-conscious about actually doing.

Given her chair moves, I have no idea how I could hit the dance floor with her. After a few more songs, Lilith whips the car from the left lane across several lanes of traffic to take a right exit ramp, leaving horns blaring in our wake.

"Wherever we are going, I hope we make it there in one piece," I mutter.

She lets out another surprisingly disturbing giggle and barely slows down as we enter a commercial area. I frown, looking around as dark block after block full of weathered buildings and dilapidated chain-link fences pass by.

I cannot fathom where we could be going in this industrial zone that has seen better days. We make a few more turns and I see a sea of cars stretching out before us.

Chapter 37

LIESHE

ilith drives straight toward the building, and at the last second, drifts the car right up to the front entrance like we're in some high-speed car chase movie. I'm too stunned to unbuckle for a moment.

I've been on roller coasters with less speed, turns, and drama. By the time I get my seatbelt off and fall out of the low car, she's already tossing her keys to one of the enormous guards that stands at the door.

I feel like a superstar as another one of the beefy dudes stops the line of people streaming into the venue and unhooks the velvet rope to allow us to pass through the plain metal doors.

So many movies are whizzing through my head right now as I try to process what the hell I'm walking into at Lilith's side. Is it some type of mysterious and secret club?

That doesn't fit the line of people outside. Maybe an underground boxing ring or music performance? Oh my God, what if it's a sex club? I've read about those.

I follow her barely clad swaying hips past more guards and through another set of nondescript metal doors until we walk into an interior that in no way matches the outside or the surrounding neighborhood. I know my mouth is hanging open as I look at Lilith.

"Welcome to Synd," she purrs as she leads me into an enormous casino.

Extravagance greets my eyes no matter where I look,

from the chandeliers overhead, to the black and gold decor with hints of deep red, and the staff in tuxedos.

The guests are an eclectic mix of people, every race and age, dressed in everything from evening wear to sunglasses and flat brimmed hats at the poker tables.

I fall behind by a few paces as I gawk at the surroundings, hurrying to catch back up to Lilith to avoid getting lost in the maze-like floor plan. I had been to the casinos once in Atlantic City when I turned twenty-one, but it was nothing like this.

She effortlessly glides in her five-inch heels to the elevators, and I'm again thankful I had stood firm in my choice of footwear. I wouldn't have made it from the car to here in the shoes she had wanted me to wear.

We step into an elevator and start descending. I can't help but smile, thinking of my time with Luke in the elevator.

"Synd has everything your dark little heart could ever desire."

"But what is it?"

"Everything," she declares, giving me her feline smile and wide eyed yellow-green gaze that sizzles sin under the surface. "Five-star dining, luxury accommodations, casino, dance club, fight club."

"Wow, that's a lot of clubs," I reply lamely.

Lilith taps one long red pointed fingernail against her perfect pout and pretends to think. After a dramatic pause she says, "Oh yeah, and a sex club."

Just then, the doors open, and she stalks out. I quickly follow, trying to digest her last statement.

"Lilith," I hiss. "Did you say sex club?" I squeak out the words, fervently hoping she has not brought me to a sex club. Wait, is Luke at a sex club?

Shit. This night could go south really quick. What if he wants me to do *things* in a sex club? Or even worse, what if he is there with someone else? My stomach plummets at the thought.

"Don't be a baby." Lilith looks at me over her shoulder and winks. She continues to walk down the short hallway toward a set of red velvet double doors bracketed by more enormous bouncers.

"Lilith. Lilith! Stop, I can't go to a sex club!" My voice starts as a yelled whisper but slowly goes up in volume with incredulity, squeaking on the sex club portion.

I should stop, turn around, and call for a ride. Get home and put on some damn underwear.

I try to talk myself down, thinking, *big dick energy, you can do this.* Besides, surely she is joking. But would it really be surprising, considering we are under an illegal casino right now? At least, I assume it is illegal.

The enormous bouncers open the doors for her, and I'm hit with the pounding bass of dance music. Ahead, I can see club lights and fog, and I've never been so thankful to see a mass of writhing bodies on a dance floor. Everyone has on at least some level of clothing, so I assume this isn't the sex club after all.

I follow Lilith along the wall and up a spiral staircase after yet another bodyguard admits us. I wonder at the level of security here, but I guess underground clubs may draw the wrong type of people.

She leads us to a red velvet booth on a balcony looking over the dance floor below. The sound is a little less likely to induce bleeding ears up here. A hot waiter comes by, not in a tuxedo. In fact, he's not in much of anything.

Lilith playfully walks her fingers up his arm as he leans in for her to whisper in his ear. As he turns and leaves, I see he is not in bikini cut bottoms as I first thought but in a full out thong, revealing a mighty fine ass.

I can't help but admire his physique. There's just so much of him on display.

"Put your eyes back in your head before Luke breaks the poor thing's neck."

I whip around to meet her eyes, but her face is flat, and I can't tell if she is joking or not. She must just have an awful sense of humor. Luke wouldn't kill some guy just because I was ogling him. Would he?

To cover my concern, I comment on the wait staff. "I'm glad it's not just women expected to put themselves on display. Everyone needs eye candy."

She nods, saying, "All the staff here love what they do. We all have a fantasy. For some, that's exhibitionism. What's yours?"

"Oh. Well, uh, hm," I sputter, taken aback. I mean, I sure as shit don't know how to answer her. I was hoping Luke would help me explore my fantasies. But I'm not quite certain where we stand right now after the cryptic text exchange earlier.

Lilith blinks her yellow-green eyes at me, contemplating me like a cat contemplates a mouse. She smoothly changes the subject. "I ordered us drinks, then we'll go dance. Don't tell me no either, I can see you checking out the dance floor and you're already bopping along to the music. Just let go and have fun."

Let go. Exactly. That's why I'm here tonight. I'm going to have fun and let go. I'm going to dance my underwear-less ass off. I love dancing, but I'm just always so self-conscious. It's not like I'm going to see any of these people again. Why shouldn't I do something I enjoy?

Lilith's confidence is contagious. I realize I have a choice.

I can bask in the pain of a shattered heart, or I can dance my ass off and move on. I'm tired of being unhappy. I want to live. I want to dance.

The hot waiter reappears with a tower of drinks topped with sparklers. I raise a brow at Lilith, but she just laughs and claps her hands delightedly. It is a pretty display. With a lot of drinks. *Good thing I'm not working tomorrow*, I think, as she passes me one and we clink glasses again and again.

I have no idea what we are drinking, but they go down so smooth and easy. The more I have, the funnier Lilith is. Soon enough, we're laughing like old friends over nothing.

Next thing I know, our tower is sadly empty, and she is pulling me up by the hand and leading me off to the dance floor below. And I'm actually excited to go.

I try to tell her my purse is still back at the booth, but she waves me off, telling me it's fine with all the security and points out a camera on the ceiling. Once she shows me, I notice them everywhere. This place is like Fort Knox.

She pulls me to the middle of the floor where the mass of writhing bodies swallows us up, moving as one to the steady pounding of the heavy bass. The flashing lights are hypnotic, and for the first time in my life, I just let go.

It's exhilarating to feel confident in the way my body moves to the primal beat. I echo some of Lilith's dance steps, and she smiles encouragingly. I feel part of something larger than myself, part of a collective whole.

The crowd moving together to the pulsing beat feels somehow familiar, like I've done this same thing long ago and far away. My feet move, my hips shimmy, my hands caress my body.

I feel so alive. My brain is at peace with my physical form instead of being so damn critical. The leather skirt sticks to my heated skin, the corset tight against my body. My hair is plastered to my neck and a lone drop of sweat trickles down my spine.

The booze courses through my veins, liquid courage. I lift my hair to cool my neck and let the music fill me, guiding my body, just existing, thoughtless in this moment.

Bodies press and retreat in a fever dream of thumping bass. I'm pulled back to conscious thought when I become aware of a presence looming behind me. I open my eyes to see Lilith's face light up and her smile widen before she slinks off into the crowd.

I think Luke must finally be making an appearance like she teased about, but above the body heat and sweat of the people, the smell of leather and tobacco tickles my nose just as solid cool marble presses into the heated flesh of my back.

Stalky Hottie.

Here.

Oh, shit.

Fuck it.

I've long since lost coherent thought, having sacrificed it to the Gods of alcohol and dance. I channel my new found big dick energy, throw my arms up, and twist my body, writhing to the beat and grinding back against the cold wall behind me. My eyes widen in surprise as I feel him begin to move with me.

His large hands encircle my wrists in the air and then slide slowly down my arms, skirt the outside of my breasts and grip my hips, pulling me even further back into him. My breath quickens as he grinds me against the impressive bulge that got me off so spectacularly what seems like so long ago.

I'm thrilled to find he isn't unaffected by me either. I can't decide if I am surprised he is here or not. I open my heavy-lidded eyes to see Lilith watching us from a distance, a strange glint in her eyes. If I didn't know better, I would almost think she looked–jealous?

I cock my head as I study her face. When she catches me watching her, she schools her face into an unreadable mask and disappears into the crowd.

I feel the pounding bass from my fingertips to my toes. It fills me, buoys me up until I could ride this wave forever. The enigma of a man behind me traces the skin exposed by the laces on the sides of the skirt with his fingertips, and it makes me shiver despite the heat of the dance club.

He slides one hand forward over my stomach while his other hand drifts down my thigh a little further and then up the back of my leg. My breath catches as I realize he is quickly going to find out I don't have any panties on.

He glides his fingers up, hitting the hem of the too short skirt and I feel it creep up in the back. I hope his body is shielding me from being on display to the entire club, but no one is paying any attention, and I'm certain I've seen other people on the dance floor doing far more than this.

He traces the lower curve of my bottom and inches inward, leisurely exploring until one of his fingers is teasing at my opening. Bringing his lips to my ear, he whispers, "My beautiful bare one. Were you hoping for me to find you this way tonight?"

He sinks one thick finger into me and then pulls out, dragging my arousal up to my clit. One slow circle and then he drags it back down and thrusts it into me again, only to repeat the process.

This is insanity, to let the same man who broke into my apartment into my body, but I lose what little remains of coherent thought as he continues his exquisite torture. His slowness is agonizing, a direct contradiction to the pulsing beat of the music and frantic need rising inside of me. I'm desperate for more.

I widen my stance to allow him better access and grind down into his fingers, running my hands sensually down the front of my body. Time warps into a slow motion phantasmagoria of bodies and relentless bass and roaming hands.

Vague memories of beating drums and dancing around a bonfire silhouetting my strange stalker filter through my brain, and I wonder at the image of him with blood covering his mouth and dripping down his chin. I can't tell if this is a waking dream, or some alcohol fueled fantasy, the music, heat, and booze infused haze overshadowed by his hands on me.

The haunting and horrific image strangely fuels my desire, a lifelong love of Dracula transposed over my anger toward the heartbreaker dancing behind me, determined to get me off. Just as I feel pleasure building deep in my belly, he freezes. My eyes snap open as I'm met with heat and cinnamon at my front.

Luke!

The air fills with ozone and sulfur, like the gates of Hell have just snapped open in a thunderstorm.

Stalky Hottie keeps me held tight against his body as he withdraws his hand from my skirt and brings it up to his mouth, slowly and deliberately sucking the finger that had just been inside of me while staring into Luke's eyes.

His cheeks hollow with the force of his suction until he pulls it out with a pop. He licks his lips, followed by a sinister smile. I have never seen this side of him, dark and forbidding. My unfulfilled desire pulses harder in my core.

I turn my head to Luke. This is a thousand times worse than having these two face off at my front door. My buzz instantly fades when I see Luke is absolutely furious, his eyes black in the flashing lights.

Luke reaches out to me, but before I can choose, Stalky Hottie wraps a cool hand around my arm and thrusts me behind him.

Luke's voice carries easily over the pulsing music, quiet and lethal. "Too late, *chien*. I already marked her. She's mine."

Incensed at them both, I try to step back out from behind McHottie, but his grip is unbreakable steel. I ineffectually pummel his back with my unrestrained arm, but it's like hitting a brick wall. Suddenly, I'm shoved backward as the two men fall on each other in an all-out brawl.

The crowd parts like the red sea, encircling the guys as they grapple, each trying to land a hit wherever they can reach. I'm shocked to see them fighting, covering my gaping mouth with a hand before I scream.

I scan the sea of people for Lilith, finding her standing nonchalantly in the front row of the surrounding crowd, arms crossed and hip cocked, looking on with a satisfied smirk. I fight my way over to her, the volume of the horde increasing with their bloodlust.

"Lilith," I yell as I get close. "Lilith, you've gotta stop this. What the fuck is happening?"

She wrinkles her pert little nose at me. "Why would I stop them?"

I throw up my arms and look back at the guys. They circle each other, looking for an opening, dancing on the balls of their feet. Hottie steps forward and throws a mean right hook and rather than dodging it, Luke steps directly into the hit, head rocking back as the enormous fist smashes into his nose, resulting in a spectacular nosebleed.

Luke throws his head back and laughs, looking maniacal

with the dark red liquid running down his porcelain skin and soaking his pointed beard crimson.

He licks the blood off his lips, staining his teeth red. He fists his hands at his sides and lets loose a primal scream that silences the crowd and sets every hair on my body on end. Every muscle clenched, head tipped back, neck tendons ready to snap. Luke is raw power. He's never been hotter.

I thought Hottie had felt like a predator, but Luke is clearly the apex predator here. Hottie takes a step back and Luke takes a running leap, landing a roundhouse kick to the kidney.

I gasp, thinking Hottie is done for as he falls to the ground, but he bounces right back up in a defensive stance. They continue their vicious assaults on each other, kicking and punching at an impossible speed.

Their fight is so fast and brutal it is surreal. I blink my eyes several times in disbelief at the events unfolding in front of me.

Luke is a few inches shorter and more compact, but also faster and more brutal in his hits. He is looking to inflict maximum pain, aiming for the kidneys and the same spots repeatedly. His face is fixed in a maniacal smile as if he is genuinely enjoying this.

Stalky Hottie is taller and broader, a little slower, and not quite as vicious. He is more methodical, waiting for the right opening to strike. And although fury guides his strikes, they still somehow seem maybe less evil?

They are both frenzied, and I can't quite believe this is all over me. For a place with a million bodyguards and cameras in the ceiling, why is no one coming to break up this fight?

Time drags on, the lights keep flashing, and the music pounds a strange soundtrack for such a savage scene. The whole thing is unreal. As the brawl rages on, I'm sincerely worried that they will seriously injure, or even kill, each other with their brutality.

Bleeding and dripping with sweat, they cautiously circle until something simultaneously snaps in each of them like the berserkers of old and they launch themselves at the other, going down to the floor, rolling across it as they fight for dominance.

I scream as all hell breaks loose when they roll into the crowd, knocking people down in the fray. Suddenly, everyone is fighting and pushing. Drinks are flying and the music cuts out.

I'm shoved backward, no longer able to see the guys or Lilith anywhere, as I'm swallowed by the chaos. Red flood lights kick on as an alarm sounds. Panicked, people run for the exits. I spin around, trying to find the best exit path out of pandemonium.

Just as I start to hyperventilate, realizing that we are deep underground, and my phobia rises to the surface as I try to contemplate escape, an angel reaches his hand out to me. I stand there staring at him. Even in the chaos and red lights, I can see he is beautiful.

Not only is he beautiful, but this is the exact man from my childhood. The exact shade of white blonde hair, the beyond handsome face. I can't see his eye color in these flood lights, but I know the exact shade of the navy ring around a light blue iris that would be there if I could. This is my guardian angel.

Shocked, I hesitate to take his hand. But as I get knocked again by the surging crowd, my mind shifts into survival mode, and I trustingly put my hand in his outstretched one just as I am pushed forward and fall into him.

Chapter 38

y rescuer pulls me into his side and yells in my ear above the cacophony, "We gotta get out of here!"

I nod woodenly, trying to wrap my head around the apparition of my childhood imaginary friend, and let him lead me through the crowd, his bulk buffering the pushing and shoving. I knew I wasn't making him up.

He skirts us around the perimeter until we reach the back corner, away from the mass of people, and pushes through an emergency exit door, pulling me up the metal staircase behind him.

My lungs burn, but I keep running as fast as I can, fueled by rising panic at being trapped deep underground and getting trampled. The noise of the people fades away, but the blaring alarm is deafening. Unable to take the overstimulation anymore I clap my hands over my ears.

Eventually, we come to a door to the outside and he leads me out into the breaking dawn. He surveys the parking lot and then races us over to a group of motorcycles.

I huff as we jog over to the bikes, thankful at least we are done running up stairs. My rescuer helps me onto the back of a sleek white Harley Sportster and then climbs on in front of me.

I wrap my arms around his waist tightly and hang on for dear life. Another long desired first, although I never thought my first bike ride would be like this.

"Is this your bike?" I yell against his back.

I feel his chest rumble as he chuckles and throws back, "I'm just borrowing it."

He kicks the bike on and the engine leaps to life with a deep throaty purr. We take off like a shooting star out into the breaking dawn. He weaves us through the parking lot, dodging cars and people with expert precision as I try to lean when he leans, my fists bunched in his shirt.

The noise of the panicked crowd leaving the building behind reaches a fever pitch, and then he launches us off the curb and onto the street, pushing the bike faster and harder, until all I can hear is the rumble of the engine and the wind whistling past my ears. My breathing slows as my heart rate maintains its frantic pace.

I squeeze my eyes tight against the wind, whipping my hair into my face, and wrap my arms tighter around him until he eases up on the throttle and pats my hand where it is in a death grip on his shirt. I marginally relax.

Now that we are no longer going breakneck speed and seem to be out of danger, I open my eyes and dare to sit up a little straighter. The breaking dawn around us is beautiful, and the cool wind feels amazing as it rushes past my overheated skin.

The alcohol has long since worn off with the adrenaline and my body quickly chills. I realize I am on the back of a bike, pressed up against a stranger in a short skirt with no underwear on, my bare ass on a stolen motorcycle seat. The realization makes me swallow hard.

This is not how I thought tonight would end. Or any day ever in my life. I knew Lilith was trouble.

My angel winds his way back out of the industrial complex, and the freedom of being on the back of the bike, leaving an epic cluster fuck behind us, both literal and figurative, bleeds the tension from my body.

He sways the bike side to side playfully, and I find my body instinctively following his, my center of gravity shifting with the bike. It's so joyous a laugh bubbles up from my throat, pulling the fear and disbelief at tonight's events out with it.

Life is a wild ride. Despite everything that has happened tonight, I haven't felt pure joy like this in ages. It's the oddest juxtaposition. He makes a few more turns and we pop into a cute suburb where we pull into the parking lot of a quaint little restaurant that looks like a cottage.

My rescuer smoothly dismounts and gallantly offers me a hand as I struggle to slide forward and then off the bike with everything under my skirt on full display. He keeps his eyes on mine as my face heats, embarrassed even though he doesn't so much as sneak a peek. He really must be an angel.

I'm thankful for his steadying hand. His chivalry gives me the courage to say, "This is going to sound so crazy, but I swear you look exactly like my guardian angel from when I was a little girl."

"How do I look for my age?" he asks out of the side of his mouth while waggling his eyebrows at me.

I laugh in response. There is no way I could have been seeing him for close to thirty years. He doesn't appear much older or younger than me. He would have had to age over that amount of time, unless he really was an angel. Wait, *do angels age?*

"You better tell your guardian angel to fly faster to keep up with you. I'm just Gabe," he says.

"Well, just Gabe, I'm just Lieshe," I reply. His answer was so kind, he didn't laugh at me or make me feel small. I'm thoroughly programmed not to speak of my imaginary angel, so it's refreshing to be able to say something out loud.

He doesn't release my hand, even after I'm steady on my feet, instead tucking it into his elbow as we walk along the landscaped winding path into the quaint restaurant. The sign above the door simply says, "Eden." I'm shocked it is open at this odd hour.

"The food here will change your life," he says as he holds open the door.

The interior is cast in a welcoming golden glow, with a few tables and mismatched chairs. Plants fill entire walls. A small, wizened old lady with a grandmotherly smile and a twinkle in her blue eyes comes over.

She passes us two menus, and I'm nervous to take a peek. I hate it when my dietary restrictions cause a fuss, but I needn't have worried. The menu is filled with organic whole foods. Not a grain in sight.

Suddenly, I'm ravenous, and my mouth is watering as I see the offerings. While I glance over the menu, trying to narrow down my choices, she brings two mugs and a French press carafe. I think I just fell in love with her. When she sets down a small pitcher and says it's oat milk, I know I'm in love.

I order the manna smoothie bowl and Gabe simply says, "Make that two."

In the soft lighting, I take in his face. He has a beautiful jawline, full lush lips, and piercing ice-blue eyes. His harsh beauty is softened by his hair falling to his shoulders in platinum waves, artfully tousled by our ride. He even looks like the angel he acts like.

"I should thank you for rescuing me. You really are like an angel swooping in to save the day."

His laugh matches his beauty. "My pleasure. I'm only glad we both got out of that mess safely. What happened?"

"Oh, um," I stammer. "There was a fight..." I trail off.

"I wonder what started it?"

"Well," I draw out. "Me?"

Gabe quirks an eyebrow, replying, "I can see why."

I don't get it. I'm just me, nothing and no one extraordinary. Shaking my head, I stir a generous amount of oat milk into my coffee. The first sip is heavenly, the rich taste of the French press coffee flooding my mouth. I love it but never bother with it at home. I should, it's delicious.

I probably ought to feel uncomfortable sipping coffee across from a polite and charming but complete stranger while being commando, but the conversation flows easily, and we are both laughing as much as talking. Gabe is as easy to be with as he is on the eyes.

"So, when you're not inciting riots, what do you do with yourself?"

Bragging about Grimm comes naturally, so I happily do so.

"Your family and your boyfriend, or should I say, boyfriends, must be so proud."

I bite my lip to keep it from quavering. His eyes look so warm, and he is so genuine that I find myself spilling my guts. I don't usually open up to strangers, but even though Gabe as my guardian angel is an impossibility, his presence is so familiar he feels like talking to an old friend.

Next thing I know, I've shared my difficult relationship with my father, the loss of my mother, my loneliness and searching for love in all the odd places, and my hurt and confusion about the two men who just had that ridiculous fight over me.

We finish our smoothie bowls as we talk, and I think we

are both on our third French press by the time I've brought him up to speed on my entire thirty years.

Smiling, Gabe says, "Your story is as beautiful and unique as you are. You deserve love and you deserve to be happy. These two guys, though, I just gotta say, not everything is always as it seems. You are smart to guard your heart and remember, you only get one soul. This is your love story, and you are the key to it. Write it for you."

I try to ponder his words, think through some of the odd turns of phrases he uses, but despite the copious amounts of coffee I just consumed, I let out a large yawn. I really want to keep talking with him and bask in his warm and friendly nature, but I just hit the wall.

"I guess I should get you home," Gabe says as the sweet little old lady drops our bill on the table.

Seeing the bill, I realize the dilemma I am in. "Gabe! I left my purse back there. I'm so sorry, I don't have my wallet. Oh no! My phone, my ID, and credit card. This is going to be a nightmare with my upcoming trip," I lament as I drop my head into my hands.

"First things first. Let's get you home. Then you can get it all sorted," he assures me. He drops too much cash on the table and stands up, taking my hand and tucking it into his elbow as we walk back to the motorcycle.

"Why were you at the club tonight?" I ask him.

"I was there to rescue you, of course," he replies. The morning sun is behind him, lighting his blond hair up like a halo. He looks like the angel I accuse him of being, ageless perfection.

I shake my head at my exhausted and fanciful thoughts and, with his help, attempt to mount the bike gracefully. While he gets on, I simultaneously try to hide my bare bottom from the world and pull my skirt down in the front.

Now that I know what to expect, I thoroughly enjoy the motorcycle ride. I give him directions as we drive, and all too soon, we are pulling up beside my vintage beetle behind my building.

I'm again impressed with Gabe's chivalry as I flash the entire neighborhood dismounting from the motorcycle. This skirt will never see the light of day again as it's being banished to the depths of my closet.

I can't believe I let Lilith talk me into going commando. I hope she made it out okay. But even in just the brief time I've known her, I have a feeling she is like a cat and lands on her feet no matter what.

"Thank you again—for breakfast, for saving me, for my first motorcycle ride. What a wild night." I cast a glance at the sky and say, "Or morning."

Gabe just smiles and wraps me up in his arms with a warm embrace that feels like home. His warmth seeps into my body, and I swear it lights up my very soul. I wrap my arms around him and hug him back.

I should be exhausted, but as I break off the lingering embrace, I feel like he's recharged my batteries.

He smiles like the sun, saying, "I better get this bike back."

I force myself to walk away from him and climb the stairs to my door. I reach into the porch light next to my door, take out the spare key, and unlock the door. Having successfully opened it, I turn to wave to Gabe who was gallantly waiting to be sure I got in.

He gives me a two-finger wave and then peels off on the Harley into the rising sun as I stash the spare key back in its hiding spot.

I really hope I can see him again someday. It was so nice to have a friend when I really needed one. And I'd love to go back to that restaurant. I'll have to see if I can find it online. I thought I knew all the local-ish places, but I have never heard of Eden.

I walk in and close the door behind me. As I turn around to lock it, I let out an audible gasp as I see a new clutch sitting on the table next to the door. I grab it up and look inside to find my phone and wallet.

I turn the clutch over in my hands and I'm in love. The jeweled knuckle duster hardware with a skull is exactly my style. Below the hardware, I can see the brand name engraved in elegant font. I squint and read aloud, "Alexander fucking McQueen!"

I pick my phone up and see it has blown up since I last had it. Opening my text messages, I start with Lilith's, which truly seemed panicked and concerned, asking where I am and if I'm ok. Then I switch over to Luke's, which started last night, before the fight broke out.

LUKE

I see you in my corset, mon petit chou. I want to pull those laces tighter, make you pant for me.

LUKE

If that ass is bare, I'm going to spank it until it's on fire, ma petite fille coquine.

LUKE

Fuck, I see Lilith has corrupted you.

One more text is from just an hour ago.

LUKE

That was not how I wanted to end the night with you. I hope you like your present. Text me. And for fuck's safe, don't hide a key in the light. You are asking for a break in.

I can't help the goofy smile that breaks out on my face at his concern. And the purse is incredible. It is exactly what I would have picked for myself if I had substantial amounts of discretionary income.

I should have known it was from Luke the second I saw the matte black hardware. With my upcoming trip, I'm so thankful he was able to get my things back to me.

I walk to the kitchen and chug a glass of water, then head to the bathroom to wash my face and get out of this ridiculous outfit. As I brush my teeth, I worry about both guys.

Guess Luke is okay enough to text. It was a hell of a fight. I've never seen anything like it and still can't believe they were fighting like that over me.

There must be something else in play. Maybe they had a prior grudge with each other? Lilith had that strange look when McHottie had shown up. What was that about?

Finishing in the bathroom, I drop the skirt and fight my way out of the corset using the front buckles, not feeling like dealing with trying to reach the laces. Throwing on my robe and bunny slippers, I head up to my room, prepared to get a few hours of sleep since Anna is covering the store today.

I flop onto my bed and glance over at the vase of dried roses I had kept. I had thrown hundreds of them away as they wilted, but the vase next to the flamingos I just couldn't bear to part with, so I had let them dry and kept them on the table next to my bed. I don't dare delve into the psychology of keeping a token from a stalker.

I roll over and try to close my eyes, but every time I do, I picture the fight all over again. Annoyed, I pull out my phone to surf some social media as a palate cleanser.

I soon become irritated with the highlight reels of everyone's lives when I'm over here trying to figure out what the hell is going on with mine and the hot guys that keep popping up.

Where have they been for the past ten years I've been looking for love? And where are they now? I don't even know how I'd get in touch with Gabe again. Luke is like a damn Tsunami, and Stalky Hottie blows in and out like a nor'easter. I can't wait to get away to Europe just to have an ocean of space between us.

I toss my phone on the end table and fall on my old tried-and-true method of falling to sleep by counting backwards from 333. I picked that number as a little girl as a nod to my angel when I read that it was an angel number. It's served me well ever since.

Chapter 39

I must be dreaming. Gabe is here, but he has enormous wings and a flaming sword. I reach out to touch the great white feathers, but before I can stroke their iridescent length, Gabe takes my hand and leads me along a path. As we walk, he nonchalantly swings the flaming sword beside him.

The sound of the fire as the sword rhythmically swings is hypnotic. Swoosh, whoosh. Swoosh, whoosh. It fills my consciousness until my heart synchronizes its beat to the sound. Swoosh, whoosh. Lub, dub.

The world turns dark, and everything except the sound of my beating heart floats away. There is nothing here. I wonder if this is my earliest memory of the womb, dark nothingness.

My ears strain to catch the start of a note, like nothing I have ever heard before. The sound builds and builds to a crescendo of an all-consuming symphony that invades every part of my being. I am filled with sound until I feel like I am becoming sound.

I know there is something special to this deafening harmony. Suddenly, a blast of light bursts forth in the unrelenting darkness. Entire galaxies appear, stars and suns and planets flash into existence and hurtle outward, leaving behind the familiar blue planet I know as home.

I blink, and in the strange timeline of dreams, I find myself sitting on a large smooth rock, warmed by the sun.

Water trickles merrily by and the dappled shade stipples me with sunlight. The scent of the forest is light and fresh.

I watch the water ripple over stones, forming little currents. I've never noticed how beautiful the water is before. How clear and pure, reflecting the light.

I can see every tiny detail, from the veins on a leaf floating by to the small crayfish peeking out from under a rock covered in velvety moss. A shadow falls over the critter, and I look up to see Gabe. Standing next to him is another Gabe.

They look at me and the name Michael comes to my mind, despite no one speaking. As I glance from one to the other, I see slight differences, but they could easily pass for identical twins.

Michael is wearing the sword on his back now, and it no longer shimmers with flames. Gabe leans forward with a smile and hands me a beautiful white lily. They look at me with matching enigmatic smiles as I take the lily and breathe in its scent; the pollen encrusted stamen tickles my nose.

I close my eyes to appreciate the light floral fragrance, and when I open them again, I am startled to find a great serpent curled up on the rock next to me, basking in the sunlight. I eye the endless loops of the body, as thick as my thigh in places.

The snake stares at me with great yellow-green eyes and I find myself leaning into its gaze, falling into the depths of the slit-like pupils. A forked black tongue flicks out, scenting the air. The mouth curves up at the corners in a reptilian smile, triggering me to smile back.

The sudden silence of the forest is deafening, even the song of the merry babbling brook seems to dampen. I continue to smile at the friendly-looking creature, missing the unease that is obvious to the rest of the forest.

I feel lost in his yellow-green depths, enthralled until I could drown. When the serpent lashes out, the shock barely registers. It seems so out of character for its smiling countenance.

I lean back, narrowly missing the strike, and scramble to my feet. Michael steps forward and hands me his sword, again consumed by white fire. I hesitate to take it, but Gabe gives me an encouraging nod.

I reach out my hand and take the blade, surprised to find the handle feels cool to the touch despite its flames, and the weight is comfortable regardless of its enormous size.

Both angels, as I am certain that is what they must be, stare at the snake, and I know in my heart they wish for me to kill the creature. I look between their eyes and back at the yellow-green gaze of the serpent.

Although the sword is light and well balanced in my hand, I feel the gravity of the task I am being asked to perform reverberate into my soul. The shimmering fire licks painlessly up my arm and engulfs me. I feel the power there for the taking.

I look at the great coiled snake, and despite its attempt to strike me, I cannot bring myself to hurt it. Serpents strike, it is in their nature. How can they expect me to kill something just for being itself, as if by fulfilling the very purpose it was created for, it is somehow imbued with evil?

I cannot fault the serpent for being a serpent any more than I can be faulted for being a human.

Just as clearly as I *heard* the name Michael in my mind, I hear him say to Gabe, "She is not the one."

I'm not sure who Michael is looking for me to be, but I want nothing to do with them. I will not deliver judgment. The flaming sword clatters to the rock with a sound like the crashing of great cymbals as I cast it away. I squeeze my eyes tight as I flinch away, and when I open them again, I'm in my bed.

I blink a few times, surprised and yet not by my surroundings. I can vividly recall every detail, from the color of the serpent's eyes to the weight of the flaming sword in my hand. Rolling over, I grab my phone, shocked to see I've slept for hours.

My stomach growls in a loud protest. I have not been able to take care of myself with all this craziness. I need a decent meal and a decent night's sleep without Gabe and his friend making an angelic appearance to ask me to kill a smiling but dangerous huge-ass serpent.

Part of the dream is easy to explain. Gabe had been my knight in shining armor. But the guy with the flaming sword made no sense. And seeing the start of the universe? That was amazing, but again, not sure where it came from. My brain really pulled out all the stops with that one.

Part of me blames Lilith and her alcohol tower. The dramatic night also added fuel to the fire. All in all, a bad setup.

I need to listen to my body and put in some quality self-care. Despite my intentions to quit living life at high speed, the world just keeps turning, faster than ever. I swing my legs over the side of the bed and into my bunny slippers to pad down to the bathroom.

My mouth feels fuzzy, so the first thing I do is grab my toothbrush and put a nice dollop of toothpaste on it. I start to brush, looking up into the mirror. My mouth falls open and my toothbrush buzzes uselessly as I stand frozen, staring.

The mirror image of me stares back in shock, watching as I reach up to wipe the tip of my nose. I tear my eyes away from my reflection and look down at my finger. I rub my finger and thumb together, smearing the orange powder that looks disturbingly like the pollen of a lily.

I grab a washcloth and scrub furiously at my nose until it glows red. Then I scrub at my fingers as if removing all traces of the physical remnants of my strange dream will make this seem somehow less real.

I can't wait to leave for my trip so I can physically and mentally escape the cluster of my current life. I head to my closet and dig out soft leggings and an oversized shredded band t-shirt.

My stomach launches into another loud protest, so I head to the kitchen to ransack the fridge. Nothing looks good, so I settle for a frozen entrée from the back of the freezer.

I throw it in the microwave and chug a glass of water. While I wait, I dig out my planning binder for my trip and start updating my lists and notes. Organizing my thoughts helps me to rebuild some semblance of control and normalcy after such an eventful summer.

My phone dings with an incoming text and I mutter, "What fresh new hell is this?"

When I open my messages, I'm relieved to see one from a known contact. I can't handle any more unknown callers.

MY LORD

You didn't check in.

I try to plan a response to Luke. I'm hungry and tired and a little overwhelmed at the moment. Not really a good setup for any type of meaningful conversation, so I settle on something easy.

LIESHE

I was exhausted and had to sleep. Thank
you for the amazing bag.

I almost type that the purse is too much, and I can't accept it, but there is no way in hell I am giving it up. I'm not sure if accepting such an extravagant gift is the right thing to do or not, but it's kick-ass and I'm keeping it.

I rationalize to myself that I deserve a luxury gift after our every meeting seems to get weirdly interrupted, and the brutality of their fight keeps running on a loop in my head.

I want to know what the hell happened, but I'm scared to ask. Do they have a backstory? Were they seriously fighting over me, or is there some deeper beef between them?

LUKE

Reminded me of you, mon petit chou.
Beautiful and edgy.

I feel my face warm as I smile at the compliment. As I wrack my brain for what to say in reply, I see the three little dots pop up, so instead I decide I will wait for his reply.

LUKE

I want to see you again. Alone.

Do I want to see Luke again? Much less alone? My mind drifts back over our times together. The first charming encounter at the expo followed by the thrill of performing with him and the steamy after-party. The sweet way he came to drop my coat off after I forgot it at the hotel.

My smile is stretched so wide that my cheeks are beginning to ache at the thought of what could have happened if we weren't interrupted when he came to my place. But then I remember him and Stalky Hottie beating the shit out of each other and my face falls.

Who is Luke? And do I want to see him again? I honestly don't know. Stalky Hottie had warned me away from Luke. Gabe had warned me about everyone not being what they seemed. What does any of this mean?

Hopefully, time and distance will help me decide, but I need a response for now. I start and stop typing several times, attempting to strike a balance between figuring out these relationships and putting myself first with some big, damn healthy boundaries.

LIESHE

I'm getting ready for an overseas business trip. We will have to sort things out when I'm home.

That sounds good. I'm not saying yes, I want to see him again, or no. Just that we need to figure this out. It's all I have energy for right now. I'm trying to prioritize my needs, and what I need is to house this frozen dinner, hydrate, decompress, and get some quality sleep.

I take the frozen dinner out of the microwave and make myself an iced seltzer. I grab the remote while the food cools and scroll through shows until I settle on the cooking channel.

It's my go to for when I just want to relax and not think. I'm hoping it will act as a palate cleanser before I go back to bed. Despite not loving cooking or doing that much of it, I love to watch cooking shows. Especially the competitions.

I balance the little plastic tray of my dinner on top of a paper plate and snuggle into the sofa. The first bite is scorching. I blow out, trying to keep from burning my mouth, once again cursing microwaves for their uneven heating.

Lucifer saunters over from wherever he had been sleeping his life away and jumps up to sit on the coffee table where he can watch me eat. He's a beautiful cat, with his midnight black coat and yellow eyes, but the prickliest animal I ever met. His notched ear gives him a roguish air.

He narrows his eyes at me and flicks his tail as if he can read my thoughts. I break off a piece of whatever indistinguishable meat is the protein in this frozen culinary delight and set it in front of him as a peace offering.

He glances down at it, sniffs the air, turns to flash me his kitty rear and jumps down. Under my breath I mumble, "Judgy, persnickety bastard. It's not that bad."

I take another bite and sigh. Lucifer is right, this food sucks. I carry the offending plastic tray to the trashcan and dump it. Oh well, guess I'll have to eat gelato for dinner after all. I'll endure the hardship.

Heading back to the couch with the container and a spoon, I sit down and try to focus on watching the cooking competition. But my mind keeps circling back to thoughts of Luke, McHottie, and now Gabe.

I hope Gabe is okay and not rotting in jail for grand theft auto, since I haven't heard from him. I really want to ask him about how to find that amazing little cafe again. *Oh, crap, we didn't exchange numbers,* I realize. Not that I want another romantic interest, I just want a friend to eat manna smoothie bowls with.

I debate going next door to check on McHottie just as there is a knock on my door. I walk over, surprised to see the very man I had been thinking of out the peephole like my thoughts had conjured him. I run my hand over my messy bun and glance down at my ripped shirt and leggings.

Shrugging, I open the door to see McHottie standing there with his hands in his pockets, head down. I expect to see a busted-up face, but when he looks up at me, I'm shocked.

"Hey. I'm glad to see you're okay, but, um, why don't you have a scratch on you?"

"Good evening. I wanted to make sure you got home safely," he says in his oddly formal way.

"Yeah, I did. But are you really okay?" I reach out my hand and grab his chin, turning his head side to side, inspecting him for damage, surprised there isn't any visible.

He takes my hand and steps into me, forcing me to look up into his eyes. He drops my hand and reaches up with both of his, so large they cover my jaw and most of my neck as he leans in, nose to nose, and stares deep into my eyes.

I lose myself in the amber depths of his, my lips parting as I wait for his kiss. He ghosts his lips over mine, whispering against them, "You cannot see him again. You promised me you would not put yourself in danger. Luke *is* danger."

I frown, pulling out of his grasp. "Luke? Luke isn't dangerous."

He shakes his head, narrowing his eyes. I get a flashback to the sinister look on his face the night of the fight. Luke is fire, wild, and unpredictable. Just like fire, he never behaves as I expect, but Luke has yet to actually hurt me. He isn't *dangerous*.

But I'm starting to wonder about my neighbor.

"We barely know each other. You give me emotional whiplash you're so damn hot and cold. For all I know, you're the dangerous one. And I'm not yours. You can't tell me who the hell I can and can't see."

He steps back, dropping his eyes to the ground. He gazes up at me through his lashes, surprising me when his mouth curves up into his signature panty melting smile. Lifting my hand to his lips, he kisses my new ring with the red stone.

"Oh, my little *Roză*," he growls with a smoldering gaze. "You have no idea just how mine you are."

I break out of his grip, step backward into my house, and close the door, shooting the deadbolt. I hear him walk down the stairs as I sag against the door. What the fuck was that about? I am not his.

I stomp to the kitchen, muttering about alphaholes, as I get out a rocks glass and throw two skull ice cubes in to pour a shot of tequila over. Probably not the best choice, but necessary, nonetheless. So much for a little R & R.

"I don't need your help," I mutter out loud to my traitorous body, who seems more than happy with his declaration. Guess vaginas don't care about toxic masculinity. "Down girl!"

That damn smile of his gets me in the ovaries every time. I put the melting gelato back in the freezer before it becomes soup and flop back down on my couch, images of my hot but insufferable neighbor dancing through my brain.

Eventually, I click off the TV and drink the last of my tequila, leaving the glass in the sink for tomorrow, get ready for bed, and head upstairs.

Chapter 40

I kick off my slippers and robe, crawling naked under the covers. I'm not super tired after this morning's sleep, but just want to sprawl out on my bed. Maybe I can just read and mindlessly scroll social media for a little.

I get settled and enjoy a few hours of delightful brain candy. Just as I am setting my alarm for tomorrow, another text comes in from Luke. With a heavy sigh, I open my messages. Good thing I took a nap today, sensing the inevitable chaos that is Luke will interrupt my night. But probably in the very best way.

MY LORD

Send me a picture of you.

I roll my eyes. I'm in bed, no make-up, crazy hair. Opening my photos, I scroll through, sending him a cute selfie I took a while ago.

MY LORD

Not what I meant. Where are you now?

LIESHE

Now? Bed.

MY LORD

I want a picture of you in bed.

Oh. *Oh!* This is the next level. Does he mean like my face

in bed or like the good stuff? I don't want to embarrass myself and send an X-rated picture when he just means a face shot.

Shit. I have no idea what the right answer is here. I decide to be on the safe side, so I bring up my camera and experiment with the lighting and angles until I get what I hope is a kinda sexy selfie. Editing it to be black and white, I end up pretty happy with the result. I hit send and wait to see what happens.

MY LORD

Tu es tellement belle.

A quick internet search has me melting. My fire god thinks I am beautiful. My neighbor had made me feel beautiful in the mirror. Lilith inspires my confidence. Gabe smiled at me like I was the angel. Even I am beginning to believe, really believe, I am beautiful.

LIESHE

Thank you

MY LORD

As much as I love seeing your gorgeous face, I need more.

More? He said "needs." Swoon. I love the idea of him needing more of me. I swallow hard, wondering where this conversation is going. Like dirty pictures more or sexting more?

Having never done either one, I anxiously watch the three gray dots, waiting for another text, and realize my battery is low. I search my bedside table, but my charger isn't there. *Why don't I put things back where they belong?*

I get up and hurry over toward my chaise to grab the one I keep there. I try to hustle, wanting to get back to our chat.

MY LORD

Send me another picture.

LIESHE

Of me?

MY LORD

Is there someone else in your bed?

LIESHE

No!

MY LORD

Good. Because I'd fucking gut them.

What is going on? Luke gets into a fight over me and now I'm the prize? This is so weird.

MY LORD

Now be a good girl and rub that pussy for me. I want her ready for her close up.

Yup. There it is. We're sexting. Will he know if I don't? I kind of want to. I kind of don't. I'm not sure I have enough hands for this since I'm unfamiliar with sexting protocol.

Like do you hold the phone or put it down? Do I take pictures with the flash, or do I keep it in selfie mode? I just have so many questions. That in itself is kinda killing the mood here.

MY LORD

Are you my good girl?

Big dick energy, I tell myself. It's go time.

LIESHE

Yes

MY LORD

Liar. Bad girls get punished. Is that what you really want? For me to punish you… turn that ass red, edge you until you beg for me? Oh, ma Reine Rouge, comme je veux que tu me supplies.

LIESHE

Can't I be both?

I give a fist pump. Damn, I'm clever. Maybe I can handle this sexting thing after all. I stare at the screen, waiting for his reply, and start walking back toward my bed to get cozy for the rest of this chat when my head snaps up.

Before I can react to the looming presence, the intruder grabs me from behind, wrapping an arm around my abdomen and capturing me against his body, muffling my scream with the other hand. My phone and the charging cable go flying.

"Abso-fucking-lutely you can. But not tonight. You lied to me. And I told you not to leave that key in your porch light, *ma petite fille coquine.* Or is that what you wanted, hm? Some stranger to sneak into your room, maybe while you are sleeping?"

My heart pounds furiously, my lungs burn as I desperately try to move enough air in and out of my nose. Luke's cinnamon smell and familiar voice growling in my ear just barely cuts through my panic.

Although I'm so thankful this is Luke, I don't know if I'll ever recover from this shock. I sure as shit will never hide a key again.

Luke spins me around and pushes my shoulders, causing

me to fall backwards onto the chaise. I stare up at him, still breathing like a racehorse. The moonlight streaming through the stained-glass windows highlights his raven mask, while his swirling black cloak blends his body into the darkness.

"Damn, Luke, you scared the shit out of me!" My voice is high pitched and breathy with fear. I clutch my chest as my breaths are still coming shallow and my heart races.

He kneels in front of the chaise, pushing himself between my knees and forcing my legs apart. Tearing off his cloak, he throws it to the side.

He leans over me and wraps his hands around my exposed throat, whispering, "Do you have any idea how dangerous that could be?"

His words sneak into the deep recesses of my mind, worming their way to secret, dark fantasies securely kept locked away. Until now. Until him.

I know in my heart this is Luke, but his raven mask adds another level of dangerous exhilaration. The silver moonlight highlights his yellow-green eyes. For a moment, I'm transported back to my dream, drowning in the nearly identical eyes of the serpent. I blink and find Luke staring back at me intently.

"Luke," I exhale.

"Oh, *non ma belle coquine*," he whispers darkly. "Who am I?"

My heart pounds erratically as I inhale through my mouth, trying to draw enough oxygen into my starving lungs. Luke stares back into my eyes through his mask, tracing a finger down my forehead and over my nose, probing at my lips.

I automatically open my mouth and suck on it, swirling my tongue. He tastes so much darker than cinnamon tonight. He hums deep in his throat, pushing his finger further and further in, never breaking eye contact.

"*Très bien.* There's my good girl." He pulls it out just before I gag hard and, bringing it to his own mouth, sucks it with a moan that ignites my desire. "Your fear and innocence are exquisite. I could fucking drown in it. *Mais quelle belle façon de mourir.*"

He stares down at me and at this angle, the mask shadows his eyes, making them appear black, and hides the bottom of his face. He looks so strange and eerie.

Luke reaches up to the collar of his black t-shirt and rips it down the center, tossing the ruined scraps to the side. The sound of the ripping fabric has my skin rippling into goosebumps.

I should be afraid of this masked man who snuck into my room. I know that is the logical reaction. But secretly I am thrilled he ripped his shirt off and left the mask on. The very air pulses with dark mystery and the promise of fulfilled dark desires.

My eyes trace the moonlight and shadows highlighting the peaks and valleys of his bare chest and arms, bleeding the beautiful red from his hair. Luke looks like a shadow wraith, conjured by my darkest fantasies, but feels like the devil. Like sin itself, personified in the night.

He slides his hands back around my throat and I feel my pulse thunder against his blazing skin. He's right. Anyone could have snuck in as he just proved, but he is here, and I'm fucking ecstatic to give him my fear and innocence that he so clearly craves.

His cinnamon scent and dark words pry open the locked door of my secret fantasies and I want to give him all of me, everything. His fingers tighten ever so slightly as he searches my face. I close my eyes for a second, and when I open them again, I know exactly what to do.

"My lord," I breathe out and then lean harder into his hands, taking my own breath away. I know I am blowing the lid off Pandora's box this time, but I can't stop myself. I've got to see inside. I'm fucking *dying* of curiosity.

Luke's flashing eyes are my only warning before he crashes his mouth to mine, slanted to accommodate the mask's raven beak, while tightening his hands further around my neck. His kiss steals my air as his grip continues to tighten.

The effect is fantastic. I am consumed by Luke. He is all I can feel, all I can taste. Just as my lungs burn and stars dance on the edges of my vision, he breathes into my mouth, loosening his hold on my neck.

Taking his very essence into my lungs may be one of the most erotic experiences I've ever had. I'm heartbroken to exhale his breath back out, but my body is begging me to breathe, forcing me to take deep lungfuls of air in and push them back out.

"You want both the reward and the punishment, but my dark is a long way down," he whispers into the night. He mutters, almost as if to himself, "Too dark for your innocence. *Trop sombre en effet.*"

He leans back up, running his hungry gaze down over my body. I am naked and so exposed, yet I feel shameless. His feral stare bolsters my confidence, while the visible effect I have on him improves mine.

He reaches out and grabs a fistful of my hair and wrenches me up. I let out a shocked squeal as he puts his masked face right in mine and growls, "Too dark, *ma petite vilaine.* Too dark."

I want to argue with him and beg for his darkness, tell

him I am starving for it. I look into his eyes, see his harsh breathing as he exercises incredible restraint, and recognize the alpha predator that he is, the same flashing black in his eyes from the fight earlier.

Can I handle his darkness? Do I want to?

My scalp prickles where he holds my hair, painful but not unbearable. We hold each other's eyes for what feels like a lifetime, both of our chests heaving, waiting for the other to break.

I make my choice and bring my hands up to his chiseled chest. Dragging my fingertips down, I graze my nails over his pierced nipples, rewarded by his sharp intake of breath. Scratching my nails down until I reach the button on his jeans, I pop it open and slide down the zipper, saying, "My Lord, let me taste your darkness."

Luke closes his eyes and drops his head back, letting out what I think is a string of curses in something older than French. Something that raises every hair on my body.

But he doesn't stop me. Emboldened, I grip the waistband of his pants and slide my hands down his fiery skin. After all this time, I can finally see Luke in all of his glory.

I am not surprised to find him commando beneath. What shocks the hell out of me as his cock springs free, are the piercings glinting in the moonlight. I can't help but shoot my eyes up to his, only to catch him looking back at me with satisfaction at my surprise clear in his eyes.

"You want to taste my darkness, *ma passion*?" He questions softly. His lips tip up in a smile as he says, "I'll fucking choke you with it."

Luke stands up and kicks off his pants. I can't tear my eyes away from his dick as it strains toward me. I get it now. This is the specimen that deserves description in every minute detail. Every ridge, every throbbing vein, is exquisite. I want it.

He reaches out and gently caresses my face as he turns dark and serious.

"Do exactly what I command. Do not disobey me. Fuck around and find out. Now open for me and stick out your tongue." The quietness of his voice belies the darkness of his commands.

Late-night reading did not prepare me for the reality of this situation. I am instantly aroused, positively dripping for him. I am also nowhere near expecting the sensations that come with giving up my mouth for his pleasure, the absolute liberation of turning over trust and control. The power of surrender is intoxicating.

His dark voice, smoldering with dominance, shoots straight to my core. Before I can think it through, my body decides for me, my jaw dropping open, tongue protruding.

Luke fists one hand in the back of my hair, angling my head where he wants it, and grabs the base of his impressive shaft with the other hand. Looking up at the imposing figure he cuts is dizzying. But I have little time to admire the view before he takes advantage of my hungry mouth.

His taste is exactly what I imagined. Cinnamon, heat, and darkness stain my soul. My eyes drift closed at the intensity, and Luke abruptly pulls out of my mouth, smacking my face with his cock. I open my eyes, shocked.

"Eyes always on me."

I look up at him, eyes wide, and watch his muscles ripple as his abs clench. He slowly rubs just the head of his cock lightly back and forth across my tongue. The black metal ball on the bottom of the magic cross piercing is a startling contrast to the hot velvet of his skin. His hips inch forward, filling my mouth again.

"*Tu es une bonne fille*," he praises on a harsh exhale as he feeds me another inch. As he eases into my mouth, I feel piercing after piercing slide over my tongue and can't help but wonder what they would feel like sliding inside of me.

The cool air hitting my molten core is maddening when I need so much more. My hips writhe on the chaise lounge, but I can't get any friction with him standing between my legs.

With a growl, he snaps his hips forward, filling my mouth completely. I breathe deeply through my nose, frantically trying not to choke as he hits the back of my throat. I strain to keep my eyes open and on his.

"Not nearly dark enough yet."

I keep my jaw practically unhinged to accommodate him and focus on relaxing my throat as he begins a punishing pace. I keep my eyes on him as instructed, even as they start to water. Luke drops his head down between his shoulders.

Despite letting him use my mouth for his pleasure, I feel incredibly empowered. I am unraveling this wraith of shadows, absolutely destroying the rigid control he is visibly fighting to maintain.

Fighting and losing.

The power makes me feel drunk.

He shifts, pushing me to lie down on the chaise, and puts a knee up on the edge. I brace my hands on his flexing thighs. This new angle allows him to thrust even deeper. He is beautifully wicked with his raven mask reflecting the moonlight, body painted with light and dark, as if the night itself was created only to adorn him with its shadows.

My eyes water and I continue to fight to control my breathing as saliva begins to slide from the corners of my mouth with my head now tilted. As the tears start to fall, Luke's mouth turns up into a sinful smile.

"There is the taste you so desperately wanted. I could drink your tears." He reaches out a finger and catches a tear, bringing it to his mouth and dropping it on his tongue. "Now swallow my darkness, *ma belle coquine*."

His hips stutter and his brutal pace slows. He draws almost the entire way out, only to snap his hips forward and bottom out in my throat. I watch as sweat drips down his chest, every muscle rigid and flexed. His breathing changes to harsh pants as he stills and holds himself deep in my mouth.

Watching him lose control is exquisitely beautiful. I feel his cock swell and pulse. Then his taste floods my mouth. I swallow him down, humming deep in my throat at the unique spicy taste of Luke.

He remains utterly still, his breathing slowly evening out. At long last, he pulls out, leaving my jaw aching. He reaches out and wipes a drop from the corner of my mouth, then uses it to draw the sign of the cross on my forehead.

I think I'm going to hell, because this? I fucking love it. I love his darkness.

I.

Want.

More.

Luke drops to his knees and grips my tired jaw in both hands. He rips his mask off and stares fiercely into my eyes, saying intently, "You are both my good girl and my wicked girl, *ma gentille fille et ma méchante fille*. You took me so well. This is only the beginning. Tonight, I have baptized you into my darkness."

He covers the drying cross on my forehead in a kiss and then claims my mouth. His tongue lashes against mine like he is a man possessed, branding his touch into my skin, claiming me as his. With his arms around me, he drags me to the floor.

He breaks the scorching kiss and continues to blaze a path of heated, open-mouthed kisses down my throat and to my breasts. He pulls a nipple deep into his mouth, cheeks hollowing out with suction.

Watching him lavish my breasts with attention adds to my rising pleasure. He looks up to find me watching him, smiles around a mouthful of flesh, and pulls off.

Holding my gaze, he works his way down, licking and sucking to the bottom of my breast, where he sinks his teeth deep into my tender flesh. I arch at the exquisite pain that quickly bleeds into pleasure as he laves the bite with his tongue.

"Luke," I squeal. He smacks my other breast sharply and narrows his eyes at me. "My Lord," I breathe out, rewarded when he uses the same hand to massage the offended breast.

His kisses drift downwards, deliciously hot and wet, as he slides his body down and presses my legs open wide with his shoulders. He slides his hands slowly up my thighs and spreads me open with his thumbs.

I feel his heated stare, and I'm thankful for the pale moonlight streaming through the stained glass rather than the more revealing light of day. He stares at my core like it is the key to the mysteries of the world.

He leans in and inhales deeply, releasing a deep hum of enjoyment. I jump when he spears my opening with his scalding tongue, but his hands hold me in place, preventing my retreat.

He licks me from entrance to clit with the flat of his tongue over and over, alternating with fucking me with his tongue until I'm writhing. My hips can't decide whether they want to retreat or grind into his face.

"So. Fucking. Delicious." He punctuates each word with a long, languid lick. "Your innocence tastes divine. Now let me taste your fear."

My eyes widen at his words, wondering what he is going to do. He leans in and bites my mound, hard. I yelp, startled at the sudden pain.

Luke crawls up my body and places his forehead against mine, reaching down between us. He grabs the base of his shaft and rubs the head of his cock up and down, teasing at my entrance.

I freeze, not sure if I'm quite ready to have sex with him. Instead of thrusting into me like I expect, he continues to rub himself up and down. Every time, not only his head but his piercings bump against my clit, I suck in a breath.

He lowers his body against mine and suddenly flips us, putting me on top.

"Use my darkness, *ma méchante fille*. Rub yourself up and down my cock. I want to be fucking dripping in your juices."

He props himself up on his elbows, staring down at where his dick strains and twitches toward me. I carefully raise myself up to my knees, bracing my hands on his hard chest. I look down to where he is trapped between us and watch his abs clench.

The sensation of the piercings sliding against me causes me to gasp in surprise as I move back and forth. Their smooth metal surface is the perfect contrast to the feeling of velvet over steel, and I grind myself down into them as I slide along the surface of his pierced cock.

I feel pleasure building deep in my pelvis at the erotic sight and the feeling of so many textures against my flesh. I lean back and move my hands behind me to his thighs, arching my back to change the angle and grind down harder against him.

"So good, just like that," he grunts, reaching up to grab both breasts. He expertly toys with my nipples, tugging further, pinching tighter until the pain and pleasure bleed together.

The added stimulation throws me over the edge, and the tightening in my belly turns to fire, licking out along my limbs, pulling moans from my lips. My entire universe tightens and releases in waves until stars dance before my eyes.

Luke slides his hands down to my hips as I lose myself in my orgasm and picks up the rhythm, wrenching out every last wave of pleasure from me.

I feel him tense beneath me and then he, too, groans, and I feel his hot release mixing with the warm wet mess I've created all over him.

We stare at each other intently as our breathing slows, locked into place, his hands on my hips. Neither of us wants to break the connection. Despite his heated skin, I feel our combined release cooling.

Before we become permanently glued together, I carefully position my legs and try to elegantly stand up from him. They are quivering like Jello as I slump back onto the chaise.

Luke rises like a graceful panther from the floor, all long limbs and rippling muscles. The moonlight and shadows reach out to caress his form.

I feel like a sea lion on an iceberg next to him. He drops a kiss to the top of my head and then pulls on his pants, leaving them unbuttoned, barely clinging to his hips. Unfair how he can look so effortlessly sexy.

He finds his ruined shirt he discarded on the floor and comes back to me where I'm perched on the chaise. He nudges my legs apart with his knee, reaches down, and wipes me off with the remnants.

I lift a hand to stop him, but he just reaches out with his other hand and laces our fingers together while he raises his shirt up to his face and inhales deeply.

His head tips back and his eyes drift close as he proclaims, "Dark innocence."

He reaches into his pants pocket and pulls out my spare key, holding it up between us. Winking at me, he says, "Mine."

Luke gives our joined hands a squeeze and then let's go, grabbing his cloak and mask from my floor. Turning around, he walks out.

My racing heart slows to normal as I rest on the chaise, mind reeling. I hear the front door shut as he lets himself out. All I want to do is crawl into bed, but I know I should go to the bathroom first.

With a sigh, I head back downstairs. I don't bother with the light as I go to the bathroom and wipe up a little more. Luke's cleanup had been pretty effective and pretty freaking hot. *What are his plans for that shirt?*

I walk to the sink to wash my hands. I look up at my shadowy reflection in the mirror and see a dark smudge on my forehead, and frown. I'm thankful it had been dark upstairs as well and hope Luke didn't see some weird stain on my head.

I flip on the lights so I can see what the hell this is. I stare at my reflection in shock, taking in my wide eyes and open mouth. A black upside down cross vividly slashes across my pale skin. What could have caused such an ominous mark?

As I think back through tonight's encounter with Luke, his words float back to me. Something about baptizing me into darkness. I can't recall his exact words that didn't seem to matter in the heat of the moment, I can only remember how I wanted more of it.

But now, alone in the dark, my doubts weigh me down like a stone. I lean down and hurriedly splash my face with water, scrubbing at my forehead until it feels raw. The chilly water soothes my overheated skin.

I check my reflection again in the mirror, but now there is nothing to see except a red spot from rubbing so hard. I pat my face dry and head back upstairs, grateful to fall into bed.

As tired as I am after an incredible night with Luke, my mind is buzzing with what has happened. Is that really what I saw? Or is my imagination acting up? Could I have had a split-second waking dream again without realizing it?

My thoughts spiral darker as I remember McHottie's warning words about Luke. Am I wrong about everything? I finally got a taste of the darkness I knew Luke could bring out in me. But at what cost? Is Luke actually the dangerous one?

Flashes of Luke carousel through my mind, snippets of fire and darkness and red.

So.

Much.

Red.

With a huff, I throw off the covers and drag myself out of bed and down to my closet. If I can't sleep, I might as well get some answers. I pull on black leggings and an oversized Grimm long sleeve black shirt, then slip on my Converse, not bothering with socks.

I shove my phone into my leggings pocket and head out the door. I creep down the alley like a burglar and slip around the corner, past Grimm, to knock on my neighbor's door.

When he doesn't answer, I wait a minute and rap again, a

little firmer this time. Still no answer. Taking decisive action, I try his front door, surprised when it opens.

Shit. I had counted on it being locked. Well, no going back now. I throw open the door and call, "Hello? Hello? Anyone home?"

Nothing. I shift nervously from foot to foot, torn between leaving before I'm caught or indulging my curiosity. *Fuck it. One good breaking and entering deserves another,* I rationalize.

I quietly shut the door behind me, fervently hoping he's not just a sound sleeper who also keeps a gun under his pillow. The house feels heavy around me, the dark decor eerie in the night. I peek into the kitchen, faint moonlight glittering off the black countertop through the window.

Driven by curiosity, I decide to start snooping. I creep to the fridge, curious about what kind of food he eats. Cracking open the door, I blink at the bright light after my eyes have been adjusting to the darkness.

Squinting against the sudden brightness, I gasp. The fridge is completely bare. Not even a bottle of ketchup in the door. Weird. How's this guy eat? He seems too fit for that much takeout.

I open the freezer and find a lonely tub of pistachio gelato. A wave of guilt at the reminder of our wonderful movie night washes over me. Closing the doors, I turn and start looking through his cabinets. All empty except the one he pulled our plates from has two other lonely plates in it. Has he not unpacked yet?

My curiosity on overdrive, I even open his dishwasher, which holds just our clean dishes from our dinner. Giving up on the kitchen, I sneak out to the living room. The paintings are creepy in the darkness, so I quickly head to the stairs. I'm torn between getting caught upstairs and figuring out just who the hell this guy is.

High on adrenaline, I creep up the stairs. I bypass the movie room since I've already been in there. I cautiously open door after door off the hallway, finding each room empty. No furniture, nothing on the walls. Just a shell of a home. Finally, I come to the attic stairs.

Hoping I've found his bedroom, I tiptoe up. I consider calling Jo, remembering her silly support when I had been worried about someone being in my home. Considering I'm now the trespasser, though, I think better of having an accomplice. Besides, she would have questions that I don't have answers for.

Every step ratchets up my heart rate until it is all I can hear, thundering in my ears. I'm halfway up the stairs when I hear the faint wail of a siren. I hold my breath, trying to gauge the direction.

In my rising panic, I can't decide whether there is a siren on its way to get me for my law-breaking ways or if it's just heading somewhere else. Shit, is there some type of security system here?

My paranoia gets the better of me and I turn and flee, feet flying down the stairs, all stealth out the window. I race back down the hall and thunder down, almost knocking off a picture at my breakneck speed as I round the corner, careening off the wall.

The siren continues to wail in the night. I peek through the window in the door and see flashing lights off in the distance. Taking this as my cue to get the hell out of Dodge, I open the door just wide enough to slip through and hightail it to the alley, up the backstairs, and back to the safety of my own house.

Safe inside, I collapse back against the door, gulping air, legs burning. I clutch my chest and my heart pounds back against my hand. Suddenly, I feel boneless and slide down the door into a heap. Fuck, that was just about the stupidest thing I've ever done.

I lay slumped in a heap until my breathing evens out and my racing heart gradually returns to normal. I berate myself for not only being massively out of shape but also illegally nosy. Especially when I didn't even find anything good!

The sirens fade into the distance, and I breathe a little easier, realizing an orange jumpsuit is not in my immediate future. I hoist myself up using the end table and make my way to the kitchen on wobbly legs where I grab my bottle of tequila before collapsing onto one of the bar stools.

I don't even bother with a glass, instead taking a healthy swig straight from the bottle. I prop my chin on my hands and think about my life's choices. I'm a thirty-year-old single cat lady with a weird store who sees shit. At long last, I manage to meet two hot guys and there is something seriously wrong with both of them. Hell, I don't even have a good relationship with my cat.

I take another swig and rest my head on the cool granite of the breakfast bar. As the tequila warms my belly and relaxes my limbs, I realize this is *not* the life I want. I'm being tossed around in the storm. I sit up with sudden conviction.

"This is bullshit," I say out loud to my empty house. I've been pushing so hard to fall in love, to keep up with Luke, to figure out McHottie, that I forgot to focus on myself. What I need, what I want, what I *deserve*. And I deserve to be fucking happy. I let the realization wash over me, stiffening my spine.

Lucifer jumps up onto the bar, something he has never done before. He saunters across the bar to face me. Just as I go to scold him for being on the counter, he bumps his head into my forehead and purrs a growling rusty noise that suits him. Great, now that I'm a bad guy, too, he finally likes me.

Emotion thickens my throat. I thought this cat hated me, or at least was unaware of my existence. But he does see me. If this mean old cat can see me, then surely someone else can, too.

I'm not one of the bad guys. And this isn't me. My life is going off the rails and I'm out of control. It is time to write my own story rather than being pushed around by the maelstrom of my life. I'm done with hot stalker neighbors, done with masked men poking around in the dark recesses of my brain, and I'm most definitely done with my fledgling criminal career.

My phone buzzes on the counter. For the first time ever, I feel I can scoop up my cat. Sure enough, he lets me. Nuzzling his soft fur, I carry Lucifer up the stairs with me to get some sleep, leaving the phone buzzing behind me. I'm tired. I need sleep. I need me.

I.

Am.

Enough.

Epilogue

HIM

J stalk the streets of the inner city, looking for a target. I curse my size for scaring away the danger that lurks in these alleys when I'm spoiling for a fight. My vision pulses red, my veins run with fury.

I replay her voice in my head. She wants darkness. I'll show her the fucking darkness.

I turn a corner and there next to a dumpster, holding a woman against a wall, is exactly what I need. Some piece of shit no one will ever miss. Someone who deserves to die.

I grab his shoulder and spin him to face me, feeling the bones crunch satisfyingly beneath my grip. The woman wisely takes off running, sensing the predator in me.

The guy is too busy screaming in pain from the crushed bones. Oops. He tries supporting it with his good hand, the damaged shoulder hardly taking the weight of the useless arm hanging at his side.

I reach out and grab him by the neck, lifting him into the air and pinning him against the grimy brick wall. Even the smell of the dumpster, redolent in the sticky summer night, cannot compete with the scent of his blood, thrumming just below his skin. I watch with total apathy as he pisses himself.

I watch the darkening stain move down his pant leg, not bothering to look him in the eyes. Death is all he sees in me.

"I want to taste your darkness," echoes on repeat in my head, followed by *his* fucking French bullshit. He's not even

French! The heartbeat of the asshole in front of me adds its staccato rhythm to the terrible soundtrack until I can't take anymore.

Desperate to stop the noise, I use my free hand to punch through his flimsy chest wall and pull out his still beating heart.

After hundreds of years of deprivation, drinking directly from the source is divine.

Pure bliss.

I bite into the heart, drinking deep, but it rapidly cools, and the taste turns bitter in my mouth. I drop it to the ground, where it lets out a sickening squelch on impact. Shrugging, I don't bother cleaning up the scene. As the kids these days say, I've got a serious case of the fuck-its.

Feeling infinitesimally better, I turn and walk away, delicately patting my mouth with a silk handkerchief. I toss it over my shoulder when I'm done with it. Let them run my DNA if they find it. It's of no use to them.

I stalk deeper into the alleys of the worst parts of the city. It may not be an advancing Ottoman army, but there must be a few more souls bound for Hell that I can make a meal of. And as I've proven before, I can do this forever.

I may not understand the world today. I may not understand my *Roză*. Hell, I may not even understand myself. But this, *this* I understand. Death and destruction are the same in any time, any language. I will drown the world in red. Again.

Vlad's back, baby. Vlad's back.

Epilogue

LUKE

$\mathcal{I}$ hold the white chess piece in my hand, twirling the king through my fingers like a Vegas magician in a steeplechase flourish. With a flick of my wrist, it disappears, and resting in its place is *ma Reine Rouge.*

I.

Will.

Win.

A Message From The Author

Dear Readers–I hope you have fallen in love with Lieshe, McHottie, and Luke. I hope that even Lucifer has wormed his way into your heart. I started writing one weekend after a trip to a small town very much like the one in this book. I had grown tired of reading what felt like the same book over and over. So, I set out to write something different and I think I succeeded. I hope you agree and continue with Lieshe's story as the Immortal Redemption series continues. If you thought book 1 was a wild ride, buckle up buttercup. Book 2 will be darker, hotter, and push you ever deeper into this world.

To the Bookstagram Community–I don't even know who everyone is who supported me and encouraged me. But thank you. I promise to support future Indie authors and be a force for good. Special shout out to Danelle (@biblio.barbie) and Sarah & Sarah.

To my wonderful friends and family–Every single one of you believed in me. I'm not sure how I was able to convince you all that I could do this, but I did. And you in turn, convinced me when I didn't think I could. To my mom–I know you are proud, and I miss you every damn day. Thank you for my love of reading. To my dad–thank you for always telling me I had "the world by the balls" and for feeding my book habit. To my husband–your unwavering support has been nothing short of incredible. To my kids–I'm not sure I ever want you to get to this message in the back of my book but here we are. Follow your dreams, you can do anything. To the real-life Mindy and Lieshe–thank goodness you didn't know that I would take years of tidbits of our friendship and stick them in a novel! You have both saved me more than you will ever know. To Sam–the best alpha reader and unpaid assistant on the planet. To Taylor–the best PA ever! And finally, to my sister–this is all because of you. You taught me to read and have always been my biggest cheerleader. I love you just as much as you love me.

Follow me @CassandraElizzabeth and keep an eye on cassandraelizzabeth.com for updates and to subscribe to my newsletter.

My Eternal Love,
Cassandra

P.S. Luke says, "Be a good girl, *mon petit chou*, and leave a review."

About The Author

Cassandra Elizzabeth is an exciting new indie voice, known for her immersive storytelling and vivid imagination. Her writing journey started when she could not find the books she wanted to read. Cassandra weaves themes of self-discovery, friendship, love, loss, and acceptance into a tapestry of macabre and spicy fiction, with a dash of murder, mayhem, and mystery. When not lost in the world of words, Cassandra can be found talking to the flowers or spending time with her family.